Kaa

KU-710-218

A
STUDY
in
MURDER

A STUDY in MURDER

ROBERT RYAN

SIMON &
SCHUSTER

London · New York · Sydney · Toronto · New Delhi

A CBS COMPANY

First published in Great Britain by Simon & Schuster UK Ltd, 2015
A CBS COMPANY

1 3 5 7 9 10 8 6 4 2

Simon & Schuster UK Ltd
1st Floor
222 Gray's Inn Road
London WC1X 8HB

www.simonandschuster.co.uk

Simon & Schuster Australia, Sydney
Simon & Schuster India, New Delhi

A CIP catalogue record for this book is available from the British Library

HB ISBN: 978-1-47113-506-4
TPB ISBN: 978-1-47113-507-1
EBOOK ISBN: 978-1-47113-509-5

Typeset by Hewer Text UK Ltd, Edinburgh
Printed and bound in Great Britain by CPI Group (UK) Ltd, Croydon, CR0 4YY

To Gabriel

And for T. J. and Mike Gostick

AUTHOR'S NOTE

During the course of *A Study in Murder*, Major Watson alludes to a story he is writing. For reference, the complete tale – 'The Girl and the Gold Watches' – is printed in the appendix.

1917

PROLOGUE

Harzgrund POW Camp, Germany

Sometimes, the dead talked too much. It was a babble of voices when they broke through – many tongues, all tripping over each other as they tried to make themselves heard. Which meant, of course, that none could be understood, not by a small, insignificant conduit still imprisoned in a mortal body. The noise reminded him of the howling Atlantic gale that did for the *Naronic* – out of Liverpool, en route to New York – killing all seventy-four aboard, including his father. It was his dad who had first come back to him, when he had just turned six, to inform his son that he had The Gift and that he could act as an opening to the domain of the dead. But latterly that opening had become clogged and chaotic.

It was, he supposed, due to the sheer volume of the newly parted being released each day. He often imagined the entrance to the afterlife, a long line of silvery souls, stretching into a far distance, waiting their turn to be admitted. Battalions of them. Many would still be baffled, disoriented, not wanting to accept that they had taken the step over the threshold and would never have to face the privations and torment of war again. Death, though, once you embraced it, was the ultimate freedom. Of that he was certain. He didn't pity the dead. Sometimes he envied them.

He found that total isolation from his surroundings improved his chances of a successful contact. So, with the room lit by just one candle, he had taken to wearing a black hood, fashioned by one of the orderlies from thick silk. Where the man got it heaven alone knew, but the touch of the material on his skin soothed him, helped him relax as the voices jabbered about him, until one recognized him for what he was – an earthbound friend – and deigned to speak through him.

This evening, sitting around the same table as the medium were three other men, two believers and a sceptic. The latter had been persuaded to part with ten camp marks for the chance to hear from his brother, killed at the Somme. Whoever made contact, it would be an ordinary person, he knew, one of the faceless masses. Not for him some North American savage king, Peter the Great, Napoleon or Nefertiti. His dealings were with Everyman, the humble and the hardworking, the soldier and the servant.

He strained to try to make something from the cacophony swirling around in his head. There were snatches of laughter, not in gaiety but with a cruel aspect. He was being mocked, perhaps. Ridiculed for his feeble attempts to penetrate a world where the living had no place.

He pulled up the hood, opened one eye and glanced down at the table, where the blood was pooling. There was enough for even the hungriest ghost. He reached for the glass of clear liquid before him, shuddering at the thought of the taste and the burn. It was like drinking paraffin. But it was part of the ritual they had developed.

'To those on the other side about to make contact, salutations!'

The three men drank. One of them gagged. Then, silence around the table, each man lost in his own thoughts and hopes. The medium pulled the hood down once more.

Then, the smell.

It made his nostrils twitch. It was pungent and far from pleasant. It spoke of caverns deep in the earth, of lava beds and hot gases. It was always the first sign that he was through.

'Jesus, what's that stink?' asked the sceptic.

'Ssh,' said one of the others. ''Tis the fires of hell.'

There was no hell, no eternal damnation; the dead were most adamant about that. So he had no idea of where the fumes originated. But the fact that even his companions could detect the aroma was a good sign.

'*Pauper*,' said the voice, causing him to jump a little.

'You'll have to speak up,' he ventured. 'We are all friends and believers here.'

'*Pauper!*'

'Are you saying you were a pauper? In this life, I mean?'

'*Pennebaker.*'

'Pennebaker? And what's your first name, Mr Pennebaker?'

A snort. Yes, a snort of disgust.

'*No.*'

He knew immediately that the fellow – for it was clearly a

man — had somehow gone back into the eddy of souls, like a twig snatched away from a riverbank, swirling off into the stream. He asked his fellow voyagers for patience.

'*Paper.*' It was the same voice, clearer now, as if its owner had stepped in closer. He could almost be at his shoulder, leaning across to pass on a confidence.

'Paper?'

'*Pen and paper.*'

'You want me to fetch pen and paper?'

'*Yes.*'

They were always close at hand and he felt them pushed towards him by his accomplices. He had experienced automatic writing, but it was not his usual method of communication. He imagined this man had something to say that he didn't trust to mere — and often misheard or confused — words.

'Are you a soldier? A British soldier?'

'*Yes.*'

'What's your name?'

Silence. Sometimes that happened. It was as if the old names no longer mattered where they were. Or they had simply forgotten them. He tried another tack.

'When did you cross over?'

The reply was garbled. He felt a sense of panic that he would lose him again. He took up the stub of a pencil and made sure it was on the top of the first page of the notebook. 'I have the writing implements.'

He felt warmth flood through him like a fever and was aware that someone, something, had invaded his body. He tried to relax, to let his visitor do as he pleased. He meant him no harm, he knew that. The spirit world was sometimes playful and mocking but never truly malicious.

His hand twitched of its own accord and he heard a gasp from around the table. He felt the pencil begin to skate across the page, jerkily, the movements like a child's. The words forming would doubtless be shaky, but it wasn't a matter of calligraphy. How often does one get a missive from the dead? he thought. The medium concentrated hard on keeping his breathing steady and his heart rate down, even though he could feel his excitement rising. Within minutes the scrawl covered five sheets of paper, before coming to an abrupt halt. The noises in his ears died away, followed by the hum of a loud silence.

'Hello?'

No reply. The gate to the realm of the dead had closed for the night.

He waited a few moments, removed the hood and waited for his eyes to adjust to the flicker of thin candlelight before trying to decipher what the spirit had written in his spidery hand. It was a sequence of apparently random words, not a complete sentence among them, but that wasn't unusual; the channels to the afterworld took time to work smoothly sometimes. But it was also unsigned. Who was he, this unknown soldier? Names might not be important over there, but they still mattered on this side of the divide. Ah, well, the medium thought, he would get it from him next time.

And, although he didn't yet know it, that name would be the death of him.

ONE

It was the rattle of chains and the squeal of unoiled hinges that drew Major John Watson to the window of the infirmary that January morning. The metal gates of the Krefeld II *Offizierlager* had swung back and Watson watched a new arrival walk through them, accompanied by the grizzled Feldwebel Krebs. It was unusual for new prisoners to appear at the camp so early in the year. With the armies on the Western Front hunkered down for the winter, the supply of fresh faces – and therefore up-to-date news of the war and of home – tended to dry up until the inevitable spring offensives, which always generated a substantial influx of POWs from both sides.

The new man shuffled, even though he had on a stout pair of boots – many of the prisoners were reduced to wearing wooden clogs – and his shoulders were slumped. His bag of possessions was clutched tightly to his chest and he dumbly followed the *Feldwebel*'s instructions without glancing around to take in his new home. His face was oddly immobile, as if it had been paralysed or covered by a flesh-coloured mask. You didn't have to be a doctor or detective to know that the man was broken. Krebs led him to Block 2, which formed the base of the U-shaped building that comprised the officers' billets, herding him like a sheepdog with one of its charges until they disappeared inside.

Watson turned back to his ward. In his morning surgery he saw dozens of minor complaints from prisoners, but there were only four in-patients that day: one bad case of boils, another of what could be TB, one with frostbite from trying to dig out under the fence on the coldest night of the year, and Private Martins, whom the other patients suspected was malingering. After all, the infirmary was the one room in the prisoner-of-war camp that was kept warm round the clock, with a ready supply of wood always available. So it was a magnet for those who simply fancied a spell in the heat.

In the main barracks – converted from the stables of a once-grand estate – the men had taken to burning their bunks in the freezing days of the new year. January had been mainly kind since then, but still a few hours in the infirmary were much coveted. However, Watson had come to the conclusion that Martins's symptoms were very real, as he had missed the Sunday football match against the Germans. He couldn't play very well, but he was rather skilled at barking the shins and clumping the ankles of any guard foolish enough to get the ball. It was the highlight of the man's week.

'Well, Martins,' Watson asked, 'any improvement?'

Martins, a sharp-faced fellow in his thirties, was an orderly, one of the other ranks kept on site to look after the officers. They had their own barracks and were little more than glorified footmen. The alternative for such non-officers, though, was forced labour, in German factories, quarries or the salt mines. Complaints, therefore, were few and far between.

'Still can't stand up, Major. Room spins and I fall down. Like I just got off a merry-go-round. And I see that flashing.' He used his fingers to demonstrate the on-off bursts of coloured lights that had been plaguing him.

'That's the migraine.' Watson had determined he was suffering from Ménière's disease, probably caused by the shell that blew Martins out of his trench and into no man's land, where he was taken prisoner by the Germans. Not that the diagnosis did either of them much good. There was no treatment for the sudden, debilitating attacks of dizziness, nausea and the accompanying visual disturbances.

'There's nothing wrong with him, Major,' said Captain Tyrell, the man with a cluster of angry boils on his bottom that were so bright they could double as streetlamps. 'He was bounding around the place like a March hare before you came to do your rounds.'

Watson raised an eyebrow as a query to Martins.

'It comes and goes.' The private lowered his voice. 'They don't like sharing a ward with a regular soldier, that's the truth of it, sir. Think they should have an officers-only ward.'

'We're lucky to have an infirmary at all.'

It was Watson's third POW camp. He had been captured in no man's land in France, having been blown out of a tank near Flers. From there he had been taken to a field hospital behind the German lines, then a giant holding and processing facility on the Belgian border, a mainly French camp near Cologne, and finally shipped on to join his fellow countrymen at Krefeld II.

This was by far the most benign and well equipped of the three. Halbricht, the commandant, had even built the prisoners a theatre and, although food was desperately short, he made sure that at least one meal a day was something more than potato water and turnip skins. It was best, however, not to ask about the provenance of the meat the kitchen produced.

'You ever play tennis, Martins?' Watson asked.

'Tennis?' he replied with some degree of incredulity. 'I'm from Bermondsey, sir.'

'I think we can rig a net up over by where that Canadian has his hop, step and jump. Eye-to-ball co-ordination, that's what we'll try. Retrain your brain.'

'Good luck with that,' muttered Tyrell.

Watson looked down across the unoccupied beds at the officer, but the words his mouth formed were snatched away by the blast of wind that swirled in with the dried leaves from the open door. Feldwebel Krebs was there, along with Lieutenant Barnes from Block 2. Between them, hanging from their necks, was the newly arrived prisoner. And from the look of him, he was busy bleeding to death.

TWO

The section of London between South Kensington Tube Station and Knightsbridge was the nexus of the operation to try to feed and clothe the thousands of British servicemen being held prisoner in France, Belgium, Germany and beyond. The War Office's Central Prisoners of War Committee had moved into premises at Nos 3 and 4 Thurloe Place, in the shadow of the mighty V&A. The Red Cross occupied an adjacent building. A short stroll away, the British Prisoners Aid Society was now situated in an elegant home overlooking Hans Gardens. It had been donated by Lady Greatlock, rent free, and its four floors were stuffed with supplies to be parcelled up and sent to the prisoners. A similar arrangement pertained at 22 and 25 Thurloe Gardens, the home of the British Prisoners of War Food Parcels and Clothing Committee. These grand houses had been gifted by Sir Richard Burbidge, the managing director of Harrods, with No. 25 used for administrative work and parcelling and No. 22 acting as a storage depot.

It was in the main packing room of No. 25 that Mrs Gregson, formerly of the Voluntary Aid Detachment and, subsequently, a spy for Winston Churchill, chalked a list of POW camps on a board, while behind her three dozen women sat at benches, deftly assembling parcels from the various foods laid out before them. Most wore gloves. Despite the stoves and open fire, the house remained cold. Day after day, the temperature outside was struggling to stay above freezing. It made many of them even more aware of the plight of the prisoners.

'Right, ladies,' Mrs Gregson said as she copied the names from a piece of paper provided by the Red Cross. 'The camps here are the ones that are confiscating tinned goods. Holzminden has been added to that list in the past day or so, and there are reports from Dortmund of seizures. Where there are no tins allowed we substitute jars or packets of jam, bacon, sausages, extra cigarettes, rice, oats, maize, curry powder, dates and raisins, Oxo and Marmite. Now we also have a list here of new prisoners, so I need some volunteers to help make up a set of New Capture parcels. Miss Hood, thank you, Mrs Nichols, Miss Kinney.'

She moved the three women into an adjacent, windowless room which, as well as tables laden with food, contained shelves of clothing and 'comforts' such as razors and tooth-brushes. Every new prisoner received a parcel of towels, shirts, vests, drawers, handkerchief, a muffler, a cardigan and gloves as well as shaving and bathing equipment, hairbrush and comb, a knife, fork and tin opener. They just had to hope that the recipient wasn't moved before the parcel made its tortu-ous way over the Channel and through a neutral country to the designated camp.

Mrs Gregson, although the head of department, also mucked

in with the creation of the boxes, carefully following the kit list pinned to the wall. Once she had learned that her friend Major Watson was a prisoner of war, she had thrown herself into the work of alleviating the suffering of the incarcerated men. Repatriated prisoners had told of terribly harsh conditions in some camps and that only parcels from home had enabled them to survive. It wasn't a deliberate policy of privation, they said — the Allied blockade of the ports meant most of the German population was also suffering from malnutrition.

She tried not to think too much about exactly how Watson was faring in all this. It made her lose focus, and even feel a little weepy, when she pictured him in a freezing hut some-where in Germany, eating his Maconochie rations from a tin. They had been reunited in Suffolk, when she had been asked by Churchill to be his eyes and ears at a top-secret establish-ment developing the so-called 'tank'. These adventures had brought her and Watson close although, if she was being frank, the exact nature of that closeness eluded her. It didn't do to dwell too much on those feelings. He was her friend and confi-dant — she had even told him about her brief affair with a married officer, now killed — which was enough to be going on with. And, whatever the ultimate reason, she very much wanted him home in England.

'So, have you news, Mrs Gregson?' asked Miss Hood, a bird-like creature in her late teens who could sometimes be heard lamenting the devastation the war had had on her social life since she came out.

'About?' Mrs Gregson asked.

'Whether the Queen is coming?'

This was a constant rumour. Queen Mary had already visited the premises of the Central Prisoners of War Committee and the Red Cross. The feeling was that BPOWFPC deserved a show of royal approval.

'I have not,' said Mrs Gregson truthfully, 'although I know the secretary has put in a request.' The secretary was related to the Queen's lady of the bedchamber, so the petition was likely to find its way to the keeper of Her Majesty's appointments. At least she hoped so – Mrs Gregson had to admit ignorance of the machinations of the Royal Household, whereas some of her subordinates had encyclopaedic knowledge of the hierarchy at Buckingham Palace and the other royal residences. And if they had contacts within one of those residences, they were quick to mention it. Mrs Gregson was doing important work, she knew, but the constant reminders and reaffirmations of social status that occurred minute by minute at the voluntary organization were ultimately very tiresome. There were those, she was certain, who resented her elevated position at No. 25 simply because she was not mentioned in Debrett's.

'Don't forget to put in the PR postcard,' said Mrs Gregson, scooping one out of the rack and laying it on top of the socks and shirt. The men were meant to send the Parcel Received card back to show the supplies were getting through.

There was a knock at the open door. Mrs Gregson looked up to see the slender form of Major Neville Pitt of the War Office. He had his cap in his hands and a slight colour on his cheeks as he always did when confronted with a room full of women. He reached up and tugged at his moustache, as if checking it wouldn't come away in a stiff breeze.

'Mrs Gregson,' he said, 'do you have a moment?'

'Of course.' She tried not to catch the eye of the others as she put the final item in the box.

Pitt, of similar age to Mrs Gregson, was relatively young for a major. He had been denied front line service because he had lost an eye, now replaced by a false one, in a polo accident; he was, by all accounts, still a useful player. He was a good head taller than Mrs Gregson and as she stepped out into the hall he stooped down to whisper in her ear. 'Do you have time for a cup of tea?'

'Well . . .' She glanced into the New Capture room, where the three women were apparently engrossed in creating their parcels. A giggle, though, escaped from within, followed by a very unladylike snort. 'Possibly.'

'I have some news,' Pitt said, pushing home his slim advantage.

'Really? About?' Not the bloody Queen again, she thought.

'About Major Watson.'

A suspicious cast clouded her features. 'Good news?'

What kind of fool was he to bring glad tidings about a man he considered a rival for this woman's affections? Not that Pitt had ever met this Watson, but he knew the man once boasted some minor celebrity, and that Mrs Gregson clearly bore him some affection. Some deep affection, he might add. However, he told himself for the hundredth time that Major Watson could only be a father figure to someone like Mrs Gregson. He himself was a far more suitable match. Some considered her too frisky and forthright, but, Pitt thought with her confident manner and red hair, she made all the other women look positively bland. And news of the old boy brought such palpable joy to her, that he could use the lift in her spirits to suggest a dinner before he travelled to The Hague.

'Very good news, Mrs Gregson,' he said, managing what he hoped was a shy smile. 'Very good news indeed.'

Before he could say any more she had turned on her heel and left to fetch her hat and coat.

THREE

After lunch and the afternoon *Appell* – the camp roll call – Watson took a brisk turn around the main compound with Colonel Isbell, the Senior British Officer at the camp. The tall, elegant Isbell had been incarcerated for two years, but managed to keep himself whip-smart. His hair was neat and oiled, the uniform beautifully pressed and he was shod with the glossiest boots in the camp. Having a pair of dedicated orderlies at his beck and call helped in such matters, of course.

The compound echoed to the sound of hammers striking nails. A stage was under construction for the scratch orchestra that was being assembled from the inmates. It would double as an open-air theatre for the reviews that were proving so popular that no single hut could contain the ever-growing audience. The Krefeld Players had been forced to put on matinées of *Two Merry Monarchs* to meet the demand. At the moment the weather was benign, but winter could sweep back in just as rapidly as it had departed, scotching the idea of outdoor shows until spring. Still, the labour was a reward in itself for the prisoners, many of whom welcomed the physical exercise of sawing and hammering.

Watson often wondered about the wisdom of not requiring officers to work; sometimes, enforced idleness could be as much a punishment as forced labour.

'How is the patient?' Isbell asked.

'Hanson? He'll live,' said Watson of the new arrival who had tried to slash his own throat. 'Most of the blood came from his ear. Krebs managed to get to him before he sliced through anything major.'

'Good. You know he played rugby for England?'

'He's that Hanson? Scrum half for Cornwall? Played in the Olympics?' Where, Watson didn't bother adding, Australasia — basically the Australian rugby team — had slaughtered them 3–32.

Isbell nodded. 'Yes. Graduate of Camborne School of Mines. He was captured making a recce into no man's land for the most effective placement of explosives. Affected him quite badly, being captured. The Senior British Officer at Friedberg, his last camp, requested a transfer here as he felt the regime more conducive to his recovery.'

They had reached the innermost of the camp's twin perimeter fences. Beyond them was a ploughed field, the soil stiff and cloddy and varnished with the evidence of the morning's frost, its furrows awaiting the next crop of mangels. Further on was a copse, its skeletal trees tantalizingly close, the spindly branches seeming to beckon as they waved in the lusty breeze coming, fortunately, from the south. 'Seems that at Friedberg he tried to walk into the kill strip,' Isbell said, nodding at bare earth between the two fences. 'Lucky he wasn't shot.'

'Perhaps he wanted to be shot,' said Watson.

'Only been in a few months, y'know. Wire fever usually takes longer to take hold,' said Isbell. 'Before men do anything quite so reckless.'

'There is a particularly black sort of wire fever,' said Watson. 'I've seen men try to scale those fences in full view of the guards. And I've seen guards oblige them by shooting them in the back.'

'Good Lord. In cold blood?'

Watson nodded.

'Where was this?'

'Karlsruhe camp.'

'You complained?'

'In writing. To the commandant and the Red Cross. Precious little good it did me.'

'Well, whatever you call the fever, I think Hanson has it bad. The thing is, I knew his brother at school. I was wondering if you could keep an eye on him for me? Just until we can get him to snap out of it. Find him something useful to do?'

'Such as?'

'The Escape Committee. Always needs extra hands.'

The Escape Committee's role was to dream up ever more elaborate ways to go over, under or through the wire. In truth, few succeeded. Hauptmann Halbricht might be a reasonable, some would say soft, commandant – there were far tougher camps in the system – but he was no fool. He also had the knack of swooping down on any plotters at the last possible moment, meaning the Escape Committee had to start all over again when its precious stock of forged documents, German marks, maps and railway timetables were confiscated. However, Watson was aware that the thought of escape, the minutiae of its planning and execution, kept many a man sane, even though the schemes might come to naught. And in some camps, the planning bore fruit – he had heard of men who escaped nine, ten, twelve times. And the exploits of those who made a 'home run' – including Lieutenant-Colonel Crofton Bury Vandeleur, the first man to 'nip out' from Krefeld, as he put it – became the stuff of legend around the camps.

'Of course I will,' agreed Watson. There was the flat report of a distant shotgun and a whirl of crows took to the air, looking like moving ink splashes against the pale blue sky. 'It will give him a sense of purpose. Of continuing the fight.'

'That's the spirit.'

'And once he is discharged from the infirmary, Hanson can come into my billet. There's a spare bunk.'

'Good man,' said Isbell. 'I appreciate it. Strange how some can't take it, eh? Even a fit chap like Hanson.'

Watson turned his back on the outside world as the nervous crows settled on the branches once more, flexing their wings in anticipation of further flight. 'Incarceration? The fact is, Colonel, none of us expected it. Death, yes. Maimed, gassed, also very likely. But this –' he swept an arm across the expanse of the camp – 'to be locked up as prisoners in Germany? They feel a failure, diminished as men.'

Isbell grunted as if he was talking rot, but Watson knew he understood. The man's meticulous grooming and adherence to a strict daily routine was a way of keeping such thoughts at bay. Watson had his patients, and therefore a role to play. Everybody else had only time to kill, and it lay heavy with many of them. There were only so many football matches and concerts with pretty adjutants in frocks one could stomach.

'And how are you bearing up?' Isbell asked.

'Me?' Watson asked.

'Burned, weren't you? In one of those bloody useless tanks, I hear.' The colonel was well informed. Isbell had been taken prisoner when the tank was still a glimmer in Churchill's imagination. But the wire fences were porous, fresh prisoners updated inmates, and news in letters sometimes slipped by even the German censors. And then there was the camp 'Marconi', the gossip machine that spread information – some of it even true – about every inmate and, as if by magic, sometimes let news leap from one camp to another.

'I was well cared for,' Watson said, which was the truth. He had seen the propaganda posters of German nurses pouring water onto the ground in front of thirst-racked and wounded British soldiers, but his experience suggested it was just that: propaganda. When Watson had been blown out of the tank at Flers, he had been picked up by a German patrol in no man's land and delivered to a field hospital where German nurses had dressed his burns and cared for him to the best of their ability. 'There's scarring, of course, but not too bad. And it's on my back, so I don't have to look at it. It's healed well, for a man of my age.'

'Good.' Isbell pulled down his jacket and ran a hand down the buttons, although it was hardly creased. 'There's something you should know.'

'About Hanson?'

Isbell took the major's arm and guided him away from the small clump of men who had gathered at the fence to smoke and exchange news from their letters.

'Halbricht had me into his office yesterday,' said Isbell. 'I expected the normal housekeeping, but he told me an exchange is being negotiated, whereby some prisoners will be released to spend the rest of the war in neutral Holland, in or around Scheveningen. They will play no further part in combat, but . . . well, it's freedom, of a kind.'

'And you are telling me this because . . . ?'

'Halbricht says the first tranche will be any prisoners over the age of forty-eight. Which means you and Digby Rawlinson. Plus any medical men are also to be released, which means you've hit two sixes there, old boy. Time to leave the crease. It'll take a few weeks to finish the formalities, apparently, but your name has gone forward, Major Watson. To all intents and purposes, you are going home.'

FOUR

The dead came calling once again. That night the four men sat around the table, with the curly-haired lieutenant, Archer, leading the proceedings as he always did. It was after curfew. They could hear the prowling dogs yelping and snarling bad-temperedly as they padded between the two outer fences of the camp.

Archer laid his hood to one side as Harry, the orderly, put out the flask of drink and four glasses and then retreated.

Archer raised his glass. 'To those on the other side we are about to contact. Salutations.'

'Salutations,' the others replied, and all four threw the corrosive liquor to the back of their throats.

'Concentrate, gentlemen,' Archer said as he pulled down his silken hood. 'Who are we attempting to contact tonight?'

'My brother. Jimmy Hulpett,' said one of the men, the sceptic about communication with the other side who, nevertheless, had been intrigued enough to come back a second time.

'I suggest we all hold hands while you tell us something about your brother.'

'Jimmy is — was — younger than me. We both joined up at the same time. I had been through cadet school, so I went to officer training. Jimmy didn't want to have anything to do with that. He went in as a private, although he was a corporal when he—'

'His personality,' chided the medium gently. 'Tell us about his character.'

'Jimmy was a joker. A practical joker. Loved to play tricks. Fill your boots with sand, make papier mâché spiders to leave in the lavatory for our sister, Sylvie, to find. Always had a joke, Jimmy, not all of them clean. He didn't get on well at school. The teachers thought he was lazy or stupid, but he had a sharp mind. Just not for letters. Numbers he was good at, which is why he started the betting ring that got him expelled . . . Blimey.'

The smell.

'Go on,' said the medium. But the moment the words left his mouth he felt a rush around him, a dozen voices ringing in his head at once. He felt a mix of elation and nausea.

'Quiet, quiet, please, gentlemen,' he pleaded, and squeezed the hands of those on either side of him.

'You all right?' one of the regulars asked Hulpett. 'You've gone quite pink.'

'It's that bloody drink. Worse than last time.'

'Shush.'

The medium let his breathing become steady and even as he waited for the cacophony to subside. So many dead now, they had to jostle to be heard. He imagined only the strong made it, even on the other side.

'Jimmy?'

'*Not Jimmy. No.*'

'Who then?'

'*Paper.*'

A *frisson* of excitement ran through the medium. It was his unknown soldier, the one who had written the unintelligible pages through him on the last firm contact with the dead. Archer was ready this time. 'I need to know who you are,' he said firmly, as if he could really influence the actions of the dead.

Archer clutched the pencil tightly and at once it moved over the paper, in a series of shaky but flamboyant loops.

'Oh, for God's sake,' said Hulpett.

The voices faded and the pencil clattered onto the table. 'What?' Archer demanded of the man who had broken his concentration. 'What is it?'

'This.' Hulpett snatched up the paper with the spirit's signature. 'Captain Brevette.'

'What about him?' Archer asked.

'Captain Brevette's still alive,' Hulpett said. 'We had a postcard from him. He's probably having a whisky at his club as we speak. Well, it proves one thing.'

'What's that?' Archer raised the hood. 'What are you saying?'

'It can't be Brevette.' There was genuine disappointment in the voice, for Hulpett had hoped to make contact with poor Jimmy. Now, he simply felt foolish for believing that was possible. He jabbed a finger at Archer. 'You're a bloody charlatan, just like the rest of them.'

Hulpett sprang to his feet, knocking the home-made chair

over as he did so, and strode from the rec hut, muttering as he went. Archer cleared his throat and picked up the pencil once more. 'Gentlemen,' he said as he slipped down the hood, 'shall we continue?'

FIVE

The familiar name leaped off the page, but the German officer made sure he showed no emotion. He looked up at his opposite number, a Major Pitt from the British Office for the Welfare of Prisoners of War, and frowned.

'Is something wrong?' asked the third man in the room, a Dutch colonel by the name of De Krom.

The Kaiser's man lit a cigarette. His fleshy features relaxed, although what he said brought dismay to the other two men around the table. 'I am afraid there are men on this list who do not deserve to be released.'

'Oh, for crying—' began Pitt before he caught himself. The three officers were in a private meeting room at the Hotel Europa in The Hague. Outside the window, a prosperous country, only sideswiped by war, went about its business. For months now representatives of the warring governments had been trying to finalize a plan whereby elderly prisoners and those in need of medical treatment could be repatriated to neutral Holland, to serve out their time in relative comfort. It was a generous offer from the Dutch. Both sides wanted it. And

Holland would be paid handsomely for its hospitality. But now the German was backsliding on the agreement.

Pitt glanced at the pasty-faced De Krom, who seemed equally unhappy. He was repeatedly running a hand through his wispy blond hair, a nervous tic that was probably responsible for his incipient baldness.

'Look here, we have been through all this,' said Pitt, trying to moderate his tone. He knew he could be hectoring at times. 'All of those men are special cases.' He read from the list of qualifying conditions. 'They have diseases of the circulatory system, serious nervous problems, tumours and severe skin diseases, blindness (total or partial), serious face injuries, tuberculosis, one or more missing limbs, paralysis, brain disorders like paraplegia or hemiplegia and serious mental illnesses, or are over the age of forty-eight or qualified medical practitioners. As I say, every single person has one or more of those afflictions. Every single one. None of them will be released to contribute to the war effort, no matter how vital they might be. We have approved everyone on the list you gave to us. And, I might add, you are getting an allocation of thirty more men than we are.'

The German stubbed out his cigarette. 'Calm down, Major. There are just three names I object to. You can put replacements forward, of course.'

'Object? For what possible reason?' De Krom asked. It was almost midday and he already had his mind on lunch.

'I don't have to give you a reason. I know that these men are a threat to the security of the German Imperial State. That they cannot be trusted to keep their bond. I'm sorry.' He stood and straightened his tunic. 'But if they remain on the list . . . I am afraid our work here is over.'

He glanced at the door. Outside were civil servants from each of the three countries, the cogs in the machine that had worked out the fine details of the exchange. With them were members of the Red Cross and both British and German organizations responsible for prisoners' welfare. And the press, waiting for the announcement they had been promised, some of them armed with cameras the size of sea chests.

Pitt wondered whether to call his bluff. But he thought of the hundreds who would benefit from this arrangement, some of them likely to die before the winter was out if the negotiations fell through. As if to underline the point, a few flurries of snow spiralled past the window to fall onto the formal gardens below.

'Very well,' he said. 'You'll share the names with us?'

The German simply nodded, his face impassive, as if his victory gave him no satisfaction. He sat once more and looked down the sheets before him, shuffling the papers, searching through the lists. In truth, there was only one name he recognized. But he didn't want this to appear to be a personal vendetta, the act of petty revenge he knew, in his heart, it was.

'Captain Arthur Cameron,' he said, and put a line through the entry. His eyes continued to rove down the columns of prisoners.

'Lieutenant George McArthur.'

Now he was on the final page and there it was, glowing as if written in blood. 'And Major John Watson.'

'Watson?' spluttered Pitt. 'What on earth has he done to Germany? And what kind of threat could he possibly be? He's sixty if he's a day. Good Lord, man—'

'Major!' De Krom snapped. Pitt muttered a fruity oath under his breath, knowing the fury and disappointment he would face at home. Mrs Gregson would shut tight like a steel trap.

'But Major Watson. What kind of threat is he?' Pitt repeated.

Von Bork had met Watson but once, in August 1914, when his famous friend and companion had humiliated the German on the eve of war. Von Bork had waited a long time to exact some kind of retribution, no matter how trivial. And for a man of Watson's age, what he was about to do would be more than a slight inconvenience. In the same way that Sherlock Holmes had snatched victory from Von Bork, he would pluck away the promise of home and comfort from the doctor.

'The worst kind,' he replied. 'The sort you don't expect. No, my apologies, but this is a matter of principle.'

That was no kind of answer, Pitt appreciated, but he had a feeling his opponent wasn't going to budge his shiny boots on this one.

'I think you are playing games,' said Pitt, standing, half inclined to storm out. But how would that look to his superiors? And surely he could work on getting Watson out later. He could square this with Mrs Gregson. She would understand the impossible situation he was in, faced with throwing away months of tortuous wrangling over the fate of one man. 'I would like to lodge a formal protest.'

'By not signing?' asked the German, with a raise of one eyebrow. 'That is your privilege.'

The chiming clock filled the silence with its sonorous declaration of noon. When it had stopped, Pitt said, 'No. We sign. For the sake of the others. And then we, at least, can all go home.'

'Excellent,' said the German, pushing the list back across the table. 'Then we can proceed.'

De Krom passed Pitt a leather-bound document case, which he opened to find the formal agreement in all three languages. Every word had been pored over by the civil servants outside, so Pitt had no need to read it again. He signed, and carefully blotted a signature that was less elegant than usual. He repeated the process twice more and then passed it across to the German.

'Well, I hope you are satisfied now,' said Pitt, his voice shaking with suppressed anger.

'Oh, I am,' Von Bork replied, allowing a small smile to illuminate his puffy aristocratic face as he wrote his name with a flourish. 'I am most satisfied.'

SIX

Thursdays were designated as Prisoner Walk days at Krefeld, so after breakfast Watson presented Hanson at the camp entrance and requested permission to leave the compound with his patient. Watson was handed the oath card by the camp's duty gate officer, a *Leutnant* with a blast-mangled face who, despite his injury, bore the British and French little obvious hostility. He even shared a joke with the captives sometimes, although today he didn't seem to be in the mood for levity.

'Can you read it out please, Major,' he said through his twisted lips.

'Of course,' agreed Watson. 'It says: "I herewith give my word of honour that I shall not, in case of my taking part in a walk, make an attempt to escape during such walk, i.e. from the time of leaving camp until, having returned to it at the agreed time, strictly obeying any orders given to me by any accompanying officer, and not to commit any acts that are directed towards the safety of the German Empire." There.' Watson made to hand the card back.

'Other side, please.'

Watson turned it over and read the unfamiliar passage more slowly. "'I know that any prisoner of war who escapes, despite having given his word of honour, is liable to the severest possible punishment." This is new, isn't it?'

'Yes,' said the *Leutnant* with a shrug. 'It means we can shoot you if you try to escape.' The poor man's misshapen smile looked like a terrible leer. 'And you, Captain Hanson, please. If you will read.'

Hanson was dressed in his standard-issue British Warm greatcoat, a large red cravat tucked in at the neck to hide the self-inflicted wound. He had said nothing since the suicide attempt. His sullenness seemed to chide all and sundry for saving him.

'Captain Hanson doesn't speak,' said Watson, pulling down the material at the throat to show the still-livid scar.

The *Leutnant* flinched, even though his own injuries made the mark look like a razor nick. 'He must speak the words and sign the card.'

'I'll sign for him.'

The German shook his head. 'Major Watson—'

'Look at him, man. He's not worth a candle. And look at me. We're hardly the most dangerous men in Germany right now. Let me sign for both. I'll "p.p." for him.'

'Pee-pee?'

'*Per procurationem*,' said Watson. 'It means on behalf of.' It didn't quite, but he didn't feel up to arguing the subtleties of Latin phrasings with a German soldier. It was almost eight o'clock, lunch was in three and a half hours, with the second of the day's *Appells* at one p.m. They'd have to be back for that at the very least.

'I'm not sure,' the *Leutnant* said.

Watson reached into his overcoat pocket and took out a single Huntley & Palmer, carefully wrapped in greaseproof paper. He held out the biscuit to the German. 'This will be crumbs by the time we get back. Can you look after it for us—'

It was gone in an instant. Two cards were presented on the counter top, Watson signed both, 'p.p.-ing' for Hanson, and the signal was given to open both sets of steel gates. It was always a heady moment, and Watson hoped Hanson appreciated it, to take that first step beyond the fences, barbed wire and look-out posts, the searchlamps and the dogs, and breathe free – albeit German – air.

'Halt!' one of the guards shouted.

Hanson, who either didn't register or ignored the command, continued on. Watson heard the familiar sound of a Mauser bolt action, took a series of rapid steps and placed a hand on the captain's shoulder. The man froze where he was. Watson, once he was certain Hanson wasn't going to do anything foolish, turned to confront the guard. 'Yes? Something wrong?'

'*Sie können nicht allein ausgehen.*'

Watson's German had improved considerably over the months of captivity, but this one, a beefy, round-faced boy barely into the shaving years, had a thick, impenetrable accent, as if he was speaking through a mouthful of aniseed balls.

'*Bitte?*'

The German repeated himself, looking over his shoulder at the gate *Leutnant* for confirmation. It was a moment before the duty officer appeared in the side window of the hut.

'*Nein, es ist in Ordnung,*' said the *Leutnant*, wiping some crumbs from his lips, then waving them on. '*Sie brauchen nicht eine Eskorte.*'

Watson caught the last bit. The guard had thought they should have an escort for the walk, as was common, although unescorted solo perambulations were not unknown. Watson mimed running and then put his hand to his heart and gave exaggerated breaths, as if about to collapse from cardiac failure. He could hear the *Leutnant* laugh at the pantomime, but the guard just scowled and lowered his rifle.

'*Komm nicht zu spät, oder ich werde kommen suchen,*' he mumbled, and swung the gate closed behind them. Watson didn't catch a word, but he was fairly sure it was a threat about what would happen if they didn't return.

The road from the camp took them between two large ploughed fields and, eventually, to the village and its railway station. But they had been warned not to venture there. The villagers, many of whom had lost sons on the Western Front, were sometimes violent towards the prisoners. They thought the POWs lived a life of well-fed comfort, while they suffered the privations and indignities that were the result of the Allied blockade.

So as they approached the woods, Watson steered his charge to the left, towards a plantation of fir trees that formed part of the same estate as the camp. From there they could walk through to a small river, which would normally be home to some wildlife, although anything edible, Watson knew, had long ago been snared or shot and cooked. But it was a charming spot, where you could sit and watch the dancing, silvery waters and pretend the war didn't exist or that a camp hemmed in by barbed wire would be calling you back all too soon.

Watson turned up the collar of Hanson's coat, pulled down his cap and began to talk.

'I thought I might tell you a story. Just to pass the time. There was a time when I was driven to tell them. To write things down. Every day an idea popped unbidden into my head, demanding to be shared. Plus, my old friend and colleague provided more narrative than one scribe could hope to have published in a single lifetime. But there is one tale that has come back to me of late. Careful here.' They stepped over some fallen branches. Above them the crows kept up their constant complaints. Behind them, one of the painfully thin horses – apparently the only breed available – was dragging a dray towards the camp gates, plodding with terminal weariness towards its destination, like, thought Watson, Germany herself.

'It was April 1890,' continued Watson, 'as the debilitating bone-chill of a lengthy winter had finally begun to relax its grip on the metropolis, when my friend Sherlock Holmes turned his attention to what the daily press was calling The Rugby Mystery, and others, The Girl and the Gold Watches. Holmes had recently completed his investigation into a most gruesome business, involving jealousy and murder.'

They stepped into the quiet and gloom of the pines, the shrill voices of the birds suddenly muffled, the needles underfoot crackling like pork skin. His voice seemed small and insignificant amid the sturdy, straight-backed trunks of the evergreens, but Watson carried on, enjoying the rhythm of the story.

'The solution to the case had put him in a rather sombre mood. "What is the meaning of it, Watson?" he had exclaimed, not for the first time. Peering into the darkest corners of the human soul often caused him to recoil in revulsion at the depravity of his fellow man. "What object is served by this circle of misery and violence and fear? It must tend to some end, or else our universe is ruled by chance, which is unthinkable. But what end? There is the great standing perennial problem to which human reason is as far from an answer as ever.'"

'Oh, for all that is merciful, man, do be quiet.'

The sudden exclamation, blurted into the cathedral-like space, did, indeed, shock Watson into silence.

'Can we double back through here to the village?' asked Hanson, pointing to the north.

Shocked by this sudden volubility, Watson began to answer, 'That's not a good idea. There have been incidents—'

'Don't worry about that. Give me a hand with my coat.'

Watson instinctively helped Hanson shuck his greatcoat. He held it while the man took off his boots and lowered his trousers.

'What are you doing?'

'Doing? What do you think I am doing?' echoed Hanson, his voice still carrying a trace of Cornish burr. 'Getting out of this godforsaken place.'

'You can't do that.'

Hanson turned the trousers inside out. Now, the dark stripe that marked him out as a POW had disappeared. He quickly pulled them back on and buttoned up the fly.

'Can't?' He took the British Warm back from Watson and began to turn that, too, inside out. The interior had been dyed a dark navy blue. From the lining came a civilian hat, which he placed on his head. 'I have a map, a train timetable, money.

Documents. I came to Krefeld fully prepared for this. Good Lord, do you know how close the Dutch border is?' He pointed a finger east.

'It's that way,' corrected Watson. 'You'd need a compass. But even if you had one, that border is impenetrable on this side. Men have tried for nigh on three years—'

Hanson was in Watson's face now, so close he could feel his breath on his cheek. 'Men haven't tried hard enough. I risked being shot to get myself to this, this *health resort*. You don't know what the rest of the camps are like.'

Watson was only too aware how cushy they had it at Krefeld, but didn't stoop to arguing with the man. 'Then stay where you are. The war will be over—'

'Ah, you've gone soft, man.'

As Hanson wriggled his arms into the coat, Watson grabbed the sleeve. 'I gave my word.'

'I didn't,' Hanson reminded him.

'I gave it on your behalf.'

Hanson laughed at him. 'Oh, please. *Por procreation* or whatever it was? You're not still clinging to some outmoded notion of honour, are you? A gentleman's word is his bond and such rot? If that isn't dead already, it's busy dying out there in the trenches amid the gas and the flamethrowers. Honour? There's no honour in this war.'

Watson felt a flush of anger. He gripped the man's arm harder. 'There has to be. There has to be some shred of honour left. Anyway, if you go running off, you'll be captured within three or four hours . . .'

'Let go of me.'

'. . . and you'll be denying scores of men this small freedom. These walks keep some of them sane. It's why I brought you out here.' Although, he now appreciated, Hanson had duped him on that score. The suicide attempt, like the phoney shell shock he had affected, had clearly been a bluff to make him seem a suitable candidate for these therapeutic walks. 'You think after you break the trust they'll let anyone leave the camp—'

The fist took Watson by surprise. The blow was an awkward one, without the full body weight behind it, but still it felt to Watson as if he were lifted off his feet as he was dashed against a tree trunk. His head spun and for a second he thought he might vomit.

'Look, old man, tell them I overpowered you. That'll be a nice shiner by tomorrow. I came here for this chance and I intend to take it.'

Hanson turned and began to stride towards the village. Watson knew he couldn't let him go. There was too much at stake for every other man in the camp. He bent one leg and used his foot to drive himself off the tree. It was a long time since he had performed a rugby tackle, and it was as much a stumble as a charge, but he caught the man in his lower back and he felt Hanson's legs buckle at the impact. Watson kept his weight on top of him as he fell towards the floor, making sure all the breath was driven from Hanson's body when he crashed down into sparse undergrowth.

Watson, too, was winded and the younger man recovered first, with a vicious elbow to the face. The padding of the man's greatcoat softened the force of the impact, but even so, Hanson managed to wriggle free as Watson reared back to prevent a repeat performance. The speed of the man was impressive. He hopped to his feet and began to work with his fists. Watson covered his face as blow after blow rained down on him, a savagery born of a desperate, irrational urge. Watson lashed out blindly with a foot and made contact with a shin, giving him a moment's respite so he could try and struggle upright.

The pause was short-lived. The moment he was on his feet an uppercut clacked his jaws together and the iron tang of blood filled his mouth. Watson had never had Holmes's facility as a pugilist, but he knew even he was performing poorly here. He managed one solid punch of his own, before a left to his ear set the world a-ringing and he went down again, into the carpet of sharp pine needles.

Watson rolled on his back. He knew the fight was almost out of him. His lungs felt as if they were being caressed with a blow-torch and his sinuses hummed with pain. Hanson, who had only been in captivity a matter of weeks, was still in good shape, still carrying muscle that hadn't been wasted by near starvation. And he was half Watson's age.

Excuses, Watson. Remember the principles of Bartitsu.

'That was you, Holmes. Not me,' he said to the phantom voice, which was as unreliable and infuriating as ever.

Hanson had stepped away from him, walked over to a nearby pine trunk, bent at the waist and then began snuffling like a truffle pig with exertion as he straightened. Watson hoped it was because he had managed to hurt him, to salvage some pride from the beating he had taken. Perhaps he'd broken a rib or two. But when Hanson stood, Watson could see he had managed to prise free a large rock from the soil. That was what had required all the grunting effort. There was certainly nothing wrong with his ribs.

Watson kicked his heels, beetling backwards through the needles until his head rested against sharp bark. He had nowhere left to go. His only option was an appeal to reason, and he was certain that was in short supply in his assailant's brain.

The would-be fugitive approached slowly, clutching the heavy stone that, in a terrible irony, looked to Watson as if it were shaped like a rugby ball. 'I can't have you raising the alarm. Not now I've come this far.'

'Hanson—' Watson began, his arms lifted in a feeble attempt to try to protect his head.

'Sorry, old chap. Needs must, you know.'

Hanson, his expression somewhere between a grin and grimace, lifted his arms above his head and Watson closed his eyes, waiting for the blow that would crush his skull.

SEVEN

'What do you mean, he's not on the list?' said Mrs Gregson, her words snapping like a coachman's whip.

'Ssh, please, Georgina,' pleaded Pitt, as the patrons of the Connaught swivelled their heads to take a closer look at the woman who was disturbing their luncheon.

Mrs Gregson pushed away her bowl of quail consommé, slopping it onto the tablecloth. She clicked her fingers at the waiter and signalled she would like a refill of burgundy. A crusty-looking diner with walrus-style moustaches tutted at her crassness, but she fixed him with a stare that sent him back to his *Suprêmes de Volailles Jeannette.*

Pitt had hoped that a meal in the dining room of a hotel that, despite the shortages apparent beyond its walls, still managed a decent show, would soften Mrs Gregson. But the gilded furniture, silk-panelled walls and pendulous crystal chandeliers seemed only to inflame her more. It was, perhaps, ill-judged to bring a woman who spent her days packing fish paste for prisoners to somewhere quite so conspicuous in its celebration of the finer things of life. A Lyons Corner House might have been more appropriate, he thought mournfully. And a damn sight cheaper, too.

With her glass recharged, Mrs Gregson took a generous mouthful, but appeared not to savour it. 'You'd better start at the beginning, Neville.'

So Pitt explained the tedious machinations of the negotiations to try and alleviate the suffering of the most vulnerable prisoners of war on both sides. How committees had given way to one-on-one negotiations and how, at the last moment, Watson had been denied a place in the first tranche of the repatriated.

A waiter appeared at her shoulder to clear away the neglected soup course. Like every man of his profession in London, apart from those with obvious disabilities, he was of a certain vintage. 'Is everything all right, madam?' he asked in a French accent that might even have been genuine.

'Yes. I'm not as hungry as I thought I was. Perhaps we could have a pause before the next course?'

'Of course, madam. I shall inform the kitchen.'

She turned her attention back to Pitt. 'You said there were three men who were struck off. Was there any common theme? Any link between them?'

'I didn't think to look,' admitted Pitt, lighting a cigarette to stave off his hunger pangs. He hadn't felt he could plough on with his soup while Mrs Gregson had clearly lost her appetite. But after a few days of what the Dutch called food, he had been looking forward to a substantial lunch. He hoped she didn't scupper his highly anticipated dish of lamb noisettes.

'You didn't think to investigate what the connection might

be? Regiment or school or battle? The same London club? Perhaps they are related in some way.'

He admitted, somewhat shamefacedly, that he had not thought to pursue the matter. The noise she made demonstrated her frustration to a good portion of the dining room.

'And this man who denied Major Watson?' she continued.

'Von Bork? What about him?'

'Yes, Von Bork. Have you looked into his background? What do you know of him?'

Pitt shook his head. 'Very little, I am afraid. Only that he was the nominated representative of the Imperial German Prisoners' Welfare Command. The equivalent of me, really.'

'And that's all you can offer?'

He flinched at the dismissive tone she had adopted. 'I don't think we were too concerned about who the German representative was at the time. Just that they had one.'

'And look where that has landed you.'

Despite his years and rank she was making him feel like an errant schoolboy caught scrumping. His false eye was itching in the socket, but he couldn't risk scratching it lest something unfortunate happened. Fishing a rogue peeper out of the lunch was not the done thing at this stage in a relationship. If there was to be a relationship. He could sense her ardour cooling by the minute. His own wasn't far behind. There were plenty of unattached women in London at the moment and a majority of them were far less challenging than Mrs Gregson. And younger.

'Look, Mrs Gregson,' he said, not daring to use her Christian name now, 'this is just a trial run, as it were. In six months there will be another exchange—'

'It is January, Major Pitt. If you think London is cold, what about Germany? He is not a young man . . .'

Precisely. Why all the fuss?

'. . . he could be dead by spring.'

Good riddance.

Pitt concluded he must be tipsy. He had been swilling back the burgundy on an empty stomach. He had to be careful not to speak these uncharitable thoughts out loud. He reached across to cup Mrs Gregson's hand, but found himself grasping only starched linen.

'I'm very disappointed, Major,' she said coolly. 'Very disappointed indeed.'

'I can tell, Mrs Gregson. As am I.' Although not, perhaps, for reasons she fully appreciated. 'Very much so.'

'Is madam ready for her sole now?' asked the waiter, who had glided up to her shoulder as if on castors.

For a second, she thought of declining and leaving, not wanting to go through the rituals of such formal dining. But she had to eat. There was talk of rationing if the German submarines continued their campaign against merchant shipping. But she was in no mood for picking delicately at her dish. 'Off the bone, please.'

'Of course, madam.'

An idea was formulating in her head. Not a sensible idea, perhaps, but one that would give her forward momentum. The thought of another six months or a year packing and labelling parcels appalled her.

'When the men are repatriated to Holland, they will need medical attention, won't they?'

'Yes, of course. The Dutch Red Cross has undertaken to provide care for the sick and injured.'

'You are in touch with them?'

Pitt frowned. His alcohol-blunted brain couldn't quite see where she was going. 'I am.'

'Can you get me in?'

'Where?' he asked. 'The Red Cross?'

'Holland. I want to volunteer my services.'

'But the Parcels and Clothing Committee? That's vital work—'

'Vital work that any empty-headed housewife can do. Just ask Mrs Nichols or Mrs Priestley.'

'Well, I don't know. Do you have any medical training, Mrs Gregson?'

If the lamb and the sole hadn't interrupted, she might have exploded. Instead, she showed him her hands. 'I didn't get these from packing parcels.'

He had noticed them, of course. Rough-skinned and scarred, hardly becoming for a woman of any standing above the servant class. In fact, he had wondered if she had been in service and had bettered herself through the marriage to the late, apparently unlamented, Mr Gregson. If he *was* late, he realized. She had never actually confirmed she was a widow, he had simply picked up that snippet from the gossip at the Clothing Committee HQ.

'Carbolic and Eusol does terrible things to a woman's skin,' she said. 'I was in Belgium and France for two years. I don't think Holland will be a challenge.'

'Well, I have to go out and make provision for the first arrivals. I will make enquiries.'

'I will come with you.'

'Mrs Gregson, I don't think that's . . .' He struggled for the word.

'Possible? Likely? Agreeable? Feasible? The done thing?' she prompted him.

'Appropriate.'

'Oh, I can make it appropriate,' said Mrs Gregson, thinking of favours owed. 'I can make it very appropriate.'

Pitt let out a sigh. He couldn't help thinking of Pandora's box. What had he unleashed with a little innocent flirtation?

'*Bon appétit,*' Mrs Gregson said with a grin that, in a man, he might have described as wolfish. Pitt stared down at his noisettes. He found, with some considerable dismay, that he was no longer hungry.

EIGHT

Hauptmann Halbricht's office, with its twin stoves and crack-ling fire, had trumped the infirmary as the warmest room in the camp, and Watson soon found himself perspiring under his greatcoat. Still, it was too much effort to remove it. He was sitting on an admiral's chair in front of the commandant's desk, wedged in between the arms, and his body was aching from the thumps and bumps he had received. In the heat of the moment, he had felt very little pain. Now, his frame was reliving the tussle with Hanson blow by blow, right down to telling him his knuck-les were not designed for making contact with muscle and bone.

As Halbricht fussed in one of the cupboards, Watson looked around the room. It featured several items he had forgotten he missed: a carpet, for one, soft under the soles of his boots. A pair of ornate table lamps with shades, suggesting quiet nights of reading. A splendid Winterhalder & Hofmeier mantel clock, from an era when time didn't drag its heels. And there was art. Above the fireplace was a portrait in oils of Halbricht in his younger days, posed holding a substantial tome under one arm and wearing what looked like a college gown. Adorning other walls were English hunting scenes, the usual confection of red jackets, horses, horns and hounds. It made him homesick for a good coaching inn and a pint of ale.

'Ah, here we are,' Halbricht exclaimed, pulling free a bottle from the rear of the cupboard. 'Port!'

Watson, who had been expecting schnapps at best, said: 'Splendid.'

'It's a habit I picked up in England,' Halbricht said. 'Along with marmalade. When I was younger and thinner.' His eyes glanced up to the portrait.

'You taught there?' The gown in the portrait indicated a teacher; the marmalade and the port suggested, perhaps, a spell at High Table. Could the marmalade be Frank Cooper's? 'Oxford perhaps?'

'For five years,' he confirmed. 'Jesus College. You know it?'

'I know it helps if you speak Welsh.' While he was in Cairo researching blood transfusion, Watson had met an alumnus of the college called Lawrence, who explained that because Jesus was founded by a Welshman, some connection with the country helped facilitate entry. Lawrence, although brought up in Oxford, had been born in Tremadog. One day, Watson thought, he must write down his Egyptian adventure with the diminutive Orientalist and spy.

'Oh, no longer. Although we did discover a Jones on my father's side, which smoothed my tenure. But I had to return to Germany ten years ago. My wife hated it there. And she wanted my boys brought up in the German way.' He looked wistful for a moment.

'Are they well?' Watson asked with some hesitation, only too aware that Germany's sons, like Britain's, had paid the highest price for this war. 'The boys?'

'Yes, thank you. They are fifteen and twelve, so have not been part of this dreadful business. I know what you are thinking. What is an old man doing with such sprats? My wife is younger than I, Major. I came back to Germany one long vac and found we had delightful new neighbours, who had an equally delightful daughter . . .'

He handed over a glass of the port to Watson and raised a toast. 'To the swift end to this nonsense between our countries.'

Watson couldn't disagree with that. 'To peace. May we both live long enough to enjoy it.'

He sipped, enjoying the once-familiar warmth and the rich, fruity overtones of the port. Now, relaxed, he felt the terrible import of what he had done descend on him, like a shroud of thick chain mail. His shoulders slumped.

'This is some business, Major,' said Halbricht, his tone suddenly glum. 'You are sure nothing is broken?'

'Bruises. A little ringing in the ears. This eye aches. And I am sure my torso is an interesting colour. My orderly, Sayer, strapped up my ribs. Did a good job.'

'You must let him spoil you, Major. A good orderly is invaluable. You are not as young as you once were, when you were running around London with Mr Holmes all those years ago.'

'You don't have to remind me of that.' Except it seemed like centuries, not decades ago. A different life altogether. He supposed it was. London would never be the same again, for better or worse, even when the conflict was over. The people returning from this abominable war would see to that.

'I really have to thank you.' Halbricht offered Watson a cigarette and, when it was accepted, lit it from a sturdy silver desk
lighter. 'It was a brave, honourable thing to do.'

'It doesn't feel like it,' Watson said gloomily.

'You gave your word—' Halbricht began.

'Perhaps Hanson was right. Perhaps such words are meaning-
less in war.'

Halbricht shook his head. 'The man was deranged. You know
he wouldn't have got very far. The villagers would have flushed
him out in a second. He would only have brought down retribution on his fellow Englishmen. Even I have to be seen to play by
the rules. Lose a man for even twenty-four hours and the local
army command wants to know how and why and who is going
to pay. Too many escapes and then you can look forward to a
new job as foreman of a slate mine. Like most of the men in the
camp, I am just biding my time here, waiting for the war to end.'

'And yet poor Hanson is dead,' Watson reminded the
commandant.

'And this is not your fault.'

'Not technically. Morally, perhaps.'

The Englishmen's voices during the argument and subsequent tussle had carried through the trees, drifting over to the
camp. The moon-faced guard with the Mauser had gone along
to investigate and arrived just in time to see Hanson about to
dash Watson's brains out with a stone. He had shot Hanson in
the chest, killing him instantly.

'What will the report say?' Watson asked.

'That Hanson was shot while trying to escape. No mention
will be made of the exact circumstances. His family will be

satisfied he was doing his duty as an officer. My superiors will be pleased that I prevented a hue and cry for a POW. And you . . .'

The pause grew.

'You can take some comfort in being an officer and a gentleman who is as good as his word.'

Watson threw back his drink. To his surprise, Halbricht topped him up. He didn't refuse, despite his unease at the fraternization. 'It's scant comfort.'

'It was the devil and the deep blue sea,' said Halbricht. 'And I face the same dilemma.'

Something in the tone halted Watson's slide into self-pity. The cosy room, the port, the cigarette. He was being softened up for an announcement of some description. He pushed himself upright in the chair. 'What is it, *Hauptmann*?'

The man looked pained, as if he were the one who had suffered a beating. 'There is no easy way to break this news. I was hoping the drink might help. But it has made it more difficult, this moment of . . . camaraderie.'

'We're not comrades. Not yet. I am still an enemy officer. I am afraid no amount of port will alter that.'

Halbricht nodded, his expression hangdog. 'You are right, of course.' He took a deep breath, steeling himself for the blow he was about to deliver. 'Major Watson, I regret to inform you that you have been refused a place on the repatriation list.'

It was only at that moment that Watson appreciated how much he had been banking on getting out of Krefeld. Perhaps that was why he had been so adamant about stopping Hanson, he had been – subconsciously – worried it might jeopardize his own release. And now this. It made him all the more wretched.

He felt a crack zigzag across the dam that was holding back the waters of despair. He struggled to keep his voice even. 'And was any reason given?'

'They don't have to give explanations, Major. "Request denied" and a rubber stamp is all they require.'

'You could ask why,' said Watson. 'And put in an appeal. You could also petition the Red Cross.'

As the *Hauptmann* nodded his features collapsed into what looked like pity. 'The devil and the deep blue sea, as I said, Major. I could object, kick up a fuss, as you say. But I know there are those in the Army Group that runs this sector who consider me too soft. Too considerate. To be a lover of all things British. I am tainted, in their eyes, by my years in Oxford. My sense of honour, such as it is, tells me I should try my damnedest to get a man like you out of here. My sense of survival tells me not to rock the boat. Unlike you, Major Watson, I am not a brave man.'

'Brave? Me? I think not. The brave thing to do might have been to go along with Hanson.'

'And then I suspect I would be drinking alone, perhaps a toast to two fallen men.'

Watson raised the glass. 'To the fallen, all of them. And those left behind to mourn.' He took a slug of the port, quickly so as not to betray his shaking hands. He placed the glass on the desk before him and made to rise but the expression on Halbricht's face pulled him up short. He sat back down again. 'And, *Hauptmann*? There is something else, I feel.'

Now the Anglophile wouldn't catch his eye. The commandant examined his port as if he had spotted something floating on the surface. He licked dry lips before he spoke. 'You are to be transferred from here. There is a *Lager* with no British medical personnel to speak of. You have been ordered there.'

'Which camp?'

'You understand that these orders are from Tenth Army Corps, from the office of Von Knobelsdorf himself.'

Watson doubted the head of the Tenth Army concerned himself with one elderly prison doctor. 'Which camp am I being transferred to, *Hauptmann*?'

The word came out like a hound clearing its throat. 'Harzgrund.'

Watson nodded. He had heard of it. Everybody in the system had. It was also known as The Worst Camp in Germany. If the rumours were true, Major John H. Watson of the Royal Army Medical Corps had just been handed a death sentence.

NINE

There wasn't much to pack in his canvas kitbag. Watson carefully folded his underwear and spare shirts and placed them in the bottom, followed by the 'comfort' requisites he had received in parcels, a few precious jars of food and an English copy of *The History of the Decline and Fall of the Roman Empire*, which he had managed to pick up in hospital.

Sayer, his wiry, jockey-sized orderly – he had served in one of the Birkenhead 'Bantam' regiments, created from the pool of willing men who were less than regulation height – was inconsolable when he heard the news and fussed around Watson as he packed that morning. He had made certain Watson had filled up at breakfast, even pushing him to two cups of the acorn coffee. It might be a long day ahead, he counselled.

'The thing is, Major Watson, most of the others treat me like the lowest footman. Make the tea, wash the crockery, make my bed, wipe my arse, there's a good chap.' Watson laughed at his faux-plummy voice. Sayer might be crude, but he was always entertaining. 'For them, 'tain't no different to being at school.

With you, at least I got a break now and then and a bit of respect. I'll miss you, sir. Where they sendin' you again?'

He repeated the name. It didn't sound any less unpleasant than when the commandant said it. *Harzgrund.* It was like a Teutonic gargle.

'Where is it, exactly?'

'Harz Mountains, I believe. Further into Germany, at any rate.'

'That's a cruelty, that is, you ask me. If you'd been going to Holland, I'd've been glad for you, but this . . .'

Watson put a hand on the little man's shoulder. 'I know, Sayer. But we sometimes have to bear the unbearable, don't we?' Sayer nodded. 'I've left you some cigarettes and tobacco and a pipe over there. No, it's fine; I am trying to smoke less.' Watson thumped his chest and winced at the flash of pain from one of his many bruises. 'Find it affects my wind these days.'

'Not as much as that bloody cabbage soup,' said Sayer.

'Not that kind of win——' he began before he caught Sayer's wink.

'And I'd like you to have these, sir,' said Sayer, producing a pair of thick-knit socks from under his tattered tunic.

'I can't, Sayer. Good socks like that, worth their weight in real coffee.'

'My mother knits them, sir. I can get plenty more. Please. I haven't worn them. Well, not more than once or twice. And I washed them.'

'Thank you, Sayer. I appreciate it. Now, there are two things I'd like you to do for me. One is post my letters. I'm stretching my allowance, but I'm sure they'll pass it this once.'

'Right you are, sir. And the other?'

'Tell the Red Cross where I have gone, so the parcels are redirected.'

'A pleasure.'

The door to the billet opened. A sombre-faced Feldwebel Krebs stepped in. 'It is time, Major,' he said. 'The truck is here.'

'How long is the journey?' Watson asked.

Krebs screwed up his face at the thought of what lay ahead for the prisoner. 'Seven hours, perhaps more.'

'And it's a truck?'

'Yes.'

'Not, I assume, fitted with Pullman recliners.' Watson scooped up the straw-filled pillow off his bed and tucked it under his arm. 'I am sure you can scrounge another for whoever takes my bunk,' he said to Sayer.

'Leave it to me, sir. Here, let me carry that.'

Krebs looked puzzled. 'Just one case?'

'Yes.'

He looked at Sayer. 'Your things too?'

'No, chummy. I'm staying here.'

Krebs shook his head. 'No. Hauptmann Halbricht was most insistent. Major Watson needs to be looked after, Private Sayer. You are going with him.'

The lorry, a wheezing Horch with loosely secured canvas sides that did little to keep out the wind, left Krefeld II just after midday and struck east. Sayer tried to put a brave face on the *fait accompli* of his involvement in the transfer; Watson had complained vociferously and demanded to see Halbricht but was informed that, as in any army, orders were orders. Sayer would accompany him to Harzgrund. In manacles, if need be.

From the open rear of the vehicle, beyond where their two escorts sat smoking, Watson could see the meagre traffic on the road consisted mainly of horse-drawn vehicles with, as always, skeletal nags between the shafts. The people, too, looked grey and wan, in need of a substantial feed of protein, he thought. Only a motorcycle rider who roared past them, leather coat flapping, looked to be in decent health.

'Bit posh, all this, isn't it?' said Sayer as he carefully rolled a cigarette.

'What's that?' Watson asked.

'A truck all to ourselves. Luxury, that is.'

Watson nodded. Prisoners were normally transported by train, third class if they were lucky, cattle if not. With the shortage of fuel across Germany, he too was surprised at the extravagance of personalized transport. He hoped it was simply a kind gesture by Hauptmann Halbricht. If so, it was, like his dispatching of Sayer, a misguided one. The solid tyres and the rutted roads meant Watson's ribs, still tender from his forest tussle with poor deluded Hanson, were giving him trouble. Sayer noticed the series of grimaces that accompanied each jolt.

'You want me to restrap you up, sir?'

'No, Sayer. Perhaps when we stop.' Watson raised his voice. 'I assume we will stop at some point.' He looked over at the guards, but the pair, one of whom was too old for the front line, the other a young man missing several fingers, either didn't understand or ignored him. The grizzled one had lung problems, his breathing audibly damp even over the sound of the Horch's engine, but Watson reckoned him too elderly to have picked up gas damage at the front. Some kind of industrial emphysema was most likely.

The truck grumbled on. Watson accepted a roll-up about as thick as a pipe cleaner from Sayer and tried to get comfortable on his purloined pillow. To pass the time, he mentally composed more of the story he had begun to tell Hanson on their walk, 'The Girl and the Gold Watches', as he now titled it.

He must have nodded off because the squeal of the brakes sent him sprawling along the metal bench towards the cab. Only Sayer's swift handiwork prevented him ending up in a bundle on the floor. The guards dropped the tailgate, hopped out and indicated the prisoners should do the same.

'Exercise. Stretch legs,' wheezed the older of the pair.

'Where are we?' asked Watson, blinking away sleep and trying to focus through watering eyes.

'Middle of bleedin' nowhere,' muttered Sayer. 'We turned off the main road about half an hour ago. At a place called Haaren.'

Watson shook his head to show it meant nothing to him. 'How long have we been going?'

'About three hours. You need a hand, sir?'

'No,' said Watson, shuffling towards the rear.

Watson climbed down gingerly from the truck, with some unasked-for assistance from the young guard with the missing digits on his left hand. Watson wondered if the wound had been self-inflicted. He had seen plenty of those in his time. If so, the man was misjudged: those serious about escaping the war alto-gether always made sure their trigger finger on the right hand – and the boy was definitely a right-hander – went. Then again, the injury had gained him this soft posting, so perhaps there was more cunning at work than Watson gave him credit for.

He looked about as he straightened his spine and did a few mild stretching exercises. Sayer was right. It was the middle of nowhere. They had pulled over on the verge of a narrow road, as straight as a rule, which, a few feet of soil and grass apart, was hemmed in on either side by densely packed pine trees. A plantation of some description. There was no other traffic and the silence, broken only by the tick-tick of the Horch's cooling engine, felt oppressive. His breath clouded in the air. It was already colder than in the west of the country.

The driver, a weathered specimen with a face the colour of walnut, was already out of the cab, smoking a cigarette and drinking coffee from a vacuum flask, which he clearly didn't intend to share.

'You want me to take a look at the strapping?' Sayer asked.

'Come.' The old guard indicated towards the trees with his rifle barrel.

'What's this? Ablutions?' asked Sayer.

Watson noted that his bladder did indeed need emptying and stepped towards the treeline.

'No!' The guard was indicating Sayer, who had followed Watson. 'Only him. Not you.'

Sayer put a hand on Watson's shoulder. 'What's he playing at, sir?'

The second guard brought his Mauser down on Sayer's arm, knocking it away. Sayer swore at him with some vigour which, fortunately, the German didn't fully understand. But he got the gist. He prodded Sayer back against the side of the truck with the muzzle of his Mauser.

'Come,' repeated the older man, 'with me.'

'Don't do anything foolish while I am gone, Sayer,' warned Watson. 'I'll be fine.' *There's no point in us both getting killed*, he almost added.

He had heard of this scenario, of course. A train or a lorry stops for a rest break. The prisoners 'stretch their legs'. They are then shot 'trying to escape'. Well, perhaps this was fate's payback for Hanson. It was possible he deserved such an ending after what had happened to his fellow Englishman.

The trees seemed to absorb both light and heat and he pulled the greatcoat tight around him as he shuffled into the semi-darkness. He could hear the whistle in the old guard's breathing quite clearly now. He wasn't a well man. But could Watson take him? He glanced over his shoulder, reducing his walking speed as he did so. The German was a good five strides behind him and he slowed to match Watson's new pace. He gestured with his rifle that Watson should keep moving. Watson did so. It was then he noticed white smudges on some of the trees they passed. He ran a finger along one. Fresh lime wash. Markings. He was being led down a particular route through these trees. But to what?

He smelled the smoke first. Pipe tobacco. Something intense and spicy, although he couldn't say more than that.

Latakia, Watson. Unmistakable.

As usual, he ignored the fraudster.

The smoker was leaning against a tree on the edge of a small clearing. There was a Puch motorcycle on a stand in the centre and an access pathway led off towards the north. It was a prearranged rendezvous between truck crew and the rider of the Puch.

Von Bork was dressed in a long, leather coat over the sharply tailored uniform of an *Oberstleutnant* in the *Oberste Heeresleitung*, the Supreme Army Command. Watson had last seen the man one sultry night in August 1914, when Holmes had disrupted his spy ring. Then, he had been in civilian clothes and favoured cigars. He had been expecting to be welcomed like a returning hero in Berlin; Holmes had ensured the plaudits were replaced by recriminations.

The well-cut tunic could not hide the fact that Von Bork had put on weight. During his time in England he had been keen on yachting, polo and hunting. Now, with his nascent belly and jowls, he looked like a man who was trapped behind a desk and indulged only in good lunches.

'Dr Watson,' said Von Bork, tapping out his pipe on a tree trunk. 'It has been some years.'

'Von Bork,' he said, trying to keep his voice steady. 'How unexpected.'

'How are you, Doctor?'

'Major.'

'Oh, we can dispense with that nonsense. You aren't in any army now, not in my book. It's back to Dr Watson. The faithful companion, the not-so-reliable biographer. You know I often think back to those four years in England. Some of my happiest times. The clubs, the women, the weekends in the country. All so civilized. Until that night when Holmes played his hand. How is he?'

'Keeping well.' Which was true, although he had moved

cottage to be closer to Bert, the young boy who was proving an invaluable companion and quite the beekeeper. It also made it harder for the admirers and the inevitable scribblers to track him down. The latter were always trying to ferret out what, exactly, was Holmes's contribution to the war. 'He has his hobbies and his health.'

'I'm sorry to hear that. I was hoping for sadder news,' he admitted with a wry smile. 'You know, I always expected, one day, to see your great triumph in print. "The Adventure of the Gullible German Spy", perhaps. Have I missed it?'

'Your story has not seen the light of day,' said Watson. 'Who knows if it ever will? It is hardly a tale of great detection or deduction. Merely one of tenacious pursuit.'

Von Bork narrowed his eyes. 'Oh, I think it will bubble to the surface, like scum on a pot, Watson. The great man's final case? How can you resist a curtain call for your consulting detective?' The sourness in the voice was striking, years of resentment curdled into hate.

'It was you who took my name off the repatriation list, wasn't it?' Watson said as the mental tumblers clicked into place.

Von Bork now permitted himself a wide grin, as if his work was something to be proud of.

'And arranged my transfer to Harzgrund?'

A nod. 'I said I would get even with you. If it took me the rest of my life. I have not yet acquired the means to take down Mr Sherlock Holmes, but I can imagine his suffering when he hears of the conditions prevailing at Harzgrund.'

'Holmes is a virtual hermit. He will be oblivious to any suffering I might experience.'

'Under normal circumstances, perhaps. Yet you write to him.' From his pocket, Von Bork took two envelopes. 'And to . . . Mrs Gregson . . .'

Watson started forward but a half-gargled bark from the guard stopped him. 'You scoundrel,' Watson said. It sounded so feeble. He wished for Sayer's artful facility with oaths and curses. 'Those are personal letters. How did you—'

'Oh, as a member of the POW committee, I can do anything. Even take the mail for censoring. Personal letters?' He held the envelopes aloft. 'Or full of secret codes? I shall let our cryptographers take a look. And I shall send them on, do not worry, suitably edited, if need be, but with a little additional information to worry Mr Holmes and this . . .' he looked at the address, '. . . Mrs Gregson. A sweetheart perhaps? A widow to keep you company in your declining years?'

'My goddaughter,' he lied, trying to recall if anything in the letter would betray his true feelings for Mrs Gregson. But he was not of the generation that indulged in florid admissions of emotion. And there were no coded messages. He had not had time to insert the deliberately misspelled words that were the key to the cipher he used when corresponding with his old colleague. 'So I am to be the instrument of suffering for Holmes? Is that your grand scheme?' Watson tried to make it sound as pathetic as possible, but he feared there was method in this cruelty.

'Until I come up with a better idea.'

'Why not shoot me and have done with it? Holmes would mourn me, I am sure.' He was serious. It was a valid alternative to what the German was proposing.

'Oh, no,' said Von Bork. 'What would another death count?

Death has lost all currency in this war, don't you find? But misery and starvation? No, an ongoing punishment, a constant drip-drip of pain to the Great Detective, is far more satisfactory.' He consulted his watch. 'Now, I am needed in Berlin, so I must leave you.' He wrapped his pipe in a pouch and slipped it into the leather coat. 'Rest assured, the camp commandant will keep me updated on your . . . progress.'

'I wouldn't want any special treatment.'

Von Bork laughed. 'Very good, Doctor, very good. I do miss that laconic sense of humour you British have. I'd wish you well, but . . . it would defeat the whole object of this meeting, wouldn't it? Gunther here will take you back to continue the journey.'

Von Bork walked to the Puch, threw a leg over it and kicked away its stand. Before he could operate the starting lever, Watson said: 'I have one question, Von Bork.'

'Yes?'

'What tobacco do you smoke?'

Von Bork examined the enquiry, looking for a trick or a hidden barb, but could find none. 'Tobacco? I have a taste for Latakia, although it is rather hard to find except in Berlin these days. Why?'

I'll be damned, Watson thought. 'No matter. I just collect such facts. You never know when they might come in handy.'

'Well, if it's a present you are thinking of,' Von Bork smirked again, 'my birthday is in December. If you should live that long.'

The sudden roar the engine smothered the possibility of any further conversation, and Von Bork manhandled the bike round, gave the throttle a quarter-turn and disappeared down the path through the trees. Watson wondered if the German could feel the imaginary daggers he was throwing him penetrating that expensive leather riding coat.

'I am sorry,' said Gunther in his halting English.

'It's not your fault . . .' Watson began, then stopped himself. 'Sorry for what exactly?'

The sound of the rifle shot zigzagged through the woods, ricocheting off the trunks until a blurred version of the report reached their ears. Watson didn't wait for permission, he began to sprint as fast as his reluctant body would carry him, back to the road.

They've shot Sayer, said the voice in his head.

And, because his phantom friend had been right about the Latakia, Watson knew this was true too.

TEN

At first the diners on that Friday evening in the Savoy's River Room thought it was thunder, but that was simply the initial ignition, which did indeed sound like a low rumble in the heavens. The noise of the second, more powerful blast came half a minute later, followed almost immediately by a strange sickly orange glow, as if the sunset had gone into reverse. The percussion wave arrived while many customers had vacated their tables and moved to the windows – which had not yet been fitted with their blackout panels – to see if this was a German Zeppelin attack or an early sortie by the new German bombers the papers were talking about.

The glass simply shuddered to begin with, the reflected light from the restaurant's electric lamps dancing and shimmering as the panes distorted. And then they imploded, showering guests with shards that sliced through cloth and skin. The screams of wounded patrons and staff almost drowned out the third explosion, which unseated the few remaining sections of glass, sending them spinning across the room like a magician's knives.

Mrs Gregson was fortunate. Seated on the far side of the restaurant's small dance floor, she was peppered with the finest of glass particles, one of which entered her eye, causing stinging and irritation. Her dining companion, Robert Nathan, a senior member of the Wartime Constabulary, was blown backwards off his chair and cracked his head, but soon struggled to his feet.

Mrs Gregson rose and picked her way through a scattering of shattered glass, broken crockery, cutlery, half-eaten dishes and bottles of wine busy glugging their contents onto the Savoy's carpet. She could see the bright blooms of fresh blood on some individuals over near the windows, but she could tell that a significant proportion of the people on their feet were simply dazed.

'I need everyone who is uninjured – I repeat, uninjured – to go through to the foyer,' she shouted over the moans and groans that that were now replacing the shriller screams that had filled the room in the immediate aftermath of the detonations. 'Now, please, in an orderly fashion. Perhaps any staff could stay and help? Thank you.'

Still that unnatural light washed over the river outside, lending the Thames a hellish cast. 'Those who are able to walk, but are wounded, I want you over on the left. Next to the bandstand. Please . . . we need access to the more seriously injured, so if you can move away . . . Mr Nathan, can you please make sure the house physician is informed at once that we have casualties and that ambulances have been called?'

There were, she knew, only six ambulance stations in the whole of London, and it was likely they would be deployed to the site of the explosion. 'And get the doormen to commandeer some taxis,' she added.

Nathan, who was facing up to fifty, but still fit – his pig-sticking and cricket regime in India had ensured that – didn't question Mrs Gregson, but vaulted the low railing behind him and walked briskly to the main foyer. She heard his voice booming out, issuing orders rather than requests, as if addressing his servants in Calcutta.

She looked around the damaged room. 'Maître d' . . . maître d'?'

'Yes, madam?' The Frenchman stepped forward. He had a razor-thin cut along his cheek, running down to the corner of his moustache, but there was little evidence of blood. His previously oiled-down hair, though, was sticking up at crazy angles, like a chimney sweep's brush.

'Ah, there you are. I'll need clean napkins and tablecloths in lieu of bandages for the moment. And any first aid kits from the kitchen.' She addressed the room. 'Does anyone have any medical training? Anyone? No?' She lowered her voice. 'Right. Just me then.'

She had reached the first of the prone figures, an elderly lady who appeared unconscious, with a nasty gash on her forehead. Her dress had ridden up, revealing her undergarments and Mrs Gregson quickly made her decent. The woman still favoured antiquated tight corsets and panic had made her breathing dangerously constricted. Mrs Gregson set about loosening the woman's stays, using a discarded steak knife to rip through the material and laces. The woman groaned.

As she worked, Mrs Gregson signalled to a waiter. 'That

man over there needs a tourniquet at the top of his arm. Can you do that? I'll be over in a second.' The bindings free, she turned the woman on her side. Using a napkin extracted from a holder on a nearby table, she dabbed at the blood along the hairline. There was a triangle of glass embedded in there and she carefully extracted it, mopping up the welling blood that oozed from the wound.

The lady's eyes fluttered open. 'George.'

'I am sure George is fine. And so are you. Just hold this in place, can you? Thank you. I'm sorry about your clothing. But you've been lucky. But I'd wear looser corsets from now on, though.'

Mrs Gregson looked up at the waiter trying to treat the man with blood running down his fingers and a large fragment of glass in his forearm. 'No, cut his jacket sleeve before you tie the tourniquet . . . Oh, let me do it. No, madam, do NOT touch your face. You will cause scarring. Don't let her touch her face. Where is that blasted house doctor? Look, this is how you tie a tourniquet . . .'

An hour later the Savoy staff were sweeping up the debris in the River Room and glaziers were boarding up the glassless frames. Nathan took Mrs Gregson to the American Bar for a stiff drink. Nobody seemed to mind that her dress was spattered in blood or that Nathan's evening dress was askew. In fact, the Sangarees were on the house.

'At least if I spill some, it won't show,' she said, holding up the red-wine cocktail.

'You were magnificent in there,' said Nathan with undisguised admiration. 'I can think of no man who could have coped better and a great number who would have done a damned sight less.'

She couldn't quite untangle the compliment and she let it pass. 'It was just like old times,' she said, with a shudder, thinking of the months when every day was a stream of constant horrors at the Casualty Clearing Stations.

'Is your eye all right?' he asked, leaning forward. 'It's frightfully bloodshot.'

'I think there is something behind the lid. I can feel it when I blink. I'll irrigate it when I get home.'

The manager of the hotel approached them, gave a little bow, and said: 'I thought you might be interested to know, the damage was caused by an explosion at the Silvertown munitions factory. The blast ignited a gasometer in the Greenwich Peninsula.'

'But that's miles down river,' said Mrs Gregson.

'We were unfortunate. The explosion seems to have funnelled straight down to us. Nearby buildings are unscathed. Somerset House has a few cracked panes, that's all, apparently.'

'There will be a serious number of casualties,' said Nathan glumly. 'Explosion of that magnitude.'

'I assume so. But there is no news of that yet. I won't detain you. I just wanted to thank you again for your efforts. If there is anything we can do . . . I'd like to have madam's dress taken care of . . .'

She waved the suggestion away, not wanting a fuss. 'No, it's fine. It's not the first blood I've seen.'

'Mrs Gregson nursed on the Western Front,' Nathan explained. She didn't bother to correct him that she'd been a VAD, an auxiliary, rather than a nurse.

'In which case, at least some luck was on our side in that you were dining with us. I insist you return for dinner at your convenience as my guest. It's the least we can do.'

'We will, thank you,' said Mrs Gregson.

When he had left them, Nathan said: 'Well, I'd like to come again if you would.'

'At some point, perhaps. But there was a favour I was about to ask you, Robert. Before Silvertown exploded.'

'Personal or professional?'

'Professional.'

A shadow of disappointment crossed Nathan's features. 'Really? I thought you'd given up all the life of skulduggery now Holmes has retired once more.'

Nathan had met Mrs Gregson in London in the aftermath of the Elveden affair, when she had been Churchill's spy in the unit that was secretly developing the tank. Nathan had helped in the hunt for Miss Pillbody, the German agent who had murdered her way across Suffolk and Essex. Although his official title was as a member of the Wartime Constabulary, in fact he was with the secret service, mostly charged with uncovering Indian seditionists at home and abroad. He had thwarted a plot by anti-Raj agents to kill Kitchener, only for the field marshal to die when his ship struck a mine en route to Russia some six months later. 'Or are you in cahoots with Winston again?'

'No, I haven't seen either Holmes or Churchill since last year when we collared Miss Pillbody.'

'Then I can't imagine what favour MI5 could do for you, Mrs Gregson.'

She took a sip of her Sangaree and gave a tired, lopsided smile.

Pitt had proved such a disappointment — he hadn't even managed to get her assigned to the Red Cross in Belgium — but she had high hopes for Nathan. 'Oh, you'd be surprised what MI5 could do for me, Robert.'

ELEVEN

Watson's German escorts bundled up the body of Sayer and placed it in the cab, so at least he wouldn't have to look at the poor chap. He had shouted himself hoarse when he had reached the lorry, yelling in the face of the driver and the young guard. They remained impassive. They repeated the same phrase over and over again. *'Er versuchte zu fliehen.'*

Watson knew what it meant. He was trying to escape. To flee the scene. That would be the official report. Shot while trying to escape.

Eventually, tired of his histrionics, they had pushed Watson into the back of the Horch and the truck had set off again, heading north-east on smaller roads now, the sun falling in the sky, the temperature dropping with each kilometre, or so it seemed to Watson as he shivered in the rear.

Why had he done it? Why had Von Bork ordered the death of an innocent man? Possibly because some of his own agents had been executed in England. Unfortunate to face trial after the declaration of war with Germany, two of his men, Hollis and Steiner, had been hanged as spies. Watson, Holmes and even

Vernon Kell of the Secret Service Bureau had objected, on the grounds that Great Britain had agents on the Continent and, if caught, they would now face the same fate. But public opinion — in a country brought up on the jingoist espionage fictions of Le Queux and Erskine Childers, and egged on by the *Mail* and the *Express* — had demanded the rope for the fifth columnists.

Watson, though, doubted the murder of his servant was a simple tit-for-tat. No, Sayer was a last-minute addition to the transfer to Harzgrund. But he suspected it was no part of Von Bork's plan for Watson to arrive at camp with a friend — for that was what Sayer had been — and an ally. Von Bork had wanted Watson to suffer. And suffer alone, without solace.

Two can play at that game.

'Yes, they can,' Watson muttered to himself in reply. But he knew better than to dwell on what might be, on the glimmer that some revenge might be visited on the German. Such a concept might nurture some people, provide sustenance, but Watson knew it could equally turn corrosive. He had seen first-hand in the trenches how an ancient grudge could lead to a morbid dementia, a case that ended with yet more deaths out in no man's land, at least one of which he was responsible for. And now, poor Sayer . . .

'Zigarette?' asked Gunther, the older guard.

Watson scowled and uttered an oath at him. The German shrugged, to show it was his loss, and lit up. The smoke drifted over and Watson almost regretted his hasty reaction. But he couldn't just flick away the crime that had been committed. It wasn't water under the bridge, not with Sayer wrapped like a mummy in the front of the truck. It was murder, not war. He would write a report at the first opportunity. Surely, when this madness was over, there would be a reckoning for such callous actions away from the battlefield?

One dead man among millions? Do you think they will care? Can anyone afford to care?

It was flat, unsentimental and it was very likely the truth.

'I will care,' Watson said out loud, his voice thick with venom. 'I will damn well care.'

The pair of guards exchanged glances that showed they thought he had taken leave of his senses. The younger guard said something under his breath and laughed and Watson felt a murderous urge come over him, alien and terrifying in its intensity.

Not now, Watson, not now, said a soothing voice. *All in good time.*

Good time? Would he know a good time ever again? Would anyone? The very concept seemed to have been swept away from Europe in a slurry of mud and blood. Watson pulled his coat around him, arranged the pillow on the bench, lay down and closed his eyes, letting the swaying of the truck lull him into a fitful, angry sleep.

It was dusk when Watson was jerked awake by a poor gear change. They were climbing and the Horch was struggling with the incline. The driver was working hard with throttle and gears to take the sweeping bends. From the tail of the truck, Watson could see the lights of villages below. What he couldn't see was many trees. This mountain appeared to be denuded of vegetation.

Gunther had unwrapped a length of sausage from a cloth

and he sliced off a chunk and held it out to Watson. After a moment's hesitation he took it. Accepting the earlier cigarette would have served no purpose other than to show weakness, but a sausage – even one he discovered was mostly sawdust – would help keep his strength up. And, even without knowing what Von Bork had in store for him, he was sure he would need all his reserves to survive.

The altitude made his ears pop and now his breath showed within the truck. He shivered. A sensible man would ask for Sayer's coat and gloves and the contents of the kitbag that lay next to his own, strapped in place with thick webbing against the cab's bulkhead. But decency prevented him from doing so. Probably he would be refused anyway. In Germany, as in most countries affected by the war, clothing was strong currency, and the guards would split the garments between them. He patted his coat to make sure those socks Sayer had given him were still there.

'Not far,' said the young German with the missing fingers. 'Soon.'

Watson ignored him. As if he was in any hurry to reach Harzgrund.

The brakes gave a squeal of alarm, and Watson slithered along the bench once more. The Germans clung on to the tail-gate, swearing loudly, and the lorry skewed across the road before it came to an undignified halt. The engine was still chugging when the driver appeared at the rear and began to declaim in rapid German. Apart from the fact he was far from happy, Watson could barely make out a word from the man's thick dialect.

The older German managed to calm the driver down and he lowered the tailgate and slid out into the gathering night. Watson could see the first stars appearing in the deep blue sky.

The guard reappeared. '*Wir müssen von hier zu Fuß.*'

The young man used two fingers to make the universal sign for walking. 'We must make foot,' he said.

'How far?' Watson asked, struggling for the translation. '*Wie . . . wie weit?*'

A shrug. '*Zwei Kilometer.*'

'*Warum?*' Weariness meant his German failed him. 'What's going on? Is there a blockage on the road?'

Fingerless grabbed Watson's kitbag from the webbing holder and tossed it down onto the ground. 'Come.'

Watson climbed out into the sharp night air. Cold rose up from the earth to greet him. Somewhere in the far distance a dog yapped, audible over the grumbling engine. Others offered a howling rejoinder. He imagined German shepherds, bad-temperedly patrolling the corridor between two walls of wire.

He ran on the spot a little to get his circulation going and walked around the side to see what the trouble was. The road was rutted beneath his feet and he stumbled on one of the ridges. Heavy traffic had passed this way, corrugating the surface. Watson steadied himself and peered ahead. The road, a sandy ribbon of grit, curved out of sight but the lorry's feeble headlamps had picked out a metal sign on a steel pole, with the camp's name written on the plate in gothic script. But there was another rectangle tied beneath it, this one wooden and makeshift. There was no mistaking its intent, even if you didn't understand the single word, *Fleckfieber*, for it was adorned

with a crudely daubed red skull and crossbones. In fact, Watson
did, for once, know that term. He knew it in several languages
and it made his already shivering body shake that little bit
more. *Fleckfieber.*

Typhus.

TWELVE

Despite the cold mist rising off the lake as the light faded, Von Bork was sweating as he rowed. A sheen of perspiration covered his shoulders as he dug the blades into the water, exhilarated by the rhythm he had found – the old, relaxed varsity stroke he had once mastered so easily – and the way the nose of the tiny craft leaped forward with each pull. He had missed this, the burn of muscle and lung that physical exercise brought. He could see now that the last few years had been blighted by a form of depression, caused by his failure in England. Now, at least, he had engineered a partial revenge for his humiliation and it had brought a fresh burst of vitality.

It was a pity he had been forced to order the killing of the orderly. But he wasn't part of the plan. He wanted Watson to feel alone, as he had, bereft of friends and acquaintances. Ostracized. And it did have the benefit of causing Watson even more anguish, once he realized that he, indirectly, was responsible for the private's death.

Von Bork glanced across at the rococo villa that stood on the lakeshore to his right, its lights blazing with profligacy, as there was only him and his host – plus the servants – in residence. But Admiral Hersch was not one to let the privations of war affect him too much. As a senior commander in the *Nachrichten-Abteilung* – Naval Intelligence – Hersch was well aware of how much the Allied blockade was strangling the country, how the shops of Berlin mainly displayed hundreds of square metres of dust. But he didn't believe in sharing the suffering of the Kaiser's subjects. Hersch insisted that men like himself needed to be kept in tiptop condition to win this war. He and his team required their full vigour to outfox the British and the French. So, tonight Von Bork was expecting a table full of sausages with no barley and sawdust makeweight filling, the best pork knuckle, oysters, foie gras, brandy and cigars.

Von Bork could see Hersch standing on the jetty, his bulk silhouetted by the electric lights behind him. Broad of shoulder, with cropped steel-grey hair, he was still attractive to women, with his unlined face and square jaw, despite being well into his fifties. The duelling scar on his upper left cheek did little harm, either. Nor did the signet ring that proclaimed him a member of one of the oldest Prussian families, albeit some moves away from the main bloodline. He had a wife – although God alone knew where she was kept – but more often than not he squired a young widow on his arm, consoling her for her loss in one way or another.

'Are you going to stay out there all night, man?' boomed Hersch, his voice skimming over the water. 'We have company arriving.'

Von Bork slowed and began to dig his right oar deeper into the water, turning the vessel towards where his former

spymaster stood. Hersch had been one of the more understanding of his superiors when Von Bork had returned from
England in shame. He alone had thought there was only a
little chagrin in being outwitted in the game of spies and
spying by a man like Holmes. Von Bork suspected Hersch
would have kept him on, but back then he lacked the influence the war years had given him. So he'd reluctantly cut Von
Bork adrift, left him to work his way up through the backwa-
ter of a bureau concerned with POWs.

Meanwhile, Hersch had created the Sie Wölfe, a group of
female assassins and spies, which he had released across Europe.
True, their losses had been comparable in percentage terms to
officers on the Western Front, but many had gleaned valuable
information. There were those in the old guard who abhorred
the use of women in war, especially in espionage, but the results
had silenced them.

As Von Bork drew level with the wooden pier, Hersch stooped
down and grabbed the craft, steadying it while Von Bork climbed
out, the exposed areas of his body steaming in the night air like
a racehorse in the winner's enclosure.

'Don't overdo it now, Von Bork,' said the admiral with a grin.
'Lottie has sent us some girls. Their car should be here shortly.
Save a little energy for yours.'

Lottie was the best-known, most expensive madam in Berlin.
This was something else reserved for those in the upper eche-
lons. An air of stiff, unyielding morality held sway in Berlin.
Dance halls, cabarets and brothels had been closed. It was
considered poor form to indulge in the pleasures of the flesh
while Germany's young men died in their thousands. But

Hersch was convinced that, as with a good diet, men of power needed their relaxations.

The admiral tossed a towel to Von Bork and secured the scull to a cleat with its bow-rope.

'You know, it's good to see you again,' Hersch said as Von Bork towelled himself dry, as if the thought had only just occurred to him.

'You too, sir.'

'Lukas, please. Just for tonight.'

Von Bork nodded, knowing he would never actually allow himself such familiarity. They began the walk back to the villa.

'I had my cryptographers take a look at those letters of yours.'

Von Bork stopped rubbing at his arms. 'And?'

'Nothing. No code that we know of. I suggest we let them through and examine what comes in return from Holmes and this Mrs Gregson.'

'Yes. Good idea.'

Hersch put a hand on Von Bork's shoulder. 'You know, we have discovered of late that a lot of the information you got for us in 1914 was, in fact, quite accurate.'

A liveried footman was waiting at the bottom of the stone steps that would take them up to the mansion's driveway. He held a silver salver, with two large balloon glasses, each containing two centimetres of Obstler. Von Bork dropped the towel at the man's feet and took one of the glasses, waiting until Hersch had his before he raised a toast and drank. The aroma of distilled apples and pears warmed his sinuses.

'Excellent. Sorry, you were saying?'

'Well,' said Hersch as they ascended the staircase. 'You were told that the information you had gathered had been falsified. In fact, only a small proportion of it had been. Most of it was, in fact, pure gold, had we known it at the time.'

'Good grief.' Von Bork had to be careful not to squeeze the glass so hard it shattered. 'Why was I not told this sooner?'

'Because, my dear Von Bork, we had no way of knowing what was the truth and what was a fabrication. Your adversary threw all of the documents into doubt.'

'The bastard.'

'Come, you have to admire the cunning of it. Did you not wonder why the British let you go free with war on the horizon? Why Sherlock Holmes spelled out that the reports you had purloined suggested the battleships were a little slower, the guns a little less powerful, than in actuality?'

Hersch laughed, but Von Bork had no inclination to join him. The liquor, so refreshing a moment ago, seemed to curdle in his stomach like week-old milk.

'In fact, the weapons were exactly as described in many cases. He was merely indulging in hyperbole. Playing games with our minds.' He shook his head in what might have been appreciation.

'So my . . . my exile, my humiliation, was for naught?'

'Well, not entirely. Holmes had fooled you, hadn't he? Wormed his way into your inner circle. No, Von Bork, he had the better of you.'

'I wish he were here for me to put a bullet between his eyes.' Von Bork tossed back the last of the brandy and left the glass on the balustrade of the steps up to the house. He could hear the distant purr of an engine. The girls were coming. Suddenly, the night ahead seemed like an ordeal.

Hersch slapped him on the back. 'Come now. All is not lost. You have this Dr Watson to torment.'

'Watson?' Von Bork hissed. 'The Judy to his Mr Punch? He had very little to do with the case, he was . . . a chauffeur. Oh, he'll have basked in his friend's glory all right. One day he'll get equal credit for fooling the German spy.' If he lives that long, he added, without voicing the thought. 'But you must have read his stories about their adventures – Watson was only ever a lapdog.'

'Lapdogs have their uses.' Hersch cocked an ear, now aware of the approaching vehicle. 'Hear that? Hurry, we must get changed. You really don't want to greet our companions looking or smelling like that, do you?' He began to take the steps up to the column-flanked entrance two at a time. One of the fancy doors swung open, to reveal yet another servant, this one a scrawny, aged specimen with a pronounced stoop, ready to welcome them.

'Wait. How do you mean?'

Hersch paused. He turned and began unbuttoning his tunic, impatient to change out of his uniform. 'You have your white tails with you? Tonight is not a military affair.'

'No,' Von Bork admitted. 'I was not expecting—'

'No matter.' Hersch pointed a finger at the servant and ordered him to fetch some suitable clothing for their under-prepared guest. The man looked Von Bork up and down, like an undertaker appraising a future client, and disappeared.

'Sir,' Von Bork insisted. 'Useful how?'

Hersch frowned, tired of the game now, aware that tyres had turned onto gravel, the final stretch of the drive. 'I would have thought that was obvious, Von Bork. You are in charge of trading prisoners. You offer Dr Watson in exchange.'

'For whom?' he asked.

Hersch tutted at the man's lack of insight. 'For Mr Sherlock bloody Holmes, of course. Now, do get a move on.'

THIRTEEN

Watson awoke shivering and itching, the taste of metal in his mouth, a succession of horrible images still stalking through his brain. Sayer was there, stuck and bleeding out in no man's land, as if he were a genuine casualty of war. Fantasy. But as he came back to reality he recalled clearly the sight of him crumpled on the ground at a godforsaken roadside. Murdered in cold blood. All too factual.

He threw back the coarse blanket in anger and took in his surroundings once more. He had arrived in darkness, weary and footsore, and well after the camp had finished serving its meals, so had been allowed to keep a tin of bully beef to eat. Everything else of value had been confiscated by the camp guards upon his arrival. He had been assigned an area at the far end of Hut 7, part surgery and examination room and part bedroom, separated from the dozen other men by what looked like an offcut from a large, threadbare carpet. This makeshift curtain gave a modicum of privacy to the patients, he supposed, but also reduced the amount of heat that reached him from the hut's pot-bellied stove.

It wasn't much of a surgery. A medicine cabinet, an eye chart and an illustration of the circulatory system were fixed to the walls. There was a desk, a lamp and a set of chipped and rusted weighing scales. From what he had seen of the inmates he didn't need that ancient machine to tell him that most prisoners were malnourished. A cabinet of drawers and cupboards filled with a jumble of medical instruments and dressings completed the inventory. Oh, for a good, efficient nurse. Oh, he thought, for Mrs Gregson, she would soon whip this into shape.

A image of her formed in his mind's eye, sitting on a bed in Belgium, a steaming mug of tea in her hand, head thrown back in laughter as she told tales of her days competing in motorcycle hillclimbs with Miss Pippery, or of the foolishness of her superiors or the cheekiness of her patients. The mental picture warmed him almost as much as that stove might have done, yet at the same time left him with a hollow feeling low in his abdomen.

He scratched again, aware that he had picked up some lice. The mattress, no doubt. He prodded it. Not even straw. Wood shavings. That was going to be a battle. The typhus sign had suggested that fighting the lice would be a priority. It was lice that carried the fearful disease, that much was known. But there was no cure, no vaccine. Constant delousing was the only possible defence.

He swung out his legs, pulled on his trousers and looked for his boots. He remembered taking them off and placing them at the end of the bed. Yet the Trenchmasters were nowhere to be seen. Instead, he found a pair of old hobnailed artillery boots, one of them broken so that the toe had peeled back, as if it were grinning at him. Still in his stockinged feet he threw back the heavy curtain, intending to bawl out his fellow inmates.

But the hut, and its row of bunk beds, was empty, except for two orderlies, hastily tucking in blankets and folding and packing away discarded pyjamas and slippers.

'Where is everyone?' Watson demanded.

The two men, both sallow-faced and unsmiling, barely glanced at him and went back to their work.

Watson was not a man to pull rank, but the insolence inherent in that behaviour, and the events of the previous day combined to create another surge of rage. 'You will stand to attention when addressed by an officer! Damn your eyes, you look at me or you will be on a charge after I'm done with you.'

Fists clenched, he took a step forward and if they thought that a man twice their age in stockinged feet suggesting he could thrash the pair of them was a ridiculous proposition, they didn't show it. Both sprang to taut attention and faced forward, expressions blank.

'Names?'

'Parsons, sir.' This one was the older and taller of the two, his skin badly marked by smallpox.

'And you?' Watson pointed to the shorter of the pair, a ruddy-faced lad with ginger hair and freckles.

'Wallace.' A beat. 'Sir.'

'Where is everyone?'

'*Appell*, sir.'

'*Appell*?' he said. Roll calls were sacrosanct at camps, as integral to the rhythm of the day as prayers in a monastery. 'Why wasn't I woken?' Not to mention why he wasn't woken with a cup of tea, as had been the normal routine with Sayer.

The orderlies exchanged furtive glances. 'We was told not to,' said Wallace.

'By whom?'

'Rather not say, sir.'

Missing an *Appell* could earn a prisoner a week's solitary. Someone wanted him to get into trouble. 'Really?' Watson pointed at his unshod feet. 'And do you know anything about a missing pair of Trenchmasters?'

Their heads shook in unison, far too eagerly for his liking. 'No, sir.'

'All right, we'll talk about this later. Get on with your work. You're my orderlies as well, are you?'

'Well, we do this hut,' admitted Parsons. 'So I suppose so.' He didn't sound very enthused about the prospect.

'How does *Appell* work here?' There were several ways of organizing a prisoners' parade and it varied from camp to camp. 'Alphabetically or by hut?'

'By hut,' Parsons admitted.

'By hut, sir,' Watson corrected.

'Sir.'

'Hut 1 on the far left of the parade ground, in order to Hut 20 on the right,' offered Wallace. Parsons looked at him as if he had just given out the King's telephone number.

'In groups of?' The Germans liked to break the lines up to make counting easier.

'Five, sir.'

'And each hut holds how many men?' Wallace made to speak, but Watson snapped his fingers. 'You, Parsons. You answer me. How many?'

He let out a sigh, resenting his silently insolent routine being disturbed. 'Most huts contains four bunkrooms like this one . . . sir. Each with at least a dozen men. Sir.'

'All British?'

'A few French,' offered Wallace. 'Hut 18. Keep themselves to themselves. But mostly British, yes, from every service. Navy and RFC as well as army, I mean.'

'So including the orderlies, we have, what? Just over a thousand men in camp?' Watson asked.

'Eleven hundred,' corrected Wallace.

Still, it was a relatively small camp. Some had ten times that number and a mix of nationalities. 'Very good. Get on with your work. And I expect a cup of tea when I get back from *Appell*. Understood?'

Both men nodded.

Watson, already tired from the exertion of impersonating a martinet, returned to his cubbyhole and, with no alternative on offer, pulled on the old and cracked artillery boots, slipped into his greatcoat and hurried outside, pausing only to scowl theatrically at the orderlies. The sky was gunmetal grey and as he looked up small kisses of moisture brushed his cheek. It was starting to snow and it was settling on the frozen ground.

Well done, Watson. The voice was loaded with sarcasm.

What have I done now? he asked his tormentor.

Not twelve hours here and you already seem to have made enemies.

Watson grunted. He couldn't argue with that.

In daylight Watson could take in the structure of the camp. It sat in the lee of a grand, turreted château-style house that had once been a mansion, hotel or sanatorium. A first-floor terrace allowed what he assumed was the commandant to step out of a salon and examine the massed ranks of his charges without having to enter the compound through the gates. The prisoners were confined inside a triple layer of fencing, topped with coils of barbed wire and electric lights. Judging from the foul deposits sitting on the soil, which was whitening as the dusting of snow fell upon them, dogs patrolled in the corridors between the fences. He could hear their whines and yaps from wherever they were kennelled by day. Twelve leggy wooden watchtowers loomed into the sky like contraptions from an H.G. Wells novel, one at each corner of the main compound and a further eight situated at intervals along each perimeter.

There were twenty huts, each one raised off the ground on blocks, in four rows of five plus a kitchen and a shower block, a 'tin room', where Watson's confiscated foodstuffs had been taken, a 'rec' or recreation hut, a cluster of latrines and, at the far end from the main house, a sports area, marked out as football field and with a rather sad tennis court, a piece of twine standing in for a net. Beyond that was another compound, entirely separate, with its own entrance to the outside world. It was a third of the size in area and had just a single, solitary hut in the centre. And next to that, a large crop of wooden crosses sprouting from the hard earth. It looked as if this was where the unfortunate went to die. This was where Sayer would be now, no doubt.

Surrounding the camp were the mountains, but this was no picturesque alpine scene. There were startlingly few trees, for a start. The slopes had been denuded of cover, leaving only ugly stumps, and in some places there had been excavations or perhaps collapses due to erosion. Certainly, rain and meltwater flowing unchecked by any vegetation had left deep scarring running down many of the slopes. One peak looked like a giant magnification of Parsons' pockmarked face. To Watson's eye it was a mountainside as envisaged by Hieronymus Bosch, tortured and flayed.

Watson counted off the rather shambolic rows of prisoners and hurried across to that of Hut 7, aware of the comical slapping sound his flapping boot was making. He joined the rear of the line just as a one-armed *Feldwebel* with a clipboard reached it.

'You are?' he demanded.

'Watson. Major. Royal Army Medical Corps.'

The clipboard was held horizontal from his chest by a metal contraption, so he could tick off the names with his single limb. 'You aren't here,' the German said.

'Perhaps he's the invisible man,' someone from the next group shouted.

'Quiet.'

'New arrival,' said Watson. 'Last night.'

The *Feldwebel* took a pencil and added the name, checking the spelling. Watson needn't have rushed after all; this camp's bureaucracy was no better than any other.

'You haven't called Aubrey's name! Aubrey du Barry. Why haven't you called him?'

A slight but intense figure, his eyes sunken and wild, had detached himself from further along the line and was coming down between the rows, wagging a finger at the *Feldwebel*. 'Du Barry. Check the list. He's back there.'

'Oh for God's sake,' someone muttered. 'Leave it out, Pickering. Every fucking day.'

Pickering, a captain, was at the German now. 'Du Barry. Shall I spell it?'

'D-U-B-A-R-R-Y,' the one-armed guard replied.

'Well, why haven't you called him, Brünning?'

The German spoke as if he was tired of the sentence he was uttering. 'Because we have no du Barry here, Captain Pickering.'

Watson grasped what was happening. He had seen it before. Prisoners, like children, sometimes invented imaginary friends. Most of the time this was a harmless delusion, but sometimes the phantom acquaintance became flesh and blood, a solid presence. He had seen men go to astonishing lengths to make sure their chums had enough rations to survive, turning a blind eye when others helped themselves, satisfied that their friend was at least eating well.

Watson stepped forward and put a hand on the captain's shoulder. 'Captain Pickering, is it? My name is Watson—'

The Englishman spun round at the touch and wrinkled his nose as if he had just caught the first whiff of gas. 'Watson!' He made a hawking noise in the back of his throat, and before Watson could step back he spat a slimy blob of phlegm in his face. 'Get your hands off me you damned traitor!'

FOURTEEN

It was in the company of Robert Nathan, with her arm through his elbow, that Mrs Gregson skirted Trafalgar Square, en route to a small suite of offices just off the Strand. There was yet another war rally on in the square, addressed by famous authors, among them Kipling and Wells. As always, a recruiting office had been set up. A year or two previously there would have been a snake of enthusiastic men at its door, falling over each other to serve. With conscription in place, there were far fewer customers offering to do their bit. Most men were content to wait for the summoning envelope through the door rather than rush to be shipped off as a green replacement to France. Few had any illusions now about the outcome of charging German machine guns at dawn.

The aim of the rally was mostly to try to keep morale high, especially in the aftermath of the film *The Battle of the Somme*, which had been seen by twenty million people. Its depiction of trenches and the dead had backfired as propaganda. People now appreciated why the lads on leave came back with those long, empty stares and were plagued by nightmares. They understood why they sought out the company of other soldiers, because only those who had experienced the front could relate to each other.

'Something for the maimed and blinded?' asked a Salvation Army officer, stepping in front of them. Nathan put some coppers in his tin. 'You're a Christian gent, sir,' the man said, before moving on.

The White Feather girls, the Shameladies, were also in evidence once more, although in smaller numbers than at the start of the conflict, when men of serving age had to swat them away like flies. As they passed them, some examined Nathan's face closely, trying to decide if he should be presented with the symbol of cowardice. There was talk of the conscription age being raised to fifty-one and some of the more aggressive women were already pre-empting that by targeting older men. But whenever the Shameladies received one of Nathan's just-you-dare scowls, they invariably walked off in search of a more suitable victim.

Nathan pointed at a barrage balloon rising into the winter sky behind St Martin-in-the-Fields, its wrinkled envelope slowly plumping as it consumed the gas being fed along its umbilical. 'Remember the rides at Vauxhall?' he asked. 'You ever do that?'

Mrs Gregson nodded. There had once been two tethered hot-air balloons on the Embankment and for thrupence you could take a ride in the gondola and have a wonderful view up and down the Thames before sinking slowly back down to earth. They had disappeared within days of war being declared. 'Tobias took me. It was all terribly exciting. It seemed so daring at the time.' She nodded at the inflatable, which had been joined by a saggy companion, its folds like elephant skin, to the north of the square. 'I assume those aren't for pleasure rides?'

'Noooooo,' Nathan said slowly, as if he knew more than he dare let on. 'Just some trials by Balloon Command, I believe.' He gave what he obviously thought was a reassuring smile and patted her gloved hand. 'Nothing to worry about.'

Mrs Gregson bristled at the new patronizing tone, and wondered if they were to defend against the German bombers they all knew were coming eventually. But she didn't press him.

'Robert, thank you for finding out the information about the German. I could have gone to Churchill, but . . .'

'Think nothing of it. Just pulled a few strings. Glad to be able to help.'

Nathan had examined the file on Von Bork and, although Mrs Gregson was not allowed to see it, he had given her an outline explaining why the man might have a lingering grudge against Watson and Holmes. Apparently the latter, in particular, had been instrumental in dismantling and discrediting Von Bork's spy ring. So, it was possible he had blocked the release of Watson as some form of petty retribution. Now she had this information, she felt compelled to act on it. If the German were intent on doing him harm, Mrs Gregson had to find a way to counter him, even from afar. She owed it to her friend to explore every avenue to keep him alive, no matter how madcap.

'You know Kell tells me there was a request recently to exchange your Miss Pillbody? For one of our boys in Berlin.'

'She is not *my* Miss Pillbody,' Mrs Gregson corrected with a shudder. 'As you well know her name is Brandt. Ilse Brandt.

And she is a monster. A She Wolf. And I would have thought we'd be glad to see the back of her.'

Ilse Brandt, a member of the Sie Wölfe group of female spies specially trained in Germany for infiltration into Great Britain, had almost killed Holmes and Watson out on the treacherous sands off Foulness in Essex. She had been apprehended and Mrs Gregson had fully expected her to be shot at the Tower, given the trail of bodies she had left across England. Then the Germans shot Edith Cavell for spying and it was decided that Britain's right to moral outrage – and the propaganda value of the poor nurse – might be blunted if they, in turn, executed Ilse Brandt.

'Did they agree?' she asked. 'To exchange her?'

Nathan shook his head. 'No. The authorities are biding their time. There are several cases of civil murder against her – an old, defenceless woman in Essex, for one. My guess is they'll wait until after the war and hang her.'

Mrs Gregson was still analysing how she felt about that when an excited voice boomed through a megaphone from the fringes of the meeting behind them, and a dozen skittish pigeons took off, skimming over their heads. 'Stop the war! Sue for peace! No more killing!' Nathan turned and looked at the young man, who was barely of conscription age. It was a peace protestor, perhaps even a 'conchie' who would refuse when his call-up papers came. There was a time when the mob would have lynched him, but his tirade was simply cut short when two policemen bundled him away, one of them kicking the youth's ankles as they went.

'I was wondering if we could try dinner again, without the excitement of the windows being blown in,' Nathan said once they resumed their walk. 'The Café Royal perhaps?'

There was something about the hopeful gleam in his eye that made her hackles rise. She tried not to show her resentment at the usual problem of a quid pro quo raising its head. She had thought Nathan above the ploy of getting her information and expecting dinner – or more – in return. 'Perhaps tea,' she said. 'Might be more appropriate this time.'

'Tea? I was hoping that . . . well, Mrs Gregson, the thing is . . . Georgina . . . I hope you know . . .'

It was her turn to squeeze his hand. How bizarre that even the most eloquent of men become tongue-tied when it came to discussing their emotions, she thought. Of course it could be worse, he could put his feelings into poetry, as was the current vogue. That would be intolerable. 'Robert. Not now, eh? We have business to attend to.' She gripped his forearm, steering him to the right. 'Here we are. First floor.'

'Of course,' he muttered. 'Bad timing. Story of my life.' He gave a staccato laugh.

Once through the street door, they began to climb the wooden stairs. 'Please don't think me ungrateful,' she said.

'I never would,' Nathan replied, with a slight pout that suggested he thought just that.

'It's just that I have to focus on one thing at a time. My personal life isn't important right now. What matters is getting my friend Major Watson out safely.'

'And once you have achieved that?'

'A celebration might be in order,' she said gaily.

'Splendid.'

But not necessarily with you, poor Robert, she added to herself.

They had reached the door of a small set of offices. Nathan rapped the pane of glass with his umbrella handle and they entered. The bulk of the room was hidden by a screen of oak panels topped with stippled glass, the entrance guarded by a solitary, elderly clerk who looked at them over pince-nez. 'Sir? Madam? What can I do for you? I am afraid the editor is at lunch.'

'No matter,' said Mrs Gregson briskly. 'I am sure your good self will suffice. My name is Gregson, this is Mr Robert Nathan, late of the Indian Army, now a senior member of the Wartime Constabulary. We wish to see your subscribers' list.'

The clerk frowned, moving his bald head from side to side with great deliberation. He removed his glasses and rubbed the bridge of his nose, squeezing his eyes shut as he did so. 'I'm afraid that is impossible. The *British Beekeeper's Journal* does not simply hand over private information willy-nilly.'

'I am pleased to hear it,' said Mrs Gregson. 'But there is nothing willy or, indeed, nilly about this.' She took a half-step to one side to cede the stage to Nathan.

The SSB man approached the clerk's desk, leaned over it and produced an identity card of some description from his inside pocket. 'I am afraid this is a matter of national security, sir. One that comes under the DORA regulations.'

The clerk visibly flinched. He pursed his lips, as if sucking a particularly astringent dose of sherbet powder. 'I see.'

'It is but one subscriber we need to access the details of,' said Mrs Gregson with abundant reasonableness. 'We are fairly sure this chap wouldn't be without his copy of the *British Beekeeper's Journal*. I assure you, the source of this information will go no further than these four walls.'

A STUDY IN MURDER 101

Nathan nodded solemnly to show his complicity.

The clerk sighed and pushed his chair back, preparing to rise and fetch the documents. 'Very well. What is the name of this subscriber?'

Mrs Gregson smiled at her victory and said, with all the flourish of a magician at the twice-dailies removing a rabbit from the hat. 'A Mr Sherlock Holmes.'

FIFTEEN

When the *Appell* broke up and he wiped away the insult from his face, Watson became aware that he was the subject of some curiosity. As the clumps of men drifted back to their huts, there were sly glances and bold, almost challenging stares. One chap, a spindly, hunched lieutenant with a riot of unkempt curly hair, stood ten yards away, appraising him as if he were an ox he was about to bid on. When Watson returned the gaze the man broke into an unexpected grin and nodded, before turning on his heel. Another deranged specimen, Watson thought.

He was about to make his way across to the messing area, where a breakfast of sorts was being served, when he spotted an old friend. Or rather, a pair of old friends. Three men were standing smoking, each wrapped in a smart, nearly new great-coat and woollen scarves. The centrepiece of the group was a man who had the air of a matinée idol, his hair gleaming with oil, the black moustache well trimmed. He looked for all the world like he was waiting for the two forty at Ascot to begin. And on his feet were a pair of well-cared-for Trenchmasters.

'Good Lord,' Watson blurted at the impertinence. The trio

slowly became aware of him. The one with his boots examined him with a languid, unhurried gaze through a curtain of cigarette smoke. Watson was just about to stride across and give the man a piece of his mind, when he felt a tug at his shoulder.

'Watson, is it? Would you care to take a turn round the camp with me? Be ever so grateful.'

The voice was surprisingly soft and velvety, with a slight air of world-weariness that suggested standards at the club had slipped.

Watson pointed across to the group. 'That man has my—'

'Never mind that, Major,' he said, gently guiding him away with a hand on his shoulder. 'I'm Lieutenant-Colonel Critchley. King's Own Yorkshire Light Infantry. And I have the misfortune to be the Senior Officer in Charge here.'

Watson made to salute, but Critchley gripped his arm.

'No need for that, old chap. Not at this precise moment. Come, I'll show you the lie of the land. Then we can have a spot of breakfast at my quarters. One of the perks of being Senior British Officer is you can eat with some privacy.'

The snow had stopped, leaving the ground a mottled patchwork of white and brown, firm underfoot. They walked towards the wire fence and began a slow circumnavigation of the perimeter.

'You must have plenty of questions, Watson.'

'I do. Why wasn't I woken for *Appell*? Why did that man spit in my face . . . ?'

Critchley stroked his lantern jaw, as if checking the quality of his morning shave. 'I am afraid newcomers are always treated with some hostility. Especially as we heard about that unfortunate incident at your last camp. And on the way here. To lose one fellow soldier to German fire might be considered unfortunate . . .'

'My servant was murdered,' Watson protested. 'Shot in cold blood.'

'That's as may be. But the word is you might be a chat. A German chat.'

'Chat?' It was slang for lice, but he doubted any camp needed the Germans to add more.

'Spies. *Agents provocateurs.* Put in here to find out about any escape attempt.'

'I am no spy,' Watson protested.

'I am afraid the *Lager* Poldhu has different ideas. It went into a frenzy yesterday and then you pop up.'

Poldhu, like Marconi, was prisoners' slang for the grapevine that spread rumours and gossip and even, sometimes, genuine news both within camps and, by some means nobody could ascertain, throughout the entire chain of *Lagers* in Germany. Poldhu in Cornwall was the location of Marconi's pioneering radio transmitter.

'And you come trailing a dead soldier, with orders for him to be buried at once without a by-your-leave. Like they had something to hide.'

'Sayer, you mean? I know nothing about that. And they do have something to hide. They murdered him in cold blood, on the way here. Said he was trying to escape. Where is Sayer buried?'

Critchley ignored the question. 'And why should a man of your vintage end up here? We heard that any man over forty-eight was being sent to Holland.' He paused. 'You are over forty-eight?'

Watson appreciated the reason for his uncertainty — the constant accretion of tiny privations meant men in POW camps often looked a decade or more older than their biological age. 'Of course I am. But my transfer was blocked.'

'Blocked by whom?'

'Let me tell you my side of things,' Watson offered.

'Very well.'

By the time he had outlined his story — holding back the exact detail of why Von Bork should hate him so much, simply alluding to pre-war animosity — they had reached one of the watchtowers and Watson looked up. A German guard peered down and used his Mauser to indicate they should keep walking.

'So, there you have it. I am no spy, sir.'

'Well, I'll have to take your word for it,' said Critchley. 'I mean to say, I believe you, old chap. I know how vindictive the Hun can be when he feels slighted. I just hope the others do. Mud sticks, Major Watson; you'll have the devil's own time shaking the suspicions of some of the men.'

'But why should they put chats in at all? I thought this place was escape-proof?'

'In a manner of speaking. Not so much physically. There's no such thing as an escape-proof camp. But the commandant says he will shoot two British officers for every one who goes over the wire, recaptured or not. Well, if you know your best friend might be put up against a wall if you go over it . . . quite a disincentive.'

'I would imagine so. Is that approach entirely . . . ?'

'Legal? Allowed under the Hague Convention?' Critchley's shoulders shook with a mirthless laugh. 'I am not sure Mad Bill worries about such things.'

'Mad Bill?'

'Commandant Wilhelm Kügel. Late of Indiana, where he travelled in ladies' underwear . . .' Critchley gave a weary smile. 'At least that's what the wags say. He was certainly some sort of salesman and he speaks English with an American accent. What you have to understand is that Mad Bill runs this camp for profit. You'll be charged a hundred camp marks a week for messing. You will be encouraged to get funds from home. A camp mark is worth half a real mark, but is the only currency allowed. You have to keep all your transactions in a special black book.' He tapped his pocket. 'They cost two camp marks.'

'This is outrageous. I had heard this was the worst camp in Germany, but . . .' Watson was momentarily lost for words.

'Not the worst exactly, although it has its difficulties, God knows. It's simply the most profitable. For the Germans, that is. All Red Cross and personal parcels are searched and any suspicious items that might be used for an escape confiscated. Especially food. Although, oddly, you can often buy the items back later.'

Watson said nothing, simply seething within.

'And if you object to these arrangements? There are solitary cells – Stubby, as we call it – in the basement of the big house, where Mad Bill lives and the guards are billeted. Now, they really are pretty grim and he uses them at the drop of a hat. He didn't appear on his balcony this morning, but he often does, perhaps eating a plate of sausages and drinking a brandy, just to taunt us. Our food's abysmal, needless to say. In fact, it probably is the worst of any Allied camp in Germany. I hope you like soup. Make friends with Hugh Peacock in your hut. Manages to have a bloody feast most days. Must be costing him a fortune. Questions?'

'Red Cross visits?'

'You've seen the typhus signs? On the road?'

Watson nodded.

'It doesn't refer to us. Well, not always; we've had some cases in the past. Hence the isolation ward.' He pointed to the lone hut in the separate compound. 'But the worst outbreaks are at the Russian camp over the ridge there.' He was talking about a jagged, treeless piece of skyline. 'The Red Cross are as terrified of typhus as the Hun, so Mad Bill makes sure they think it's endemic in here. Which means their visits are . . . fleeting, shall we say. It's on the C list inspection roster – which means hardly ever.'

'There's method in this Kügel's madness, then.'

'Oh, yes. He'll probably end the war a rich man. We'll just end it thin. If we are lucky. It gets damned cold here. Careless men lose fingers and toes. This is a mild spell, believe me. When that wind comes from the east, the stoves in the huts can barely cope. Get some sweaters sent over or start knitting. Preferably both.'

'How long have you been here, sir?'

A rueful grin spread across his face. 'Me? Two years. Before that, various camps . . . well, I got nabbed in 1914. Haven't seen much of the war, to be honest. Just a lot of fences.'

They paused, looking through the wire across at the cluster of crosses that constituted the graveyard. 'He's in there? Sayer?'

'Yes.'

'I am going to lodge a complaint.'

'Write it and save it. In fact, hide it from prying eyes. Chickens will come home to roost eventually. But don't get yourself marked as a troublemaker. You've seen Pickering, I know. And Archer? Eyes like Rasputin? Obsessed with the dead.'

Watson recalled the man who had stared at him at *Appell*. 'I think so.'

'Both of them were subjected to harassment. Solitary confinement, adulterated rations, repeated searches, sleep deprivation. Both are damaged up here.' Critchley tapped his temple. 'Both had threatened to reveal the profiteering, you see. But who is going to give any credence to their words now? One has an imaginary friend and the other talks to the dead.'

'This du Barry Pickering was talking about – he's imaginary?'

'Oh, as good as. He was some school friend of his. Blown to bits, apparently, before his very eyes.' He sighed. 'Still, you'll find this hard to believe, but it could be worse. We could be digging the mines, for one. The mountains out there are worked hard.'

'What do they mine for?' asked Watson.

'Gold, silver, iron ore. Whole mountain riddled with shafts. If anyone did get over the wire they'd probably end up at the bottom of some hole with a broken neck.' He shivered, apparently shaking off a feeling of melancholy, and was much brighter when he spoke again. 'And look, it's not all gloom. We have a theatre group. An orchestra. Do you play?' Watson shook his head. 'Pity. Short of brass. There's a magazine, *Harz and Minds*. Do you write or draw?'

'I have been known to put pen to paper.'

'Not poetry, I hope.' Critchley flashed that apologetic grin again. 'Over-bloody-whelmed with poets.'

'No, short stories.'

'Good man. Always willing to consider submissions – I'm the editor, by the way. No promises, though. Got some professional scribblers in the ranks, so standard is high. I turn down ten for every one published.'

Watson discovered he had lost the feeling in the toes of his right foot and continued with the walk to try to get the circulation moving. 'Sir, about my boots . . . I have been the victim of a substitution.'

Critchley glanced down at Watson's feet. 'Hmm. Dirty prank.'

It was, in Watson's eyes, more than a prank. 'I know the man who has them. Chap who looked like he was about to go on at the Gaiety. Oiled hair, no cap—'

'Henry Lincoln-Chance. Link, to his friends.'

'I'd like them back,' said Watson, wriggling his chilled toes.

'That might be tricky.'

'Why? I thought you were senior in the camp?'

'Only officially,' Critchley said with some regret. 'In reality, Link and his chummies wield significant . . . shall we say, influence.'

'Why is that?'

'Oh, they are the Escape Committee.'

SIXTEEN

After a breakfast of tongue, bread, marmalade and tea in Critchley's office, Watson exchanged some of his marks for camp currency and then ordered fresh funds from Cox & Co. on the Charing Cross Road. From the tin room he purchased a black book – the price had risen to three camp marks – and a pencil, plus a packet of his own biscuits.

He kept an eye out for his Trenchmasters and their new owner, but the snow returned with renewed vigour and he made his way back to his own hut without spotting the thief. He had agreed with Critchley that he would run surgeries for patients twice daily, at 10 a.m. and 4 p.m., starting the next day. Apparently for serious cases a German doctor could be summoned, and there was a hospital some ten miles away, but Mad Bill was loath to use it.

And what of this three-man Escape Committee, he asked. What use was one in an escape-proof camp? But Critchley told him it was a matter of morale, of showing they hadn't caved in completely. Watson supposed he was right, but the matter of his boots still grated. He would have to put this Link right at the first opportunity.

As he entered the hut he shook off the snow from his shoulders and was greeted by a fug of woodsmoke and unwashed bodies. Showers, apparently, were available only on Fridays. It was Thursday. The volume of conversation dipped momentarily, and the soldiers, airmen and couple of naval officers that made up Hut 7 went back to their cards, chess, letters, or just their own thoughts.

Watson could feel the suspicion clouding the air. He walked through the barracks, nodding to anyone who caught his eye, feeling the stares at his back. Was it Von Bork who had spread the lie of him being a 'Hun lover' in their midst? If so, it was a very clever turn of the screw.

He stepped inside his surgery and pulled the curtain across, aware of a drop in temperature as he did so. Perhaps, Watson mused, he could find a way of securing his own stove. After all, patients often had to undress; it would help if the room were heated. He took off his greatcoat and the hobnails, changing to two pairs of dry socks to keep his damp feet warm.

Watson sat on the bed, put his elbows on his knees and let out a long, ululating sigh. Despair was only a heartbeat away, he knew. Everything he held dear was further from him than ever. Furthermore, he seemed to have been pitched into a camp right out of Edward Lear. The land where the bong tree grows, he thought glumly.

There was a sudden rise in the volume of conversation from next door. Watson, not paying much attention, caught only snatches.

'. . . in there.'

'I'm ill, I tell you.'

'Bloody traitor.'

'. . . fuck you.'

The curtain was flung back and the young lieutenant from the parade ground, with his distinctive mop of unruly brown hair and staring eyes, was standing before him, hopping from foot to foot. Archer, Watson recalled from his conversation with Critchley.

Watson pulled himself upright. 'Yes? Can I help?'

The man nodded vigorously. 'It's my heart. Palpitations, Doctor.'

'Major,' Watson said.

'Sir.'

'Take a seat.'

Conversation had resumed in the rest of the barracks and the newcomer seemed to relax. Watson opened a page in his notebook.

'Name?'

'Archer, sir.'

'What's your unit?'

'The 4th Dragoon Guards, sir.'

'Age?'

'Twenty-four, sir.'

Looks older, Watson wrote next to it.

'Height?'

'Six foot, give or take.'

'Hop on those scales for me, will you?'

Watson peered over. Eight and a half stone. 'How long have you been a prisoner, Archer?'

'Eighteen months, sir.'

'Tell me about these palpitations.'

'Well, they start whenever I try to go to sleep. No matter where I lie I can hear my heart. Thump, thump thump. Loud in my ears. Then it goes all . . . peculiar.'

'Where are you from, Archer?'

'Colchester.'

'You went to the Royal Grammar?'

'I did, yes.'

'Field commission?'

'Indeed.'

Temporary gentleman, he wrote, even though he despised the phrase. Grammar school boys from the ranks didn't start being seen as officer material until the cream of the public schools fell to German machine guns, snipers and shells. Then they were allowed above their station in life. But only with visiting rights.

It sounded like an anxiety attack to Watson. Many of his shell shock patients had complained of an over-loud heartbeat. He found prescribing any tablet, from quinine sulphate to liver, did the trick. All they needed was the illusion of treatment to quell whatever fears were causing the arrhythmia or tachycardia.

'Drink much tea? Coffee? Or what passes for them here?'

The man shook his head. 'It's running a bit fast now. Want to have a listen?'

'Very well, slip your shirt off.'

Watson fetched the rather perished stethoscope he had found in one of the drawers and placed it in his ears. When he turned,

Archer had pulled up his shirt and vest with one hand. A finger of the other was pressed against his lips.

But that wasn't what caused Watson to start. There was something written in ink across his chest.

The Dead talk to me.

When Watson went to speak, Archer shook his head. He turned around and pulled up the rear of his shirt. Written on his back was: *The rec hut. After curfew. Come alone.*

Come alone? Who on earth would he bring? He was a pariah in this place.

There was an explosion of yelling from the next room and the sounds of a scuffle. Men began shouting encouragement to the combatants. There came the crash of chairs overturning.

Taking advantage of the racket Archer stepped in close. 'I know who you are, Major, or should I say Doctor, Watson. I know you like a mystery. Here.'

From his top pocket the man took two pieces of paper, both folded into tiny squares.

'I'll explain tonight.' Then, as the hubbub in the hut subsided, with more volume: 'Thank you, Major, I will.'

Watson, though, had spotted something. He grabbed the man's right wrist and turned it over. There were scars, some white and fibrous, of an age, but others still raw and fresh. The left wrist was the same.

Archer leaned in and whispered. 'I will explain tonight. It is not what it seems.'

'It seems you are a very clumsy suicide.'

'It's not that,' he hissed.

Archer pulled down his shirt and vest, tucked them in and, with a rather insubordinate wink, he was gone.

Watson found himself writing in his book the phrase written across the man's chest.

The Dead talk to me.

He supposed that Archer meant through spiritualism of some description. He had acquaintances – including writers and scientists – who believed in such things as the afterlife and being able to access the spirit world. Some even accepted the existence of fairies. Holmes, the rationalist, never countenanced such things – he believed only what his senses told him; Watson, as a medical man, considered the world beyond this one outside his remit. But he knew such thoughts gave comfort to the millions of bereaved created by this war. He rarely sought to dissuade patients when they professed the belief that a son or husband was somehow 'with' them. The devastated needed all the comfort they could get, even if it was with, like Pickering, an imaginary friend.

He had even heard of accusations from beyond the grave, accusations of murder from the supposed victim, transmitted through a 'sensitive'. But none that had stood up to scientific rigour. No, he suspected this was another inmate driven by incarceration to seek comfort in the outlands of the human soul. Hadn't Critchley said Archer had been subjected to a regime of harassment?

And what of the marks on the wrist? They were relatively shallow cuts, by the look of them. Hesitation strokes, they were known as, when a suicide makes some tentative slashes, either hoping to be discovered before he did more serious damage or while he summoned up the courage for the surprisingly deep incisions needed to make a human being bleed out from the ulnar artery.

He took the squares of paper that Archer had given him and unfolded them. Both contained signatures, executed in a rather jerky hand, although that was all the pair had in common. He would have sworn they had different authors. One said: 'Lieutenant George Threadglass'; the other: 'Captain Martin Brevette'. Watson knew of a family called Brevette that lived in Oxford. They had made their fortune as merchants, trading woad from the city of Toulouse, before indigo became the blue dye of choice. But by then they had invested wisely in other businesses. Could this Brevette be one of them?

Watson folded the papers and slotted them between the pages of his notebook. Would he go to the rec room to clear this little puzzle up? He laughed to himself. Damn the man, he knew who he was, knew he was cursed with a curiosity. Presumably it was easy enough to cross to this recreation room without being seen. Yes, he would go. But that was some hours away. It wouldn't do to dwell when he didn't have all the facts before him.

He heard the peal of laughter from beyond his makeshift curtain and suddenly felt very alone and bereft. He found himself wishing for that phantom voice in his head, which surely was only one step removed from Pickering's delusion. He had to chuckle to himself. Well, if that voice wouldn't come, he could conjure it up. He had promised Critchley a story. What better way to escape the grim confines of the camp than to slip back in time, to the clack of horses' hoofs and the shouts of

costermongers and paperboys? He laid what was per page probably the world's most expensive notebook on the desk, took up
his pencil and began to write the story he had started telling to
the unfortunate Hanson back in the woods near Krefeld.

SEVENTEEN

Sitting at the desk, Watson began to write, slowly at first but with gathering confidence that he could still find his old style and pace. It was almost a physical exhilaration when he did, as if he had rediscovered his rugger legs and lungs.

It was April 1890 (and not 1892 as some accounts would have it), as the debilitating bone-chill of a lengthy winter had finally begun to relax its grip on the metropolis, when my friend Sherlock Holmes turned his attention to what the daily Press were calling The Rugby Mystery and some others The Girl and the Gold Watches. Holmes had recently completed his investigation into a most gruesome business, involving jealousy and murder. The solution to the case had put him in a rather sombre mood. 'What is the meaning of it, Watson?' he had exclaimed, not for the first time. Peering into the darkest corners of the human soul often caused him to recoil in revulsion at the depravity of his fellow man. 'What object is served by this circle of misery and violence and fear? It must tend to some end, or else our universe is ruled by chance, which is unthinkable. But what end? There is the great standing perennial problem to which human reason is as far from an answer as ever?'

By the time he put the pen down from between aching fingers, two hours had passed in blissful immersion elsewhere and Watson swore he could feel the heat of the Baker Street fire, when the curtain was thrust back.

'Emergency *Appell*,' said Parsons, before adding, 'Sir.'

Watson looked out of his window. Snow was falling in large flakes now, an impenetrable wall. 'In this?'

Parsons' pockmarked face stretched into a grin. 'The colder and wetter the better for Mad Bill.'

Watson pulled on the unfortunate boots and his greatcoat and went into the main section of the hut, where he found the other men doing likewise, all grumbling loudly.

'Bastard. What about lunch?'

'That bloody bread? That's not lunch.'

'What you having for luncheon, Cocky?'

'I thought I might have grouse.' This from a captain, who must be Hugh Peacock, the bon viveur that Critchley had told him about. He was certainly plumper than the average inmate, dark-haired, baby-faced, neat moustache as black as coal. His boots, too, Watson noted with envy, were a cut above, knee-high and fur-lined.

'Come on, gentlemen, hurry along.' It was the one-armed *Feldwebel*, Brünning. 'Do not keep the commandant waiting. Or it'll be Stubby for you.'

'I wouldn't mind a bit of solitary,' someone piped up. 'Can't be worse than sharing a room with Cocky's grouse farts.'

'The commandant—'

To Watson's surprise, the whole hut burst into song, drowning out the remainder of the *Feldwebel*'s sentence.

> Mad Bill, Mad Bill,
> He's been sent to torment us.
> Mad Bill, Mad Bill,
> Always on a percentage,
> Mad Bill, Mad Bill,
> Says us guys are swell,
> Mad Bill, Mad Bill,
> Yet makes our lives hell.

Peacock took up a cod-operatic solo refrain in a surprisingly fine baritone.

> He used to sell silken knickers,
> To the gals of Indiana,
> But we only want to show him
> The size of our Vickers.

The others then came back in with a chorus.

> Mad Bill, Mad Bill,
> Likes to eat a banger,
> Mad Bill, Mad Bill,
> One day will come a clanger.

Even the *Feldwebel* gave a half-smile and then looked puzzled. 'But isn't it to drop a clanger? Don't you come a cropper?'

'Artistic licence, Rufus, old chum,' said Peacock with a smirk.

Brünning's smile faded at the familiarity and he shook his head vigorously. 'You must hurry, or you will be writing your verses on a prison wall.'

Outside the ravaged mountainsides had disappeared beneath a shimmering grey screen of cloud and the snow was falling steadily. Watson followed the inmates of his hut over to the designated line. This time, Wilhelm 'Mad Bill' Kügel was standing on the balcony, one of his junior officers holding an over-sized umbrella above his head. The commandant was a stocky fellow, but broad, with a well-nourished face and, as far as Watson could ascertain, deep-set eyes. Kügel's arms were crossed and his gloved hands were tapping his biceps impatiently. As soon as the prisoners were in line he accepted a megaphone from his aide-de-camp. When he spoke, with a bizarre German/Midwest accent, he sounded like an American fairground barker.

'Gentlemen. You disappoint me. It has come to my attention that last night escape equipment was found in the tin room. A compass. A saw. A map. Jesus, fellas, have I not been fair and square with you? This man, this foolish man, threatens the lives of all of you. He will, of course, be punished. But you all share responsibility. You will remain here for one hour. And the lunch ration is cut by half.'

There was an almighty groan, an almost bovine noise rising from the crowd. Watson, too, made a grunt of irritation. The snow was already blowing into the open toe of his boot. An hour in these conditions and he risked chilblains or worse. He looked around and eventually found Lincoln-Chance, who no doubt had feet as warm as toast. As soon as they were released from the line-up he would go over and have it out with him.

'And so, *Stubenarrest*,' Mad Bill continued, looking down at a sheet of paper that was handed to him, 'for the man who tried to smuggle in the proscribed items. Step out of line, Major John Watson.'

EIGHTEEN

The cottage was some five miles from Holmes's original home on the South Downs. Nathan had told her he had moved because journalists had begun to seek him out to ask his opinion of the war and to wonder why the 'Greatest Mind in England' was not doing more for his country. Holmes had kept the new address even from MI5, insisting he could be reached via the classified advertisements of *The Times* if they ever needed his services. Which was unlikely. All at MI5, and its sister organization, MI6, knew that Holmes was a spent force, his remarkable energy exhausted, seemingly permanently, by his exposure to the Black Sands of Foulness. The man deserved his retirement and a peaceful twilight with his bees.

The cottage was modest but handsome enough, single storey, whitewashed, thatched — albeit in need of patching — with a small front garden, but a generous walled area to the rear, which was, perhaps, where he now kept his bees. Mrs Gregson asked the motor-taxi driver to wait and proceeded to knock on the door. It had been a long, slow train journey from London to

Lewes and she felt a surge of disappointment when there was no immediate reply.

She gave a holding sign to the cabby and walked round the side. There was a wooden gate to the walled area and, when she tried the latch, it opened. The space beyond contained a few fruit trees and, at the rear, a row of hives, shut down for winter. The lawn needed a scything, but it was by no means overgrown.

She walked round the rain butt and tried the handle of the door that led to the kitchen. It turned freely, she leaned her shoulder against the glass and the swollen door broke from the frame with a squeak. It swung back on oiled hinges.

'Mr Holmes?' she hissed. 'Are you in there?' Then again, louder. 'Mr Holmes? It's Mrs Gregson. Georgina. May I come in?'

She took a breath, aware of her heartbeat thumping in her ears. Steel yourself, Georgina. He's an old man and he lives alone. Anything could be waiting for her within. There was a slight tremor in her voice when she spoke again. 'Mr Holmes?'

It was dark within the thick-walled cottage. The deep-set windows admitted little light. There was no sign of electricity. She found an oil lamp and a box of matches and lit it. She checked the temperature of the stove. Cold. As was the kettle. There was a dish in the sink, unwashed, the food crusted on hard. Mr Holmes had not been there for a day or two at least. She walked through to the sitting room, as stuffed full of books and magazines as she had expected, although a large stack of unopened brown boxes suggested there were more to see the light of day. She could smell pipe tobacco.

An oblong table dominated the room, a fine piece of oak

made for a much larger, grander dwelling. Several books lay open on its surface, and the matching chair had been pushed back, as if the reader had recently got up and moved to another room.

She crossed to the fireplace. Again, the embers were cold, a few nuggets of charcoal, topped by a pile of burned, flaked paper. She sat in an old armchair, its red velvet seat and headrest shiny from use, one side darkened by smoke from the fire.

'What are you doing, Mr Holmes?' she asked herself. 'Where are you?'

She felt her body sag with weariness. The tension was exhausting her, she knew, though she had the resolve to go on. But why? She hardly dared explore her feelings fully, for she was ashamed of herself. Ashamed at how she was toying with Robert Nathan, using whatever feminine charms she still possessed to jerk him around like a puppet. But it was in a good cause. It was for Dr Watson, the man she . . .

She what? She certainly held strong feelings for him, but once again she backed off from examining them too closely. Watson was twenty-five years older than she, at least. Yet he didn't think or act that way. But could she imagine a life with him, after all this was over? Again, doubt clouded her vision of the future. But one thing was clear – if he died in some camp over there, she would never get to find out what she truly felt. And she would never forgive herself if she believed there was more she could have done to free him. It was, she knew, a selfish motivation, but if the end result was freeing Watson, who would complain? Not John.

The cabby's horn parped with a brittle impatience.

Should she wait until Holmes returned? Perhaps take lodgings nearby? Or seek out Bert Cartwright? What she wanted was
information on this Von Bork. Nathan had done her a service by
uncovering the circumstances under which Holmes, Watson
and Von Bork had met, near Harwich on the eve of the war.
Clearly, Von Bork harboured some grudge against Watson,
which was why he had struck him off the repatriation list. But
what, exactly? Nathan had said the written records were sketchy
in the extreme. All he knew was that a German spy ring had
been broken just in the nick of time.

If only Watson were here to explain what role he had played
in this particular adventure. Breaking spy rings didn't sound
like the John Watson she knew. No, it was Sherlock Holmes who
would have been the prime instrument of espionage. It was he
who liked subterfuge and disguise, not Watson. This Von Bork
was simply lashing out at anyone involved in his defeat, when
he should have been after Holmes . . .

Holmes! Perhaps he was the ultimate target.

She moved the lamp closer to the fireplace, to the embers she
had touched. She picked them out one by one, trying to discern
a scrap of writing, a postmark, any solid piece of evidence that
could give truth or lie to her new suspicions. But there was
nothing. The papers had been thoroughly burned.

She moved over to the desk and examined the books. There
was one on beekeeping, a pamphlet on blood typing, a guide to
the birds of England, a pre-war Baedeker, *La Hollande et la Belgique*.
As if anyone would want to be a tourist in Belgium these days.
Holland, though, had at least been spared the worst effects of
the war, but again few tourists . . .

She snatched up the book and rifled through the pages, until she found what she was looking for. Or, rather, didn't find it. The map at the rear of the book had been torn out, an act of vandalism that suggested a man in a hurry.

Holland. Sherlock Holmes was going to Holland. And she knew what the motive was – she even understood it, after a fashion. But she also knew that Holmes had to be stopped. Yes, John, she was certain, would want her to stop him. No matter what the cost.

NINETEEN

'Know your beard,' Holmes had once told him. 'It is a reliable measure for the passage of time, when *in extremis*.' Back then Watson had been hard put to imagine a situation where he would have to rely on stubble to tell the hour, but in that dank cell, four paces by five, with just the odd snuffling rat for company, it had proved a godsend. Three nights, his fingertips told him. Three nights since he had been plucked out of line and frogmarched to the house and into the basement, where six 'Stubby' cells lined a corridor.

His prison consisted of a bed with a straw mattress, a bucket, full to overflowing, which he had not been allowed to empty, and a tiny slit of a window near the ceiling, which admitted the gloomiest of light, even at noon.

The whistles for *Appell* should also have helped him keep time, but there had seemed more than usual, five or six a day, perhaps as a punishment for his fictitious transgressions. If so, it was guaranteed to make the inmates hate him more than ever. He had grudgingly to admire Von Bork. He had orchestrated his torment perfectly. The instrument of his death would be his

own countrymen, as they grew increasingly tired of the depri-
vations caused by the new arrival. Sometimes even the British
turned on their own, like hyenas might on a wounded pack
member.

Watson lay down and let himself cough as freely as he could.
There was fluid on his lungs. He could feel it in his tubes. When
he awoke each morning he was forced to clear his throat and
spit up a golf ball of phlegm. As far as he could tell there was no
blood in there, but that would only be a matter of time if he
spent much longer in the cold and damp cell.

Chin up, old chap. If you succumb to despair, Von Bork will have won.

Von Bork had already secured victory. What chance did one
old man, alone and ailing, have against a machine determined
to crush him?

*As I have said before, my mind, and I believe yours, rebels at stagnation.
Give me problems, give me work, give me the most abstruse cryptogram or the
most intricate analysis, and I am in my own proper atmosphere. I crave mental
exaltation. You must do the same.*

'Holmes,' he said out loud, 'will I ever truly be free of your
platitudes?'

Watson pulled the greatcoat around him and allowed
himself to doze off. As he did so, Holmes's words echoed
around his drifting consciousness. Something about him being
one fixed point—

'Stand!'

Watson snapped awake at the command. After months of
captivity his muscles seemed to know what to do even before his
nervous system had sent the appropriate messages. He pushed
himself to upright with a minimum number of groans and

shuffled away from the door, which had been cracked open by the German orderly.

Once Watson was well back, the wan-faced veteran stepped in, eyeing the prisoner warily, as if he presented some kind of threat. Out in the corridor Watson knew an armed soldier waited. It would be a foolish man who tried anything with the orderly. But, Watson suspected, after a week or two in these conditions any man could become foolish.

The orderly placed the circular metal tray, which held the usual wooden bowl of soup and a slice of KK bread, on the bed. Made from *Kleie und Kartoffeln*, bran and potatoes, the bread was like eating the contents of the mattress, and about as nutritious. The man's suspicious gaze never left Watson as he backed out and clanged the door shut.

Watson waited until his eyes readjusted to the half-light after the brightness of the bulbs in the corridor and sat next to the meagre offering. A finger told him the soup was barely warm. Grease was already congealing on the surface into an opaque skin. He quickly snapped the bread into small pieces and dropped it into the liquid, then gulped down the resulting mush, hoping it didn't linger long enough to sully his taste buds.

A coughing fit exploded after he had barely managed half of the loaf and he shuddered as he caught the tang of something rancid. Sometimes the meat they put in the soup was worse than no meat at all. He wiped his chin and tried to breathe as evenly as possible. He would have to take his time. Choking to death on this slop would be an even more ignominious way to go than consumption or hypothermia.

As he waited, he thought of Holmes's words. A mental

exercise was needed. He put down the bowl and began to feel along the dust and dirt of the floor. It was close to the aromatic bucket that something stabbed his skin. He picked it up and examined it. A shard of brick. It would have to do, he thought, and set to work.

TWENTY

The German agent known as Miss Pillbody had memorized every inch of the bathing closet that served the landing they had assigned her at Holloway. It was about twenty feet long, nine feet wide and ten in height. There were two baths in this room, separated from each other by a wooden partition, so two female prisoners could bathe at the same time. But she always bathed alone, after the incident where she was forced to near-drown the Dryden woman in scalding water, just to show her who was boss. For months afterwards Dryden had stared out from eyes sunk into shiny, scarred skin and each time the gaze of hatred had been held by Miss Pillbody. After Dryden's husband visited for the last time, just before his wife's release date, she had hanged herself in the laundry. Miss Pillbody wasn't sure what her roughhouse of a husband had said about welcoming home a mutilated monster, but she could imagine.

Adjoining the bathroom was a small store of prison-made clothing, carefully arranged on the shelves, consisting of dark grey jackets, vests, skirts, socks and shoes. There was also a large chest of drawers containing linen, stockings, flannel shirts, and drawers. This was the domain of Mrs Gray, the bathing wardress.

Miss Pillbody piled up her stockings, drawers, petticoat, dress, apron and cap and slipped on a chemise, taking her shoes with her. There would be freshly laundered clothes waiting for her upon her return. She was taken by a landing wardress to the medical room, where she was weighed by a matron, who noted the figure in a ledger, and then returned to the bath closet, where the bathing wardress had already drawn the water and was waiting to gift her the cube of carbolic soap she was allowed, plus an oatmeal-coloured linen towel and a rag of flannelette.

'Ten minutes,' the ferret-like Mrs Gray said.

'Fifteen, please, ma'am,' Miss Pillbody replied, head to one side, eyes as wide as she could make them. She thought of a dormouse or a cute rabbit as she did so.

'Twelve,' said Mrs Gray, her voice losing its sharp edge. 'Shout if you need anything.'

'Yes, ma'am,' the prisoner replied. 'And thank you, ma'am.'

Once the sour-faced bitch was next door, Miss Pillbody quickly kneeled and, using what fingernails she had left after stitching webbing belts for the British soldiers, she levered up a loose hearth tile and slipped out the piece of metal she had been working on for weeks now. She had spotted it, glinting in the corner of the exercise yard, close to a drainpipe. She had resisted the urge to look up, to see where it had come from. Where it had come from didn't matter. Where it was going did. Stooping to apparently retie her shoelaces, she had managed to secrete the metal up the sleeve of her prison jacket, and to keep it hidden until the next bath time.

It was around fifteen centimetres long, perforated with four drilled holes, two at each end, and with blunt, rounded extremities. A fixing strap of some description, intended to repair the drainpipe or gutter or part of the roof. About as threatening as a baby's rattle. No matter, it was not made of lead or zinc or copper or any other useless metal, but galvanized steel.

And so each bath time she used the hardest pumice stone to work on one of those curves, masking the sound by splashing enthusiastically with her feet, ever alert for the footfall of Wardress Gray, honing and honing until now, more than a month after she had begun, a definite point was beginning to emerge.

She wasn't quite sure what she would do with it. She had considered taking Gray hostage, but that would leave her trapped in the bathroom with no further card to play. True, she was sure that there was a way to the prison's roof space, following the pipes, if one had time to tear down the ceiling. Perhaps even get onto the roof. What then? It was a long way down to freedom without a ladder of some description. And the prison had searchlamps and sharpshooters, and the governor wouldn't be afraid to use them.

She had to do something to get free. She had been reprieved once, that was true, but she knew she was an itch the British Government would love to scratch into oblivion. One day, they would find the means to retry her and hang her. Whether it was when they had won or lost the war would make no difference. Whatever the outcome, she was a loose end to be tidied away – a German spy and a multiple murderer who once had the temerity to try to kill the great Sherlock Holmes out on the sinking sands of Foulness island. Hanging, she imagined many would think, was too good for her. Of course she could be wrong, they might just leave her to rot into old age, in many ways an even worse fate.

No, sometime, somehow, the chance to escape would present itself and she would be ready.

The banging on the door made her jump and she quickly pushed the makeshift weapon under her thigh.

'Wardress Gray!' She recognized the gruff voice as belonging to Jefferys, the big-nosed senior warden of this wing. The door was unlocked, but he would not enter a room where there might be naked ladies, much as she suspected he might enjoy that. One thing that had been a pleasant surprise, none of the male staff had ever tried to molest her. Perhaps they had heard what happened to Gray's predecessor, who liked to help the prisoners clean all their most intimate places. Slipped on the soap and cracked her skull, the report said.

Wardress Gray came through and opened the door a notch. 'Yes, sir?'

'Tell Pillbody to hurry along.'

Pillbody. She had thought it best not to use her true German name. It would be a constant reminder to both guards and inmates of why she was in prison.

'I have only just got in,' she protested from the tub.

'Yes, Missy, but you have a visitor.'

A visitor? She thought. Nobody ever visited Miss Pillbody. Her curiosity got the better of her. She moved the crude knife towards her buttocks, lifted one cheek, wedged it in the crack and clenched hard. She would find a way to return it to the hiding place or locate a new one when the opportunity arose. She carefully levered herself up.

'Can I have a towel, ma'am?' she asked, excited, despite herself, at the prospect.

A visitor!

'Who is it, Mr Jefferys?' she asked. 'Did you get a name?'

'There's a Mrs Gregson to see you.'

Miss Pillbody almost fell back into the water in shock. Of all the *Fotzen* to come out of the woodwork, it had to be that one.

TWENTY-ONE

It had taken two days of careful negotiation to get what he wanted from his warders. Watson had scratched his offer in the surface of the metal tray, but it was hard to read. So he had cut himself with the edge of the brick shard and rubbed blood into the grooves. The message was small enough to be hidden by the bowl, but at least it was legible. Ten marks for a notebook and pencil, it offered. Ten more for a lamp.

The orderly had replied with scraps of paper, also hidden under the bowl. Fifteen for a notebook. Fifteen for a lamp. Five for matches.

Eventually the man had settled for thirty marks all in, to be paid on Watson's release. The German had insisted on a furtive handshake. Someone else who believed that an Englishman's word was his bond, thought Watson. And so it was, at least in this case. Despite being an astronomical sum of money – it was to be paid in real, not camp, marks – Watson would honour the debt. Even when, at the last moment, the orderly wheedled five more marks by offering Watson a clean, empty bucket. That, he decided, was the real bargain in the deal.

And so, with a lamp that seemed to be burning oil hardly worthy of the name, producing more black smoke than an ocean liner, and a hazy light that reminded him of the sun shining through a peasouper, he settled down with the notebook – even more extortionately priced than his other one – to follow Holmes's suggestion of keeping his brain active. He continued the tale of the man in The Girl and the Gold Watches, picking up from when the Manchester Express pulled into Rugby five minutes late, and a most remarkable state of affairs was discovered.

Holmes leaned forward now, fingers still pyramided together and eyes blazing. 'Pray proceed, Mr Henderson,' he said.

In a very different kind of prison some 350 miles away, two burly male warders led Miss Pillbody in manacles into one of Holloway's stark, green-painted visitors' rooms. They planted her in the metal chair, which was bolted to the floor, and transferred her hands to the 'bracelets' on top of the scratched metal table, which was also affixed to the concrete floor.

She looked thinner, thought Mrs Gregson, more feral and – if this was possible – even more dangerous. On the face of it she was very docile as they transferred her from one set of metal cuffs to another, her face expressionless. But those eyes, they darted around the room, from Mrs Gregson to the door, as if calculating the distance, from her hands to the guards, and back, estimating the odds of success were she to break free. She had clearly decided those odds were against her because as the iron cuffs were snapped shut on her wrists and ankles, she seemed to relax a little, as if she were conserving energy for a time when circumstances favoured action.

Mrs Gregson, in turn, examined the prisoner. Her cheek-bones were more prominent than she recalled, the eyes a little sunken, the hair wiry, and the skin coarse. It was hard to imagine that she'd ever successfully passed herself off as a demure schoolteacher.

Mrs Gregson looked up at the warders. 'Thank you, gentle-men. If you'll leave us for a few minutes now, I'd be most grateful.'

The senior of the two let his moustache quiver. 'Can't do that. Not with this one.'

'If you check with the Governor . . .' Mrs Gregson reached into her bag and brought out a document. 'I have here authori-zation to interrogate the prisoner alone on a matter of national security covered by the Defence of the Realm Act.'

This was not untrue. She had convinced Robert Nathan that she needed to try to elicit as much information about Von Bork as possible. He had argued that the Sie Wölfe Special Naval Unit, the group Miss Pillbody belonged to, was run by Admiral Hersch, and that Miss Pillbody would therefore have little infor-mation about Von Bork. But Mrs Gregson had been most insistent on the need to quiz Pillbody.

'That's as may be, ma'am,' said the warder. 'But I have a duty to protect you.'

'If you are privy to what we say, you may end up in one of your own cells, as a risk to national security. How can you protect me then?' She reached into the bag again and drew out a police whistle. 'You can wait outside the door. If I feel in any way threatened I shall blow on this. And don't worry,' she flashed the warder a smile, 'I know Miss Pillbody of old. I fully appreciate she cannot be trusted even one of her German centimetres.'

With much huffing the guards left, slamming the door behind them. A hatch slid back on the other side, framing a pair of eyes. They really didn't trust this prisoner.

'You took your time,' said Miss Pillbody. 'I expected you at the Tower.'

'I didn't need to see you at the Tower.' Mrs Gregson reached into her bag and took out a bar of Fry's Chocolate Cream, which she pushed across the table, leaving it just within reach. Miss Pillbody examined it suspiciously.

'It's not poisoned,' Mrs Gregson said.

The spy scrabbled at it with her fingertips and pulled the confectionery towards her, closing a fist over it. 'I'll save it.'

'It'll melt if you hold it too tight.'

'People in here don't care whether it's been melted or not.'

Of course, thought Mrs Gregson. She wouldn't eat it. She could doubtless pull in some useful favours for a Fry's Chocolate Cream.

'So, you couldn't resist.'

'Couldn't resist what?'

'Coming to gloat.'

Mrs Gregson took out a pack of cigarettes and passed that over. 'I haven't come to gloat. I've come to help you.'

The eyes narrowed alarmingly and, despite herself, Mrs Gregson found she was glancing at the manacles to check that they were quite secure. 'Help me with what?'

'Miss Pillbody,' Mrs Gregson met her gaze and then dropped her voice so the words barely made it across the space between them, 'I've come to help you escape.'

Across the Channel and over the border in Germany, escape, for the moment, was the last thing on Watson's mind. He had allowed himself to pass beyond the walls of the vermin-infested basement cell and into the golden years at Baker Street, with the century not quite over and dear Victoria not yet dead. There were pipes and scones, hansom cabs and wild dashes across London. And there was Holmes. The whole confection was as nourishing as beef tea and it was with great reluctance he wrote what would have to be his last sentence for now.

'Pass the Bradshaw's, will you?'

Those final words of the new section of the gold watch story he was writing echoed around Watson's skull as he let the pencil drop from his fingers onto the blanket of his prison cot. When he closed his tired eyes they were there, written on the inside of his lids, like the incandescent bulbs of the Bovril sign in Piccadilly Circus.

The phrase made his heart beat faster even now. Passing the Bradshaw's was so often the prologue to an adventure, a fast drive to the countryside or perhaps a crosschecking of a client's account of his movements with the timetable of trains coming to and from London. With The Rugby Mystery, it had been both — verification of the details and a dash for the Manchester Express. He could smell the cinder and smoke that greeted them at Euston, recall exactly the gleam in his friend's eye as they boarded the train, 'Feeling alive once again!' as he had put it.

Oh, Holmes, that it should come to this.

Careful, old friend.

Watson let his body slump down onto the bed. He heard the notebook slap onto the floor. There came the brittle scratching of claws on concrete as, alarmed by the sudden noise, one of his fellow inhabitants scuttled away.

His throat felt tight and he laid a hand on his forehead. The skin was warm at the very least, although without a thermometer it was impossible to judge if it had tipped over into fever. Another coughing spasm came, leaving his ribs hurting, and Watson was forced to spit the contents of his mouth on the floor. Creatures were moving about his hairline, tickling him, and he brushed them away, his fingers touching the cluster of scabs at the base of the follicles from earlier bites. He moved his hand to his jaw, inspecting the tender swellings in his neck. A groan of despair and disgust escaped his lips.

Even if he hadn't been a physician he could have diagnosed himself. Fever. Congested lungs. Swollen gums. Exhaustion. Muscle ache. He couldn't give it an exact name, but he knew some malady had him in its grip and it wasn't about to let go.

He should write a note or two, before it was too late. Holmes. Mrs Gregson. His bank, of course. And a fresh will. There were some modifications he wished to make there. But the very thought of sitting up and the effort of writing made his head spin. He rode out another hacking fit, pushing the accumulated spittle out with his tongue and letting it drain from the corner of his mouth. A tear squeezed from the corner of one eye. Thank goodness Holmes couldn't see him now. And thank the Lord the voice in his head had the good grace to keep quiet. He rolled over onto his side, slowly pulled his knees towards his chest into a vaguely foetal position and surrendered to the impending delirium.

TWENTY-TWO

The attack, when it came, was no real surprise to Miss Pillbody. Why the other inmates of Holloway had waited so long was the genuine puzzle, given how she had bested them at every turn. Perhaps it was the visit by the Gregson woman that triggered it. The prison's rumour mill would have ascribed all sorts of motives for that. Including the gossip that had finally been whispered along her own landing – that the German whore-of-a-spy was going to be pardoned and repatriated. That would incense those who had been biding their time to repay the many slights and slaps she had dealt out since her arrival.

It began with an unexpected summons to the bathhouse, the usual change into the chemise and a visit to the medical office for weighing. When she returned, the bath was drawn, not to the usual four or six inches, but close to the brim.

'Ma'am?' she asked, knocking on the door of the linen room. There was no reply. The soap and square of towel had, however, been left on a stool for her.

Miss Pillbody lowered herself into the water, enjoying the feel of submerging all but her head and the tips of her breasts.

She shuddered with pleasure. What a luxury. Had the Gregson woman engineered this? Special treatment for her pet prisoner? Two bathing sessions in five days?

She was an enigma, that Mrs Gregson. Miss Pillbody could see that she despised her – perhaps even feared her. But she had suppressed all that to create a scheme that even Miss Pillbody, trained in secret missions by the Sie Wölfe, considered what the British called hare-brained. *Verrückt* for certain.

Initially the Englishwoman had wanted to talk about Von Bork, but even had she wished to, Miss Pillbody could offer her little. She had seen him but once, when Admiral Hersch had brought him for a tour of the Sie Wölfe training facility outside Mainz. Then Gregson had asked about the admiral and his loyalty to his little She-Wolves. It was only at that point that Miss Pillbody grasped exactly what role Mrs Gregson envisaged for her.

But the woman had let slip the weakness in her plan. The look in her eyes told Miss Pillbody that Mrs Gregson was acting out of sentiment. Miss Pillbody knew the feeling of old. She herself had enrolled in the Sie Wölfe because of a mixture of love for her dead husband and the desire to avenge him. That had been expunged during the training. There had been no sentiment left; even when she began an affair with Hersch it had been a pragmatic choice, a way of getting the best assignments. Oddly, it was Hersch who had shown worrying signs of emotion when it came to her deployment abroad. He had even offered her an administrative post in Berlin instead, as if that would have satisfied her after all those months of training. The putty at the core of even so-called Iron Men never failed to amaze and sicken her.

But Mrs Gregson was also pliant and malleable at heart, for she was proposing something even a She-Wolf would consider insane or suicidal or both. Still, Miss Pillbody thought, if she could turn the tables, use this deranged woman for her own purposes . . .

Lost in her thoughts, Miss Pillbody heard the rustle of feet on coconut matting just a moment too late to react. A splayed-out hand pressed down on her head, the pressure irresistible, and she was quickly under the water, fighting for breath, her limbs thrashing, fingers scrabbling for a grip on the sides of the bath. She could feel other hands on her, holding her ankles and wrists. She opened her eyes, and through the distorting lens of the broiling surface, she could just make out three figures, each with swollen, dark heads. Golliwogs were drowning her, she thought, as her airways filled with the bath's contents.

One of the trio took a fistful of her hair and she was yanked clear into the air. She expelled the lungful of water with a series of barking coughs. Before she could recover her composure, an open palm stung her face and the flannelette rag was forced into her mouth. Miss Pillbody could see now that the three attackers had pulled thick prison-issue black stockings over their heads to disguise their features; all that she could see were the eyes, burning with hatred through hastily ripped holes. She gagged against the rag in her mouth, sure she must suffocate. A sense of panic rose in her, and a silent scream filled her head.

One of the three held a pottery bottle and she cracked it against the rim of the bath until it shattered, causing a series of razor-edged shards to drop onto the tiled floor. The woman picked up one of them, a long, tapering triangle, and leaned over Miss Pillbody, who tried to twist, to kick and scream, but it was useless. She was held fast. All she could do was close her eyes once more as the tip of the improvised dagger approached her skin.

So they weren't out to kill her. Just disfigure her, as she had the Dryden woman.

A woman or man without clothes is exquisitely vulnerable. Any training is forgotten in an attempt to protect their modesty and their private parts. It was why Hersch had insisted the Sie Wölfe at his camp wrestle, run and fight naked for a good proportion of the time. Hence Miss Pillbody had few inhibitions, not once her training kicked in. And the moment it did so, the scream in her skull stopped dead.

She pulled one hand free, oblivious to the friction burns on her wrist as she twisted it from the grip. The blade hidden between her buttocks needed a few more sessions before it was a perfect prison weapon. But needs must.

The point sliced through the wrist of the attacker who was twisting her hair. As the grip loosened, Miss Pillbody yanked away, ignoring the splinters of pain rippling across her scalp as a fistful of hair came away. The eyes staring from the stockings made perfect targets and she jabbed at the woman's left one. She fell back with a squeal. Eyes had always been a Pillbody speciality.

Now for the one with the pottery shard. Miss Pillbody grabbed the wrist, pulled the woman close, felt her slap against her breasts, and stabbed up and under the ribs, before pushing her back towards the third woman. Blood was pooling and streaking the water now. She reared up from the bath, crouched slightly, ready to parry the next thrust. Miss Pillbody pulled the rag from her mouth and took in several deep lungfuls of air. The cry she let out, the howl of the She-Wolf they had practised, was amplified into something unworldly by the room's tiled surfaces.

Then, as quickly as it had started, the assault was over. The pack of imbecilic would-be assassins and mutilators were stumbling out of the door. No matter, she would be able to find at least two of them later from the wounds. And she would deal with them then.

She looked down at her glistening body. Some of that blood swirling in the bath was hers. She had a gash running from the side of her left breast almost to her navel that she didn't recall receiving. It was only now beginning to sting. She replayed the frenzied moments of the attack in her mind, but could not isolate the moment she received the cut or who inflicted it. She would have lost marks for that at the academy.

Miss Pillbody stepped from the bath, careful not to pick up any splinters in the soles of her feet from the shattered pottery, and used the linen square to dab at the bleeding. Red globules continued to well from along the break, as if someone was blowing tiny bubbles from beneath her skin. It would need a dressing.

She dropped the towel and went next door to fetch a larger piece of material. In the far corner was Gray, the bathing wardress, wrists and ankles tied and a laundry bag over her head. Miss Pillbody contemplated cutting the ropes, but that would reveal her weapon. Instead, she secreted the knife above the doorframe, pulled off the bag, removed a gag, and set about the knots.

'Miss Pillbody, thank you,' gasped Mrs Gray, blinking hard. 'But you are hurt.'

The curtain of blood busy pooling around her groin certainly looked spectacular, but Miss Pillbody knew it was a superficial injury. Still, she permitted herself a theatrical wince. 'It can wait, ma'am. Let's get you free from these first. Must be cutting off the circulation,' she said, unthreading the bindings.

From the grateful look in Mrs Gray's eyes she knew she had just gained an ally. Perhaps Mrs Gregson's *verrückt* plan might work after all.

TWENTY-THREE

Silk on skin. A hot bath, with some of those new Radox salts in it. A glass of something rich, a tawny port perhaps, or a glass of Bristol cream or . . . a brandy. A warming cognac or a Solera Gran Reserva. Or a hot toddy, a Laphroaig, a slice of lemon peel, hot water and a spoonful of demerara. One of Holmes's favourites. Even in his febrile sleep, Watson's lips smacked at the thought of these choices.

Next, clean underwear, nothing too fancy, just freshly laundered cotton next to the skin. Oh, why not something fancy? It was all a dream anyway. Why not push the boat out? So, perhaps a Smedley's Anglo-Indian combination, the softest merino wool and white silk. Like being kissed all over by Maude Fealy's lips. And new socks, straight from the packet, a pair of Morley's cashmere would do nicely and . . .

He groaned, like a man who has gorged on too much of Simpson's game pie, and turned over, his delusional state suggesting the ticking pillowcase was caressing his cheek like the softest of fingertips.

His eyes snapped open. It *was* the softest of fingertips, or at least his face was resting on gloriously fine-threaded cotton, made plump by duck down, not shredded paper. Now Watson understood, now he knew the truth. He had died and gone to heaven, or at least the place his dying mind had wished for. Perhaps these were the final few seconds on earth, before the blackest of curtains fell for ever. If so, he thought, closing his eyes once again and relishing the cool touch of the material, there were worse ways to go.

'You are awake, I see, Major.'

Watson opened an eye. There was a vast plain of white as far as he could see. He raised his head slightly and opened the other eye. Before him was a pillow, an enormous, fat, soft pillow, stretching away, like a sea of cotton he could sail across. He was aware that his legs were swaddled in something cool and caressing. Up above was a billowing canopy, sporting a family crest in the centre. He was in a bed, a four-poster. On top of his covers was a heavily embroidered eiderdown, adorned with the same family crest, writ large in gold and red thread. He lifted the top layer up, taking the sheet with it. Underneath, he had on clean underwear. Not the Smedley of his dreams, but white and laundry-fresh.

The room was bright enough to hurt his eyes after the cell and he had to squint to take in an over-ornate wardrobe, a dressing table and the man standing next to the washstand.

Watson blinked away the tears from his watering eyes until he could focus on the figure. He still wasn't certain that he hadn't passed over. This could be an antechamber, a prelude to heaven, hell or purgatory. But the rumble in his stomach and the dryness of his mouth suggested he wasn't yet beyond all earthly woes.

'Where am I?' he croaked.

'Alive, at least. Be thankful for that.' The accent was slight but unmistakable. The German had on an impeccably tailored uniform of the *Sanitätswesen*, the German medical corps. His face was sharp and sallow, and his black hair sparse. He had bags under his eyes the size of steamer trunks. He took out a packet of cigarettes and moved across to the bed. He offered one to Watson, who shuffled up in the enormous bed until he was upright and accepted it. The man lit it, then passed him a porcelain ash-tray, again with that crest, which featured two bears holding a shield that bore a maiden with flowing locks. The motto underneath was in Latin: *Aut suavitate aut vi* – either by gentleness or force. Watson thought that if it referred to the bears' intentions towards the young woman, it was in very poor taste. It was the kind of crest Hugo Baskerville might approve of.

'Your uniform has been fumigated and laundered, Major Watson. You'll be free of those little friends. For a while, at least.' Watson took a lungful of the dark tobacco and held it in his lungs for a moment. Not dead and gone to heaven, but close enough.

'I'm sorry,' Watson said, once he had exhaled. 'You have the advantage of me.'

'Dr Ernst Steigler, late of the Kaiser Wilhelm Bavarian Respiratory Clinic. Your heart and lungs, by the way, are in decent shape, considering. There is some inflammation in the left lung, perhaps, but I can give you something for that.'

'What I am doing here?' Watson looked at the doctor. 'What are you doing here?'

'Me? For my sins, I am a medical inspector for the Army Group that runs this and several other camps in this district. I was on a tour of the ones around Einbeck but was summoned back here somewhat urgently and told there were two things to take care of. A patient who must be brought back from the brink . . .'

So he was still in Harzgrund. This must be a room in the big house. 'Medical inspector? Have you been out there?' He pointed to the window. 'There is much that needs your attention.'

Steigler nodded, sadness and possibly shame in his eyes. 'I know that. And it offends me mightily,' he added defensively. 'I can only offer recommendations to the High Command and make protests to the commandants. If you saw the conditions at some other camps . . .'

'I have never really been convinced by that argument. *If you think we treat our servants badly, you should see how the Monroes down the street beat theirs . . . if you think our gas is bad, wait until you see German flame-throwers.* That someone is worse doesn't wash as an excuse for cruelty and neglect.'

'I repeat,' said the doctor more forcefully, 'it is out of my hands. I simply make my reports and obey orders.'

'So why am I here? Why have I been pulled out of Stubby to . . .' a wave of the arm took in the ridiculous opulence of his surroundings, '. . . all this?'

Steigler puffed on his cigarette. As he did so, Watson noticed how red and raw the skin was on the back of his hand. It was a common affliction among medical staff, given the powerful carbolics and bleaches used, but rare in a senior doctor. Steigler caught the appraisal. 'I am afraid the medical facilities at some of the camps are very crude. I have no nurses or orderlies to assist. I do, literally, get my hands dirty. And bloodied.'

Watson nodded. He, too, had found himself at the 'sharp end' of the medical war when he had been in Flanders and knew the niceties of the peacetime ward quickly went by the wayside. 'So what is this all about? Why am I no longer in a cell?'

'All will be revealed, I am sure, when you see the commandant.'

'Mad Bill?'

The use of the nickname didn't seem to surprise the doctor. 'Mad? Mad like a fox. You be careful. I've never known anyone be given such accommodations before. You must be a very valuable prisoner.'

'How long have I been here, in this room?'

'Two days. I gave you a sleeping draught to allow your body to recover. I shall send up some coffee. I think the commandant wants to see you. Perhaps he will feed you some of his fine pork. If you are strong enough.'

'I'm strong enough,' Watson admitted.

'Be careful. A little at a time. And chew well.'

'I am fully aware of how easy it is to overwhelm the deprived body,' Watson replied stiffly.

'Of course you are.' Steigler stood. 'You know, I don't like this situation any more than you do. I had a teaching position before the war. I would have it still, but for . . .' he paused. 'I made enemies. A few indiscretions here and there. But for those, I would still be in Munich instead of trudging from charnel house to . . .'

'What was the second?' asked Watson, recognizing an imminent dose of self-pity coming his way.

'What?'

'You said you were summoned here for two reasons. One was to treat me. The other was . . . ?'

'Death certificates. We have been reclassified as a category B camp by those meddlers at the Red Cross. They have begun insisting on death certificates for all inmates. So they can notify relatives and also to prevent summary executions, or so they say.'

'Who died?'

'Three of your fellow countrymen.'

'Three? How? Trying to escape?'

The German shook his head. 'Not exactly.'

'What did you put on the certificates?'

'Heart failure.'

Watson laughed. 'All three? Three men died of heart failure in the space of . . . how long?'

Stiegler looked agitated. 'I shall get food sent up. You can ask the commandant—'

'How long?' Watson insisted.

'The same night. They all died at the same time.'

'Of what? And do not say cardiac failure.'

The German squashed the cigarette in Watson's ashtray and lit a second, inhaling several times before he spoke. Watson bided his time.

'Are you a man of science, Major? Someone who believes all the wonders of life will one day be explained by chemistry and physics?'

'I'd like to think so,' said Watson. 'Not the wonder of it, perhaps, but the mechanics, yes.'

'I, too, but you know, as men of science even we have come across situations that challenge our beliefs.'

'Challenge how?'

'Things that suggest what we know of the world is pitifully little. Something beyond our feeble understanding—'

Watson felt his patience snap and a rush of anger brought a flush to his face. 'Steigler, for God's sake man, can you get to the point?'

'I don't believe,' Steigler said evenly, 'that they were killed by anything known to our science.'

'How do you mean?'

'Whatever killed your comrades, Major Watson, came from beyond the grave.'

TWENTY-FOUR

Von Bork walked alongside the muddy River Meuse to the north of Venlo, its surface riffled by a sharp wind blowing down from the North Sea, where Allied ships, submarines and minefields were trying to starve Germany into submission. He was on the Dutch side, heading for a small workers' café that mostly served the employees of the three boatyards that operated on this stretch of the river, to build and repair barges and tugboats. How easily they could all now have been in German hands.

Von Bork had seen the original versions of the Schlieffen Plan, which had called for a sweep through the Netherlands as well as Belgium. It had made perfect sense, but for some reason the High Command had modified it, so that in the event only Belgium was invaded. Had they taken Holland and, more importantly, its ports, the Allied blockade would have been almost impossible. On such decisions does the fate of nations turn, he thought glumly.

The German drew level with the bridge that spanned the Meuse. Its black girders were flecked with rust, although the

mechanical system displayed evidence of recent care and attention, with cables, pulleys and pistons conscientiously greased.
Across the other side was his homeland, because in 1893,
Germany had moved a small section of her western boundary
by a handful of kilometres, creating a new border right down
the centre of the river for a short distance.

He stepped out onto the span, looking down between the
wide wooden planks at the sludgy waters below. The bridge was
in two halves. The span he was walking on was fixed, running
out to mid-stream where it rested on a concrete pillar. The
second half of the bridge, the part that connected to Germany,
was hinged, so that it swung back at ninety degrees, ostensibly
to let larger river traffic pass, but in fact to ensure that only the
Dutch had control of this access point.

The Knok bridge had been officially extended half a dozen
times since the conflict began, always for some ceremonial
reason, such as the crossing of the first prisoners to be released
on their bond into Holland, and for the exchange of civilian
internees that neither side wished to hang on to.

He raised a hand in salute to the two Germans standing at the
checkpoint at the far side, and they returned the greeting. It
wasn't much more than a symbolic entry point into Germany,
just a striped pole across the road that punctured the border
fence and an adjacent rough shed for the brewing of coffee – one
perk of the posting was that the little garrison could obtain the
real thing from Venlo, Lomm or Arcen – and, further up the
road into the Fatherland, a sand-bagged machine-gun post.
Everything was manned by soldiers who were old or crippled or
both. But then the Germans knew the Dutch weren't coming

across. The Government of Holland was aware of what fate awaited armies in this war. They weren't about to allow the Allies to strike through their country nor, heaven forbid, take the offensive themselves. They'd sit this dance out, thank you very much.

Von Bork lit a cigarette and retraced his steps, back to the Dutch bank, and covered the two hundred metres to the café in double-quick time. That wind was a blade, able to open up even his Schipper overcoat. Inside the café it was warm and steamy and he shrugged off the coat and hung it on a stand by the door, ignoring the few hostile stares thrown his way. He was in civilian clothes, but his accent as he asked the proprietor for coffee and cake was unmistakable. There were some hereabouts who had been displaced by the Imperial land grab of twenty years earlier and treated all Germans as thieves.

The owner put the coffee down and pointed at a chair. 'Do you mind,' he asked in German, 'if I join you for a moment?'

Von Bork, curious, shook his head. The man sat and set about filling his pipe. 'My daughter will fetch the cake,' he said, indicating a thick-ankled woman in her thirties, her slumped shoulders and untidy hair suggesting someone who was resigned to a life of serving coffee and cake to greasy-fingered dockworkers.

'What can I do for you?' Von Bork asked.

'I have two nephews in your army. German father, you see. I look at your coat —' his eyes darted to the Schipper — 'your suit, your nails, the five-guilder haircut. You are no mere civil servant. Am I right?'

Von Bork shrugged.

'I want those boys back alive. You should stop this madness before the Americans come into the war.'

'It is hardly my decision.'

The proprietor shook his hairless head. 'Not alone, no. But what is a government? Collectively, a lot of men like you. Together, maybe, you can make the Kaiser and Hindenburg and Ludendorff see sense.'

Clearly the man did not know Ludendorff. The term 'iron will' could have been coined for the humourless, friendless martinet.

'We'd all like the killing to stop. But not on terms that will damage Germany.'

The man gave a bitter laugh. 'Fifteen kilometres over that bridge you seem so interested in, I've seen fatherless children starving in the streets, reduced to begging. Ah, here is your cake.' He stood while the daughter placed the plate before him. 'Enjoy.'

Von Bork considered walking away without touching it, but he wouldn't give him the satisfaction. 'And another cup of your excellent coffee, please,' he said, scooping up a forkful of *taart*. The owner gave a frown as he stood and retreated to the kitchen.

Perhaps the interfering fool was right, Von Bork thought as a little capsule of meringue exploded in his mouth, releasing a tangy citrus flavour. But he had smaller fish to fry than the war. While he savoured the cake, Von Bork pulled out the telegram he had picked up from the *postkantoor* in Venlo. Reading it for the tenth time washed away all the sourness that the conversation had built up.

Agree all terms. Need a week to tidy affairs in London. Leave all details of exchange at Hotel Bilderberg. Holmes.

It was the reply to the proposal he had sent the great detective. And now he had him. Von Bork had Sherlock Holmes at last.

TWENTY-FIVE

Herbert Greenhough Smith, the editor of the *Strand Magazine*, was dressed, as always, in his old-fashioned frock coat. It marked him out as a man from another age, Mrs Gregson thought. Someone who would love to use his pages to rail against lounge suits and straw boaters. But people bought the *Strand* for escapism, not politics, and so the readers were spared his anachronistic views. He shifted uneasily in his chair as he examined Mrs Gregson one more time, as if unable to quite believe what she was offering him. They were in his office above Southampton Street, the noise of the apparently endless road repairs outside drifting up to them.

'I'm . . .' Greenhough Smith paused and stroked his moustache, wondering how to phrase this. The offer she had made was tantalizing in the extreme. His breath was short at the very thought. But he had to be careful. 'Do you have the authority for what you are proposing?'

Mrs Gregson shook her head. She had known this would be the trickiest part. 'Not exactly, but I can assure you—'

'I don't need assurances, Mrs Gregson,' he interrupted, 'I need a contract with the author.'

'I can't give you that,' she said flatly.

Greenhough Smith swivelled slightly in his chair, and stared at the artwork on his walls, including an enormous portrait of his predecessor, George Newnes, before he rotated back. 'Then I am afraid I have to decline your offer.'

'I can have a legal document drawn up saying I will deliver. If I fail to do so, then the monies will be refunded in full. I shall put a charge against my parents' house.'

'Will you? And they'll be fine with that?'

Once she explained the situation, perhaps. 'Yes.'

Mrs Gregson waited, hands clutched firmly on the handle of her large handbag. He was clearly tempted – who wouldn't be? – but he was also a businessman. 'I don't see what you have got to lose.'

He laughed at this. 'Only money.'

'But I just explained—' she began.

'No matter how you dress it up, it's still a promise. Everything you are saying is just a promise. I'd be betting you are as good as your word. And, frankly, Mrs Gregson, I don't know you from Eve. You claim to be an old friend of Holmes and Watson—'

She unclipped the catch of her bag and took out the small bundle of letters. She slid them across the desk. 'These are personal, you appreciate,' she said. 'Which is why I didn't use them unless I had to. Perhaps you would simply examine the signature.'

Greenhough Smith picked up the stack, undid the ribbon and leafed through the flimsy papers quickly, as if anxious not to let his eyes fall on any stray sentence. When he was satisfied, he carefully retied the bundle. 'They would appear to be from Dr Watson, yes.'

'I have heard no word from Major Watson for some time now,' she said as she scooped the correspondence back up. 'I think that does not bode well. Which is why I am anxious to act.' She felt a surge of emotion well up inside her. But she was not going to cry, even though her eyes were stinging. That wasn't how she was going to win over an old trooper like Greenhough Smith. She began to sob.

'I'm sorry, I'm sorry.' She reached into her bag once more and pulled out a handkerchief. 'I didn't mean . . . it's so . . . I'm so weak. It's not very professional. But, well, as you can see, I care for the major.'

'You must care for him very much,' said Greenhough Smith softly.

She smiled as she dabbed at her eyes. 'I won't argue the point, Mr Smith.' Mrs Gregson cleared her throat and composed herself. 'I have a scheme to help him, and that scheme will cost me money. The most valuable asset we have – I have – is Dr Watson's talent as an author and Sherlock Holmes's celebrity. As editor of the magazine that made both their names, I don't have to remind you of that. I am offering you at least one case from Baker Street that the world is not yet aware of.'

'I cannot deny what a coup this would be, Mrs Gregson. And I feel for Dr Watson, as you do. He is an old friend. He has been very loyal over the years.' Greenhough Smith glanced over his shoulder at the portrait of Newnes once again, as if looking for his approval from the old man. He turned back, slapped the desk with the flat of his hand and grinned at her. 'I say, let's do it, Mrs Gregson. Let's get Watson home. And let's give the public what they have been baying for – the further adventures of Sherlock Holmes!'

Mrs Gregson tried to keep the feeling of satisfaction from showing in her features. 'In which case, my price is two thousand pounds.'

As the magnitude of the sum sank in, the smile slowly faded from Herbert Greenhough Smith's face.

'In advance.'

TWENTY-SIX

Robert Nathan had never considered himself a man in need of a wife. Harriet, his first, had died, along with her child, soon after they had arrived in India. Since then his needs had been fulfilled by a succession of widows and, on occasion, other men's wives. But remarriage? It had never occurred to him. Until he met the blasted Mrs Gregson.

He was sitting in one of MI5's cars, a sleek six-cylinder Napier, which Kell had commissioned directly from the company, claiming priority because they were for 'the war effort'. Nathan wasn't entirely sure what he was doing for the war effort sitting opposite the Diogenes Club off the Strand, while Mrs Gregson was engaged in what she called 'a fund-raising mission' with an editor.

Asked what else she needed to bring her plan to fruition she had smiled and said: 'This project requires four more things: a magician, a lighter-than-air machine, a dead body and a meeting with Mr Sherlock Holmes.'

It was a queer business, all right, but the woman certainly had the means to bend men to her will. Although he wouldn't

officially sanction anything she did, Vernon Kell had agreed that
the country owed Holmes and Watson enough of a debt to lend
Mrs Gregson the use of Nathan and Hiram Buller, the young,
bucktoothed driver sitting behind the wheel.

Nathan consulted his watch. 'Why don't we just go in there
and get him, sir?' Buller asked, nodding at the porticoed entrance
to the club, with its fearsome bulldog of a doorman, all jowls
and scowls for anyone approaching his precious steps.

'Apparently, it will bring down the Government,' said
Nathan.

'What will?'

'Going in there.'

Buller laughed, suspecting a joke. 'How's that, sir?'

'I don't know, lad. It's not like the Overseas or The Empire or
The East India. It has its peculiarities, shall we say. If we were to
simply barge in, so the Guv'nor says, it would reflect badly on
the service.' And Kell was all about making sure that MI5 ended
the war stronger than it had begun it.

'I see,' said the driver, his brow furrowed in puzzlement.

'No, neither do I, Buller. But softly, softly catchee monkey.
You see, Mr Holmes has committed no crime, put nobody in
danger, except perhaps himself. So we can't be involving the
police and warrants. We have to persuade him to come along.'

'What if he won't, sir?'

Nathan patted the Webley Self-Loading pistol in his pocket.
'Oh, I am sure we can convince him.' He took it out and checked
the action. A lovely little gun, but prone to jamming unless it
was kept scrupulously clean, which, of course, he did. But at
least it didn't spoil the hang of a jacket the way a revolver did.

Nathan had been out of the country for much of the Sherlock Holmes fever that had swept the nation. He knew of some of the more famous adventures – the rather silly one about the dog on Dartmoor, which he could scarcely give credence to, and the one involving a speckle-banded snake – equally unlikely – and thought Holmes and Watson must be little more than tall-story merchants. Consulting detective, my eye, he thought. A Jack of Tall Tales more likely. But Kell assured him that Holmes had performed valuable service for both King and Country over the years, right up to August 1914. And of course he had also helped capture the Ilse Brandt woman, who by rights should be lying in an unmarked grave within the confines of the Tower.

'Is that him, sir?' asked Buller.

Nathan looked over as a stooped figure slowly descended the steps, aided by the doorman for the last few. He had a Gladstone in one hand and a stout cane in the other, which he leaned on. He was wearing a flap-eared travelling cap, of the sort popular twenty years earlier, and a tweedy paddock coat. As he turned to speak to the doorman, the profile was unmistakable.

'Wait here,' Nathan instructed.

He was out of the vehicle and across the street in a series of lengthy strides and was at the man's side before the doorman could hail the member a cab.

'Mr Holmes?' he asked.

The rheumy eyes turned to look at him and he was surprised by the vacancy in there. The greatest mind in Europe seemed to be curiously absent. 'Yes. I'm sorry, do I know you . . . ?'

'No, sir, but Mr Vernon Kell sends his compliments.'

'Does he indeed? And why is that?'

'I'm afraid I'll have to ask you to come with us.'

'And you are?'

'Robert Nathan. A representative of Mr Kell.'

'Ah.' Holmes seemed to slump a little further. 'How did you . . . ?'

'Find you? I'm afraid we have the authority to read all telegrams sent from this country.'

'Ah. That blasted DORA, again?'

'I am afraid so. We know your intentions, sir, regarding Von Bork and Major Watson, and can't let you do this, no matter how noble your motives.'

Nathan carefully prised the Gladstone from the bony fingers.

A sparkle came into Holmes's eyes, like the embers of a dying fire offering one last flare. 'He's my friend, you know. Watson. An old friend.'

'I know, sir. But I think it's time to leave the adventuring to others, don't you?'

'This gentleman bothering you, Mr Holmes?' asked the doorman, thrusting his chest out in challenge. Nathan discreetly lifted the flap of the pocket containing the Webley, just in case.

'Oh, no, Henry. Just offering me a lift.'

The doorman didn't look convinced, but stood down as Nathan guided Holmes across the street to the Napier which, thanks to its electric starter, had burbled into life. Buller was already out from behind the wheel, holding open the rear door and doffing his cap.

'As a matter of interest, where are you taking me. Mr . . . ?'

'Nathan. Robert Nathan. Mr Kell keeps a suite at the

Connaught for unexpected guests.' One with barred windows, outside bolts and a boxroom for a guard to sleep in.

'Splendid,' said Holmes, with a sly smile. 'If one is to be imprisoned, one could hardly do better than the Connaught.'

TWENTY-SEVEN

'Mad Bill' Kügel didn't look particularly mad. 'Well-Fed Bill' might have been a better name for him. He was the first man with a healthy glow to his cheeks Watson had seen in many a month – Captain Peacock excepted – and he had the moon face and the girth to match. At least someone was having a good war, he thought as he walked slowly across the ruby-red carpet to where the commandant stood, gazing out of the French windows that opened on to the terrace overlooking the camp.

The room was triple height, with an ornately plastered ceiling, lined with bookshelves that held leather-bound volumes in complete sets, arranged by author. Only for a moment did a flash of vanity make Watson wonder if one of his own were there: before the war he had enjoyed a happy relationship with a German publisher. But he kept his eyes from the 'W's.

An imposing table of polished walnut dominated the centre of the room; along its spine was a series of silver platters, the contents hidden under cloches. A trio of decanters stood at one end, the spirits within ranging from a light straw colour to a deep, syrupy brown. A marble fireplace directly opposite the French windows held a flickering log fire, although the amount of smoke puffing into the room suggested it was burning green damp wood and that the chimney might be in need of a good sweep. No matter, it was warm and welcoming, and as he made a slow, but he hoped stately progress, across the carpet, Watson allowed himself to revel in it for a few moments.

Despite the cotton sheets, the bath and the clean, deloused uniform, Watson could feel the effects of his confinement. His old bullet wound throbbed with a rhythmic precision – a lack of fresh fruit could cause old wounds to reopen, he knew – as did, strangely, one of his Achilles tendons. His knees felt a trifle more fragile than they had, with even more clicking and crunching if he kneeled. His back, too, had suffered from the hard surface. He had often railed against the march of time, but he now knew he had been premature. This was what old age truly felt like. He could only hope it was a temporary preview.

He looked at himself in the gilt-framed mirror – in need of resilvering – over the mantelpiece. Had the frail figure been a patient, he would have sent him to bed with copious quantities of beef tea and Mrs Hudson's steak puddings.

There was a very unseemly crack splaying out from behind the mirror and, he noticed, another fissure zigzagging across the ceiling mouldings. It couldn't be shell or bomb damage this far from the front. The building was collapsing like a tired soufflé. He felt some sympathy – physically, Watson felt in a similar condition.

'When I was a boy, a very young boy,' said the commandant in his strange drawl, 'my father took me hunting for boar in those forests.' He pointed to the naked hillsides. 'The ones that aren't there any longer.'

He turned to face Watson.

'Shocking. I've seen it in America, of course, strip-mining coal until all that is left is a black desert. Out there it was gold. Gold extraction ravages the land, poisons the water, you know. At least coal and iron and copper benefit mankind. But gold? Baubles and teeth, baubles and teeth. Sit down, Major Watson.'

He would have preferred to stand, but his weary body accepted before his brain could object and he sank into one of the cushioned chairs at the table. His nostrils caught the piquant scent of food from the salvers. Kügel walked over and indicated the decanters. 'I have whiskey, brandy and a navy rum.'

'Rum,' Watson said.

'I'd like to apologize for your treatment of late. Apparently, I was misinformed. Instead of a dangerous enemy of the State, you are something of a hero. Such is war.' Kügel handed Watson the glass with a good inch of liquid in the bottom. Watson sniffed and inhaled a thick coil of molasses. 'Such is politics.'

Watson drank and all but shuddered with pleasure.

'You know how the British Navy knew it was the good stuff? They'd mix it with gunpowder and see if it burned true. Because the rum was kept below decks with the gunpowder, should the two mix, they had to be sure the powder would still work.'

Watson had heard this before and was fairly certain it was hokum. But he didn't want to get into a discussion on the mythology of the high seas. 'What is this all about, Commandant?'

Kügel helped himself to some whiskey. 'A bourbon,' he explained, even though Watson couldn't have cared less. 'I got the taste in America. You don't much approve of me, do you, Major Watson?'

'It is exceedingly difficult to approve of anyone who operates a camp as you do. For personal gain.'

Kügel sipped and smiled at the taste. 'Takes me right back. Right back to the Appalachians. I am sure you've heard that I travelled in ladies' underwear? Yes? That's just a rather poor example of the British sense of humour. I travelled, true, but in machine tools. German machine tools. Pittsburgh, Pennsylvania, Virginia, West Virginia, Texas, California. Anywhere men were cutting, digging or drilling. I loved America. For its ambition, its scale, its sense that anything is possible. What I am doing here isn't much different to what the Vanderbilts, the Astors, the Rockefellers did in the United States. I am a capitalist. I know, as they say over there, how to turn a buck. Is that a crime?'

'It is when men suffer while you turn your buck.'

Kügel frowned. 'You do understand the principles of capitalism, don't you, Major? Someone always suffers. The Chinese who built Huntington's and Vanderbilt's railroads. The blacks picking Duke's tobacco, the miners in Osgood's pits, the labourers in Carnegie's steel mills. It's the traditional way of capitalism.'

'The tradition of fleecing those weaker than yourself.'

Kügel shook his head. 'You are a naïve man, Major. And I'm inclined to throw you back in your filthy cell. But I have my orders.'

'Which are?'

'To look after you.'

Watson felt a creeping sense of unease. The order to improve his treatment could only have come from on high. From Von Bork. And what possible motives would he have for such a volte-face?

Kügel reached over and lifted one of the silver cloches. 'Sausages,' he said. 'Without a trace of sawdust. We have kidneys, too. And dumplings.'

Watson wanted to say that he couldn't eat in such company, but his stomach shouted him down as it contracted in anticipation. He despised himself for the groan that squeezed from his lips. 'There is something I want to ask you before we eat.'

'Go ahead,' Kügel said, a hint of suspicion in his voice.

'Your man Steigler, the doctor, tells me three men died in the camp while I was incarcerated.'

'That is true,' admitted Kügel. 'Most unfortunate. I am opposed to any death. For me, each one means one less sheep to shear.' There was a twinkle of humour in his eyes.

'Your doctor insists they died of supernatural causes.'

'Steigler has a vivid imagination. It was suicide. Of a sort, anyway.' He mimed the slashing of wrists.

Watson thought of the marks on Archer's arms. 'Suicide? When was this?'

'Several days ago.'

'The day you had me put in Stubby?'

Kügel thought for a few moments. 'I guess it would have been, yes.'

The night Archer asked Watson to meet him. He could easily have been with him that night. Would he, too, have committed "suicide"?'

'How did it happen?' Watson asked.

'Apparently they were taking part in a séance.'

As he had thought. *The Dead speak to me.* But he played dumb. 'A séance?'

'To contact the dead. Have you ever been to one?'

Watson had. He, Holmes and the magician Maskelyne had exposed some of the most notorious charlatans in London. He had nothing but contempt for characters such as the Davenport Brothers, who prayed on the bereaved and the bereft. It was, so he had heard, a booming and fraudulent industry back in Britain, now that so many had lost sons, lovers and fathers and were looking for comfort.

'The aim of a séance is to contact the dead,' said Watson. 'Not join them.'

'Do you believe that they can contact the dead?' Kügel asked.

Watson shook his head. 'I have never seen anything either in person or in photographs that could not be explained by science and trickery.'

'I agree,' said Kügel with some relief. 'The notion of an afterlife where we pay for our sins . . . well, let's just say I don't buy it.'

'And you certainly must hope you are right. Given the magnitude of your sins.'

Kügel's mouth twitched with displeasure. 'My sins are between me and my conscience.'

'Quite. Tell me about the suicides. Wrists were slit?'

'So they say. I didn't examine the bodies myself.'

'Really,' said Watson loftily, enjoying the annoyance on Kügel's face. 'You surprise me. What blade was used?'

'An open razor was found at the scene.'

'Just one?'

'Yes.'

'So they would have taken it in turns?'

Kügel clearly hadn't thought of this. 'I reckon.'

'It's unusual that one of them didn't lose his nerve while the others were carving.'

'Perhaps. But the men had also been drinking, to make them more "receptive" to the spirits.'

'Drinking? Drinking what?'

'What we called in Virginia, white dog. Moonshine.'

'Made from what? The inhabitants of your camp hardly have any ingredients to spare for distillation.'

Kügel shrugged. 'The ingenuity of man in pursuit of intoxication knows no bounds. Whatever it was, Steigler found a jar of it next to the table. The thing is, as I know from experience, the stuff fries a man's brains, like tossing them into a skillet of hot fat.'

'Dutch courage, you think? Maybe so,' said Watson. 'Although it could be the drink that killed them, not the cuts. If the batch contained enough methanol, for instance.'

Kügel shrugged. 'Does it matter? Whether they were playing with the supernatural or with some home-produced poison? They are dead. They aren't coming back. Not unless you want to set up a séance, Major, and ask them what happened.'

'Have they been buried yet?'

'I'm not certain. You'd have to ask the camp chaplain. We only have a Roman Catholic one, so he might have a view on what kind of burial is appropriate. Shall we eat?'

'I can't believe you have taken the death of three men in your care so lightly. If care is the right word for what you are doing.'

Kügel downed his bourbon. His face had reddened and not all of the colour was from the drink taken. 'Perhaps lunch can wait a little longer. I want to show you something. Come.' His voice was full of a new impatience. 'Now. Come.'

Watson sighed at the thought of leaving the sausages, kidneys and dumplings. As he stood a rocket of searing pain shot up the back of his leg and his knee bent. He reached out and steadied himself on the table.

'Are you all right?' the German asked.

'Yes. Just my knee.' He put the weight on the leg and winced at a second blade of pain. 'A cane might help.'

'There is a selection downstairs by the entrance. We are taking an automobile trip,' said Kügel. 'So it will be under no strain.'

'Very well.'

'Don't worry too much, Major Watson. You will be able to have it seen to soon. My orders tell me you are to be transferred. To Holland. And then . . . then, I think you will be going home.'

The stick Watson chose from the basket by the doorway was a Wurzelstock of chestnut, with a four-inch metal ferrule at the tip, and a leather lanyard for him to hook over his wrist. It was more a hiking staff than a supporting cane, but he wasn't quite ready to hobble around like a cripple with something smaller. With the Wurzelstock at least he could pretend he was out for a stroll in the woods, rather than a lame old man.

Once he had selected his support, Kügel loaded him in the back of a well-appointed Argus tourer, all leather and red velvet, which had a hint of the mobile boudoir about it. There was a driver up front – a facially scarred *Feldwebel* with an eye patch

– and a guard, armed with a 'broomhandle' Mauser pistol. Watson wondered if the man with the weapon was in case he made a break for it. If so, the precautions were redundant – he wouldn't get far with one good knee.

Kügel climbed in beside him and offered him a cigarette. Watson took it, if only to kill the hunger pangs.

'Dramin, please, Emil,' Kügel said to the driver.

The Argus pulled away smoothly and they made stately progress down the mansion's driveway. It, at least, still had its colonnade of trees, albeit bare of leaves at that time of year.

At the gates they turned left and Kügel pointed to a smaller, single-storey building built in the same style as the château they had just left. 'The stables. They once housed sixty horses. Now there are twelve and we have to guard them day and night.' He turned and faced Watson. 'The meat, you see.'

The tourer headed east until it hit the road that Watson had come up, the one where Sayer had been murdered. Then it turned north and began to climb further uphill. More snow had clearly fallen while he had been in solitary, and the brutalized landscape looked less bleak in its swaddling of white, as if a remedial coat of limewash had been applied. The road, though, showed signs of heavy traffic and the borders were blackened by the filth from engines and the splash from tyres.

As they negotiated a series of switchbacks, Watson looked over his shoulder at the shrinking camp. He could see the two compounds quite clearly, but he now saw that the mountain at the rear of the camp's plateau had been scooped out, as if by an enormous spoon. There was evidence of buildings and rusting machinery and a number of spidery tracks led down to the old workings, and there were decayed wooden chutes, no doubt used to carry water from the churning, slate-grey mountain rivers that they crisscrossed at intervals. The rushing water was flecked with little flags of white and Watson spotted debris in there – of both natural and human origin – being purged away, down the hillside.

The Argus struggled as the incline increased and, after cresting a rise, the camp was lost to view. Here were a series of dark ponds; a scum of ice had formed on some of them. Again there was evidence of industrial machinery, most of it rusted or rotted.

The road forked. One way indicated what Watson assumed to be a village, called Zellergrund; the other had a large wooden arrow with the word *Fleckfieber* on it – typhus again – and the crudely daubed skull and crossbones. They took the path towards the disease.

There were a few trees in evidence here, evergreens that, despite the name, were mostly brown, their branches dusted with snow on their dorsal surfaces. Beyond them was another range of mountains with a saw-toothed outline, steep enough that snow had only settled in the crevices and gullies that fissured the flanks. At the base was another camp, much larger than the one Watson had just left. This plateau seemed more exposed than the lower levels and he could feel the wind buffeting the Argus as they approached the steel and mesh gates that blocked their path. A barbed-wire-topped fence ran over the undulating terrain on either side of the gateway.

Signs indicated it was *elektrifiziert*, electrified, something the Germans had grown rather skilled at, having strung electric fences the entire length of the French–Belgian border. A second type of warning showed the silhouette of a figure being struck by a lightning bolt. The fence was charged with enough voltage to kill a man.

The guards opened the gate to allow the car in, peering in at Kügel as they drove through, then saluting. As the Argus bumped down the track towards the main camp, which was surrounded by a triple layer of wire, with the centre one displaying the electrified signs, Watson felt his mouth dry. To the right of them was a row of gibbets, twenty in all, each with a hinged platform at the base that acted as the trapdoor. Nine of the nooses were occupied by bodies, in various stages of decomposition. All were naked, all looked like anatomical models designed to show off their skeletal structure, such was the detail with which bones protruded through grey skin. Beady-eyed crows were removing strips of flesh from those with enough left to pick at and as the vehicle purred past them they stared at the newcomers and fanned their wings for a few moments before settling back to their gruesome work. Liquid rose in Watson's gullet, scouring his throat. He swallowed and it was like gulping acid.

'Why have you brought me here?' he asked.

Kügel tapped the driver on the shoulder. 'Stop here, will you, Emil?' He turned to Watson. 'Can you manage a short walk? A few metres?'

Watson nodded and stepped out of the car. The smell that hit him reminded him of the stench of the waste barges on the Thames. That and an abattoir. There was something else, too, the acrid bite of rotten eggs. Sulphur dioxide was in the air.

Beyond the wire fence he could see men moving, shuffling

with a gait that suggested their legs were shackled. But there were no shackles. They were mustering together into ragged lines, pushed into some semblance of order by guards with their rifle butts.

Reluctantly, Watson moved closer, the wind whipping at his words as he spoke to Kügel. 'What is this place?'

The commandant bided his time. A few of the inmates looked through the wire, a glint of curiosity flaring in otherwise dead eyes. All the men looked strangely alike – the sharp angles of cheekbones in gaunt faces, skin pulled taut over shaved heads, limbs that seemed to carry no muscle whatsoever, just sinew. They each wore a greasy uniform of coarse blanket material, entirely inadequate for the winter.

'This is what they really mean by the worst camp in Germany. Not mine,' said Kügel. 'These are the damned.'

'Where are they from?'

A truck drove by towards the gate, belching fumes. Watson glanced in the rear at German soldiers who looked alarmingly similar to the inmates in their flat expressions.

'Commandant, where are these prisoners from?'

There came the distant sound of gunshots, three, in rapid succession.

'And where are they going?'

'Russian, mostly. Some Serbians, Greeks, Romanians. They are about to go into the mountains for the next shift.'

'Of what?'

'There are two mines up in those foothills. About a three-kilometre walk. Copper and silver. Some zinc, too.'

'Those men can't work.'

'You'd be surprised what a man can do on one potato a day.'

'But this is monstrous. It's against all humanity. How will they survive in these conditions?'

Kügel looked genuinely puzzled by the question. 'They are not meant to survive. Those mountains are full of old mine shafts to dispose of bodies in. New prisoners can easily be drafted in to replace them. We have a million Russians in this country. Enough to keep the mines going for very little cost.'

'And the Red Cross?'

'Does not know this place exists. Who will tell them?'

Me, thought Watson. *I will.*

Another rifle shot boomed down the valley. 'What's that firing?'

'The previous shift returning. Those without the strength to make it back . . .' He mimed firing a rifle at a figure on the ground. 'I'll admit it is a harsh regime.'

'Harsh? Harsh?' Watson spluttered. 'It's mindless murder, that's what it is. I assume there is a point to showing me all this.'

'Only a very oblique one,' said Kügel. He passed Watson a small flask of schnapps. Watson took a hit from it and for a few welcome moments his nostrils were purged of the smell of decay and filth. 'This camp is operated by the Eighth Department of the *Großer Generalstab*, the German High Command. The silver- and copper-bearing ores are mined here, and then, you see there is a small-gauge railway there? That runs the ores to the processing factory. French prisoners work in that. Treated rather better. The army then sells the silver and copper on the open market.'

'For profit?'

Kügel laughed. 'Of course for profit. Which then lines the pockets of various colonels and generals, as an expediency in case things don't go Germany's way. If, as we said, America enters the war, for instance. The same department also operates my camp. I have a sum I have to deliver each month, or I will be relieved of my post. No excuses. If I can't raise it as revenue, I have to make up the difference from my own accounts. Now, you think I am cruel? You think I exploit the men in my care? Let me tell you, the man who runs this camp has often said he would prefer my job to his at this charnel house. Who can blame him? Look.'

In the far distance he could make out a shuffling line of more ragged men, heads bowed, if it were possible moving even slower than the men behind the wire. They were stooped as if great rocks had been placed on their shoulders.

'There is a saying, Major, better the devil you know. I'm the devil you know. The men who run this place? They make the devil look like one of the good guys. Seen enough?'

Another rifle shot, a sharp crack, much closer. One of the prisoners collapsed out of line. The guards dragged him to one side, and the herd of men continued on its way.

A terrible sense of shame overtook Watson. Shame that men could treat their fellows like this. Shame that he should be powerless to do anything about it. Shame that he wanted to turn on his heels and run as fast as his aged limbs could carry him, never looking back.

'We still have that lunch,' said Kügel, directing him back to the car.

'I think I've rather lost my appetite,' said Watson as he took the first step back towards the Argus. 'Just take me back to the camp, will you?'

The lunch did not go to waste. Once Watson had been returned to the camp, Steigler and Kügel stacked up their plates with the food and shared a bottle of Hock. After they had both commented on the quality of the sausages and the wine, Steigler asked: 'Will he do it, do you think?'

'Watson? I'm not sure. I am certain, however, that a direct appeal would have done little good. He would never countenance working for a man like me.'

Steigler helped himself to a dumpling. 'Even though you showed him the conditions up the mountain?'

'I think he thought it was like Nero saying, "Look, it could be worse, I could be Caligula," or Attila the Hun protesting: "You think I'm bad, you should see my brother Bleda."'

Steigler laughed. 'Did he believe the story? About the General Staff running the mines for profit?'

'He had no reason to doubt it. Most of what I told him was true. They are working the Russkies to death up there. But the silver and copper goes straight into the factories of the Ruhr. Given what he knows about how we operate here, the lie that the High Command are lining their own pockets would seem perfectly plausible.'

Steigler dabbed at his mouth with his napkin, finally approaching satiation with the rich food. 'He's no Sherlock Holmes, you know, our Major Watson.'

'No, but I suspect he has something of the terrier about him. Presented with the facts, the scientist and the medical man in

him will chafe. Three men die in one evening? We blame it on
them trying to contact the dead? No, he'll get to the bottom of
it if he can. After all the years with Holmes, he won't be able to
help himself.'

'But he only has a week.'

'Less, I suspect. It will be forty-eight hours, seventy-two at
most, before Von Bork has him moved.'

'No time at all.'

'We'll see. Look, Steigler, I know you said that it is an internal
matter for the prisoners, but I am not convinced. I think those
three men were murdered. But why? What are those bastards up
to? There's something else happening here, something we don't
control and that makes me uneasy. And three fewer men means
three fewer bank accounts to empty. I have a bad feeling about
what will happen to Germany in future. Every mark will help.
You've done what I suggested?'

'Moved everything into Swiss francs, yes.'

'Good. So, all we have to do is sit and wait.'

'For?'

Kügel poured himself a healthy glug of the Hock and toasted
the doctor. 'For Watson to solve our little crime for us.'

TWENTY-EIGHT

Mrs Gregson was well aware that Nathan had thought she was joking when she gave him her 'shopping list' for her scheme, but she hadn't been. A magician was essential to its successful execution, and not any old music-hall conjuror with a hat and a rabbit. She needed something far more sophisticated. She needed the very best in the business. She needed David Devant.

But her heart sank when Devant opened the door of his apartment on Haverstock Hill. To her dismay, he was a shadow of the man she had seen on stage five years earlier – he was stooped, his skin waxy and his moustache untrimmed.

'Mr Devant? I'm Mrs Gregson. I'm the one who sent the telegram. You were kind enough to say you would see me.'

He nodded, releasing a small spray of dandruff, and retreated down the hall, walking with an odd, stiff gait. Mrs Gregson followed, closing the door behind her. She tracked him into the living room, which had an oblique view of Hampstead Fever Hospital, now being mainly used for military patients.

'Can I fetch you something?' he asked.

She looked at the tremor in his right arm and said, 'No. Thank you.'

'Please be seated.'

Mrs Gregson sat in one of the armchairs, while Devant took the couch. The room smelled of neglect and dust. The owner himself looked careworn, in a threadbare jacket and slippers whose soles had had an argument with their uppers. It was hard to believe this was once a man who strode the stages of London in capes of red and gold, turbans with glittering rubies, and shirts of the finest silk.

'You'll have to forgive me,' he said. 'Not been too well of late.'

Mrs Gregson smoothed out her skirt and removed her hat. 'When did the symptoms first appear?'

'I'm sorry?'

'Mr Devant, I have some medical training. Mostly in treating gunshot wounds and the aftermath of gas attacks.'

'Golly.'

'I was at the front for some time,' she explained. 'But I have seen this before. Paralysis agitans.'

A long sigh escaped from him. 'That's what the doctors say.'

'Can I make some tea?'

'That would be wonderful,' he said with a smile. 'At least you won't spill half of it.'

The kitchen was long and narrow, like the galley of a ship, and before she started she quickly wiped down all the surfaces, which had attracted a sticky film of grime. A veritable necropolis of flies lay at the bottom of the small window. She lit the gas, put the kettle on, rinsed the metal teapot and rifled the cupboards. She found an unopened packet of Nyasaland tea. She looked around for a cool box.

'There's . . . there's . . . there's no fresh milk, I am afraid,' Devant shouted from the other room. 'Just condensed.'

She went back to the cupboards and found it behind a jar of Camp coffee and some tinned asparagus. 'That's fine. I acquired a taste for it in Belgium.' She examined the label. Libby's, an American brand, part of that country's food aid and, thank goodness, unsweetened.

Once she had made the tea and located sugar, cups, saucers and a strainer, she carried the tray in and placed it on a low table. 'I brought the Dorset Knobs, just in case.'

'Splendid.'

As she poured the tea she glanced at her host. He was around fifty, although the strain of his condition had aged him considerably. She suspected he wasn't too far from giving up entirely. 'I thought there was a Mrs Devant?' she asked.

'I sent her and the boy away, back to her parents in Ireland. The Zeppelins, you know.'

'And you didn't think to go?'

'My audience is here. I'm expecting another engagement once this improves.' He held out a hand with dancing fingers.

She put the tea on the arm of the couch next to him, with a biscuit in the saucer. She sat and said quietly: 'It doesn't get better, Mr Devant.'

His face crumpled for a moment and she thought that she was telling him something he didn't know. He took a deep breath. 'I've been told as much. But a little voice tells you that they don't know everything, do they? Doctors, I mean. They could be wrong. Miracles do happen.'

Mrs Gregson nodded, as if in agreement. 'Mr Devant, I saw you at the Palace Theatre. You were a miracle in yourself.'

'Did you?' He seemed pleased. 'And the Egyptian?'

'No, I never saw that run,' she admitted. 'But I have never in my life laughed so hard as I did during A Boy, Girl and Eggs.'

Devant beamed for a moment, then remembered something that made him blink away a tear. 'Nevil isn't well either, you know. Nevil Maskelyne. We make quite a sad pair these days.'

'I am sorry to hear that. I was hoping to make use of Maskelyne's equipment for the Vanishing Pilot.'

He gave a croak of a laugh. 'The trick that nearly burned down the Empire Liverpool?'

'I want to do it out of doors,' she said.

'Sensible. Well, I have access to all Nevil's props. They are in Camberwell. Have to ask his permission, of course. Simple enough illusion.' He looked around the room. 'I'd just have to remember what I did with the key.'

'And a pilot?'

'Oh, yes, yes . . . now, where did I . . . ?' He pursed his lips in concentration.

'You don't have anyone who does for you here? A girl?'

'Ah, we did. Two, in fact. Both went off to work in the munitions factory.' He held on to the cup with both hands as he took a sip of the tea, then, with great concentration, placed the cup back in the saucer with a minimum of rattling. He smacked his lips. 'Very good. Better pay in the factories, you see.'

'I can find you a girl,' said Mrs Gregson. 'I have contacts with some of the Prisoner of War charities. They have a surfeit of willing helpers.' The ladies who packed parcels wouldn't stoop to domestic work, but the army of messenger girls and cleaners might provide a willing candidate.

'Well . . .'

'And I'll pay for her.'

'Pay? Why on earth would you do that?'

'For services to be rendered?' One thing she was certain of was that two thousand pounds wasn't quite the fortune she had envisaged.

'And I think there are ways to alleviate your condition. I have heard tell that velvet beans help. And certain physical regimes.'

He wagged an admonishing finger. 'Don't dangle false hope in front of me, young lady.'

There was no malice in his reproach, but she apologized. It was true that she had heard of various treatments for the disease Parkinson had described. But she could not promise any actually worked. 'I'd . . . I'd just like to help.'

Devant went through the painful ritual of drinking more tea, then lay back and looked at her, as if for the first time. 'Who are you, Mrs Gregson? And what are you doing here?'

They were good questions. Not that long ago all she had wanted to be was a woman serving the soldiers on the front. Then she had fallen in love with one of them. And he had died. And now? She wasn't certain who she was. She hoped that a certain major might be able to show her.

'I'm here to save a friend.'

'And what do I have to do with that? You said you wanted to engage me. I had thought in a professional capacity.'

'Oh, I do, Mr Devant,' she said. 'I want to engage you very much.' From her bag she extracted the sketches she had made. 'I want you to give the performance of your life.'

The magician and the props secured, she needed the second item on her requirements list. A dead body. Which was how, an hour after leaving an elated Devant – thrilled that his talents were required once more – she was staring at the internal organs of a collection of deceased individuals. Mrs Gregson was very familiar with the inside of the human body. During her time in France and Belgium she had seen far too many organs that were designed to be hidden from human view. Young men turned up day after day, their skin unzipped by shrapnel and bullets, insides glistening with vital fluids draining from ruptures and punctures. Yes, she could tell a spleen from a kidney from a duodenum. Yet she had never seen a liver like the one on the shelf before her.

It was elongated for a start. Whereas the lobes of the liver fanned outwards over the stomach, pressing up against the diaphragm, this one was funnelled to the vertical. It looked – in shape if not in texture – like a towering thundercloud, nipped in here and there before billowing out again. It was difficult to see how a human abdomen could have made room for such a distorted organ.

'A tight lacer,' the voice behind her said.

She turned and looked across the student teaching room of St Barts at the tall figure that had entered the room. Like Greenhouse Smith, he was a throwback to another era, with his long, dark frock coat and mutton-chop whiskers. His skin was as grey as the specimens that lined the walls of this triple-storey demonstration room.

'Mr Valentine?'

He gave a small bow. 'I haven't got round to cataloguing that one yet. I am sure women of this day and age will suffer no such deformities, but the generation passing on now, a remarkable percentage have internal damage from lacing their corsets too fiercely for fifty or sixty years.'

'Yes,' she said, thinking back to the elderly woman she had treated at the Savoy and her over-tight stays. 'I have come across it.'

'And what do you think of our display?'

He waved an arm to take in the whole room, which was indeed impressive. Wrought-iron staircases led up to balconies that ran the perimeter of the room, which was illuminated by a full-length glass ceiling, like something from the greenhouses at Kew. Each level was packed with the morbid, the exotic and the freakish, from miscarried conjoined twins to the overgrown skeletons of those suffering from Paget's disease. Whole sections had rows and rows of hearts, split open to show the many and varied types of damage that could occur to valves, vessels and ventricular muscle. There were similar displays of diseased or damaged lungs, livers and kidneys. All human suffering – at least of a medical nature – was here, in one form or another.

'Remarkable,' she said truthfully.

The curator flicked on the electric lights, which spluttered into life after a number of false starts. 'The skylight doesn't give us quite enough in winter. When it was built thirty-odd years ago it was all candles and oil lamps – the daylight was a blessing. But, Good Lord, it gets hot in here in summer. Especially when you have thirty students and a freshly dissected corpse. Quite ripe, if you'll pardon the expression.'

'I have nursed under canvas in high summer in France. I would imagine it is similar.'

Valentine looked impressed by this admission. He took out a pair of folding spectacles and placed them on the bridge of his nose, as if to examine this rare specimen more closely. 'A nurse, you say.'

'A VAD,' she corrected.

He nodded. 'You said in your letter you were acquainted with Mr Holmes and Dr Watson.'

'Major Watson, mostly.'

'Major?' he chortled. 'I heard he'd gone back in.' He shook his head. 'A man of his age . . .'

'Now a prisoner of the Germans.'

Valentine's face took on a grave aspect. 'Oh dear.'

'This is where they met, isn't it? Holmes and Watson.'

The curator nodded. 'In the hospital, yes. Not this room. Next door in the pathology block. And Watson used to scribble his stories in a little office next door when he did a few months' training here.'

'Wasn't Holmes flogging a body or some such?'

Valentine laughed at the memory. 'Indeed. You couldn't get away with that now, of course. He was beating a body with a cane to see how bruises developed after death.'

'I have reason to believe Mr Holmes is also in danger, Mr Valentine.' She gave him an outline of her plans, including the role that David Devant was to play. It was a calculated risk, for such shenanigans might outrage the man in the street. But she suspected this creature of formaldehyde and twilight was no ordinary citizen.

'I am thinking of a plaque,' he said when she had finished.

'I beg your pardon.'

'I am thinking the hospital should erect a plaque. To commemorate the meeting. On this spot, Sherlock Holmes and Dr John H. Watson were first introduced with the words, "You have been in Afghanistan, I perceive." What do you think?'

'A fine idea,' she replied, unsure of where this was leading.

He nodded furiously. 'I think so. They have given people so much pleasure. I would hope they live to do so again. But, Mrs Gregson, I am afraid your scheme is foolish in the extreme.'

'Risky, I will grant you—'

He whipped off his glasses. 'Risky? Going over Niagara Falls in a barrel is less risky than what you propose.'

She sensed there was more. 'But?'

'But . . . I could not live with myself if I failed to offer my assistance to any undertaking that might save those men. Foolish or not.'

She felt the warmth of relief course through her. 'Thank you, Mr Valentine.'

'I am not,' he said, slipping his glasses back on and looking down his nose at her, 'in any way condoning it. Foolish it was, foolish it remains, with or without my help.'

'Still, I am grateful. But it is not without risk to you.'

Valentine relaxed a little and the pomposity was gone from his voice when he spoke. 'Only three times in my career here

has Mr Holmes sought my help or advice. On two of those occasions, he came with requests as outlandish as yours. On the
third, he simply wanted help identifying the effects of white lead
poisoning. Therefore I shall pretend it is Mr Holmes in front of
me, making one of his more unusual requests. So, tell me what
it is you desire of me?'

'It is very simple, Mr Valentine. I shall require one fresh
cadaver. Female. Thirty or thereabouts.'

Mrs Gregson had to suppress a smile as Valentine's jaw hinged
towards the floor.

'And I need it within two days.'

With the magician and corpse ticked off Mrs Gregson's list, all
that remained was for her to tackle Mr Sherlock Holmes. Not
relishing the thought of trying to persuade him that she knew
what was best for Watson, she stared gloomily out of the motor
taxicab's window. London was being assailed by a spiteful black
rain falling from the heavy sky. The roads and pavements looked
as if they had been painted with creosote. Extended umbrellas,
pulled-down hats and turned-up collars made the city's inhabitants even more anonymous than usual.

The *Evening News* hoardings were proclaiming that America
was threatening to sever all diplomatic ties with Germany, but
few were stopping to buy from the drenched vendors. Perhaps
they didn't realize there was more in that single sentence than a
diplomatic spat. Help – no, salvation – might be on the way for
their battered nation.

Robert Nathan had told her about an intercepted telegram,
an invitation from Germany to Mexico to invade the USA, with

a promise of German money and arms in support. The idea was for Mexico to reclaim lands such as Texas and parts of California. The intent was to distract America from Europe. The British had decoded the telegram and were about to reveal its contents to the Americans. Nathan was sure it would tip the Americans into entering the conflict on the Allies' side.

Nathan, of course, shouldn't have told her any of this. She was fully aware that he was trying to win her favour with such confidences. She rather liked him, a no-nonsense man who was used to getting his own way. But that certainly included women. A courtship gave little indication of what lay ahead in an engagement or marriage. She suspected that, once the war was over, Nathan would become bored with grey old England and itch to return to India or perhaps apply for a new posting in Africa. She would be a memsahib, or whatever the equivalent was in Kenya or Egypt or Rhodesia. And that didn't appeal one jot.

So, yes, she was toying with him but without Nathan she would never have been able to secure the telegram traffic from the Post Offices around Holmes's house, which led her to the one he had sent to Venlo.

Agree all terms. Need a week to tidy affairs in London. Leave all details of exchange at Hotel Bilderberg. Holmes.

But you didn't need to be Sherlock to work out what was being planned at or near Venlo. Or where he might base himself in London to tidy his affairs, now Baker Street was no longer available. Which is what made the intercept of the detective at the Diogenes so straightforward.

And what of Devant? Was she simply using that great magician's talents and goodwill too? Well, he was in no fit state to take too active a part in her enterprise, but his thoughts on the matter were inspired, if suitably bizarre. The man was a showman, after all, someone who had introduced the theatreograph to the West End. A man who lived for the limelight. Engaging his mind could – no matter what her motives – only be to the good. He had certainly seemed a darn sight more sprightly when she had explained what she had in mind than when she had arrived. 'A show!' he had exclaimed.

But would it work? She had to believe so.

Meanwhile there was Holmes to interrogate. She needed to know as much about this Von Bork as possible, to see if the second part of the ruse would fly. She was sure the old detective would be furious with her, but he would have to see that she had both Watson and Holmes's interests at heart. Much as she wanted Watson home, she couldn't sacrifice his old friend to do that. It would, for one thing, destroy Watson if Holmes offered himself as a sacrifice to save him, which is what he fully intended to do. Watson, on the other hand, would rather they perished together than he survive at the expense of his companion. He had demonstrated that out on the Black Sands off Foulness.

A cascade of gloom washed over her and she could hear her mother's voice, chiding her. *What are you doing meddling in the affairs of men? You are attempting to undermine the play of nations. All for a pointless infatuation. Go back to packing parcels.*

'We are here, ma'am,' said the cabby, interrupting her thoughts. 'The Connaught.'

She shook herself, like a dog emerging from a pond, flinging off the negative voices. She paid the fare and entered the hotel, taking the lift up to the fifth floor, where Kell's comfortable prison was located. At the end of the corridor was a bowler-hatted man, reading the weekly *Herald*. Mrs Gregson recognized him as one of Nathan's colleagues.

'Turning pacifist on us, Mr Cusack?' she asked, for the *Herald* was violently anti-war and had opposed conscription. 'You'll have the Shameladies on you.'

Cusack smiled beneath his moustache. He was an ex-army man, a fervent patriot and admirer of General Haig. Only his limp, caused by a bullet through his pelvis, had kept him away from the front line. 'Just keeping abreast of what the other side are up to, ma'am. Know thine enemy, especially when they publish their own newspaper. Mr Nathan is inside, if you wish to go through.'

'And how is our guest?'

Cusack grimaced. 'Demanding.'

She nodded. 'That's not unexpected.'

Cusack unbolted the weighty black door and swung it open. She was immediately aware of raised voices.

'You do not believe me? In a word, then, there was a famous trial in Paris, in the year 1890, in connection with a monstrous scandal in politics and finance. How monstrous that scandal was can never be known, save by such confidential agents as myself. The honour and careers of many of the chief men in France were at stake. You have seen a group of ninepins standing, all so rigid, and prim, and unbending. Then there comes the ball from far away and pop, pop, pop – there are your ninepins on the floor. Well, imagine some of the greatest men in France as these ninepins and that this Monsieur Caratal, who was on the train, was the ball which could be seen coming from far away. If he arrived, then it was pop, pop, pop for all of them. It was determined that he should not arrive.'

As she entered the room she took in the scene. Nathan was sitting on the sofa, smoking. At the window stood Holmes, far more substantial than when she had last seen him. There was an impression of bulk and, in his movements and speech, an undercurrent of impatience.

Nathan leaped to his feet, ever the eager puppy. 'Mrs Gregson, there you are. Come in. Mr Holmes is just telling me a fantastical story about a lost special. A train. Apparently it was all a French Government plot to make sure a certain Frenchman never arrived in Paris.' He turned back to Holmes. 'And you say this train lies buried in a mine? A whole train?'

'I do. Minus most of the innocent passengers, who were forced off at gunpoint. I can give you the precise location. I know the French are our allies, but it demonstrates their duplicity as a nation.'

Mrs Gregson knew all about that duplicity from a certain Levass, who was, indirectly, responsible for Watson's capture by the Germans. 'I hardly think we need—' Mrs Gregson hesitated as Holmes turned from the window, his great head enveloped in smoke. 'Mr Holmes?'

'Yes?'

Mrs Gregson felt as though she were in a lift in which the cable had snapped, plunging down floor after floor. She dropped her bag and took two steps forward. Now she knew she had been made a fool of. 'Mr Mycroft Holmes?'

'At your service.'

She spun towards a slack-jawed Nathan, all the anger she felt against her own stupidity coming out with a venomous hiss. 'Nathan, you damned fool. You've got the wrong Holmes.'

TWENTY-NINE

The applause took Watson by complete surprise. Of all the welcomes he was expecting back in Hut 7, a chorus of 'For He's a Jolly Good Fellow' would have been some considerable distance down the list, along with backslapping, the offer of cigarettes and a tot of real, genuine brandy. The men crowded around him, firing a battery of questions that coalesced into a single inquisitive howl.

'Gentlemen, please!' he managed to yell over the hubbub. 'One at a time. What on earth has caused this change of heart?'

'We owe you an apology, sir,' said one.

'Slice of tongue, sir?' offered Hugh Peacock.

Watson took it, as some recompense for the feast he had been denied. 'Thank you.'

It was sharp and salty and he relished it. Peacock had pushed to the front. 'You'll have to forgive us for our previous behaviour. Jungle drums get it wrong now and then—'

'When Brünning told us who you were—' started one of the men.

Another chimed in, '—you could have knocked us down with a feather.'

'Dr bloody Watson. Here, with us. Well, we knew then that all that stuff about you being a chat had to be a load of—'

'The thing is,' said Peacock, his rich, plummy voice drowning out all the others, 'every man jack in here has read *A Study in Scarlet* and *The Hound of the doo-dahs.*'

'Because they were the only books in English we had to begin with,' a voice piped up.

'Quiet,' said Peacock. 'It's true other volumes were in short supply. But the truth is that those two copies fell apart from so much reading.'

'I'm gratified,' said Watson, 'if they helped pass some time. Look, if you don't mind, I'd just like to have a lie-down. I feel a little light-headed.'

'Of course,' said Peacock. 'Thoughtless of us. A few days in Stubby knocks the stuffing out of any man. Move aside, let the major through to his billet. Come on, we can talk about Holmes at a later date.'

Watson groaned inwardly. If they had studied his texts in such detail they were bound to be picky about the odd lapse in dates. He hoped they hadn't got hold of a copy of 'The Man with the Twisted Lip' – the typographical error from the printer that had Mary call him 'James' had caused him plenty of grief over the years. He really must get that altered. As well as stressing he had two war wounds, although only one of them was made by a jezail bullet.

Peacock led him through to the end of the hut and pulled back the curtain to reveal a most remarkable sight.

There was a young private sitting on his bed, a man in his late twenties, a cheeky smile on his face. But that wasn't the shock.

In his hand he held a brush and he was using it to bring a shine to a pair of Trenchmasters. Watson's Trenchmasters. Watson gave a small gasp of pleasure.

'Well,' said Peacock, 'I'll leave you two to get reacquainted, sir. I'll send some tea through.'

'Splendid,' said Watson, absentmindedly.

The orderly stood. 'Hello, Dr Watson.'

'Hello . . .er . . .'

'Kemp, sir. Harry Kemp.'

'Well, Private Kemp, thank you for my boots. They are a truly comforting sight. But how . . . ?'

'Well, I was told to tell you there had been a misunderstanding. Which the gentleman in question understood at once, as soon as I pointed it out to him.'

'You went and got them back for me?' asked Watson. 'From Lincoln-Chance?'

Kemp nodded. 'In a manner of speaking. You don't remember me, do you, Doctor?'

Watson peered at the face, but no recognition came. 'I'm afraid . . .'

'I was a Boots at Baker Street. Not long after you promoted Billy to Buttons. And before Mr Holmes's long absence.'

Watson recalled the promotion of Billy and that several other lads had filled the lower position over the years. He and Holmes had the rather reprehensible habit of calling every boy, Boots and Buttons, 'Billy', as if they were all interchangeable, something he would never countenance now. 'And what happened when Holmes disappeared for all those years, presumed dead?'

'Well, Mrs Hudson helped me move on. To groom, eventually, for a most respectable firm of lawyers. I was only twelve when I came to you, sir. I'm not surprised you don't remember clearly. It was not long after the murder of Charles Augustus Milverton, the one that seemed to excite Mr Holmes so much.'

'Quite so. Well, I'm glad to hear you got on in life, Harry, although I am dismayed to see you here.'

'Well, I feel exactly the same, Dr Watson. Exactly the same. I've asked to be transferred here as your servant, on top of me other duties. I hope you don't mind.'

'Not at all. Someone who recalls the old days would be quite welcome.'

'That's settled then,' Kemp said. 'And I haven't forgotten how to shine a boot.'

'I can tell. I can see my face in those toe caps.'

Harry Kemp smiled and Watson had the sudden image of a much younger version offering the same broad grin after a nugget of praise. 'I'll go and fetch that tea. Anything else you need? See if I can get you a biscuit from Captain Peacock? Got a locker full of 'em, he has.'

'No, Harry, thank you. Oh, there is one thing,' he said, just as the lad had pulled the curtain back. 'If you can manage it before *Appell*.'

'What's that, sir?'

'Fetch me the chaplain.'

The lad looked alarmed.

'Don't worry, it's not about my immortal soul.'

*   *   *

Father Hardie was the least likely chaplain he had ever seen. He had a crown of jet-black curly hair, a nose that had seen its fair share of blows, and hands like nicotine-stained steam shovels. When he spoke Watson saw teeth the shape of tombstones and spaced as far apart. Watson noticed a pattern of scarring across his nose and cheeks, like smallpox, but tiny, shiny dots rather than pits. There were similar ones on his wrists.

'Thank you for coming, Father. Harry, can you fetch some more tea?' Watson pointed to the solitary seat and he took the bed.

'How can I help you? Are y'troubled in some way?' Hardie asked in a broad Scottish accent. Before Watson could answer, the priest asked: 'Do you mind if I smoke?'

'Not at all. I'll join you, if I may.'

Soon the room was hazed with fumes. 'Some people think I'm not paying attention if I have a ciggie in my hand. Or that it is somehow disrespectful to God. Whereas I find it enhances my ability to concentrate on spiritual matters.'

Watson waited until the tea had been delivered and Harry departed before he got to the crux of his enquiry. 'The three men who died a few days ago. Have they been buried yet?'

'They have. No point in delaying.'

'You conducted a service?' Watson asked.

'Aye. I said a few words.'

'And you had no problem with that?'

Hardie looked puzzled. 'It's my job.'

'They were suicides, so I was told.'

'Suicides?'

'Well, perhaps not deliberately so,' said Watson. 'It is possible that it was blood-letting during a séance leading to accidental death. But I thought there was enough there to give a man of your persuasion some qualms about them having a Christian burial?'

'Me being a Roman Catholic, you mean?'

'I do,' said Watson.

The priest carefully lit a second cigarette from the first. 'You know, if God was ever fussy about how a man met his end, I would imagine this war has cured Him of that. I can't be certain. For all I know, on Judgment Day, He will haul me up by my hair and say, well Hardie, a fine dobber you are. Burying Methodists and Presbyterians, Quakers and Anglicans. Aye, and ministering to the living of all those congregations and more. However, I suspect He will be more forgiving. There is but one God. I think the distinctions we fret and fight about are man-made.'

'I am sure you are right.' Watson took a sip of his tea, not adding that it was feasible that God himself was entirely born of man. 'The deliberate cutting of the wrists, though—'

'It's an old Greek tradition when you are talking to the shades. Read your Homer. Blood-letting helps summon the dead. There are hungry ghosts out there, so some say.'

'Isn't it possible that the blood loss helps make the participants more susceptible to suggestion by the medium?'

'Ah,' said Hardie, taking a tug on his cigarette. 'Now, though, you are assuming all is showmanship and fraud, being the professional cynic. The man of science.'

'An agnostic. But you sound like you believe.'

'Believe?' He gave a croaking cough. 'Believe in what?'

'That man can communicate with the dead.'

'Now, Major Watson, I am someone who has to have faith in the Virgin Birth, in the resurrection of Jesus Christ Our Lord and in the transubstantiation of bread and wine. I am in no position to start telling other men that there is no link between the worlds or that they are simply being superstitious or gullible. I personally do not believe in a bridge to the afterlife. Not one we can access from this world. But, again, I could be wrong. I wasn't always a priest—'

'You were a shipbuilder. On the Clyde. A welder, I would suppose,' said Watson.

Hardie tipped his head to one side, as if trying to get a different angle on the major. 'Ah. I had heard the rumour. That you were *that* Watson.' He smiled. 'Is this some Holmesian witchcraft?'

'Holmes never dealt in witchcraft, Father. He dealt in facts and observation. The scars on your face and arms. I couldn't quite place them at first. But now I see you had been wearing goggles of some description, which is why the area around your eyes has not been burned by the sparks from a welding flame.'

'Aye, they have better protection now.' He looked at the back of his wrists. 'Longer gloves, for one thing.' He touched his cheek. 'And full face masks. And I suppose once you had welding, with my accent, the Clyde is an obvious deduction.' Watson nodded. 'Simple when you know how. But, I was saying, I wasn't always a priest. I lived my life in the shadow of the devil, drinking and whoring. Until God visited me and gave me a good slap around the back o' ma heid. Oh, I can't explain it, given up trying. But I do believe there are higher forces at work. I think those three men were misguided to try and contact the dead.

Just like they were misguided in cutting their wrists and drinking that filth they brew in the camp. But I'll no' condemn them for it, Major. Now, would you tell me why you are so concerned about their immortal souls?'

'One of them, Archer, came to see me on the day he died. He asked me to go along to the séance. You might recall I was hauled out of line and carted off to Stubby, so I couldn't keep the rendezvous.'

'And you think if you'd gone, you might have prevented the deaths?'

'I suppose I do,' admitted Watson.

'It does not occur to ye that there might have been four bodies instead of three if you had started playing their foolish games?'

'Not at all. I think I might have stopped them.'

Hardie gave a harrumphing sound that suggested he didn't believe it. 'I knew one of the men. Not Archer. Campbell. A Scot. A proddie, but a Scot. And a good man. He was convinced that they could speak to the dead. And in the end, I gave up trying to persuade him otherwise. Because, as he said, if this war has snuffed out all those young, innocent lives for good, deprived them all of an extra forty, fifty, sixty years of the one life on this earth . . . millions of them b'now . . . that that would be almost impossible to contemplate, wouldn't it? So, he took comfort where he could. Not in my God, but in Archer's bridge to a better world.' He drained his tea. 'Now. Is there anything I can do for you, personally? Because I think we should let those three dead boys be.'

'No, thank you, Father.'

The priest stood and held out his hand, his impressive jaw jutting out even further as he spoke. 'Anytime, Major. Anytime. And God be with you.'

When he was gone Watson lit one of his own cigarettes, swung his feet onto the cot and, right up until the call for *Appell* came, wondered why he hadn't told Hardie the whole truth.

Because you want to dig them up, Watson, don't you?

THIRTY

'My younger brother is a remarkable man,' said Mycroft Holmes, filling his pipe. 'Not as remarkable as he thinks he is. Not as remarkable as me, in my prime.' He gave a little cough. 'Which I will allow you, I no longer am. But when my brother asks for my help with a little subterfuge, he doesn't actually have to give me a reason. I am glad to be of assistance.'

'I heard you were dead,' said Nathan.

'You know him?' Mrs Gregson asked, still fuming from the mistake. 'You know Mycroft Holmes and you still thought he was Sherlock?'

'I knew *of* him. *Of* him,' Nathan snapped at her, irritated at his own misjudgement and at Mrs Gregson's accusatory tone. 'Mycroft Holmes was running the British Secret Service before it was called any such thing. But we heard he had expired.'

'Retired,' corrected Mycroft. 'Although it is much the same thing. I have no power nowadays other than to get my pink gin delivered at exactly twelve o'clock every day at the Diogenes.' He stared at Nathan. 'You are right, I was once at the heart of Empire. Every secret document passed my way. I amended naval treaties and approved submarine trials. But no longer. It was made clear to me long ago that my tenure was at an end. So, I am here to provide a little support for my brother. Is that a crime?' He checked his pocket watch. 'Now, may I go? I have a luncheon.'

'Damn your luncheon,' Mrs Gregson exploded, causing Mycroft Holmes to raise an eyebrow and to cast a glance at Nathan, as if suggesting he should keep the woman on a tighter leash. 'Do you know what your brother is up to?'

'Now you listen to me, madam. My brother knew there were men waiting outside the club. Men who wanted to detain him when he was on his way to assist Dr Watson in a most delicate matter. Do you think I stopped to ask him chapter and verse?'

'Perhaps you should have,' said Nathan quietly.

'Sherlock Holmes is intending to offer himself to the Germans in exchange for Dr Watson, who is currently in a prisoner of war camp in Germany. Or perhaps you knew all this?'

Mycroft shook his head. 'I am afraid not. I heard Watson had been caught up in the tank affair, along with . . .' he furrowed his brow, dredging his memory. 'Are you the woman involved in that business?'

'One of them,' she admitted, thinking of Miss Pillbody. 'Dr Watson – Major Watson – was captured while trying to apprehend a murderer and schemer. And now the offer has come for this exchange.'

'But why would they swap one old man for another?' Mycroft asked.

'Perhaps you can tell me. The man orchestrating the whole affair is called Von Bork.'

Mycroft jiggled, as if his nervous system had malfunctioned. 'Good Lord.'

'So, I suspect this isn't about the war effort at all, Mr Holmes. I suspect this is something personal.'

'Indeed.' He frowned and looked around the room. 'I want a telephone. It might not be too late to stop Sherlock.'

Nathan hurried out to try to locate one.

'You think this Von Bork means Sherlock harm?' Mrs Gregson asked.

'Very likely,' Mycroft replied. 'But that isn't what worries me.'

This sounded rather callous to her ears. 'Really? What else could possibly matter?'

'Von Bork was a clever spy, very useful to Germany, so we made sure we destroyed him. At least, Sherlock did. He returned to Germany with his reputation in tatters and everything he had sent them for years made suspect. Of course he wants to do my brother harm.'

'But?'

Mycroft finally lit his pipe. 'But Von Bork won't be doing this alone. He'll need help from a higher authority. Or at least approval.'

Mrs Gregson was beginning to feel particularly stupid. 'And?'

Mycroft puffed for a few moments. 'Let's say that there was a German Sherlock Holmes. A man famous the world over. Respected. Admired. In terms of public opinion worth fifty or a hundred Barries, Hardys, Galsworthys or Wellses.'

These were the big guns of the literary world, still being rolled out to exhort the British public to continue the fight 'to protect the English-speaking races'. Mycroft pointed the stem of the pipe at her. 'You know the Government pressed my brother hard, too hard, to join the ranks of the pro-war faction. I, myself, I am ashamed to say, encouraged him. But he refused. He thought using the celebrity Dr Watson had conferred upon him to political ends was to cheapen his achievements in other fields. My brother can be infuriating.'

'I know,' she said.

'But imagine if you were the Germans and Sherlock Holmes landed in your lap, as it were. Think, madam, think.'

'Oh my good God,' she said, as it dawned upon her.

'The personal quickly becomes the political.'

'Robert!' she bellowed in a most unladylike manner. 'Where is that telephone?'

The *Kaiser Kombinierte Dienstleistungen* Sporting Club occupied a Gothic mansion on Thüringer Allee on the western fringes of the city, next to the grounds of the Berlin Ice Skating Club. The house had been designed by Karl Friedrich Schinkel, also responsible for the renovation and modernization of the Berlin Palace. He was a theatre designer as much as an architect, and every area had the feel of a stage set. The dining room, for example, had a ceiling showing the heavenly constellations, as well as rich dark curtains dividing the space, also adorned with stars. This was the room known as the '*Königin der Nacht*' – the Queen of the Night – and even during the day it was lit by candles, the drapes on the tall windows being kept drawn.

Von Bork had been in the building before, but not since his fall from grace. He felt himself grow a few centimetres as he strode in, another important step in his rehabilitation. He paused and took in the marble Corinthian columns of the lobby, veined with gold, and the statues of German and Norse warriors that stood on intricately carved plinths. The walls were adorned with heroic scenes from Wagnerian operas.

'Shall we go through?' asked Admiral Hersch.

Von Bork and Admiral Hersch were taken to the gloom of the Queen of the Night room and shown to a booth that, thanks to the great swathes of material suspended around it, offered first-class privacy. As they passed through, Hersch nodded to some of the other members. Although it was a sporting club, there was only one sport that qualified an officer in one of the Imperial services for membership. Even if one didn't know which particular pursuit that was, thought Von Bork, the visitor would soon be struck by the number and variety of duelling scars on show. Not that entrance was based on a current pursuit of the sport (although it was said the clearings of the Grunewald nearby sometimes echoed to the sound of steel on steel on misty early mornings) but in having fought at least three duels at some time in one's life. And survived, of course.

In the days before the war, the waiters in the room were exclusively male; now there was a smattering of women who, as a sop to the traditionalists, looked like men. The admiral, however, as a member of long standing – the duelling scar next to his right eye was almost four decades old – was assigned Lachmann, an elderly Jew who was old enough to have served at the Siege of Paris.

'Admiral, sir, welcome,' the old man said, fussing with the table linen as they sat. 'Shall I fetch a bottle from the admiral's cellar?'

Hersch nodded. 'What's good to eat today?'

'The peppered beef, sir. Swiss, I believe.'

'Sounds promising.'

'Then might I suggest a Württemberg red?'

'A Lemberger. Perhaps the Bergbauer '95.'

'Excellent choice, sir. And for your guest?'

'I shall share with the admiral,' said Von Bork.

Lachmann stiffened and pursed his lips. 'It is the admiral's custom to have a bottle to himself—'

'Ach, don't worry, Max. We'll open a second if need be.'

'Very well, Admiral.' He gave Von Bork a look that made him lose those extra centimetres he had gained on entering the club. 'So, two of the peppered beef? Excellent. And perhaps the buttermilk soup to start?'

'Yes. But bring us two glasses of Sekt and give us fifteen minutes alone before you start serving will you, Max?'

'Peppered Swiss beef?' said Von Bork after the snobbish old Jew had departed, his stomach rumbling at the thought. 'I would wager there aren't any other establishments in Berlin serving that today.'

The admiral wagged a finger. 'Don't get socialist on me now. There is a streak of hair-shirtedness in you I don't approve of. And there aren't too many of those bottles of '95 left. But you won't refuse a glass or two.'

'If it's not an inconvenience.'

The admiral laughed. 'Max is very protective of my stocks, which have dwindled of late. You see, the war affects everyone. We must all make sacrifices. If we don't finish this conflict soon, I shall be all out of Chablis. Ah, thank you, Max.' The waiter put down the two glasses of sparkling wine, gave a small bow and departed. 'Good health,' Hersch said, raising a toast. 'And I must say, you are looking well. Exercise and fresh air agree with you.'

'Being back in the game agrees with me.'

'The game? Ah, yes. And how is your snaring of the great Sherlock Holmes coming along?'

Von Bork took a sip of the Sekt. It was excellent, rich and biscuity, not the acidic muck that was served elsewhere. 'I do believe that in a few days, he will be on German soil.'

'Very good. Well, you must give me full details of where and when you plan to bring him over.'

'Why?' he asked, although it came out sharper than he intended. 'Why, sir? This isn't exactly official. And as you well know, as a rule, the fewer people who know about an operation . . .'

The admiral put down his glass and glowered at Von Bork. 'I hope you are not suggesting that I can't keep a secret?' he growled.

'No, not at all, it's just that—' he stumbled.

Hersch let out a roar of laughter. 'I am joking. You are right, of course. Keep it secure. I'll use handpicked men.'

Von Bork shifted uneasily in his seat. He didn't like the way this was going. Why was Hersch interested in Von Bork's little act of revenge? The spymaster played on far bigger stages. 'Handpicked for what, sir?'

'The cinematic film crew.'

'The . . . you want to film the exchange?' He couldn't quite believe what he was hearing. 'Watson for Holmes?'

'Yes. It would be an excellent first outing for the UFA. The Universum Film AG. Our new propaganda arm.'

'You plan to use this to Germany's advantage?'

Hersch beamed. 'Of course. Why else would I let you run with it?'

'But to what end?'

Hersch managed to look as if he couldn't quite believe his ears. 'My goodness. You have grown rusty. I knew you needed lubricating, but really . . .'

'Holmes is a retired old man.'

'Holmes is an icon. A legend. People follow him, believe in him. If we can have the great detective declaring the war has been a terrible, futile waste of British lives and should be halted at once . . .'

'Yes, yes, I see that. But I have met the man. He won't do that.'

Hersch held a steady gaze.

'Not unless . . .'

'Precisely. Not unless we break him.' The admiral drained his Sekt. 'And break him totally. Now, where is that Lemberger?'

THIRTY-ONE

It was a particularly grim second *Appell* that day. A slanting, icy rain was falling from the sky, hitting the skin like a shower of needles. Men shuffled over the mud into line, tempers ready to flare at any slight, intended or not. The guards, too, snarled and snapped more than usual and prodded and poked with butts and bayonets. Everyone on that parade ground wanted to be off it as soon as possible. Kügel, of course, did not appear on his terrace. Roll call was left to his deputy, the flute-voiced Hauptmann Musser, who had the efficient manner of a librarian who worried about his books being out of alphabetical order.

As he stood shivering, Watson thanked providence for the return of his boots. Cosy feet – thanks also to the unfortunate Sayer's socks – counted for plenty on such a miserable, objectionable day. As soon as the roll call was completed, Watson hurried as quickly as he could to the makeshift canvas marquee outside the kitchen block, where he was one of the first in line for a tin mug of the fatty globules that was the lunchtime soup. He helped himself to a large crust of bread and, as he crossed over towards the rec hut, wolfed down both elements, unconcerned about taste or texture. Fuel, he told himself, that's all it was, although pretty low-grade stuff, to be sure.

Watson knew he was being manipulated. Once back in his billet, the whole incident with the soft sheets and the wonderfully seductive bed had seemed like a strange dream. There had to be more to that whole . . . he struggled for the word . . . charade. That's what it had been: a charade. He recalled how it often took an oblique approach to ignite Holmes's curiosity. Watson had on many occasions pointed out in the newspaper over breakfast a tale that he thought might snap Holmes out of some torpor or other, only to be dismissed with a curt *aperçu*, which put the potential case into context or, just as often, the dustbin. However, leave the same piece of journalism lying around or, indeed, dismiss it oneself, and Holmes might just turn his beady gaze upon it and Watson would almost feel the vibrations of that great brain cranking into action.

Watson could not boast of such a brilliant mind, but he recognized an attempt by Kügel to engage such faculties as he possessed. The talk of the supernatural, the strange method of dying, the hasty burials. Kügel and Steigler suspected foul play in their camp but assumed – correctly, Watson thought – that it would be impossible for any German to get to the bottom of it. They also gambled on the fact that considering such a case might help Watson pass the time until his release, minutes and hours that were otherwise sure to drag their feet, as if they had been snapped into manacles.

There is something not quite right here, Watson. Can you smell it? Feel it? An air of corruption, of decay pervades this place.

Watson ignored the fanciful ghost in his head and entered the recreation hut. He was pleased to find he had it to himself. His fellow prisoners were still waiting in line for their meal or had retreated to their billets to eat in the relative warm and dry. There were signs of recent occupation, hastily abandoned cards, a chess set frozen in something close to the endgame, although he resisted the temptation to move to checkmate. The hut contained a home-made dartboard, studded with wooden darts, a ping-pong table, a library of well-thumbed books – Verne, Childers, Scott, Conrad, Hardy, Stevenson, Dickens, Collins and, as Peacock had said, a scattering of his own works.

There were four smallish round tables with matching chairs, all rough-hewn but well constructed. Three of the tables had been in use, but the fourth was bare of any evidence of games or other occupation. This, he surmised, must be the site of the séance and death.

A close look at the surface confirmed that thought. The wood was stained with something the colour of aged claret. Blood, he assumed. When he had first met Holmes at St Barts, the detective had been working on a method for detecting bloodstains. Watson remembered him running towards him shouting: 'I have found a re-agent which is precipitated by haemoglobin, and by nothing else.' Sadly, the re-agent had proved unstable and, therefore, unsuitable for everyday police work, but Watson wished he had some of it with him at that moment.

He carefully examined the tabletop, then the chairs and finally dropped to his knees and put his nose close to the floor, as if he were a supplicant, praying to his god.

'Major Watson, are we disturbing you?'

Watson banged his head on the table as he struggled to his feet. It was Lieutenant-Colonel Critchley and two other men, one of whom he recognized as Henry Lincoln-Chance, boot thief. Watson straightened his clothes. 'Gentlemen.'

'Might I ask what you are doing?' Critchley demanded.

Watson cleared his throat. 'I heard that three men passed away here a few nights ago. As camp doctor—'

'Look, Watson, I don't have to tell you what being in a place like this does to the minds of some men.'

'Pickering and the like,' said the unknown newcomer. 'Forgive me, Major, I'm Rupert Boxhall, Royal Flying Corps. It's a pleasure to make your acquaintance.' He held out his hand and Watson took it.

As they shook Watson gave a quick appraisal. He certainly looked like a flyer; he had the floppy hair and swagger of the newest service. Pilots often reminded Watson of over-enthusiastic cocker spaniels. 'Boxhall of the furniture makers?'

His eyebrows shot up in surprise. 'Yes. How did you know?'

Watson pointed at the tables and chairs. 'These are your work?'

'They are. Although not quite up to Father's standards, I am afraid. Been a while since I was on the shop floor. How . . . ?'

It was an educated guess, given the fresh calluses on his right hand, as if he had been gripping a hammer or similar implement. 'Oh, we used to have a Boxhall desk at one of my practices. Very sturdy. And it's not a common name.'

Lincoln-Chance stepped in and also offered to shake, his eyes glancing down to Watson's boots. 'And I'd just like to say I'm sorry for the misunderstanding. We'd been bowled a bit of a googly when you arrived. If we'd known then who you were . . .'

'Yes, well,' said Watson, taking the man's hand without too much enthusiasm. 'I'm just glad to have them back.'

'They were damn fine boots. Sorry to see them go,' he said with a winning smile that dimpled his chin. The man must have broken plenty of hearts back home, Watson thought.

'I will have to ask you not to investigate this matter any further, Major,' said Critchley once the pleasantries were concluded.

'Why is that?'

'Morale,' said Lincoln-Chance. 'Such mania as these three had,' he pointed to the empty chairs, 'can be as contagious as typhus. As you know from Colonel Critchley, me, Rupert here and a chap called Hulpett make up the Escape Committee. Nobody really escapes, but we work as if they do.'

'And one day,' said Boxhall, 'when Kügel and his thugs are on the back foot, we'll have a mass break-out.'

'But at the moment, we simply plan,' said Critchley.

'That's all very well—' Watson began.

'Major, as senior officer in the camp I am ordering you to desist. We all know your background, but I am afraid we don't want any of your Sherlock Holmes shenanigans. These three men believed they could talk to the dead, which as we all agree, I hope, is complete tommyrot.' Critchley had grown red in the face. 'I hear you will be leaving us shortly. So please do us the courtesy of not interfering with the smooth running of the camp. We'll still be here when you have your feet up in front of the fire in Holland sucking on a Sumatran cigar.'

Lincoln-Chance and Boxhall nodded their agreement.

'Well, if you put it like that . . .' said Watson.

'I do,' said Critchley, relaxing. 'Sorry to pull rank. I have a couple of favours to ask. Do you think you can still run your surgeries for the next few days? It would be a great help, clear up the minor complaints.'

'Of course.'

'Splendid. I'll circulate a book, see who needs an appointment, eh? I'll have it delivered to your hut this evening and you can sort out a roster.'

'And the second?' Watson snapped, impatient to be away now he could no longer continue with his inspection.

'Bit embarrassing this, Major. But had I known who you are, I would have jumped at the chance of a story for the *Harz and Minds* magazine. I can't believe I hesitated. Like asking Charles Dickens to take a written test before accepting anything by him.'

'I'm hardly in—' Watson began.

'Before you set off for Holland, do you think you could leave us something?'

'Most of us have read everything there at least two or three times,' said Boxhall, pointing to the sad library. 'And some of the blighters who get books from home simply won't share them around.'

'Something fresh would be most welcome,' agreed Lincoln-Chance. 'From a real writer, like yourself.'

'I'll see what I can do,' said Watson, still stinging. He wasn't about to be paid off so easily with some flattering remarks. But he could see there was nothing else he could achieve in the hut. His mind ran through his next moves. First, find out if Steigler was still on site. He had something he needed. Second, get the money he owed to the German in the solitary block – one never knew when one might need the good graces of such a man again – and thirdly, task Harry with catching him a couple of rats. 'Can't be hard in a place like this.'

'I beg your pardon?' asked Critchley.

Watson discovered he had spoken out loud and quickly said: 'Finishing a story. Can't be hard in a place like this. Not much else to do.'

'Very good,' said Critchley.

'If you'll excuse me then, gentlemen, I have work to attend to.'

But not the sort they imagine, eh, Watson?

In fact, back in his billet Watson did take up his pen once more, allowing time to slip, so that he was catapulted back into the long-lost world of the 1890s.

The Manchester Express left that Monday evening at two minutes past five, with the usual cacophony of steam, whistles and slamming carriage doors. Holmes and I had a carriage to ourselves, a smoker in the same portion of the train as the one that the gentleman with the cigar would have used. We both used the opportunity to light a cigarette and, replete after a late lunch in Simpson's, I felt like snoozing. Holmes was having none of it. He was on his feet as soon as the train left the station, examining the doors and latches and, at one point, throwing himself on the floor and rolling under the seat.

Watson had some trouble with the end of this section, trying hard to create something that might, for instance, make a reader of the *Strand* instantly crave the next issue. In the end he settled on: *At that moment I heard the slamming of the door and looked around to see that Sherlock Holmes had left the carriage.*

Watson stopped the account when Harry came back with a jute sack that was twisting and spinning in his hands. 'Blimey,' he said, holding it at arm's length so Watson could see for himself the turmoil within. 'I reckon they'll kill each other if you don't get 'em out of there soon.'

'Much trouble catching them?' Watson asked.

'Best you don't know about that, sir. There's more around that kitchen hut than might make you comfortable, if you get my drift. You know those days when meat suddenly appears in the soup? I reckon—'

'Yes, quite, Harry,' said Watson quickly, not wishing to dwell on the fact that he had found tiny bones in the bottom of his dish on more than one occasion. 'I want you to ask Peacock out there if we can borrow one of the wicker baskets he gets sent from home.'

'Righty-oh.' Harry expertly knotted the neck of the sack and laid it on the floor, where it continued to writhe.

'And some sugar, if he has any, Harry.'

'Sugar? I'm sure he has.' Harry left and Watson looked back over what he had written. Just one more chapter, he estimated, with the denouement and it would be done. Not quite a classic Holmes story, perhaps, and not one where the detective produced the solution with a flourish. But that might act as a corrective. He was only too aware that he had celebrated successes and relegated most of the failures to his locked files, now with Cox & Co. He stood and looked out of the grimy window. The sleet has coalesced into snow, falling lazily with a seesawing motion. The churned ground was already covered in a fresh blanket and he could see it settling on the roof of the rec room, the tin hut and the other barracks. As before, he marvelled at how that flattering dusting could transform even the meanest of scenes into something approaching beauty. But his breath against the pane told him there would be a sting in this snow-fall's tail as the thermometer dropped further.

'Here we are, sir, one basket. And six sugar cubes.'

'Right. Give me a hand, will you, Harry? If you have time?'

'I got to do Hut 3 after evening *Appell*. I tell you, sir, you'd think some of them fellas was born in a barn and lived in a pigsty. The Temporary Gentlemen aren't too bad, but some of the others I swear don't know how to wipe their own arses. Sorry for being so crude.'

'No apologies necessary, Harry.'

'Then I have to clear the rec room – put the cards back, make sure there's 52, British style, not 48, pack away the chess pieces . . . same thing really. Most of the officers think there's an invisible army trailing after them, clearing up. Thing is, for many of them, that's exactly right. Although I reckon a lot of those invisibles have been killed these past few years. I think they's in for a rude awakening when they get back, the toffs. Servants'll be like gold dust.'

'I'm sure. Pass me that kidney dish, will you?'

From beneath his bed he produced a screw-top jar, half filled with a clear liquid.

Harry looked at the contents of the canister with suspicion. 'If that's what I think it is, I'd go easy, Dr Watson. You want, I can get you the good stuff. Not sure where you got that.'

'It's not for me.' He removed the lid and sniffed. It was fortuitous that Steigler had kept the liquid recovered from the séance and that he was willing to hand it over to Watson. It confirmed what he had thought. Kügel and Steigler were using him as a surrogate. But if foul play had been done, it didn't matter who was calling the tune for the investigation, as long as it got to the truth.

The fumes from the container clawed at the back of his throat, making his eyes water, but not before he got the fruity smell of esters, redolent of pears and bananas. Despite the acrid overtones, the scent of those fruits made him feel hungry for fresh food. Perhaps he would go over to the tin hut and buy some of his peaches back; not fresh perhaps, but healthier than rat broth.

'Place the sugar cubes in the bottom, please.'

Harry did as instructed and Watson carefully poured about half of the Virginia Dog over them, watching them collapse and crumble until he had a thick, viscous fluid. He sniffed. 'Not very scientific,' he said to Harry. 'But I think the rats' love for sugar will overcome any aversion to what may or may not be in here.'

Harry lowered his voice. 'Is that from the rec room, then? You reckon that stuff might have . . . y'know, done them in?'

'What makes you think that?'

'I heard you was over there. I figured, if Dr Watson is interested, something must be a bit queer. You think they was poisoned?'

He was impressed by the lad's insight. 'I don't know. But you get a bad batch of any distilled product and it can have serious consequences, although not normally death. Imagine if there were a bad batch of this, though. Might someone want the evidence disposed of as quickly as possible?'

'I dunno, sir. But I tried that stuff once. I had a headache for four days.'

'I don't doubt it, Harry. I'm not sure if rats get headaches. But they can be poisoned. Now, you think we can get those rats in this basket and close the lid without spilling all of the liquid?'

'Give it a go, sir. I remember you and Mr Holmes was always up to strange 'speriments. The smell was right awful sometimes. Didn't Mrs Hudson go on.'

Watson laughed and felt a sudden flood of warmth towards the young man. He had been right. How good it was to have this link back to his past, something solid, flesh and bone, rather than the untrustworthy, disembodied voice in his skull. 'Good man, Harry.'

With a series of swift, co-ordinated movements they had the rats in Peacock's basket, the sound of their claws on the weave filling the room.

'They'll eat their way out eventually, sir. You know that?'

'I do. In the absence of a glass cage, however, it will have to suffice. Let us hope the pair fancy some libations before they start on the willow, eh?'

'Sir. I'd best be going.'

'Right. And Harry?'

'Sir?'

'Thank you. It's a pleasure to have you with me.'

'Pleasure's all mine, sir. Life was getting dull before you turned up.'

When he had gone, Watson spent a few minutes standing over the basket, listening to the movement of the rats within. The frantic scrabbling had subsided, replaced by sudden bursts of activity and then moments of quiescence while they explored their immediate surroundings. He would give it until the evening *Appell*, he decided, then, if they had drunk the potion and if they showed no ill effects, he would let the blighters go. And just hope he didn't run into them anytime soon, in a different context altogether.

So far his only theory was thin. The three men had been poisoned by alcohol. It could be accidental. It could also be deliberate. But if the latter, why? Who would gain from their deaths? It was all very well finding the method, but he needed motive. And for the moment he simply couldn't conceive why anyone – British or German – might kill a group of men misguided enough to think they could speak to the dead. Or why they would bury them in such haste.

Watson sat down and picked up his pencil and paper again. Soon he was writing once more, oblivious to the rodents a few feet away from his bed. Where had he got to? Ah, yes, Holmes had just disappeared from the carriage.

He wrote until his fingers ached once more, something that had never afflicted him before. It was with great sadness he laid out the final paragraph for now, for it pained him to recall those lost years when Holmes had been plucked from him.

Neither of us realized then that it would take five long years for the Rugby

Mystery to be solved and, in the interim, my great friend would appear to be lost to the world forever.

After *Appell* and the evening meal of cylinders that managed a convincing impression of sausages, and a boiled vegetable with the consistency, but not the taste, of cabbage, Watson returned to his billet, stamping the snow off his boots at the entrance to the hut and pushing through the bodies towards his surgery.

Peacock hailed as he passed. 'Chocolate, Major?'

Watson hesitated, then moved across to where Cocky was holding up two squares of Dairy Milk. He took them with a thank you.

'Not finished with my basket?'

'Soon,' Watson said.

Cocky moved in closer. 'I don't know what you are playing at, Major, but don't rock the boat.' It was not a threat, but a plea. 'I'll go mad if you do.'

'How do you mean?' Watson asked.

Cocky looked around to make sure nobody else was listening. His well-fed face had reddened, and Watson wondered about the man's blood pressure. 'I'm up next, is all.'

'Up next?'

'Cocky, you going to share that with your chums or just with your betters?' asked the lieutenant called Laine.

Peacock snapped back and scooped up the remains of the chocolate bar. He tossed it over to Laine. 'That's it till the next parcel.'

Watson pulled him closer once more. 'Don't do anything stupid, Peacock,' he said softly.

'Like what?'

'Like a séance.'

Peacock shook his head vigorously. 'No, don't worry. Nothing like that.'

Back in his room, Watson could hear the rats. If they had drunk the liquid, it hadn't affected them. He took a lamp close to the lip of the hamper, undid the straps, and eased up the lid. Two sharp furry faces, whiskers twitching madly, appeared at the crack, flinging themselves at the opening with such force Watson almost lost his grip before he slammed down the lid and redid the fastening. But he had seen what he needed. The kidney dish was empty.

Watson returned to his bed and looked at the inch of fluid left in the jar. Rat physiology was different from humans'. There were poisons they could process without harm that would fell a man. It could be that. It was a silly, inconclusive experiment. Oh, for a proper laboratory, analytical equipment, controls, assistants.

Watson took the lid off the jar and raised it to his lips, his eyes prickling as he did so.

Didn't you just tell a man not to do anything stupid?

Aye, I did, thought Watson as he braced himself for the burn and drained the jar in two big gulps.

THIRTY-TWO

Winston Churchill entertained Mycroft Holmes in a minor drawing room, relatively restrained by the standards of Blenheim, but still opulent by any other benchmark. The wallpaper was hand painted, every cornice and curlicue gilded, all the artwork venerable and valuable. They sat on a pair of couches, arranged in parallel in front of a roaring fire, under the black eyes of famed and framed ancestors. A manservant brought two enormous balloon glasses of brandy and then retreated from the men sitting before the grate, the flickering flames giving them a devilish hue.

Churchill was in his early forties, four decades younger than Mycroft, but a spectator might think they were of the same generation. Years of political infighting – and a daily intake of brandy, cigars and champagne – were beginning to take their toll on the younger man. His physical state was not helped by the strain of waiting for the report of the Dardanelles Commission, as Mycroft well knew. Churchill's political future rested on whether he was condemned as a reckless adventurer who gambled away men's lives or as the engineer of a noble failure.

'How are you, sir?' Mycroft asked, deferring to the younger man.

Churchill sipped his brandy. 'Well enough. Although my enemies are all powerful today and my friendship counts for less than nothing. I am simply existing.'

'Until the report?'

'Of course.'

'I am sure it will be good news.' Mycroft was certain of this because a government-appointed body was unlikely to admit to a catastrophic failure in planning and thousands of wasted lives. If they did so, Australia and New Zealand, which had lost many thousands of sons, would be in uproar. It might even threaten the Empire.

'We haven't always seen eye to eye, have we, Holmes?'

Mycroft shook his great head. 'We have had our disagreements.' It was an understatement. Churchill was a great admirer of Mycroft's brother, Sherlock, and had had reason to use his talents in the past, and had come to know Watson quite well since their meeting at the front in Belgium. But, unlike them, Mycroft was a political beast with his own ideas about how best the nation could be served and so Churchill was always wary around him.

'Well, then I can expect you to give an honest opinion about me.'

Mycroft thought for a moment and opened the bout with rather a soft jab. 'You know I think as Home Secretary you could have organized our intelligence services in a more efficient manner.'

'You can do better than that, sir.'

Mycroft took a slug of his own brandy. He didn't like the tone Churchill had adopted or the challenging one-eyed stare he was giving him. Had the man been drinking already? 'How do you mean, Mr Churchill?'

'Clemmie will tell me I am a wonderful man. Not without fault, mind, but wonderful. Lloyd George, too, flatters. But, really, I value most the opinion of those I have crossed swords with.' He leaned forward. 'Give me your assessment of Winston Spencer Churchill, Holmes. Both barrels, if need be.'

Mycroft took another generous dose of brandy before he spoke. 'It is a difficult matter.'

'Try, man. They tell me you are cleverer than your brother.'

'In some things, I am his superior, it is true. In human relationships, certainly. But like my brother, I find much that is paradoxical in you, sir.'

'Go on,' Churchill demanded gruffly when it appeared Mycroft had come a halt.

'I would say you have a clever mind, holding an above-average intelligence.' Churchill gave a little grunt of satisfaction. 'But whether that mind is always focused as it should be is open to debate. You handle great subjects in rhythmical language, which is often inspiring in the extreme. But I fear you are sometimes enslaved by your own phrases. I suspect you deceive yourself that you take broad, overarching views, when your mind is fixed upon one comparatively small aspect of the question. You admire a grand gesture, but do not always look at the motives behind it or the consequences of failure. I fear that is what happened in the Dardanelles.'

Churchill said nothing.

'Your power for good is very considerable. On the other hand, you have a capacity for unwitting harm. Your temperament, sir, is of wax and quicksilver. You would describe yourself as a statesman, but I feel you to be a politician of keen intelligence with an extraordinary set of skills, if only one knows how to apply them. I think, if used judiciously and at the correct moment, you could do great things for this country. On the other hand, should you feel slighted or betrayed, you can make much mischief. For those reasons, I would advise any Prime Minister always to have you in the Government and keep you close at hand, where your talents can be accessed.'

'And where they can keep an eye on me?' Churchill offered.

'Precisely.'

Churchill took a polished humidor from a side table and, without offering Mycroft one, lit up a corona, puffing it into life before examining the glowing tip. Mycroft thought he had overstepped the mark. 'You don't, do you? Smoke cigars?'

'No, sir. Pipes, cigarettes. Not cigars, not for some years now.'

'You should. I find they offer a sense of peace that no other smoke can.' He puffed some more. 'That was a fair assessment, I feel. I know I can be impatient and headstrong. Bloody-minded and vengeful, too. But knowing one's faults is half the battle. So, Mycroft Holmes, why have you come to the wilderness to consult with this old dog?'

Mycroft outlined what he had discovered about Watson's capture, the offer of exchange by Von Bork and his brother's disappearance.

'I remember Mrs Gregson,' said Churchill. 'Who could forget

her? Another one who is headstrong and bloody-minded. I admire her, though,' he added.

'I would have to concur. Reluctantly.'

'So, she intends to do what, exactly?'

'She isn't stupid or careless enough to share her entire scheme with me. She has an MI5 man, Robert Nathan, wrapped around her little finger and I am certain he doesn't know the whole picture. But she plans to thwart the exchange of Holmes by preventing him from travelling. Or she did.'

'But you fooled her?'

'Nathan, not her. But yes, I went along with my brother's plan, not knowing the gravity of the situation.'

'And Sherlock is where now?'

'We don't know,' Mycroft admitted. 'We've got his picture and description at every railway terminus and port. All we can be certain of is that he is heading for the continent. To Holland.'

'Holland?'

'That is where the exchange is most likely to take place.'

'Any idea where?'

'There are a number of likely spots. There is a bridge north of Venlo that they have favoured of late. Where Germany bulges into Holland. Place called Knok, on the Meuse.'

'Holland?'

'Yes,' said Mycroft irritably. Had the man taken leave of his senses? 'Holland. The Netherlands. Just over the North Sea.'

'I know where Holland is, Holmes.' He paused. 'You know we can't allow Sherlock to fall into German hands?'

'That's why I am here,' said Mycroft glumly.

'And so why doesn't Sherlock appreciate this?'

Mycroft gave a sigh that shook his frame. 'Sherlock is not a political animal. Oh, I know he did political favours for both of us from time to time, but the political wasn't why he acted. It was the challenge of the case or, as I said, as a personal favour. He will not have thought this through. He will only have thought of saving Watson.'

'I admire the man's loyalty, but it is misplaced. Now, tell me everything else you know about these shenanigans.'

Mycroft did as instructed and, when finished, gave Churchill the telephone number at the Diogenes Club where he could be contacted. After he had departed Churchill smoked his cigar for a while, staring into the flames as he considered his options. Holland. His old friend Jackie Fisher at the Board of Invention and Research could help him there. He rang for a manservant and instructed that a telephone be brought in and was eventually put through to the School of Observation at Bisley. He knew the man he needed: Major Hesketh-Prichard, whom he had met in France, but who had been posted back to set up a version of his training school back in Blighty.

'Prichard?' Churchill asked when he came on the line. 'It's Churchill.'

'Sir. How are you, sir?'

'I'm vexed, Hesky, vexed.'

'I am sorry to hear that, sir. How can I be of assistance? Although I must warn you I'm due back at Lingeham any day now.' This was the original sniper school in France, where Prichard had made his name.

'It's not you I require, Prichard. I simply need your finest sniper.'

Prichard laughed. 'I don't think you do. You'll have to settle for second best.'

'Do I seem like a man who settles for second best?' Churchill boomed into the mouthpiece. 'Who is your finest sniper?'

'Well, you won't like this, but the man who holds the top score here is actually a Hun sniper.'

'German? Who goes by the name of?'

'Bloch. Ernst Bloch.'

'I'll be damned,' Churchill muttered under his breath.

'You know him, sir?'

'Bloch? He's a prisoner because I damned well captured him.' When he was on the Western Front Churchill had led many a patrol out into no man's land to bring back prisoners for inter-rogation. Bloch, one of the German army's best sharpshooters, had been one of them. 'Where is he now?'

'You won't turn him, sir. He came up here and shot bull after bull but refused to pass on any technique or tips. Wouldn't help the British kill Germans, he said.'

'Well, that's perfect then.' In other circumstances he might have chortled at the irony of it all, but they were dealing with a man's life here. A friend's life.

'How so, sir?'

'Just tell me where Bloch is. I don't want him to kill a German,' Churchill said. 'I want him to kill an Englishman.'

I need him, he thought with great regret, to shoot Sherlock Holmes.

THIRTY-THREE

The term headache was woefully inadequate to describe the crushing feeling Watson had in his temples. As the alcohol and goodness knew what else leaked into his bloodstream invisible fingers tightened the clamp around his cranium and his heart was replaced by a big bass drum, pounding its rhythm in his ears. His tongue felt as if it had been coated in sand and a raging thirst meant he emptied his water jug down his parched throat within a few minutes.

He moved over to the wicker basket and cocked an ear. Silence. The rats had stopped moving.

He retreated to the cot bed and lay down, trying to concentrate on something else, anything else, but his mind refused to focus. He thought he had pinned down Mrs Gregson but her features were hazy and he realized with a sense of despair he couldn't really recall what she looked like. Holmes was moving in shadows, flitting from doorway to doorway, like a man who doesn't want to be found. Mary was there, dear Mary Morstan, the woman whom he thought he'd spend the rest of his life with, until fate cruelly snatched her away during those years when Holmes, too, was missing after the affair at the Falls with Moriarty. Holmes had been restored to him, to the world, but Mary was consigned to loving memory. Yes, at his low points he had been drawn to try a séance to contact both of them, but he was repelled by the characters involved in what he knew, in his heart, was fraudulent. He had left before it had even commenced.

How he had hated Holmes for his deception about the Falls. Was he such an unreliable friend that some kind of cryptic note, a hint that Holmes lived, was too much to ask? Had he not shown loyalty and discretion – so much discretion – over the years? And again in the Von Bork business, vanished for years, without thinking to tip him the wink. Of course he didn't put the anger or frustration on the page in 'The Empty House' when he reported Holmes's re-emergence after the Reichenbach Falls. As always, the story was about Holmes, not his own sufferings. But sometimes, he wished he could knock some compassion into Holmes's skull, some small concern for the feelings of others. He imagined raising his walking stick and bringing it down on that great dome of a—

'Dr Watson! Dr Watson! Wake up, sir.'

Watson's eyes snapped open and he found himself smacking dry lips, a sound that reminded him of a hungry baby. Harry was standing over him, shaking his shoulders. The headache was still there, but the marching band had moved on. He could feel the cranial band loosening moment by moment.

'Harry . . . sorry . . . My God, what time is it?'

'Bedtime. I was just bringing you some cocoa and we all heard you shouting. I came in and you were thrashing about.'

'I was having . . . having a dream?'

'Didn't sound like no dream. Didn't look like no dream. It was more . . .' His eyes widened and he leaned in, reeling back from Watson's corrosive breath. 'You didn't?' Harry looked around the room and caught sight of the empty jar. He picked it up. 'Dr Watson, you . . . why would you do that? I thought them rats was . . .'

He went across and unlatched the lid of the basket and gently raised it. No sound came from within.

'Dead?' asked Watson.

'Sleepin' it off, more like,' Harry laughed bitterly. 'They are alive but blotto. I bet they have a tuppenny hangover tomorrow.'

Watson reached out for the cocoa on the floor and almost fell as the world spun.

'Here, let me get that.' Harry put the mug to his lips. The beverage was tepid, but all the better for it and Watson slurped greedily. 'You are butter upon bacon, you are, Dr Watson. What did you hope to achieve with all this malarkey? See, if it was poison, you'd be dead.'

'I'm not sure I'm not,' Watson croaked.

'And if it wasn't, well, you just get a price on your head like them rats there.'

'I don't think you'd get a farthing for this,' Watson said, tapping his temple and wishing he hadn't. 'I was wondering if it was some kind of hallucinogen, a potion to help give the illusion of talking to the dead.' He had recently had experience of power-ful drugs at Elveden in Suffolk, where they had been used to kill and control men.

'And did it, sir?'

Watson thought about the muddled dreams and the threat of violence to Holmes. 'Is this liquor common in the camp?'

'Well, it comes and goes. I mean, sometimes there's a lot, sometimes it's scarce. But there's those that loves it and will pay through the nose for it.'

'Does everything in this camp have a price? My head excepted?'

Harry thought about it. 'Mostly. Food, drink, sex—'

'Sex? You mean there are women here?'

A thick silence settled into the room.

Watson reddened. 'Oh, I see.'

'Doctor, you aren't telling me you don't know about—'

'Of course I know about such things. Why, I am sure you heard some base rumours regarding my relationship with Holmes that have sprung up in recent years. Idle, malicious gossip from people who could not envisage the true nature of the friendship we shared.' He shook his head. 'A sign of more cynical and prurient times, I feel.'

'Nobody'd say such a thing in my earshot, because they'd know what they'd get.' Harry balled a fist and shook it. 'But you have to think on, Doctor, some of these men haven't seen a Judy for a long time now. Even those that aren't that way inclined, and there's some of them that are a bit oopsy before they get here, they might find themselves turned by a pretty subaltern. Or maybe even a servant,' he added quietly.

Watson tried not to look shocked. But Harry was a handsome boy. 'Oh. I see. Well, far be it from me . . .'

'Not me,' Harry said firmly. 'Just that I know some officers and servants whose relationship goes beyond simply fluffing his pillows. If you get my drift, sir.'

'Well enough,' said Watson curtly.

Harry stood. 'Takes all sorts, Dr Watson. Takes all sorts. Can I get you anything else?'

'Some water, please. And thank you, Harry. You've been a rock.'

'Just like the old days. Do you still think the men at the séance deliberately killed themselves? If you don't mind me asking.'

'Not at all, Harry. But I don't know. All I do know is, there wasn't enough blood.'

'What's that?'

'On the table, the chairs. It had been cleaned up, but the rough wood had absorbed enough to show the extent of the staining. There was simply not enough blood for three men to have died. And no sign of it beyond the confines of that immediate area. If they had severed an artery, then one would expect a spray of blood. No, it doesn't smell right to me.'

'But what would be the motive for murder? Here of all places?' Harry asked softly.

'It seems to me that this place is no different from any metropolis — there is greed, drunkenness, gluttony and, as you say, sex. Add to that the imperative to stay alive and get back home at all costs . . . it's almost as heady a brew as that filth I recently drank.' A wave of weariness washed over him, trailing a little nausea in its wake. 'I need a clearer head, though, to speculate much more. Please fetch me the water and I'll sleep it off, Harry.'

And do try not to fantasize about bashing my brains in, Watson.

*   *   *

But he didn't dream about detecticide. Instead his swirling imagination was haunted by a woman who seemed to be a chimera of Mary Morstan and Georgina Gregson. One moment the former – sweet and compliant always – had the upper hand, a second later a forceful stridency took hold and he knew that Mrs Gregson has thrust herself to the fore. Whoever or whatever this creature was, Watson had performed acts with her that would cause him to blush whenever he recalled them. Never again, he swore, would he imbibe liquid of unknown provenance.

Harry came in with a cup of tea to wake him and enquire how his night had been. A little fevered, he admitted. But he felt relatively refreshed. Harry reminded him that he had a surgery after breakfast, with more than two score men wanting his treatment and advice. He asked Harry to make a running order for him and set about washing and shaving.

'Any more thoughts on the dead men, sir?' Harry asked as he laid out Watson's razor.

'Not worth sharing,' he admitted. 'Why's that?'

Harry looked uneasy.

'Come on, man, out with it,' said Watson, accepting a towel.

'Just that . . . I enjoyed our little chat last night and, I know I can never be what you were to Mr Holmes, but . . . it was pleasant to be treated as an equal, sir.'

'I see.'

'I don't mean to get above myself,' Harry said hastily. 'But, well, any change of routine, even if it is sad that three men lost their lives . . .'

Watson examined his face in the mirror and used a sliver of

soap to try to create a layer of foam over his chin. Many men in the camp had stopped shaving altogether, but doctors, he felt, had to keep some kind of standards. 'Well, Harry, I would welcome a sounding board. Often that was my only role with Holmes, you know. Do you remember Mrs Hudson's brother, Alfred? About ten years younger than me. Red-headed chap.'

'I do, sir, very well.'

'He stood in for me with Holmes when I was detained with medical matters. Said he felt he could have been one of those cigar shop Indians for all the use he was. I told him Holmes liked to play his thought processes out loud, and that he would have been invaluable. But we must attend to the patients first, Harry. Do you have duties elsewhere this morning?'

'Usual. Rec room. Nothing a few camp marks to the right place won't fix.'

'Allow me to settle that bill,' said Watson taking the razor. 'It would be good to have you on board.'

Harry said nothing, but his smile almost split his face. What a shame, thought Watson, as he made the first tentative strokes along his bristles, that Mrs Hudson didn't have a red-headed brother called Alfred or anything else for that matter.

The powder-fine top layer of snow was being swirled across the camp by a keening wind. Watson tramped through the fresh deposits, enjoying the feel of his boots penetrating the crust, treading where no man had gone before. Within fifteen minutes, when *Appell* was called, it would be trampled into mush.

Watson used his staff to steady himself as he made his way across the open ground. The crisp air and the breeze, icy though it was, seemed to clear his head. Now the only trace of the damned alcohol was a slight fuzziness. He had been both foolish and lucky, it seemed.

'Watch where you're going,' he found himself saying to the hunched figure that veered in from his left, his motor skills apparently forgotten as he barged in front of Watson. The man stumbled and fell headfirst into the snow.

'Steady on, old man,' Watson said as he leaned over to help him up. 'The breakfasts here aren't worth breaking a leg for.' He recognized the face of the man who turned to look up at him, but couldn't place it.

'I'm Hulpett,' the man whispered. 'Captain Hulpett. I was at the séance.'

As the man gained some purchase and stood, Watson brushed some of the snow off the man's greatcoat, trying to remember where he had seen him before.

'Then you know what happened?'

'Not now, later.'

Watson gave the man a good stare, taking in the thin moustache, the sunken cheeks, and the sharp blue eyes. He was also missing part of one ear, an old war wound by the look of it. 'Later when?'

'Chess club.'

Watson felt something thrust into his hand and he quickly pocketed the slip of paper.

'Thank you, Major,' said Hulpett as he dislodged the last of the snow from the skirt of his coat.

'You watch your step, lad,' Watson said loudly.

'I will. Looking forward to that Holmes story.'

Watson smiled now. He had him. Hulpett. He had been the third member of the Escape Committee when Critchley had pointed them out during the walk around the camp. Link, Boxhall and Hulpett. This could be promising, he thought. I have a turncoat to match the spy they have put in with me. He looked around but none of the figures moving through the bleached landscape were paying him any attention. Head down against the strengthening wind, he continued in his quest for an early breakfast.

THIRTY-FOUR

Winston Churchill watched Clemmie speaking with the head gardener through the rain-streaked window of his study. She was discussing the spring planting already and had decided one of the hedgerows needed to be taken down. The old man was shaking his head. He didn't like change. The gardens had been as they were for decades. Why muck about with them? Churchill gave a grunt of sympathy for the man. Clemmie would simply steamroller his objections.

He turned away and looked down at the photographs that were splayed out across his desk. There were twenty of them, clearly showing the stretch of the river where the German border bulged into the Netherlands and the folding bridge that could be used to span the Meuse.

These were expensive photographs, he thought. The flying distance from Houtem in Belgium to Venlo in the Netherlands was around 270 kilometres, he had been told by his old colleague Robert Groves at the Air Department of the Admiralty, right at the edge of the Sopwith One-and-One-Half Strutter's range. And part of the route would be patrolled by the Germans' lethal new D.III Albatros. Churchill, it was implied, was asking a great deal of any Royal Naval Air Service pilot who agreed to do a reconnaissance over-fly of the bridge. I need a man to try, he had told Groves, for the good of the nation. Volunteers had been found, the mission flown, a life lost when the gunner/navigator was hit. The pilot who nursed the bullet-ridden Sopwith home was unlikely to fly again. It was, he mused again, all a very high price to pay for a few photographs. He hoped it was worth it. He made a mental note to find out the dead man's name and write personally to the family.

After a few more minutes' studying the grainy images, he asked his secretary to get Jackie Fisher on the line. When he came through they exchanged cautious greetings and talked about the Dardanelles inquiry – Fisher had resigned from his post as First Lord of the Admiralty after the fiasco at Gallipoli – and the expected slant of its findings.

'I have it on good authority,' said Fisher, 'that it'll be more rapped knuckles than being put up against a wall at dawn.'

He didn't sound too disappointed. There was a time when Fisher probably would have liked Churchill shot. But the acrimony had faded somewhat over the past months. Churchill made a non-committal noise at the news of potentially lenient treatment by the inquiry. He didn't want a whitewash, just an acknowledgement that the whole enterprise might have worked and, if it had, he would now be a hero, rather than cast out into political limbo. And if Fisher had had his way with a Baltic landing? Churchill suspected that would have been more bloody and futile than the Turkish adventure and the tables could well have been turned.

'God willing, you'll be back in harness soon enough,' said Fisher. The man was deeply religious and Churchill always had to rein in his tendency towards blasphemy when in conversation with him.

'And you'd welcome that, would you?' Churchill asked.

'I don't like to see talent such as yours going to waste. All you need is a firm hand on your tiller.'

Which was more than Fisher had provided, the old boy alternating from support for to opposition to the Gallipoli landings. But Churchill didn't want to antagonize the man. 'Thank you. I, too, hope I can be of service once more.'

'Now what can I do for you?' Fisher asked. 'I can't add to my evidence—'

'It's not about bloody Gallipoli,' snapped Churchill, hoping against hope he would never have to mention the name of that cursed spot ever again. 'It's about Holland.'

'What about it?' Fisher's voice was full of suspicion, worried that Churchill had another madcap scheme, this time involving the Low Countries. 'It's neutral, remember.'

'No, not that Holland,' said Churchill. 'The one you have at Dunkirk.'

'Ah, I see.' If Fisher was surprised that Churchill knew about one of the Board of Invention and Research's secret projects his response betrayed nothing. 'Well, what about it?'

'Let me start at the beginning. Do you remember the Poruce–Partington affair?'

Ernst Bloch, formerly one of the Kaiser's finest sharpshooters, had settled into a quiet life at Camp Belmont in Kent. The POW stockade was situated in the grounds of a house being used as a recuperation hospital for British wounded. Because he wasn't an officer Bloch had to work, but as this mainly consisted of hospital duties in the kitchen or the laundry, he had few complaints. The damaged men who came to the hospital would never be posted back to the front line. So Bloch had no compunction about assisting the work of returning them to something approaching good health.

If he were honest with himself, he was quite content. He received regular letters from home, from his father and from Hilde, his faithful sweetheart who, since their one stolen night in Brussels, had promised that, no matter what happened, she would wait for his return. Other prisoners had received letters telling them that their romance, engagement or marriage had been blown off course and had foundered on the jagged rocks of this war. But Bloch felt certain he would see Hilde again and they would have a future – and a family together.

So he wasn't exactly welcoming to the two men who turned up at the camp asking if he would accompany them to an unspecified location. One was a captain in the King's Royal Army Rifle Corps, who introduced himself as Carlisle, the other a burly sergeant from the Honourable Artillery Company. Bloch didn't like the look or the sound of either of them. The regimental titles suggested to him they had come because of his sniping ability. He had already told them at Bisley that he would not assist in any programme that led to the death of German soldiers.

They took him to one of the interview rooms, where he was

provided with tea – it was a better option than what the British had the audacity to call coffee – and cigarettes.

The captain affected a nonchalant air, smoking with his hand to one side so the smoke curled away from him, one leg crossed over the other showing boots polished to a mirror gleam. The sergeant parked his bulk by the door and glared at Bloch from under his peaked cap, as if daring the German to try to get past him. Bloch had no intention of doing anything so stupid.

'Would you prefer English or German?' the captain asked.

'How is your German?' Bloch asked in English.

'Adequate.'

'English will be fine.'

'Good.' Captain Carlisle took a puff on the cigarette. 'Scharfschütze Bloch, we have a favour to ask you,' he said. 'A favour that might develop into something to your advantage.'

'Favour?' The Englishman had made it sound as if he simply required a lift to the station and was offering to pay for it. Yet the use of his 'sharpshooter' title suggested otherwise. 'What kind of favour?' he asked. 'You understand, I cannot help the British war effort. That would be treachery.'

The captain uncrossed his legs. 'I promise you, we are not dealing with anything that would result in the death of a single German. You have my word.'

Bloch made a face that suggested disbelief.

'Initially, we simply want you to make a shot. To prove it can be done.'

'Why?'

'Well, it pains me to say this, but you are the best sniper we have on home shores at the moment.' He flicked the ash off the cigarette. 'The best of our chaps are, of course, over there.'

'Killing my comrades,' Bloch said.

'If they aren't killed by those comrades first.'

'True.' For a moment he caught an echo of the sharp tang of decay that had been his constant companion during those months out on the front line, where every day was spent trying to get a British officer in the crosshairs. And where, for a few fleeting moments, he had framed Winston Churchill, the former First Lord of the Admiralty, in his graticule. The very man who had later ambushed him out on no man's land.

'If you do this exercise, hit or miss, we will pay you. Initially, twenty pounds. If you repeat the exercise under certain conditions we will pay you . . . considerably more.'

Although Bloch wasn't particularly interested in the cash, he found himself asking: 'How much more?'

'More than money can buy.'

Bloch laughed. 'And what is that?'

Carlisle dropped the cigarette on the concrete floor and leaned forward. His features seemed to harden, the air of foppishness banished, and the brown eyes fixed Bloch with a piercing stare that made him want to squirm. He kept stock-still, waiting for the Englishman to speak. 'Follow this through,' Carlisle said quietly, 'and we'll give you your freedom. You can go home and see . . .' he clicked his fingers, '. . . what's her name, Sergeant Balsom?'

'Hilde,' the big man grunted.

'Ah, yes. Hilde. Play your cards right and you'll spend the rest of the war fucking your beloved little Hilde till the cows come home.'

Bloch resisted punching the man in the face for his crudity but the sergeant noticed his body stiffening and took a step forward. Nevertheless the words conjured up an image of him and Hilde in the hotel room in Brussels and he swallowed hard. He did want that again, more than anything.

He licked his lips. 'Tell me more.'

Carlisle took a piece of paper from the top pocket of his tunic, unfolded it and laid it out. On it was a drawing of a stretch of water, a bridge and a series of buildings, one of which, on the left bank, was marked as an observation post.

'The target is on the bridge,' said Carlisle. 'You will be up here. It's an old observation post built by the Dutch when they had this land. It is now on the German side of the border.'

'You want me to go into Germany?'

'Yes. We can get you across easily enough. The target will be here, as I say, but we do not want him, um, eliminated until he is on the German side. That is, well past halfway on the bridge – after the concrete support in mid-stream. Understand? It must not compromise the neutrality.'

'Actually, I don't understand,' Bloch began.

'You don't have to. You just have to do the job. You will have papers on you saying you have been released by the British authorities on compassionate grounds. Once you have made the shot, you will be free to pick up the various travel documents you need to get home. *After* you have made the shot.'

Bloch squinted at the map once more. He could iron out the

details later. Hilde! He could almost taste her. 'There is no scale. What is the distance from tower to bridge?'

'Around nine hundred yards – say, eight hundred and twenty metres.'

'With what weapon? Not an SMLE? I don't want to be in Germany with one of those.'

'No. We have a captured Gewehr 98 with Oige optics.'

Bloch preferred the Görtz telescopic sights. Whichever he used, the distance was still at the far end of guaranteed accuracy. He tried his best to stay focused on the matter at hand, but his pulse was racing at the thought of going home. He had been happy to sit out the war, but these bastards had opened a door to temptation and he wasn't sure he could resist.

'It has been some time. I would need to practise.'

Carlisle gave a quick smile. 'That's why we are here. That is the first part of the favour. Show us it can be done. Show us *you* can do it. There is a setup at Gravesend that mimics the actual conditions. Bridge and tower, the same. We can practise there with dummies. You manage the shot, twenty pounds is yours. Then if you agree to the real thing . . . well, it's home, young man.'

Unease squirmed in Bloch's stomach. The British were famously skilled at reeling in their prey with blandishments and enticements, delivered with a sorry-to-trouble-you-old-chap air of slight distraction. The next moment, a steel trap slams shut. 'I will need to know more.'

'About?' asked Carlisle. 'It's very straightforward.'

No, he thought, it is anything but. 'About the target. About whether I am aiding the enemies of Germany. About why you are doing this. Why do you need me?'

Carlisle banged the table, his patience seemingly exhausted. 'What you are doing, Bloch, is saving an old man from many hours of torture. It is Sherlock Holmes walking across that bridge and believe you me, you will be doing him a great service if you end his life there and then.'

THIRTY-FIVE

The final part of the jigsaw that was Mrs Gregson's grand plan needed a large green space in North London, away from prying eyes and, she had been told, to the north-west of the intended target. If the weather held, that was. After a morning scouting suitable locations on a hired motorcycle, she chose Waterlow Park. Lauderdale House, which stood on its fringes, had been taken over for the duration by the Air Defence Department of the War office but never utilized, and it was a simple matter to have Nathan seal the park itself for 'air defence exercises'. That way any curious locals were likely to think that when David Devant and George Bletchley – Maskelyne's pilot – turned up, the enormous horse-pulled dray they used was delivering a barrage balloon. Which was close enough.

With the dray manoeuvred through the entrance by Highgate Cemetery, Mrs Gregson watched the unloading of the cargo. Devant was too infirm to help, and besides he had his own work to do some distance away, and so Nathan had recruited six burly 'ruffians', as he described them. Mrs Gregson was dressed in her Dunhill motorcycling clothes, a totem of more carefree times, and she had to admit, as insane as her scheme seemed, she was enjoying herself. Inaction was anathema to her and even if the whole pack of cards collapsed at least she could tell herself she had tried her misguided best.

After Devant left by bicycle to take up his position, the ruffians, whom she discovered were professional *agents provocateurs* employed by MI5 to create or disrupt protests as required, set about unloading under the direction of Mr Bletchley. The light was fading across the park, he had to be airborne by dusk and he snapped out brisk orders on how to manhandle the giant parcel off the flatbed of the dray and where to place it on the grass. The ruffians, despite their size and strength, were sweating by the time they had finished.

As Mrs Gregson watched the canvas envelope being unfolded on the grass, Bletchley walked across to her. He was a tall, willowy chap, perhaps sixty, with the wind-beaten skin of someone who has spent a lot of time outdoors. Or in the sky. 'It's a Rozière, you know, miss,' he said with some pride, pointing at the unfurling inverted pear shape. 'Very rare.'

'Is it?' she asked.

'Uses a gas bladder in the top of the envelope. Helps with lift. Usually filled with hydrogen. That's what happened at the Liverpool Empire with the half-sized one.' He shook his head at the memory at a stunt gone wrong.

'And now? What do you use?'

'Helium. Bloody expensive, if you'll excuse my language.' He took out a cigarette and put it between his lips. 'But at least we won't go up in flames.' He gave a grin and lit his Woodbine. 'Sorry, rude of me, would you . . . ?'

'Yes, please.' She had cut down since her days of nursing, when the smoke helped mask the smell of gas gangrene and carbolic, but her heart was fluttering like a trapped bird and she needed to steady her nerves. 'Thank you.' She leaned forward into the proffered match. 'Is the wind to your liking?'

He licked a thumb and held it aloft. 'Holding up. It's fortunate we don't have to be pinpoint accurate. I think luck is on your side.'

Mrs Gregson took a lungful of the coarse smoke and held it for a while, suppressing the urge to cough. 'Let us hope so. You know, Mr Bletchley, that what we are doing is—'

He shook his head vigorously. 'Don't tell me. All I know is I have never seen Mr Devant looking so happy. Not for a while now, at least. And when he told Mr Maskelyne, well, the two had a right old laugh. If he'd been stronger, he'd've been here. OK, I admit it's a bit of a rum do. What with that.' He nodded towards the parked dray, where, next to the wicker basket, a sausage-shaped bundle lay. Valentine's corpse. 'But I'm just doing what this strange lady hired me to do. No questions asked. No, I didn't catch a name, officer.' He smiled now. 'But she paid very handsomely in cash.'

'I did.'

'Mr Devant told me it might be unconventional, but it was for a good cause.'

What with all the arrangements she had had to make and the strain of organizing this launch, she had almost forgotten why she was doing all this. To rescue Watson, of course, to bring him back, dust him down, feed him up, and see where they went from there. 'It is.'

Bletchley looked at the now enormous envelope and its long fringe of guy ropes and nodded his approval. He began to roll up his sleeves. 'Then let's get a fire going, eh?'

The breeze swirled around the roof, plucking at Miss Pillbody's clothes as she sprinted across an open area until the shadow of the chimney stack swallowed her. There, she caught her breath and scanned the night sky. It was empty, apart from patchy cloud and the pinpricks of stars.

Below her stretched the terraced homes of North London, the lights hazed by the smoke from a thousand chimneys. No wonder nobody ever tried to escape from the roof, she thought. It was a long way down and, even though she had a head for heights, she didn't fancy trying to cling to one of the drainpipes that, anyway, had spiked collars every few yards to prevent anyone shimmying up or down.

She checked the sky again. Still empty. The thought occurred to her that she had been fooled, taken in by the Gregson woman. She regretted, now, killing Wardress Gray. She could have just tied her up. But she personified the days of humiliation Miss Pillbody had endured in Holloway. She had to admit to enjoying stabbing her over and over again until the life had gone from her body, which she used to block the bolted door to the bathhouse. She'd hang now if she was caught, that was for certain. Not as a German spy but as a murderer. Even her own government couldn't object to that.

Was this what Gregson had in mind all along? To put her in a corner where she might do something like this and then leave her to face the consequences? The sky was still devoid of any unusual feature, the promise of rescue looking increasingly empty. Yes, perhaps Gregson had intended the noose all along.

She wouldn't go without a fight. She could certainly take at least one over the edge of this block, plummeting to the court-yard below on one side, or the streets of Holloway the other. Better a death like that than the cruel judicial ceremony of the hangman.

From below the sound of a hacking cough carried up from the gatehouse. There were squat towers down there with searchlamps, aligned pointing downwards at the moment to sweep walls and courtyards, but, no doubt, able to swivel up and rake the rooftops to find any escapee.

Check the sky. Still empty.

She felt disgust at her gullibility. Imagine trusting an Englishwoman who comes along and offers you your freedom. She had been duped. Now she would never see Germany again.

It was a roar, like the noise of a dragon exhaling and the light from it spilled across the slates of the roof. She stepped to one side of the chimney stack and for a second she saw the great bulbous shape, illuminated from within, like a giant version of a Chinese lantern. It had come from the opposite direction to the one she had expected. But at least now the sky was no longer empty.

As the burner was switched off the giant lantern disappeared again, leaving the sphere a darker shape against the pinpricked heavens. She could make out its shape by the way it blotted the stars. Drifting towards her, hundreds of metres away yet, blown inexorably to the rooftop by the breeze, was the instrument of her freedom.

All thoughts of hanging and hangmen dispersed from her head and she went over the instructions that had been delivered to her. She willed the lighter-than-air machine on, agonizing at the slowness of the approach. It roared again and the envelope glowed as it rose slightly. She imagined sleepy eyes were turning towards it now, guards and inmates wondering what manner of fire had arrived from the heavens. It was the fire that would take her home.

THIRTY-SIX

Watson waited until he was alone in his room to examine the piece of paper that Hulpett had given him. He read and reread it several times, hoping the meaning would leap out at him.

We made contact with Captain Brevette.

Brevette had been one of the two names written on the square of paper Archer had presented to Watson on his visit to the examination room. What was the significance of Brevette? He heard footsteps approaching and quickly tucked the paper under the excuse for a pillow. It was Harry, looking breathless and with snow in his hair.

'You all right, lad?'

'Never better, sir,' he said, clutching his heart. 'Just some of us boys having a snowball fight. One of the Germans joined in and wished he hadn't. Looked like a bleedin' snowman by the time we finished with 'im. He took it in good part, though.' He paused. 'I thought you might need a hand settin' up for the surgery, sir.'

Watson nodded. He would be glad of the company, even if he did think Harry had something other than his best interests at heart. 'As long as you aren't neglecting your other charges.'

'I told you, we've come to some arrangement, Doctor.'

'And I said you must let me pay for any expenses in that area, Harry.'

He gave a lopsided grin. 'I'll bill you at the end of the month, sir.'

'I won't be——' he began, before he realized the lad was joking. 'I'll pay you later on today. No arguments. Now, can you fetch me some boiling water?'

'Sir.'

'Oh, Harry.'

'Sir?'

'Do you know a Captain Brevette?'

Harry frowned. 'Yeah . . . Brevette. He's not on the list, is he? Must be some sort of mistake. He won't be turning up for surgery today, though.'

'And why is that?'

'He died about three months ago. Maybe more.'

'Of . . . ?'

'It was the cholera. We had an outbreak. He was quarantined in the other compound. But it killed him.'

'Just him?'

'Only one to die. Some of the others had the . . . you know, the shits, sir.'

'Diarrhoea and vomiting?' Watson prompted.

'Not half.'

'Lucky.'

'Not a word many of those affected used.'

'Lucky you didn't have a full-blown epidemic. Did they trace its source?'

'No, but that German doctor had us clean out the latrines and he rerouted the drinking water pipes. They were next to the latrines.'

'Steigler?'

'That's the kiddie.'

'Good for him. And, Harry, one last thing – where is the chess club? In the rec room?'

'No, they reckon that's too noisy for them. Horseplay, they call it. Like a bit of peace and quiet, the serious players do. Hut 15 is where you'll find them.'

'Tonight?'

'What's today?' He thought for a minute. 'Yeah, Wednesday and Friday is backgammon, chess every other night. You fancy a game?'

'I might,' Watson said non-committally.

'Well, be careful, sir. Some of them is demons and they like to suggest a little wager.'

'Thank you for the warning. I prefer to lose my money on the horses.'

'Ah, then you'll be wanting Hut 9.'

'What for?'

'The Epsom of Harzgrund, that's what it is. Only they ain't got any real horses. So they use rats. But there's bookies and everything.'

'Sounds charming. But I'll try the chess first.'

'I'll get that water.'

After he had left, Watson sat on the bed and ran the

conversation with Harry through his mind, trying to decipher what was truth and what was a lie, until his head started to thump as if he'd swallowed more of that hideous alcohol.

It was later that same day that Watson made his way across to Hut 15. More blasted snow had arrived, filling the gauzy cones cast by the perimeter lights. But the snow brought a calming quiet as all noises were muffled and even the barking of the dogs seemed distant. Most sensible men had retreated indoors to keep warm, by stove and collective body heat. In his own hut, Cocky had opened up some more of his delights, and word had whipped around the camp that there was pressed ham and tinned pilchards and pickled onions and the atmosphere had grown oppressive as more and more souls 'dropped by' in the hope of some morsels. Watson was glad to be out of it.

He wondered what Holmes was doing at that moment. Probably settling down by the fire with pipe and book. Perhaps his young companion, Bert, would be with him. Watson felt a twinge of envy but quickly suppressed it. Circumstances had brought him here and there was little he could do to alter those. Holmes would never dwell on past events that were immutable. One should only dwell on those immediate concerns that can be influenced by your actions.

So what could he influence? He could find out what lay behind this apparent suicide of men who claimed to have contacted the dead Brevette. Something was very peculiar in this camp, very peculiar indeed. But he felt as if he were looking at events through a fog, that nothing would come into focus. There was foul play at work, but the exact shape and form of it was impossible for him to grasp, as if he were trying to catch and preserve one of the snowflakes falling around him.

He walked into the shadow of Hut 8 when he saw a figure detach itself from the wall. The man made two steps and turned to block his path. 'Major Watson?'

'Yes?' he asked, trying to place the voice.

The blow from behind was both unexpected and accurate. A short, sharp tap to the temple and Watson's legs crumpled under him and he pitched sideways, heading for a soft landing in the snow.

DAILY NEWS

GUARDS FOIL DARING AERIAL ESCAPE FROM HOLLOWAY

Witnesses see 'dangerous' female prisoner attempt to climb
rope ladder into balloon before being shot dead.

Wreckage discovered on Highbury Fields — police search for
body.
Female warder murdered 'in cold blood'.

STOP PRESS: Police report finding body of escaped prisoner,
identified as Nora Pillbody, convicted of murder and spying for
a foreign power.

THIRTY-SEVEN

Watson's first instinct on regaining consciousness and realizing he was lying on his back in darkness was to sit up. He immediately struck his forehead on something hard and unyielding, sending him back down to the supine position. He kept his eyes closed until the dancing stars slowed and then faded. Then he opened them.

It wasn't darkness that surrounded him, it was total pitch-blackness, a complete absence of light. He raised a hand and his knuckles hit the same solid surface that had braked the upward progress of his head moments previously. He did the same with the other hand. Again, solid. He tapped. Wood.

Gingerly he ran his fingers along the surface and over his head, both hands this time. There was some sort of vertical screen there. And at the sides, too. He shuffled himself down until his feet were pressing against another immovable surface.

By now he was sweating, even though it wasn't particularly warm. He closed his eyes again, aware that there was a throbbing in his temple from the blow that had felled him.

Who was it who had stepped out in front of him? He tried to

replay the moment as if it were a gramophone record. '*Major Watson?*'

It was no good, it wouldn't come to him. Watson spread his fingers, reached up and pushed at the solid sheet of wood above his head. It would not yield. He attempted the same with his elbows, but it was tendon and bone that came off worse. He tried to get some movement at the panels above the head and with the feet. Nothing.

Don't panic.

That is very easy for you to say, he thought, feeling that very sensation rising in him.

Panicking will achieve nothing.

That much was true. But he had to consider that the box contained a finite amount of air. If he hyperventilated it would be used up that much quicker. Similarly, shouting would deplete his oxygen. But he had to try.

'Help! Help!' he tried, but the voice seemed trapped within the confines of the same prison as his body. He made a fist and thumped as hard as he could and yelled again.

Silence. Only his ragged breathing and the insistent thump of his accelerated heart in his ears. It was time to face the truth. The box was a coffin. He had been buried alive.

THIRTY-EIGHT

Miss Pillbody held up her shackles and rattled the chain that linked her wrists and then did the same with the one that was looped through the chair she was sitting on. 'So I have exchanged one prison for another?'

'For the moment,' said Mrs Gregson. They were in the stone-floored, beam-ceilinged kitchen of a ramshackle farmhouse to the north-east of London, en route to the Port of Harwich, which was served by the Great Eastern Railway whose tracks ran within a mile of their current location. They, though, would be driving to the port. The longer they could keep Miss Pillbody shackled, the happier everyone would be. And that would be difficult on the train.

The room was sparsely furnished, with a pitch pine table and chairs and a Welsh dresser devoid of any crockery, but it was warm thanks to a cast-iron range. Mrs Gregson wasn't sure how Nathan had located it, but it would do the job nicely.

'I don't know what you think I'd do if you uncuffed me. Bite you?'

Mrs Gregson did not answer directly but pointed behind her. 'This gentleman is Mr Nathan,' she said.

Nathan nodded in Miss Pillbody's direction and opened his jacket to show an automatic pistol shoved into his waistband.

'Pleased to meet you, too,' said Miss Pillbody.

Mrs Gregson pulled open the door of the kitchen. Outside in the corridor was bucktoothed Hiram Buller, who raised his bowler as if greeting a lady on her stroll to church. Only the shotgun held in the crook of his arm added a note of incongruity.

'Mr Buller.' She closed the door. 'Do not for one moment think we underestimate your determination or resourcefulness. Both men are fully prepared to shoot to kill.'

Miss Pillbody gave a smile and a nod of appreciation; as if this were the highest compliment she could be paid.

'Why did you kill the warder?' Nathan asked.

'Bitch. Deserved it.'

'You have put us in a very difficult position.'

'Because you feel guilty? Because if you hadn't dreamed up this plan, that woman Gray might still be drawing baths and folding towels?'

Mrs Gregson said nothing, but the damned woman had touched a nerve. Now, she was complicit in a murder.

'Send me back then.'

'You know we can't do that.'

'I do. Because you might join me on the gallows. You've been lucky so far. All that nonsense with the balloon—'

'Nonsense?' Mrs Gregson blurted. She was proud of the

scheme. 'It was a modified version of the woman-overboard escape I used at Foulness.'

Miss Pillbody snorted. 'That didn't work, though, did it?' Mrs Gregson had faked a leap from a ship and then stayed hidden on board until the hue and cry died down. She had been caught, but not due to any flaw in the plan's execution, just by dint of a keen dockyard guard. 'How long before they realize that the body isn't me?'

'Given the damage to the facial features, which are consistent with a fall from a great height, a few days, if ever. Long enough so they won't be looking for you at the ports just yet.'

Valentine from St Barts had provided the body that was dressed in prison clothes. It was the cadaver of a young woman from the East End who had died from exposure after a night – or more likely several weeks – gorging on bathtub gin.

'Can I get something to eat?' Miss Pillbody asked. 'If I am to stay in this position until morning.'

Mrs Gregson glanced out of the window. A faint overture of dawn had appeared and the birds were singing. She almost allowed the feeling of exhaustion to overcome her but took a deep breath. 'Mr Nathan?'

'There's some bread and cheese in the car. And we can make tea.'

'Tea! Hallelujah!' sneered Miss Pillbody. 'All is well with the world.'

'That will be fine,' said Mrs Gregson to Nathan. 'And fetch the clothes, will you?' Nathan handed Mrs Gregson the Webley as he left, his expression a warning to use it if in the slightest doubt.

'I think shooting me now would rather spoil the party, don't you?'

'Oh, we have contingency plans.'

'Really?' Both eyebrows went up. 'I thought you were making this up as you rolled merrily along.'

'You think you can hire the most accomplished illusionist in the country on a whim? Or one of the few balloonists who can fly over London at night?'

The plan had been both complex and simple. Miss Pillbody had never left the roof, but had hidden in the cleft of two chimney stacks, along with a length of rope dropped from the balloon, with which, after a few hours, she descended the outside wall of the prison to where Nathan and Buller had been waiting, with hood and ropes and a fast car. The woman ascending the rope, witnessed and sworn to by guards and neighbours alike, was an illusion projected by David Devant onto sheets slung from beneath the balloon, using his theatreograph system, mounted on a nearby rooftop. Mrs Gregson had assisted him, such was the shaking of his hands due to his illness, but he had enjoyed creating the show. 'What a shame there is no audience to applaud,' he had said when the masquerade was complete. But there had been an audience and they supplied something much more valuable than applause – sworn statements that the illusion was actually a genuine event.

'It must have cost a pretty penny,' said Miss Pillbody.

'Sometimes, the name Sherlock Holmes brings out the best in people.'

'Ah, but it's the other one you want to save, isn't it, Georgina?'

Mrs Gregson recognized an attempt to upset her, the gentle

press of a knife between the ribs, presaging the sudden twist. 'I want them both home,' she said flatly. 'They are old men who deserve a rest.'

'What are the clothes you mentioned to Nathan?'

'You can't travel in that prison garb. We shall be taking the ferry as Red Cross VADs. A perfect cover. And we can hide your restraints under the long cape.'

'There are submarines and mines in the North Sea.'

'We will take our chances.'

'I can't swim with these.' She held up the manacles.

'Then you will be taking somewhat more chances than the rest of us.'

Miss Pillbody stuck out her lower lip and blew a strand of hair from her mouth. 'Will you at least allow me to brush and pin up my hair to keep it out of my eyes? All this running around has made it quite wild.'

Mrs Gregson could see no harm in making her look present-able. And VADs, like regular nurses, did tend to wear their hair up. 'Yes. In due course.'

'And you are certain the Germans at the border will accept me in place of a piece of propaganda like Holmes? My masters are not sentimental types, you know. They won't even trust me, thinking I have been manipulated by the British. I will be treated with suspicion for many months. I might even end up in prison there.'

'I wouldn't put a wager on that, Miss Pillbody. Not with your silver tongue.'

A flash of a smile. 'And what does Mr Holmes think of this scheme?'

Mrs Gregson must have betrayed something with her response.

'Hold on a moment. He doesn't know, does he? Is that right? Holmes is going to offer himself up and you wish to pre-empt that.' Miss Pillbody began to laugh so hard that the metal of her chains rattled. 'Oh, perfect. At this moment you have no more idea where Sherlock Holmes is than I do.'

My Dear Watson,

By the time you get this, I will either be dead or on my way to the eternal sleep of death. The thought of this journey is lightened by the knowledge that you will be spared any more suffering and can go home to a well-deserved retirement. I would recommend bees, but I know you never shared my enthusiasm for the wonders of the hive.

I am well aware that you – and Mycroft – consider me naïve in the ways of the world and especially politics. It is true I have only dabbled in my brother's sphere when I thought I might be of some assistance to King and Country. But even I appreciate that due to my having – in no small part thanks to your commendable efforts – a certain public standing, that once I am in the hands of the Germans they will seek to exploit that position. I am old now, frailer than I was, although, again with thanks to you, much better than when we were on that blasted island together. But I have no illusions about what methods the Germans might use to bend me to their will. A man can hold out for some time but few can guarantee they will not, at some point, snap like the brittlest of reeds.

Therefore, I have prepared a poison that I will release into my body as soon as I am certain you are safe in the hands of our forces.

Do not grieve. I have feared the slow decline of old age more than any of the other evils I have faced. I have peered into the abyss of senility and know it isn't for me.

I am already in Holland as I write this. I intercepted the instructions for the exchange from Von Bork at the post office, before they were delivered to the hotel. The hotel, I have noted, is being watched. Which makes me suspect there are those who would — nobly but wrongheadedly — thwart me in this undertaking. Mycroft, whom I told only half the truth to? Or your redoubtable Mrs Gregson? Or Kell. Or Churchill, perhaps. The watchers are of English origin, at any rate, that much is obvious. A naval man and two ex-army types I have deduced. One of them plays cricket regularly.

So my task now is to make sure the exchange takes place and you are safe at home in England.

I say again, do not grieve for me. Ours was the most wonderful of times, you were the best of companions and colleagues. And friend, of course. What adventures we had. But I fear that the world that will emerge from this conflict would ill suit me. I shall leave copies of this letter with Mycroft and post one to your club and another to Cox & Co. Mycroft has my will. Do not fret, I have not left you the bees.

I wish you many more years and assure you that, should you decide to unearth some of the cases yet to be put before the public, I will be in no position to object. Just do not dim your own considerable light at the expense of mine, as you are wont to do.

I shall see you on the bridge, John. It will be a pleasure to greet you one last time.

Your friend as ever,

Sherlock Holmes

THIRTY-NINE

Watson crossed his arms over his chest and let his breathing fall back to an even tempo. If he was going to die he was going to try to do it with a certain serenity and sense of poise. He imagined he was like the Black Prince in Canterbury Cathedral, although as far as he could remember he lay with his fingers making a pyramid. Watson tried it but it didn't feel right. No, best be comfortable to face the last few minutes on earth. He 'crossed his heart' by gripping the opposite shoulder with each hand.

Would anyone ever find him here buried deep in the cold soil of Germany? That possibility gave him more pain than the thought of the breathlessness to come. That Holmes and Mrs Gregson should never discover what became of him. And that the crime perpetrated on him should go unpunished.

Why did he have to be done away with? What was the urgency? A few days and he would be gone, away from the camp. And what were they covering up?

Foul deeds, Watson.

Yes, thank you, Holmes, even I could have grasped that conclusion. What was the significance of this Captain Brevette, apparently dead but still trying to communicate with the earthly realm? And why should the medium and his friends need to be murdered? If that was what had happened.

You can't solve it from in there. Not enough facts at your disposal.

I know, I know. Watson decided to concentrate on something else. The last, unfinished Holmes story that would never, now, see the light of day. But he could complete it to his own satisfaction while he waited for the air to grow thin. He could picture the words on the page, paragraph by paragraph until he reached the release of the last line. He imagined himself at the desk at Baker Street, the air full of curlicues of tobacco, the only sound the solid tick of the wall clock and the muffled clop of hoofs on cobbles, interrupted only by the occasional grunt from Holmes as some item in *The Times* caught his attention. With a fresh Bishops Bourne writing tablet, he saw himself pick up an Onoto self-filling fountain pen – his favoured writing instrument of late – and begin the final section of the story of the gold watches.

I recall it recorded in my notebook that it was a bleak and windy day towards the end of March 1895 that Holmes received a telegram over breakfast. He scribbled a reply and said nothing more of it. A few hours later there was a measured step on the stairs and a moment later a stout, tall and grey-whiskered gentleman entered the room.

Watson had no idea how long had passed before he mentally composed the finale to the tale of the gold watches.

Mr Sherlock Holmes is retired, tending his bees, his reputation secure and robust enough to survive a tale in which he played the part of the mistaken detective.

But should this be the final tale in the entire canon? Surely Holmes should leave the public stage with a greater flourish, a final bow, rather than a case that baffled the Great Detective. It was true, Watson had long determined to bring to light some of those incidents where even Holmes's deductions had proved fruitless, but as the grand finale?

Who was he fooling? This manuscript existed only in his head. There would be no chance for anyone else to read the finished product because the words of the final section did not exist in solid form, just held in the wires and synapses of his brain, an organ that must soon see its sparks extinguished for ever.

The thought made him restless and he pushed once more against the lid. For a moment he imagined something from outside. A scuffling. There it was again. And . . . voices? Was this it? Was the end presaged by aural hallucinations? No, again there was a distinct sound, scratching against the side of his prison, although whether animal or human he could not tell. Perhaps it was a curious mole or a wayward rabbit. But he had heard human voices, of that he was certain.

He shouted again for help, but no reply came. Then he heard a distinct click and the squeak of wood moving over wood. The floor of the wooden box he lay prostrate in was moving, swinging open as a mechanism of some description was released. There came the most perplexing sensation for a man lying in a coffin as Watson fell through the base and found himself falling through the air, apparently plunging deeper into the cold earth.

FORTY

One round. That was all they had given Ernst Bloch. One solitary bullet, just in case he decided to turn his Mauser on his captors. Why would he do that? Why would he thwart the one chance he had to get back to Hilde? No, he was going to carry out this mission, this state-sanctioned execution, unless they had been lying to him. He had to face up to that possibility, be alert to the chance that the perfidious British were toying with him, manipulating him into a situation where he would strike a blow against his own side.

But that was for later. Now, as he climbed the metal ladder up the crane, he had to concentrate on making his one shot count. A truculent wind snapped at him as he ascended, his hands chilled by the icy metal rungs.

He wasn't sure where he was exactly. Gravesend, they had said, although he had never heard of the place – his British geography was poor. The morbid-sounding town was on the English coast somewhere, obviously. To his right were docks, where a score of cranes were busy unloading freight from merchant ships, dockworkers swarming over a pair of trawlers, probably being converted to mine-sweeping duties. A trio of destroyers rode at anchor just beyond the mouth of the harbour. Below him was a canal and set back from it rows of warehouses. The surrounding area was completely deserted, cleared of both civilians and military personnel while he carried out the exercise.

Bloch paused to catch his breath at the first of the platforms. He had been instructed to fire from the next one, which mimicked the height of the watchtower on the German/Dutch border that was to be his perch on the actual day. That day would be 'soon', according to Carlisle.

Which meant he could see Hilde 'soon'.

A shouted prompt from below instructed him to keep climbing. On the ground, peering up, was Carlisle and, next to him, the bull-necked Sergeant Balsom. How he wished he had an extra bullet for him. Whenever the pair had time alone the sergeant made snide remarks about Hilde, hoping, he said, that Bloch wouldn't return to find her pinned on a Prussian officer's pork bayonet. Or carrying a cavalryman's bastard child. But the jibes didn't hit home; Bloch knew from the tone of her letters that Hilde had stayed true. Still, the image of what one of his old S.m.K. armour-piercing rounds would do to the thuggish sergeant helped him keep an even temper.

As the wind tugged harder at his tunic, with the rifle slung over his back he scampered up the next section of ladder at double-quick speed until he made the perforated steel platform. Here, he walked to the rail and surveyed the scene. To the right was the bridge that, Carlisle claimed, more or less matched the one crossing the River Meuse. The scale was different – this was a much shorter span over the canal – but the distance was about right.

Bloch pulled the strap of his Mauser over his head and slipped off its protective muzzle cover. He then removed the metal caps from either end of the telescopic sight. Even without the magnification he could make out the target at the end of the bridge nearest to him. He shouldered the rifle and adjusted the optics. The man came into sharpened focus.

It was, in truth, only an approximation of a human being, the sort of dummy the British liked to use for bayonet practice. This one was dressed in a long black woollen coat and a low-crown top hat, as if ready for a night at the opera.

Bloch put down the rifle and examined his options. The wind was gusting intermittently, which was far from ideal. He was confident he could make a clean kill standing up, but decided it would be better to use the railings as support. Would there be any such resting point on the actual tower? He couldn't be certain, so he made a note to ask for a stand for the rifle like the British snipers used, a single pole that clamped to the foregrip.

Bloch dropped to one knee and rested the rifle on the rail. He took his time getting comfortable, positioning the stock in his shoulder and distributing his weight carefully. He timed the peaks and troughs of the breeze coming from the sea, finding a ragged pattern in the gusts. He put his eye to the rubber bell that surrounded the ocular lens. A series of minor adjustments followed, to the zoom ring, the focus on the objective lens and the top, elevation, turret. Finally, the windage compensation, although with a single shot to his name this was guesswork.

Stop and breathe. Through the sights he could see the torso and the head. It had to be a body shot in these conditions, he decided. A tiny miscalculation in the sighting or drift of the bullet and, at that range, he could miss altogether. No, it was a chest shot. Even if he missed the heart, it was unlikely the victim would survive a high-powered round slicing through bone and blood vessels.

He snapped his head back, away from the sights and blinked hard, his mouth unexpectedly dry. It had been a long time since he had dealt with such considerations. At one time, it was all he thought about – angles, trajectories, penetrations, kill shots and incapacitating wounds. It had been a form of madness, the mania of mass killing that had gripped the whole of the Western Front. And now here he was, embracing all that again. But in a good cause, he reminded himself. One last kill for Hilde. And this wasn't a man in his crosshairs. It was a stuffed dummy. *So take the damned shot.*

He put his eye back to the rubber bell, waited for the next gust of wind to peak, riding its coat-tails down to the moment when he squeezed the trigger, watched the world blur under the recoil, then resteadied and repositioned so he could see that the round had ripped out the spot where, in a few days' time, Sherlock Holmes's heart would be.

FORTY-ONE

It was meant to be a soft landing but the impact jarred every bone in Watson's wasted body. For a few moments he couldn't see anything, the light causing his eyes to ache and water after what seemed like hours of darkness. When he did blink away the moisture that filmed his corneas, he was looking up at the coffin and the hinged door that had swung open to release him. The coffin had been suspended on two trestles, one at either end. He had never been buried at all. The coffin was above ground. It was some kind of prank.

The anger at this made him roll to one side, off the thin mattress that had been provided to break his fall, and eager hands grabbed at him to haul him to his feet. He was in a hut he didn't recognize, but he could place most of the faces that stared at him, some in concern, others in bemusement. Critchley, Lincoln-Chance, Peacock, Harry, Boxhall, Father Hardie and Hulpett, the man he had been on his way to meet. Most surprising of all was Brünning, the *Feldwebel*.

'What the hell is going on here?' Watson demanded, his anger quickly replacing the fear he had just experienced.

Critchley started to brush at his clothes but Watson smacked his hand away.

'Colonel, what is the meaning of this?'

'I'm sorry,' said Lincoln-Chance, 'it was my fault. I feared you were about to ruin everything.'

Watson composed himself. 'Ruin everything? Is that why you put Harry in as a spy?'

Harry examined his feet.

'He was never at Baker Street. Were you?'

He gave a gulp before he spoke. 'No, sir. But I am a great admirer—'

'Never mind that,' Watson snapped. 'What is this all about? Why the trick coffin?'

Boxhall stepped forward with a cup of tea. 'It's how we escape, Major.'

Watson, despite his irritation, took the tea. 'Where are we?'

'Keep your voice down, please,' said Lincoln-Chance. 'There are guards in the towers still. We are in the isolation hut. Next to the cemetery. There is a tunnel from the recreation room to here. Although very few know about it.'

Watson was incredulous. 'You dug a tunnel between huts? Through this ground?'

Critchley shook his head. 'It was here already. Under your feet are gold workings, some of them centuries old. When we first tried to organize an escape we blundered into them.'

The cracks in the big house, he recalled. Subsidence. The workings had made the ground unstable, that was why Kügel's mansion had settled and cracked.

'Look, this is partly my fault,' said Hulpett. 'That damned séance . . . it spooked me.'

'Perhaps we should have taken you into our confidence earlier,' said Boxhall.

'But we thought you were a chat, remember,' added Peacock.

'One at a time, please,' said Watson, taking some of the tea. 'Will a designated spokesman please tell me what exactly I have witnessed here?'

The group exchanged uncertain glances, like a jury charged with selecting a foreman. 'Why don't you gentlemen return the way you came,' said Father Hardie, 'and I will explain all to Major Watson. Before we attract any attention.'

There was a murmur of assent and the group turned towards a section of the floor that had been removed. Critchley took something from his top pocket and handed it to Hardie. 'You'll be needing this.' Hardie nodded and took a piece of card.

When the men had departed, Hardie replaced the section of floorboards and dragged a cot to cover it. 'It's not the best camouflage but the Germans rarely come in here. Brünning sees to that. He's on a wage. We mumble typhus or cholera every so often and they just glance in, and if a volunteer is needed to step inside, why, good old Brünning volunteers.'

'He is playing a risky game.'

'And is suitably rewarded. Cigarette?'

Watson nodded and, after he had drained the tea, they lit up. The windows, he noticed, were tightly blacked out by thick fabric taped to the frames to prevent any light escaping to the outside world. Hardie fetched two chairs and they sat facing each other at one end of the coffin.

Watson tapped the wooden box. 'This is Boxhall's work?'

Hardie nodded. 'What makes you assume that?'

'Family of furniture makers. Rough hands for an officer. Cuts and scratches and splinters.'

'Ah, I see. Yes, it's ingenious, isn't it?'

Watson stood, went over and ran his fingers under the coffin, working the flaps to try to understand the mechanism. 'Above ground, yes. It is hard to see what use it is six foot under. These wouldn't work.'

'Oh, you can't get six foot down in this soil. Not in winter. Too hard. But we don't have to, if we know where to dig.'

'Hardie, would you like to start at the beginning?'

The priest nodded. 'It was Lincoln-Chance who discovered the gold workings when he was digging his first tunnel. He went down and followed the tunnels and stumbled across a way to break through to the outside.'

'A ready-made escape route?'

'Aye. The wee problem was, after we got two men out, Kügel introduced the punishment of killing two inmates for every man who escaped. That kindae put a damper on things, ye might say.'

'Which is why he is still here? Lincoln-Chance?'

There was something like anger in the priest's eyes when he spoke. 'No, laddie. Don't be fooled by Link's looks. Cresta Run playboy he may be, but he's no' daft. He decided there was a way to get men out without bringing down the wrath o' Kügel. Some way to keep everybody happy.'

'Which was?'

'Kill them first.'

Watson began to see where this was heading, but, playing the dunce, he said: 'Rather drastic, isn't it?'

'We find a way to fake their death—typhoid, dysentery, cholera—'

'Suicide?'

A sly smile spread over the priest's craggy face. 'Aye, suicide.'

'That's why you weren't too concerned about their immortal souls?'

'Ach, the play-acting and wringing of ma hands was never ma thing.'

'So how many people know?'

'All that was in this room, one or two more. The fewer the merrier, if you get my meaning.'

'And how do you choose those who are to seek their freedom?'

'Well, Major, first off is – can ye speak German? After all, we're a long way from the border. If not, we give lessons and if they make decent enough progress, they are in. And second – can ye afford it?'

'Afford it? You mean you charge people to escape?' Watson couldn't keep the scorn and disapproval from his voice.

Hardie lit another cigarette from the first. Watson refused his offer of a second. 'You've seen how this camp operates, Major Watson. It is entirely lubricated by money. From the very top to the very bottom. It is not cheap to arrange the papers, money, train tickets, travelling documents that an escapee needs. Oh, we can do it all right. But it costs a packet.'

'How much?' he asked, unable to keep the disgust from his voice.

'Somewhere in the region of one thousand pounds to guarantee Switzerland or Holland and freedom. Sometimes more.'

Watson whistled. It was an incredible sum. 'But who has that much money to pay in camp? Asking for that money to be transferred from a bank back home would arouse suspicion, surely?'

'Well, we'll take a cheque or banker's draft,' Hardie laughed. 'No, seriously. Hulpett was a solicitor before the war. He draws up legal documents so that the escapee promises to pay any sum owing upon their return to England.'

'An IOU.'

'Just a formality, y'see. A gentleman's word is his bond. Most think it is worth the price.'

Watson shook his head. 'It's unbelievable is what it is. So this coffin . . . ?'

'Is buried just above the workings. There is a handle inside for the poor dead man to release himself and fall through to the tunnels. We thought you might discover it for y'self. There, he finds his escape kit, map, instructions, money to smooth the path. New identity, so even if he is caught, they won't identify him as coming from this camp. That's very important. But we haven't lost one yet.'

'Are you saying you can guarantee they'll get through?'

'With enough money, you can guarantee anything, Major. Anything at all. The German civilians out there —' he pointed with the glowing end of his cigarette — 'need cash as much as anyone. Some of them rely on us to feed their families.'

'Why was Hulpett keen to see me?'

'Ach, Hulpett is a fool of a man. I told him to stay away from the séance, but he thought I was just being a God-fearing priest. Archer told him he'd made contact with Captain Brevette. On the other side. Yet Brevette escaped a few months ago. Hulpett got it into his head that he'd been caught, shot and we weren't telling.'

'Well, it might put a few customers off if that were so, don't you think?'

Hardie looked affronted. 'Major, please don't think we are only in this for the money. The operating expenses are enormous. Sourcing the wood and the tools for the coffins costs a fortune. I tell you, after the war, this will be one of the great tales — how dead men managed to get home to Blighty. You should write a story about it.'

'I'm not saying Archer really made contact with a dead man — but how do you know Brevette or any of the others actually make it?'

Hardie gave a little smile of victory. He handed over the card that Colonel Critchley had given him. It was from the Coburg Hotel in Mayfair, postmarked three weeks previously.

'Tea and Scones at Coburg. Marvellous. Keep your chins up. You'll be home soon — B.'

'It's an agreed code,' said Hardie. 'It's a home run, as it were, if ye make it to the Coburg and send us a card. We've a fair collection now. The problem is we can't overdo it.'

'Yet you took three men out at once. Archer and his fellow séancers. Wasn't that risky? And did they pay?'

'Aye, although one of them stood surety for all of them.'

'I'll be blowed. Three thousand pounds?'

'It's hard to take in, that much, isn't it? But it worked. They are probably halfway home by now.'

'And Peacock, he's out next?'

The eyes narrowed. 'How do ye know that?'

'He said as much. I didn't know what he was talking about at the time, of course.'

'Ach, he's another bloody fool,' Hardie said. 'I was always against Cocky going. He's the only man who has put weight on in this place, all the food his family and friends send over. I just hope yonder coffin is strong enough.'

'But he has the money, I assume.'

'Aye, he has that. Now, do you want to see with your own eyes?' He glanced at the floor.

'The tunnels?'

'Well, the one to the rec room in the main compound. Unless you want to stay here till morning. There's a little rope contraption enables us to pull the bed back in place once we are doon there. And we can get back to our huts easily enough with a bit of dodging of lights. I'm sorry about all the subterfuge.'

Watson now perceived just how tired he was. Even the thought of his thin, prickly mattress was tempting. Being convinced you are going to die after being buried alive was apparently exhausting. He stood slowly so as not to damage his weakened left knee further.

'One thing you might lend a hand with, though,' said Hardie as he ground out his cigarette. 'While you are still with us.'

'What's that?'

'Can you help us think of a convincing way to kill Cocky?'

FORTY-TWO

It was the queasiest sea crossing Miss Pillbody had ever experienced. The cabins they had chosen for the dash across the North Sea were in the bowels of the ship and the thump of engines and smell of fuel made her nauseous. The sudden changes of direction didn't help. Even though she was a neutral ferry, painted bright orange, the captain still saw fit to zigzag his way to the Hook of Holland, in case they ran into any colour-blind U-boat commanders.

Miss Pillbody lay on the bottom bunk and allowed herself a groan. One of her hands was manacled to the steel upright of the berths and she'd tried to free either flesh or metal and failed at both. Her only gain was a series of angry welts around her wrist. Besides, even if she could wriggle free, the extravagantly toothed Buller was out in the corridor, a cut-down version of his shotgun hidden under a greatcoat. Nathan had instructed him to blast away should Miss Pillbody appear at the door, preferably before she had a chance to open her mouth. They were taking no chances with her after the murder of Wardress Gray.

From snatches of conversation and sidelong glances she had

built up a more or less complete picture of what was being undertaken. In Holloway, Mrs Gregson had told her the truth, but had withheld certain facts. Like this hideous crossing, dressed in the scratchy, over-starched uniform of a VAD. Or that Mrs Gregson was using a man besotted with her to get what she wanted.

Nathan was in love, all right, even if he didn't acknowledge the full extent of it. Good Lord, Miss Pillbody had done her fair share of manipulating men. There were a few who had tangled with her and even managed to survive relatively intact. But all had compromised themselves one way or another in the hope that she would give herself to them. So she had knowledge of this game and she could tell that Mrs Gregson was not only playing it but winning.

Now and then she could see a flash of something like concern on Nathan's face. Miss Pillbody suspected he was bending if not breaking the rules to accommodate the woman's scheme. His other glances contained something else, that flash of lust for Mrs Gregson that effectively wiped away any doubts about his intentions towards her. What she couldn't quite grasp was to what extent Mrs Gregson was orchestrating this. Oh, she knew to some degree that she was doling out bait, like a fisherman chumming the waters, but Miss Pillbody reckoned some of it was unconscious, or possibly she was denying to herself just how risky the little dance she was involved in was.

Miss Pillbody had also gathered that she would be offered as a sacrificial lamb somewhere on the border between Holland and Germany. In exchange, Watson would be released. That was the endgame. At least, that was the finale Mrs Gregson had planned for her. But for a variety of reasons — not least the fact that she didn't like being a pawn in anyone's game — that wasn't going to be how it played out. She didn't yet know where or how, but Miss Pillbody knew that the opportunity would arise for her to take matters into her own hands. That favourable occasion might only last a minute or two, possibly even less, but she knew she would grasp it with both hands. And then, once again, someone would pay for her humiliation. Pay with their life.

Three decks above Miss Pillbody, close to a porthole that showed the churning North Sea, Mrs Gregson and Robert Nathan sat, pushing food neither could really face around their plates. Nathan was drinking an indifferent claret, Mrs Gregson was on lemonade. The ship itself was less than half full — the confirmation in the newspapers of German submarines having all restrictions removed meant only those who really needed to make the crossing did so. The dining room didn't even reflect the fifty per cent capacity — the truculent sea kept most of their fellow passengers confined to cabins or their daychairs and so the pair had it almost to themselves.

'I think the time has come for me to lay my cards on the table,' said Nathan after a large gulp of his wine.

'Robert—'

'No, Georgina.' Nathan reached over and cupped her hand with his, all but pinning it to the table. Only a struggle would remove it from beneath the paw. What hairy hands he has, she thought. It really *was* like a paw.

'You know how grateful I am to you, Robert. I know the risks you have taken.'

'I don't think you do, Georgina,' he said. 'If Kell became aware of the extent to which I have abused the authority of the service, if he even suspected I know about breaking Miss Pillbody from prison—'

'But he doesn't.'

'Not yet.'

Mrs Gregson shook her head. 'He may never.'

'He's a spy. He has men who are spies. Perhaps here. Yes, there are Kell's men at ports and on ferries. Women, too.' He looked around as if expecting to see MI5 agents at every table. 'There will be repercussions from this little adventure. Serious repercussions.'

'I am willing to accept them for the chance of success.'

'A woman died.'

'I know that,' she snapped. 'And that will doubtless come back to haunt me. For the moment I have to live with that, too.'

'And the fact that I might go down in disgrace and ignominy.'

'Oh, Robert—'

'Yet here I am, risking that for you to free another man. I think I deserve to know what your intentions are.'

He sounded like a father demanding an answer from his daughter's suitor. She laughed and his face darkened a little. 'Robert, I am not laughing at you. I am laughing at the notion that I have any intentions. I certainly didn't intend this. To be crossing the North Sea with a caged animal downstairs, hoping to use her to exchange for a man I . . . I respect and admire.'

'Is that all?'

'It is no trivial thing, Robert. As you so kindly reminded me, one woman has died already. I hope she is the last casualty.'

Nathan released her hand and she pulled it away, a small, pale thing, like a mouse scuttling away from a predator. 'Have you any affection left over for me?'

'Of course. No matter how this develops, you will always have my . . .'

'Gratitude?'

Mrs Gregson felt anger spurt through her like a geyser and it took all of her self-control not to dash the wine in Nathan's face. 'Robert, I don't have a crystal ball. You ask about my intentions. I have none beyond these next few days. You ask me about love, but the men I have truly loved have left me, one way or another. Don't ask me to analyse my feelings, because it would be like asking for a map of no man's land – churned and blasted and ever-shifting. No, if you excuse me, I think I will go back to my cabin and rest. The next forty-eight hours will be most taxing, I fear.'

She stood, gave a small inclination of the head and swayed off as elegantly as she could, given the seesawing of the floor. Robert Nathan marvelled yet again at his ability to snatch defeat from the jaws of victory and to place his foot firmly in his mouth. Shaking his head at the absurdity of it all, he reached over for the decanter and refilled his glass. Perhaps, he thought as he took another mouthful, he should just cut his losses and leave her to this old man Watson. Or perhaps he should simply make sure the old man never made it home.

Two decks above the dining room, at the rear of the ship, Ernst Bloch leaned on the rail, relishing the thrum of the engines vibrating through the metal and the wind whipping spray into his face. He had the deck virtually to himself, apart from the two men sheltering under a snapping awning. Captain Carlisle and Sergeant Balsom, his constant companions. All three were dressed in civilian clothes, their journey to Holland ostensibly to source meat supplies for England. They watched him now as he smoked a cigarette, looking out over the prancing white horses of the North Sea.

Of course it occurred to Bloch that he could thwart the British by simply leaping over the rail. He could do it before they took two steps to stop him. The sea would have him in seconds.

On the other hand, it was just possible he might get out of this alive. And the slimmest chance of seeing Hilde again was one he would grasp every time. Plus there was a chance that by killing himself on a mission like this, the truth might never come out. What he was doing – the whole scheme – was likely to be the sort of event that never made it into the history books, no matter what the outcome.

'I think we should go below,' said Balsom, grabbing the rail next him. 'Catch our death up here.'

'When I have finished this,' said Bloch, holding up his cigarette.

'Well, get a move on.'

'Beautiful, isn't it?' Bloch said. 'The sea.'

'It can be. I wouldn't count today as its finest hour, mate.'

'I could watch it for hours, finest or not.'

'Don't get any ideas, Bloch.' Balsom wiped water from his eyes. 'You know, we're going to have to hurt you.'

'Hurt me?'

'You'll have papers saying you were released on compassion-ate grounds. But for what? Has to be an injury of some description. I could use a spoon and scoop out one of your eyes.' He showed yellow teeth in a grin as he mimed the action. 'Hardly stings if you are quick enough, apparently. But I think you might need both your peepers to make a shot like that. Although, you'd look dashing with an eye patch, don't you think? Probably be treated like a hero back at home. Or, we could smash your knee with a hammer.'

'That's very kind,' Bloch said. 'But I think I'll also need both knees for the climb up the tower.'

'Oh, yes.' Balsom frowned. 'Still, we'll think of something, I am sure.' He snatched the cigarette from Bloch's mouth and tossed it in the foaming wake of the ferry. 'Let's be havin' you, then.'

Bloch hesitated, feeling cheated of the last few lungfuls of smoke and then shrugged. If by chance, he decided, they gave him more than one bullet, he really would use the second on the thick-necked sergeant.

Von Bork entered the working men's café near the bridge and nodded to the customers, some of whom acknowledged him. He had almost become accepted by the regulars. The owner, too, had softened, no longer demanding he change the course of the war single-handedly. Von Bork, cheered by the thick soup of tobacco and wood smoke that made up the atmosphere, asked for a coffee and set about building himself a pipe of Latakia tobacco. He was close to the bottom of the pouch now, and his suppliers in Berlin were claiming fresh supplies were difficult to source thanks to events in the Middle East. Von Bork knew that meant the price was about to go through the roof. He should buy all he could find on his next visit to the city.

When the coffee arrived Von Bork beckoned the proprietor to sit down. He did so and his daughter automatically fetched him his own coffee. 'This must be the best cup of *koffie* in the world,' the Dutchman said, 'given how much time you spend with us.'

'It isn't just that. Or the company. Or your charming daughter,' said Von Bork, producing an envelope from his pocket and laying it on the table.

The Dutchman looked around to see if anyone had noticed, but his clients were too busy with their newspapers or dominoes. 'What's this?'

'Payment.'

'For what?' He flipped it open with a fingernail and glanced inside. 'That buys you a lot of *koffie*, man.'

Von Bork smiled and carried on with his pipe. When he had finally stoked it to his satisfaction he said: 'It is for services to be rendered.'

It was the owner's turn to be silent as he watched Von Bork put match to bowl. 'What kind of services would that be?'

'Two of them.' A burst of puffing and sucking interrupted him. 'One, I am looking for information about an Englishman.'

'We don't get many of them hereabouts. There's some kept in Venlo. Most are up in internment camps near Groningen or Scheveningen.'

'I know that. The man I am interested in is a civilian. Well past military age. Tall, almost two metres perhaps, but stooped now.

Black and grey hair, receding, a distinctive thin, hawk-like nose. Grey eyes, which seem to look right through you.'

The Dutchman shook his head. 'Sounds like I'd remember that one.'

'Well, he's around here somewhere,' said Von Bork. He could be certain of this because he knew his instructions for the exchange had been taken before they reached the hotel at Venlo. Holmes knew the plan for the exchange and that it would centre on this river crossing. 'You just get word to me at this number . . .' He scribbled on the envelope. 'Or send a cable or a runner to this address across the border.' He was staying in a hostel next to the barracks at Holt, where the second-rate soldiers who guarded the border were stationed.

'I can do that,' said the café owner. 'But not for me. The cash will come in useful as a bribe to get my nephews away from the front. You know that can be done? People are selling safety.'

'Nobody can guarantee such a thing,' said Von Bork, well aware that fraudsters were fleecing concerned relatives by promising cushy clerical posts. 'Be careful who you hand money over to.'

The owner shrugged and rubbed his bald pate as if for luck. 'I know it's a gamble. But so is leaving them out there. You don't know anybody?'

'I can make enquiries.'

'I would like that.'

'Very well.'

'There was something else you wanted.'

'The man who operates the Knok bridge down the river there. Who opens and closes it.'

'It's not a man. It's the Meuse Navigation Company who decides when it opens and closes. The man just does their bidding.'

'I am talking about an opening of perhaps fifteen minutes. I don't want the bureaucracy.' Or the prying busybodies that would come with it. 'There must be someone who knows how to open and close it.'

Von Bork had inspected the bridge. The mechanism was electrically operated, hydraulically assisted, probably quite straightforward but was sufficiently complicated that he would rather an expert did it. Plus the controls were encased in a locked metal box, just to the left of the bridge entrance.

'You give the man some of this cabbage,' said the Dutchman, stabbing at the envelope, 'and I am sure he'll oblige.'

'You know him?'

'Know him? He's a regular.'

'Then ask him how much he wants. To open it at about eight in the morning in two days' time.'

The Dutchman's eyes flicked over to the bearded figure near the window in a coarse blue jacket and matching hat, puffing on a clay pipe while he read a Louis Couperus novel, his dark brows furrowed in concentration as if doing battle with the text.

'Is that him?'

'Old Herman, yes. A grouchy bastard at the best of times.'

'Leave him to me.' Von Bork made to rise but the owner put a hand on his wrist.

'If you'll allow me to do the negotiations . . . He'll charge you double.'

Was that greed he could see in the Dutchman's expression?

No doubt he would skim a fee off any agreed price. So be it. Von Bork glanced over at the bridge operator once more. 'Is he reliable?'

'Once everything is agreed, very. How do you think black-market goods from Holland get across into Germany? Not all of them by boat and barge.'

'I'll call by later, then,' said Von Bork. 'Let me know the price.'

The owner drained his coffee and left, palming the envelope with all the skill of a stage magician as he went.

Von Bork checked his watch. He had a meeting with the UFA cinematic people at the bridge in thirty minutes, They were concerned about 'the light' during the exchange. Could he make it an hour later? No, he could not. Eight was already an hour later than he had originally hoped for. He had already sent word for Dr Watson to be brought to Holt, ready for the piece of theatre at the bridge. And then, he would have Sherlock Holmes. He recalled their last meeting in August 1914 and the threat he had uttered when he still thought Holmes was an Irish-American double agent.

'I shall get level with you, Altamont,' he had said, speaking with slow deliberation. 'If it takes me all my life I shall get level with you!'

As Holmes would find out, that was no idle boast. Now, as that fool of a doctor used to put it, the game was afoot.

FORTY-THREE

Watson hardly slept that night. When he did it was for a few fitful hours and when he awoke he felt as if his bones were too heavy for his skin, as if they might burst through at any second. He remembered the walk under the camp, the eeriness of it, a tunnel – no, tunnels: there were unlit side passages, with dark uninviting mouths – hewn out by hands long dead. Gold had been mined since Roman times, the priest had told him, up until the turn of the century, when the seams had finally given out. Even so, he held a lamp up to show some lustrous veins in the walls. Such skeins were simply not valuable enough to return the effort of extraction, Hardie had said. Most of the excavations were tall enough for a man to stand – Watson had to admire the complex supports that had been put in place over the centuries – but in some places he had been forced to crouch and scuttle like a troglodyte through dark sections where the air tasted gritty and foul. But they had made it to the rec room, and now the whole incident felt like a bizarre dream.

As Watson shook the subterranean images from his brain, he

climbed out of the bed, straightening slowly lest his poor back protested and spasmed. He needed his staff to get to his feet and stumble over to his desk. There, written in a burst of activity by candlelight, was the final chapter of 'The Girl and the Gold Watches' story. He was gathering up the papers and adding his previous drafts when Harry entered with tea.

'I didn't expect to see you today,' Watson said curtly.

'Are you all right, sir? You don't look too clever. I'll fetch your breakfast. Sod of a wind out there, snow, brass monkeys.'

'Harry, you can drop the pretence.'

'Pretence?'

'That you are in any way attached to me. Or ever have been.'

The lad looked offended. 'It wasn't a pretence. I am a big admirer of your stories, sir. When they needed someone to keep an eye on you——'

'Spy,' corrected Watson. 'When they needed someone to spy on me.'

'I knew all of them adventures backwards. Knew you'd had lots of Boots and Buttons and Billys over the years. It was like I said, an honour to serve you. In my mind I was just making sure you didn't get into no mischief.'

It sounded so heartfelt Watson was taken aback. He grunted. Then he remembered the walk back through the old workings with the priest, only a lamp to guide them, and the rock walls seeming to close in on him. He supposed it had been that experience in the coffin that had triggered a sense of claustrophobia. He looked down at his fingertips. He had been rubbing his fingers together so hard the skin had come away.

'How do they manage to dig fresh graves in this weather? The ground must be frozen solid. And there is a rocky substratum once you get through that.'

'Ah, that's the clever bit, sir. There are three permanent graves, three coffins. They move the crosses around so that the Germans never realize they are using the same plots over and over. Once the men have dropped through, the coffins can be manhandled down into the tunnels later on, y'see, and then stripped down, brought up top and reassembled, see?'

'Ingenious. But don't you feel aggrieved that you can't have a go? That it is all based on the ability to pay?'

'No, sir. I wouldn't get ten miles. Can barely speak English, let alone German. Nah, that game is for officers, that is. Now you stay here, I'll get some breakfast. *Appell* isn't until eleven today, it being Sunday.'

'Is it?' He had quite lost track of the days. 'Can you drop these pages off to the colonel? For printing. They do have a printing press?'

'Of course, sir. For more than the magazine, if you get my drift.'

Of course, they would produce the false papers and travel documents needed too. 'I see. And, Harry, you'd best cancel my surgery today. I'm not up to it.'

Watson limped over to the cot bed, still using his stick for support, and lay back down on it. He had a residual headache from the blow to the head he had suffered. Why they had had to clump him was another mystery. As to why they chose to lay him out in the coffin so he thought he had been buried alive . . . Couldn't they just have *told* him about the coffins? Unless . . .

'Major Watson?'

His eyes snapped open. He had dozed off. It was Hugh Peacock, the overfed captain from next door.

'Yes?'

'I just wanted to say thank you for helping.' His eyes shone with happiness. 'The thought of getting out is all that kept me going. That and my food parcels.'

'I haven't agreed to help,' said Watson, swinging his feet off the bed and patting his hair back into place.

'But I thought as a doctor you were going to find a way to fake my death.'

'Captain Peacock, first I think there have been too many deaths here of late for another to go unnoticed. Kügel and Steigler are already suspicious. I would wait a month or two—'

'No! I am ready to go. I have signed all the papers, paid over the bribes.' The formerly cheerful features had collapsed into something like despair. He gripped Watson's shoulder. 'Look at me. Everyone says – good old Cocky, living the high life with his pâtés and his champagne. But I tell you, if I don't get out of here soon, I'll be cutting my wrists or measuring myself up for a new necktie.'

Watson gently removed the man's fingers, aware once more how raw his own were. 'Calm down, Captain. *Ich bin auch besorgt, das Ihr rundes Gesicht vielleicht machen Sie sich, sobald Sie entkommen sind. Die meisten Menschen sind dort hungern.*'

'What?'

'How is your German?'

Cocky took a deep breath and grimaced. '*Ich kann ein Bahnticket bestellen.*'

He could buy a railway ticket. It sounded like a bad ventriloquist was at work.

'Well, that's hardly fluent. And I said before that you might be a little well fed to fit in with the general populace out there.'

'We have thought of that. I have a hat with flaps that covers my cheeks.' He squashed his plump face together, making him look like a slapstick star of the moving pictures.

'And this?' Watson prodded Cocky's belly.

'A big coat will cover that. All we need is to convince them I am dead and I am as good as home.'

'As good as home? Do you know how far we are from the Swiss or Dutch borders here?'

'The others made it. All it takes is organization.'

'And money, apparently.'

'So you can't help me?'

'There is no safe way to mimic death. Not that would fool someone like Steigler.'

Harry entered with a metal tray. On it was a bowl of soup and two hunks of dark bread. The usual fare.

'Sorry to interrupt, sir, but Major Watson needs to keep his strength up.'

'Think on it. Please,' said Cocky, his eyes imploring.

'I can't help you.'

'Then I shall find someone who can.'

He stormed out, almost knocking Harry aside. 'Careful, sir,' he said as the level in the soup bowl yawed alarmingly. 'Touchy,' he said to Watson.

'Fragile,' he replied. Watson took the soup, which was thicker than usual, and broke some of the hard bread into it, letting the liquid soak into the honeycomb of crumbs.

'You've put the word out about the surgery being cancelled?'

'Yes, and it will be announced at *Appell*. Not that you'll be there, sir.'

'Why not?'

'The commandant, Mad Bill, he wants to see you as soon as you've finished breakfast.'

Mad Bill Kügel did not look best pleased when Watson was shown into his office. He was standing at the French doors, watching the sky gear up for another dump of snow. Steigler was seated by the fireplace, the smoke from his cigarette conjoining with that of the logs spitting and blazing in the hearth. His legs were crossed and he was gazing into the flames, as if in deep contemplation.

Watson stood, waiting for someone to speak, and while he did so he idly picked at the loose skin on his fingertips.

'Major Watson, I assume you did not discover what happened to the three suicides we told you about.'

'Was I meant to?' he asked innocently.

Steigler spoke up. 'The commandant felt sure your curiosity would be piqued.'

Kügel looked over his shoulder, his jaw set in irritation. His lips barely moved as he spoke. 'Professional curiosity.'

'I was never a professional investigator. Nor was Holmes. We left that to the likes of Martin Hewitt. We were not driven by a love of money.'

'So you found out nothing.'

He thought, but didn't say: *Only to expect a postcard from the—*

Steigler unfurled his legs and got to his feet. 'Are you all right, Major? You have gone quite pale.'

At last, you are thinking straight. Your fingers, Watson, look at your fingers.

He did so, the room spinning so that he had to lean on his staff once more. Steigler was in front of him, guiding him to a chair. He slumped into it. 'Can I have some water?' Watson asked.

Steigler went across to pour some from a pitcher on the drinks trolley.

And where have you been? Watson asked of his phantom friend.

Considering the facts, my old friend. It's murder, Watson. Murder. I am sure of it.

What is?

But Steigler was in front of him, holding out a glass, which he downed in one. 'Thank you.'

Kügel had moved away from the window. 'Well, no matter, it is none of our concern now. Not yours, not mine.'

'Why is that?' Watson asked.

'In two days' time there will be a full Red Cross inspection. We are, apparently, to be treated like any other prisoner of war camp from now on. Category A. There is also to be a change of commandant. I am being transferred to Berlin. Apparently they need people who are experts in the United States.'

'Well, you speak the language,' Watson said facetiously. 'And all that means an end to your fiefdom here,' he added.

Kügel gave his first smile of the meeting. There was little mirth in it. 'Oh, I've managed to put enough aside to see me through to the end of the war. Don't worry, though. You, too, will be free of this place.'

'Oh?'

'I have had word that you will be collected this afternoon for transfer. Your days at Harzgrund have come to an end.'

Not now, Watson, you need to stay and clear this up.

But Steigler's utterance silenced the nagging voice in his skull. 'Pack your things, Major. You are going to Holland.'

FORTY-FOUR

The party, driving in an Eysink four-seater hired at the Hook of Holland, stopped for lunch at an inn on the outskirts of Eindhoven. They requested a private dining room, ostensibly for business discussions, but mainly so they could manacle Miss Pillbody still in secret. Nathan and Buller were masquerading as doctors: an eminent surgeon and his young protégé. They claimed to be heading to the internment camp just south of Venlo to aid in the repatriation of the more seriously injured POWs. Miss Pillbody was kept in check prior to her shackling by the fact Buller had a revolver in his coat pocket pointed at her the whole time, and an expression that suggested he was quite keen to put a bullet in her.

While they waited for the food to appear in the wood-panelled annexe that smelled of years of cigar smoke, they shared a bottle of German wine – something that would have been frowned upon back home – and studied the map of the area around Venlo. Buller, meanwhile, chained both of Miss Pillbody's ankles to the table cross pieces.

'If that is the bridge,' said Nathan, 'then we should set up base as close as possible. The exchange might not happen tomorrow. Or the next day.'

'My feeling is that it will be tomorrow,' said Mrs Gregson.

'Are we going to try and find Sherlock Holmes before the exchange?' Buller asked. 'I am sure he will see reason when he knows we've got that—' he nodded towards Miss Pillbody — 'to offer in his place.'

'It might be worth a try,' said Mrs Gregson. 'But Holmes has a reputation for not being easy to find.'

'You know we are being followed?'

They all turned to look at Miss Pillbody, who had made the announcement.

'At least one car, possibly two. Both taken off that ferry. The Ford, I am sure about. There was a Vauxhall, too. The Ford has a registration plate of A7667. The Vauxhall, SA983.'

The three others exchanged glances.

'Why would I lie? I want to get back to Germany as much as I am sure your precious Watson wants to get home.'

Nathan considered for a moment. 'I did see a number of cars being craned on and off the ferry. It doesn't mean they are after us. "A" is a London registration I believe. But "SA"?'

'Scottish,' said Buller. 'Aberdeen, perhaps.'

'Unlikely they'd be using a Scottish car,' said Mrs Gregson. 'That must be a motor-tourist. Any theories who it might be in the Ford?'

They were interrupted by the arrival of plates of cold meats and cheese with a variety of pickles. Mrs Gregson made sure the knives and forks provided were kept well away from Miss Pillbody's end of the table. She could eat with her fingers.

Nathan, who had clearly been pondering the question, eventually came up with an answer. 'I suspect it might be Mycroft. Or Mycroft's people. After all, he won't want his brother falling into German hands if he can help it.'

Miss Pillbody gave a grunt of disbelief. They ignored her.

'So they'll want to flush him out, as we do. Would they stop us presenting Miss Pillbody here as an alternative prize?'

Nathan considered for a moment. 'I doubt it. They could have apprehended us by now.'

'Except they don't know how little we know about Holmes's whereabouts.'

'Which is nothing,' Miss Pillbody interjected.

'You might find it difficult to eat through a gag,' Mrs Gregson snapped at her.

Miss Pillbody scowled and folded a large circle of ham into her mouth.

'Should we disable the Ford?' Mrs Gregson asked. 'It is probably somewhere around here.'

'The problem is,' said Buller, tapping the map, 'they probably know where we are going.'

'And,' added Nathan, 'they'd soon have another car from Eindhoven.'

'And it is entirely possible,' said Mrs Gregson after a little reflection, 'that they are on our side.'

Nathan's reply was drowned out by the sound of snorting derision coming from Miss Pillbody.

'What is so funny?' demanded Mrs Gregson.

'Nothing, really,' she said eventually after thumping her chest to aid her digestion. 'It's that I've only just realized.'

'Realized what?'

'You people don't have a clue what you are getting yourselves into.'

After his meeting with Kügel and Steigler, Watson was escorted back to the compound, where he hurried as fast as he could back to the hut, leaning heavily on the staff as he went, thus leaving strange tracks in the snow that even Sherlock might struggle to interpret. His mind was whirling like the flakes falling around him. And what was his phantom voice offering?

Gold!

Over and over again, like a demented forty-niner.

As he crossed the compound he saw a group of prisoners tramping the ground in a line four abreast, pressing down the snow. Watching them was Henry Lincoln-Chance and at his feet what looked like a sled. Ah, yes, the conqueror of the Cresta Run at St Moritz was creating an ice run down the slope of the ground.

Watson burst into the hut and indicated that Captain Peacock should follow him into his surgery/billet. Cocky raised his eyebrows in hope but Watson gave a barely perceptible shake of the head.

Once inside, Watson pulled the curtain and kept his voice low but urgent. 'Cocky, you mustn't go.'

'Go? Go where?'

'You mustn't try and escape. It's a trick.'

'Well, it fools the Germans all right,' he beamed.

Watson gripped him by his plump arm, trying to convey the gravity of the situation. 'I don't know why or how, but I don't think anyone gets home. I think they are done away with en route. Perhaps a German betrays them or kills them.'

'What? Why? Why go to all this trouble . . . ?'

Gold!

'Oh, be quiet. No, not you, Cocky. Why? Money. You pay for the escape service, don't you?'

'Yes.'

'Well, what if there isn't a network of helpers, railwaymen, border guards to be bribed? What if you don't get more than a mile? What if . . . Good Lord.'

'What?'

Watson backed to his flimsy chair and sat, his left hand stroking his stubble. 'The Russian camp up the road. What if the escapees are delivered there? It's not a POW camp at all, it's simply a . . . a *death* camp.'

'Look, Major, I've done a dry run. I've seen how it works. Seen freedom. Smelled it. What proof do you have of this monstrous accusation?'

'The Coburg Hotel.'

Peacock shook his head. 'Now you really aren't making sense.'

'Brevette, the last to escape before the deaths of the three from the séance.'

'Yes?'

'There is a postcard from him purportedly written from the Coburg three or four weeks ago.'

'Your point being?' asked Peacock.

Watson stood again, excited that at least one of the whirling jigsaw pieces had made it onto the board. 'Some time ago I received a letter from a friend. I kept it . . .' Watson rummaged among the few precious possessions he still had, letters from Holmes and Mrs Gregson being a substantial part of them. 'Here. It was when I was at Krefeld.' He read out the penultimate paragraph. '"Let us hope the war is over soon and we can all be together. Dinner at the Connaught (as they call the Coburg now), says Mr Holmes. Doesn't that sound grand?"' You see? They changed the name of the hotel. It comes from Saxe-Coburg-Gotha – it might be the Royal name, but it's just too German for these times.'

'Perhaps it was an old postcard.'

'Perhaps,' said Watson without conviction. 'But you can't take that chance. There is a new commandant on the way. Red Cross inspections. Everything will change. For the better.'

'Everything will change if I stay here, Major.'

The tone of sadness made Watson look into Peacock's face. His eyes had filled with tears. 'What is it, man?'

'I have . . . had a fiancée. Margery. Margery Godman. Of the Esher Godmans.'

'I'm not familiar with them.'

'Father is Sherard Haughton Godman. A respected land-owner in those parts. He didn't like me at first. Thought I was a wastrel. It's why I joined the army. He's Scots Guards, y'see. Anyway, he gave his blessing just before I left for France. The thought of Margery has kept me going but . . . well, my older brother has been paying her court. Of late her letters have cooled somewhat.'

'Your brother? Isn't that a rather underhand thing to do? Not the action of a gentleman.'

Peacock gave a bitter laugh. 'My brother is no gentleman. He has a nervous condition that has kept him out of the war. The condition being that he is nervous he might get killed or maimed. But we have a compliant family doctor. So he works for the Treasury on War Bonds issue. And meanwhile makes love to my fiancée.'

Watson had heard similar stories too many times to be shocked. It was startling how many of his patients at the camps had emotional rather than physical ailments. As a doctor concerned with body rather than mind, it often tested his expertise to the limit. 'I can offer little comfort there, apart from the fact than I suspect upon your return she will see the error of her ways. In my experience, women do eventually see through the facile blandishments of hollow men. And your brother does sound hollow.'

'As a reed,' Peacock said. He patted his belly. 'But also as thin as one. Unlike me. So you see I must grasp any chance to leave. You bring me proof that this is but a cruel trick, and I will, of course, reconsider. But, for the moment, I shall continue with my plans.'

'When are you meant to go?'

'Tonight.'

'But you have no way of imitating your death.'

Peacock wiped his eyes and straightened his clothes. 'Link says he has bribed the German doctor for a catatonic potion.'

Watson wasn't sure which of the questions clamouring for his attention to ask first. 'Which German doctor?'

'Steiglitz, is it?'

'Steigler. There is no such thing as a catatonic potion.'

'Link says it is an Italian draught. The same one Juliet used.'

'Juliet?'

'In *Romeo and Juliet*.'

Watson suppressed the urge to laugh in his face at such naïvety. 'That is a fiction, Hugh. There's no such potion.'

'Pent— something, he said.'

'Pentolinium?'

'That's the chappie.'

Watson had come across it while researching blood transfusions. It was some kind of nerve agent that lowered heartbeat and relaxed muscles. But he had never heard of it as a coma-inducing drug. Although he had to admit he was some years behind in his reading of the *Lancet*. It was possible there was a new application.

'One, I would be very careful of any drug that interfered with human metabolism. And two, how did Lincoln-Chance get to know Steigler?'

'St Moritz.'

'Explain,' demanded Watson.

'He and Steigler met before the war. They luged and bobsleighed together.'

'I don't like the sound of that,' said Watson, a sinking feeling spreading across his insides. 'Don't like the sound of it at all. I think we have all been fooled.'

The curtain switched back and Harry's face appeared. 'Sorry to interrupt, Major Watson, the commandant sends his compliments. Your transport is here. Whenever you are ready . . .'

'I shall be a while longer. I need time . . .'

Harry shrugged. 'You don't want it leaving without you, Major.'

'Thank you, Harry.' Watson turned to Peacock once the face at the curtain had disappeared. 'Will you consider what I have said?'

Peacock nodded but it wasn't convincing. 'But thank you for your concern.'

'One thing before you go. You said earlier that you had signed the papers. What papers? An IOU?'

'No,' said Peacock breezily. 'Just a new will, in case anything should go wrong. To make sure all the monies due are paid no matter what happens to me.'

When Peacock had departed Watson put his head into his hands. His cranium felt like it might burst, such was the pandemonium of conflicting voices and images within it. Then, one clear, incisive articulation elbowed its way to the fore.

A new will, Watson? A new will? I don't have to tell you what an instrument for infamy a new will can be. Mark my words, some of these men have found a way to make others' lust for freedom pay. And pay handsomely. All you need now is to know who is perpetrating this monstrosity. And how.

He thought on those two ponderables for a few minutes before he roused himself and searched the drawers and the cupboard in the room. Tucked away at the rear of the latter he found what he was looking for, a number 22 scalpel from Dräger.

FORTY-FIVE

One of Mycroft's contacts from The Hague was waiting for them in Venlo. His name was Victor Farleigh and he had an avuncular chumminess that Mrs Gregson suspected, as was so often the case with the intelligence community, hid a core of steel. Farleigh watched with some bemusement as they shackled Miss Pillbody to the bed in one of the rooms of the house he had rented for them to the north of the city.

'Is that entirely necessary?' he asked.

Miss Pillbody gave him a wry smile in return.

'It is,' said Mrs Gregson once she was certain the locks and links were secure. It was arranged that she had some power of movement, the chain to her right hand being a decent length, but unless she took the bed with her, she was going nowhere. 'England is littered with the corpses of those who took Miss Pillbody, Ilse Brandt, at face value.'

'Do you think we could have a moment, Mrs Gregson?' Miss Pillbody asked. 'I need to talk about . . . women's matters.'

'What sort of women's matters?'

'The sort that men don't want to hear about.'

She looked at the other three. 'Buller, can you wait outside? With your gun at the ready? Robert, perhaps you'll put some coffee on downstairs for Mr Farleigh. I'm sure I won't be long.'

When the three had left, Mrs Gregson turned to Miss Pillbody. 'Yes?'

'Does it not offend you to see me like this?' She rattled her chains. 'Pinned like an animal?'

'You forget, I saw your handiwork in Suffolk. I saw what you did to poor Mr Coyle.' Coyle had been an MI5 man who had unearthed Miss Pillbody's secret – that she was not an innocent schoolma'am but a German spy – and had paid for his life with it.

'I don't forget any such thing. It's a war, Mrs Gregson. I fought it in my own way. Do you not think there is a British equivalent of me deep in Germany at this very moment? Plotting to kill my countrymen and women? It's the way wars will be fought in future. It is no different to the trenches that you know so well. I wish to be treated with respect, particularly as I am . . . due.'

'Due?'

'Due. Do I have to paint you a picture? In red?'

'Ah. I see.'

'I wondered if you could get me some Hartmann's or something similar. I am sure Dutch women have the same, um, issues.'

'I will see what I can do,' Mrs Gregson said.

'Thank you.' Miss Pillbody hesitated for a moment. 'It was nothing personal, you know, those men. In Suffolk.'

'Are you saying you didn't enjoy it?'

'I am. I felt nothing.'

'That could be even worse.'

'In the same way I won't feel anything if I have to kill you.' This came with a smile bordering on the angelic.

Mrs Gregson returned her gaze. There was no connection she could feel, no sympathy for another human being. Just an emptiness inside that disturbed her. 'And I don't think I would feel anything if I had to do the same to you,' she said.

Miss Pillbody gave a firm nod. 'Then we know where we both stand.'

'I'll see about the pads,' Mrs Gregson said. 'Wouldn't want you ruining a perfectly decent VAD uniform.'

She left, half-expecting to feel the steel of sharp daggers in her back, and sent Buller into the room with instructions to keep his distance and his weapon at the ready.

Downstairs, the kitchen smelled of coffee and Farleigh's pungent Dutch cigarillos.

'All all right?' Nathan asked.

'Yes. I might have to find a chemist is all.'

'We were just saying, Mycroft is obviously concerned for his brother,' Farleigh began.

'Is he here?' she asked. 'In Holland.'

'No.'

'Not that concerned then.'

Farleigh sounded offended. 'Fieldwork is hardly Mycroft's forte. He has mustered considerable resources to track down Sherlock.'

'I assume all hotels, guesthouses and so on have been checked?' asked Nathan.

'Twice over. Especially in the vicinity of the bridge. I fear we can do nothing but keep an eye on that and try to intercept Holmes before he crosses. Without alarming the Dutch who, of course, want no part of this.'

'We think we might have been followed. From the port. A Ford. Any ideas?' asked Nathan.

Farleigh shook his head. 'I'll have a scout around.'

Mrs Gregson poured and handed out the treacly coffee. 'Has there been much activity around the bridge?'

'On the German side, yes. There appears to be some sort of moving picture outfit involved.'

Nathan and Mrs Gregson exchanged glances.

'What is it?' Farleigh asked.

'Just that Mrs Gregson here used moving pictures to facilitate Miss Pillbody's escape from Holloway.'

'Escape? Really? You mean she wasn't released through the usual channels?'

'There are no usual channels for what we are doing, Mr Farleigh,' said Mrs Gregson. 'And besides, time was of the essence. Official channels are not renowned for their speed of action. So we used a little sleight of hand.'

'Well, I am not sure the German cameras are up to any tricks. They moved the equipment around quite openly when I was observing. Perhaps you should take a look for yourself.'

'Perhaps we should,' said Nathan. 'You'll come with us?'

Farleigh shook his head. 'Best if you take the car and drive past slowly, a married couple out for some air. I'll stay here and finish my coffee. When you get back we can discuss the fine details.'

'Did you see any lights?' asked Mrs Gregson.

'Lights?'

'For cameras. There'd be rather a lot of them.'

Farleigh shook his head. 'Why?'

She drained her coffee. 'Let's go and take a look, Robert.'

'Of course. I'll just go and check Miss Pillbody is on a very short leash.'

'Good idea.'

After days of imagining the crossing, Mrs Gregson was disappointed by the sight of the bridge and the river beneath it. In her mind it had been something equivalent to the Forth Railway crossing, a span of fearsome grandeur. In truth it was more a pedestrian bridge, wide enough for a large motor or a small lorry to cross, but only one at a time: a single lane into and out of Germany. The river, too, was wide and brown and sluggish and had been dredged and widened, so it looked more like a giant man-made canal than one of Europe's major waterways. There were strings of barges being towed by tugboats but also quite large coastal steamers that, thanks to the vagaries of the border, were crossing from Dutch waters into German and back into Dutch sovereignty again. It was clearly too complex to try to institute border controls in mid-stream.

'Can you stop the car?' she asked Nathan as they approached the still-folded bridge. 'I can't really see what is happening over there.'

Nathan pulled over and she got out. She stretched a little, like a cat confined in a cramped space too long, and strolled towards the crossing. The horizon was huge, like East Anglia, she thought, or the view out from the Essex marshes. The sky was mostly lumpy and grey, with dark bruises here and there that threatened rain.

She gazed over the sludge-coloured river, which looked toxic to her. On the far side there were small clumps of people – soldiers guarding a striped pole, a truck with the words UVF painted on the panelled sides, and a cluster of civilians near it. She stepped out onto the wooden boards, careful to keep her skirt down with one hand as the wind tugged at her clothing, the other planted firmly on her hat.

Where are you, John Watson? she wondered. Are you here yet, perhaps a few miles away, waiting for the crossing? Do you know what they have in store for you? If not, how much of a shock will it be to see Holmes striding towards you? And how heartbreaking for that reunion to be so fleeting, as each man continues on his way.

No, she couldn't let that happen. They had to find Holmes before that moment and stop him. She and Nathan had discussed how and they had agreed that, if need be, they would incapacitate Holmes with a shot to the leg. Risky, but she had tended many bullet wounds in her time. It was only to be used *in extremis*, but there was no alternative she could think of.

She looked down at a small rowing boat making its way upstream with two young men putting their backs into it. Of course, Holmes might get across some way other than the bridge and circumvent the whole business. But something told her he would stick to the procedure. That he might even enjoy a touch of showmanship. The Holmes in Watson's stories certainly did, although, as she had discovered very slowly, the man on the page and the man in the flesh didn't always entirely match up.

'*Wat doe je daar?*' asked a harsh, guttural voice from behind. She turned to see an elderly worker in blue serge jacket and cap. He waved at her with his pipe stem. '*Het is privé-eigendom.*'

Her Dutch wasn't up to much, but she assumed he was telling her it was private property. The man pointed to a sign high on one of the girders. *Privé*. Close enough to English to be pretty clear, she thought. 'I'm sorry. I didn't see that.'

The man grunted and stepped aside, indicating she should get off. She was aware of eyes on her from the far bank and when she turned a German – or so she assumed – in a long woollen coat was inspecting her. He raised field glasses to his eyes and she turned her back to him, the hairs on her neck prickling under this distant examination.

She hurried back to the car and told Nathan to drive off. 'Who was that?' he asked as he turned the vehicle around.

'The bridge man, I think. But I could see no sign of German lights, at least not big ones.'

'Meaning?'

Mrs Gregson took off her hat and ran fingers through her tangled hair. 'Why would they want to film this event?'

Nathan considered. 'To gloat.'

'Propaganda, yes. Which means they'll want good, clear shots. Those cameras need very, very bright lights or daylight. So if they haven't got artificial ones, they'll wait for sunrise.'

'Meaning?'

'The handover will be after eight o'clock, which is when it gets light at this time of year.'

'I see.'

'I could be wrong, but I wouldn't expect them to appear with John much before eight fifteen.'

'All right,' said Nathan. 'But we'll ask Farleigh to post a night-watchman just in case.'

'Good idea. And we should be in place with Miss Pillbody by seven tomorrow. And every day until it happens.'

'Agreed.'

Feeling more settled now there was some sort of timetable in place, Mrs Gregson kept silent until they had retraced their steps to the house.

'Robert . . .' she said as they got out of the car.

'Yes?'

'I know I have said it before. But I do think you are a sweet-heart for . . . well, not every man would do this for me.'

'Oh, you'd be surprised,' said Nathan wryly. 'But you are very welcome. And I hope you will reconsider that dinner when we are all safely back home.'

Where would be the harm? she thought as she pushed open the door that led to the kitchen. She could let him down gently then. 'Of course. Oh, damn.'

'What is it?'

'I forgot to go to the chemist. Oh well, I'll just boil up some rags for her. Shall I put some more coffee on? It might be a long night. Mr Farleigh? Mr Farleigh?'

Nathan put a hand on her shoulder to quieten her. He had his Webley self-loader in the other. The kitchen was empty, although Farleigh's chair had been knocked over onto the tiled floor. Some of the coffee had been carelessly slopped on the table.

Perhaps it was Holmes, she thought. He must be lurking around here somewhere. It was entirely possible he would try to thwart them so he could continue with his own agenda. He might have outwitted them once more. She uttered a small curse under her breath, or so she thought.

'Shush. Wait here,' hissed Nathan.

As he moved softly over to the hallway and stairs, Mrs Gregson crossed to the dresser, opened the knife drawer and selected a long boning blade. And then it hit her; the memory of another cottage in Suffolk, when Miss Pillbody had been unmasked as a Sie Wölfe, and the little surprise she had left for them, secreted under the body of poor Coyle. A booby trap. She could easily have done something similar here.

'Nathan!' she shouted. 'Be careful. There might be——'

But he was standing in the doorway, the colour gone from his face.

'Nathan?'

'Don't go up there,' he said, an uncharacteristic tremor in his voice.

As if a mental transference had taken place she could see the scene – the empty shackles, the slumped bodies. The smears of menstrual blood on sheets that Miss Pillbody would have used to alarm her captors and lure them in. 'They're dead, aren't they?'

'Buller and Farleigh, yes. But worse than that——'

'I know,' said Mrs Gregson, replacing the knife in its compartment. 'She took the keys to the locks from Buller. Miss Pillbody's gone.'

⋆   ⋆   ⋆

The tower stood bleak and forlorn, its grey concrete walls seeming black in the low winter light. It was a few hundred yards inside German territory, beyond two sets of wire fences and a good half a kilometre or more from any other building. Once it had looked east, watching for invaders seeking to take land from the Dutch. And that had come to pass, albeit by opportunistic political not military means, so that now the watchtower lay stranded in enemy – or at least, potentially hostile – territory.

Captain Carlisle, Sergeant Balsom and Ernst Bloch stood staring at the monolith from the Dutch side, beside the Ford that had come over with them on the ferry from England. Each smoked a cigarette, lost in his own thoughts for a few moments. To their left, a kilometre away, was the bridge over the Meuse where the exchange would take place. To the south, the town of Venlo and ahead, beyond the muddy river, lay the country and the woman that Bloch longed to rejoin.

In time they were joined by a fourth man who introduced himself as Jasper. He was in his twenties, dressed in coarse clothes and with workers' hands and fingernails. His English, though, was surprisingly good and unaccented.

'That's where you want to go?' the Dutchman asked as he lit his own cigarette and inclined his head towards the watchtower. 'The *uitkijktoren*?'

'It is,' said Carlisle. 'Is it inhabited?'

'By crows and bats,' said Jasper. 'We *spoken* use it as a landmark when crossing. Head down in some of the drainage ditches around here, you can become very disoriented.'

'*Spoken*?' asked Bloch, unfamiliar with the word.

'*Geister*. Ghosts. The men who cross the border. The men who stop Germany from starving.'

'For a price,' said Bloch.

Jasper stopped the cigarette halfway to his lips. He looked at Carlisle. 'This one is German?'

'He's the package.'

'The price will have to increase.'

'Now look here—' Balsom began, stepping forward as if to grab the man's lapels.

'As you were, Sergeant,' snapped Carlisle. 'Jasper comes highly recommended by our people. He's got many British escapees over that water and back home. Isn't that right, Jasper?'

The Dutchman didn't answer, apart from a confirming raise of the eyebrows as he puffed on his cigarette.

'I am sure there is a valid reason for the price increase,' Carlisle said, although an edge to his voice suggested a qualifier of: *there'd better be*.

'I assume you have good reason for him not just turning up at a crossing post. There's plenty to choose from.'

'We have,' agreed Carlisle. 'There might be too many questions. He might be detained. We don't want him detained.'

'Understandable. If they even suspect he might have been turned around by British Intelligence he will be shipped straight to Dusseldorf for interrogation.'

'I have not been turned around,' Bloch protested.

'Of course not. All German POWs spend time with British officers and NCOs at the border, looking up at the single vantage point that gives an overview of the whole area. Look, I'm not interested in what you are doing. But it is in my interest that you do it and get clean away. It helps my reputation . . .' He glanced at Carlisle. 'With potential employers. Furthermore, if you were captured you might mention this name – not my real one, but nevertheless – and give a description. I don't want some German kill squad coming over to shoot me while I sleep. Or setting up a trap so they can get me on the other side and take me to those cells in Dusseldorf. From what I hear, they are none too pleasant.'

All that made sense to Bloch, so he said nothing.

Jasper returned his attention to Carlisle. 'He has his identification papers?'

'Yes.'

'Good ones?' asked Jasper.

'Very good – they are the ones he was captured with. The mud and blood on them tell their own story.'

'And a documented reason for release from British custody?'

'Indeed.'

'Which is?'

Carlisle cleared his throat. He hadn't shared this with Bloch yet. Balsom had a grin on his face. 'Mental health problems.'

'What?' asked Bloch. 'I'm mad now, am I?'

'We can still do the scooping out of the eye if you'd rather,' said Balsom, with another little pantomime. 'Not too late.'

But Bloch already knew why they had gone down that route. If anything went wrong and he fell into German hands before the execution of Holmes – or indeed immediately afterwards – the British would claim the man was clearly more insane than they had thought. As if they would release someone they thought was going to shoot their own man.

'The price goes up,' said Jasper, more to Balsom than anybody else, 'because his papers must include a border stamp on the German side, to explain why he is over that side of the river. Preferably from the crossing point at Aachen. That's so busy, nobody would remember who stamped what. But that will take time and money. You haven't got much time, so we need to throw more money at it. Understood?'

The three others nodded.

'Luggage?'

'Yes,' said Carlisle. 'Two bags.'

'Money?'

'Not excessive.'

'So no gold or silver or any valuables?'

'No.'

'That makes it easier. Some people get mighty greedy when they know a package is being carried. Weapons?'

'Yes.'

Jasper paused and stroked his stubble. 'There is a crossing at midnight plus twenty. We can add you to that. It is mostly food being taken across, black-market stuff, and we leave some for the German patrols, so they rarely bother us. They'll be there, but they'll have their blind eyes on. It takes place three kilometres down there, at a spot called Grubbenvorst, so you'll have to work your way back without being seen, then climb that tower in darkness. It is on the other side of the border fence, but we can get you through there. Can you do that?'

Bloch said he could.

'We meet at Grubbenvorst church, the eastern side. In the graveyard. I'll have crossing papers, you have an extra fifteen per cent to cover that. All clear?'

When they said it was, Jasper, without a goodbye or a hand-shake, turned and walked off, shoulders hunched, puffing on the last of his cigarette.

'What now?' asked Bloch.

'You rest up.'

'I must check the weapon.'

'As you wish. Check the weapon, rest up, have something to eat. At midnight we'll be at the church. Within eight or nine hours, with any luck, you'll be a free man.'

'And Sherlock Holmes will be dead,' Bloch added, just in case there was a misunderstanding.

Carlisle grimaced a little. He didn't like mission objectives voiced. It was bad luck. He shaded his eyes and looked back down river to the spindly bridge. 'Yes. I suppose Sherlock Holmes will be dead.'

FORTY-SIX

It was probably a very foolish response, but Watson could think of no other course of action and time was short. He stormed, as best he could with a stick and through thick snow, across to Colonel Critchley's office, where the senior camp officer was in conversation with a lieutenant whom Watson didn't recognize.

'The game is up, Critchley,' he announced.

'Lieutenant, can you excuse us a moment?'

'Sir.' The man left and closed the door behind him.

'I thought you were on your way, Watson?'

'You despicable man. How can you sanction this?'

Critchley took out a block of tobacco from his desk, broke a piece off and began rubbing it between his palms. 'What are you talking about, Major?'

'This so-called Escape Committee. There are no escapes. Nobody makes it home.'

Satisfied with the pile of shreds before him, Critchley fetched his pipe from a rack. 'What are you talking about?'

'I don't know the details, but I know I shall be reporting this as soon as I get anywhere near the British authorities. You'll hang for this, Critchley.'

'Now look here, Watson. I don't know what has caused this outburst, but I would appreciate it if you tempered your language. Hang? What the devil are you talking about?'

'I am talking about a cruel deception. I am talking about greed. Avarice. I am talking about the murder of your fellow countrymen.'

Critchley lit the pipe and gave a condescending smile. 'Nobody has been murdered. We have had a successful subterfuge operating here—'

'Do you deny that Lincoln-Chance and Steigler know each other of old?'

A puzzled frown. 'No. I don't deny it. The British and Germans did mix before the war. Especially the officer class. You know that. I do believe you had some dealings with the King of Bohemia.'

'Never mind that. The hotel is no longer called the Coburg.'

'What?'

'The Coburg has changed its name to the Connaught. How can Brevette's card have come from there?'

'I—'

'Who received the card?'

'Why, Link of course.'

'Of course,' Watson sneered. 'And Archer had to die, because he knew that Brevette was dead.'

Critchley's face flushed. 'Listen to yourself, man. Archer knew Brevette was dead? How? Through a séance? You are basing all this on a piece of charlatanism being reliable? You believe, do you? That voices speak from the other side?'

Watson found his jaw working but no words coming. The wind dropped from his sails somewhat. 'I . . . no, but I am sure that you are deceiving the escapees.'

Critchley waved the stem of the pipe at him. 'I am proud that we have got men home, Watson. Damned proud. And you come in here, making wild accusations. I thought you were some sort of detective. But no, I think you have shown where the talent in your partnership with Mr Holmes lay. And it wasn't with you.'

The anger, Watson appreciated, seemed quite genuine. Either Critchley didn't know what was going on right under his nose – and feet – or he was a brilliant actor.

'I think you should stop Peacock going. Just in case.'

'Just in case of what? Who knows when we can next send someone out, what with the change of, um, management? And Cocky needs to get home, or there will be a death. His own. Do you understand?'

'I understand that you are not willing to listen—'

'I am not prepared to listen to tosh and misguided speculation. Why would someone set up an escape route and kill the people they send down the line?'

'Money. The escapees pay through the nose.'

'Link is a very rich man. He has no need of money. All that cash goes in bribes and expenses.'

'There are no bribes. No expenses.'

'So you claim.'

Watson banged the desk in frustration, as if he could knock some sense into the man. 'And the escapees make out a new will. And give power of probate and attorney. They are executors. Once they are home, Link can strip the family fortune.'

'Oh, for goodness' sake. These are Englishmen you are talking about. Englishmen! Get out, man. Get out and get to Holland and go home. Your mind has gone.'

'But—'

'No more, Watson. Do you hear? No more. If you wish to make your wild accusations, so be it. But make them somewhere else.'

Critchley clamped the pipe between his teeth and began a self-conscious study of the papers on his desk. After a few moments he looked up, as if surprised to see Watson still there. 'Safe journey, Major. I'm afraid I can no longer guarantee your story will appear in the next issue of the magazine.'

'You are either very naïve or very stupid, Colonel.'

Possibly both, Watson.

Watson turned and left. As he walked across the snow he could see Lincoln-Chance and Boxhall watching his progress from the shadow of a hut. Link raised a hand as if in farewell, but Watson simply glowered and carried on towards his hut to collect his things. It was time to leave the field, to fight another day.

The right thing to do, my old friend.

That's as maybe, thought Watson, but it doesn't make it feel any less wrong. Or cowardly.

Waiting for him at the gate were a number of familiar faces. Steigler was there, as if to see him off the premises, but also the young guard with the missing fingers, and Gunther, the older man – the pair responsible for Sayer's death – and, at idle, the Horch lorry, with its wheezing and grumbling at tick-over seemingly worse than a few days before. The driver – if it was the same one – had clearly overcome his fear of typhoid and had brought the truck all the way up to the camp entrance. The snowfall had slackened but it was still thick underfoot and Watson had to be careful not to slip. He wanted to depart with some dignity at least.

'Dr Watson!'

He turned to see Harry standing at the gate, a German soldier blocking his way. 'I just wanted you to sign this for me.' The orderly held up a battered copy of *A Study in Scarlet*.

'Let him through,' said Steigler. 'Get a move on, Harry. Major Watson has to be going.'

'Do you know what you are doing?' Watson asked under his breath. 'Getting involved with Lincoln-Chance's schemes?'

'He is paying me handsomely,' said the German. 'The game is up here, Watson. You know that. You can take that look off your face. *Populus me sibilat, at mihi plaudo, Ipse domi stimul ac nummos contemplar in arca.*'

'Don't quote my own epigrams back at me,' Watson replied curtly.

'Thank you, Dr Watson,' said a breathless Harry, holding up the book. 'I have a pen.'

'What do you want me to write?'

'Not what he said anyway. My Latin isn't that clever.'

Watson obliged. 'The public hiss at me, but I cheer myself when in my own house I contemplate the coins in my strong-box.'

Harry shook his head. 'I don't want that.'

Steigler laughed. '*Es könnte am besten geeignet.*'

'No it isn't,' said Harry with some irritation.

'No. It's a despicable sentiment.' Watson thought for a moment and wrote: 'What you do in this world is a matter of no consequence. The question is what you can make people believe you have done.' And then he signed it and handed his first novel back to Harry.

'Thank you. What's it mean?'

'Ask the doctor here,' said Watson. 'Goodbye, Harry. Stay safe.'

'You too, sir.'

Steigler watched in silence as Watson threw his kitbag and walking stick into the truck and, refusing any help, climbed up into the truck. The two Germans followed suit and Steigler walked across to help push up the wooden tailgate and bolt it in place. 'Have a good journey,' Steigler said. 'Give my regards to Holland.'

'I know what you are now, Herr Doctor. Does Kügel?'

Steigler kept his voice low, nonchalantly brushing snow from his shoulders as he spoke. 'The commandant is happy as long as his bank balance is kept healthy. His interest in the three dead men was . . . atypical. Is that the word? Quite unusual. I assured him you would solve the problem . . .'

'But thinking I wouldn't?'

Steigler gave a smile. 'Yes. And I was correct, wasn't I? You haven't solved anything, Major Watson. Not a thing. I have heard about your wild speculations that we trap escaped prisoners en route. Nothing could be further from the truth.' He began to chortle to himself, a horrible sound to Watson's ears. 'You haven't got a damned thing.'

He banged on the side of the truck, the driver engaged first gear and Watson watched Steigler shrink to a small figure at the gate, waving occasionally as if seeing a relative off on holiday at the station. Watson glanced at the two German guards, wondering if he was about to suffer the same fate as Sayer on some lonely stretch of forest road.

'We will be some hours,' said Gunther, as if reading his mind. 'Make comfortable. We were told you are special property this time.'

The younger German rolled a cigarette and offered it to Watson, who shook his head. The lad shrugged and lit it for himself. The other guard took out his pipe and ignited that. Watson closed his eyes, feigning sleep, and let his mind race away up blind alleys and dead ends.

Outside, the grainy light of late afternoon was coalescing into darkness. After forty minutes of being tossed around, as they were still descending, but beyond the blasted and treeless zone, he said, 'I need to go.'

'Go?' asked the old man.

'*Mach wasser*,' Watson said, with a little mime thrown in for good measure.

The young German said something along the lines of he should have gone before they set off. The other said something about an old man's *Blase*, which made Fingerless laugh. Bladder, Watson assumed. The young man worked his way to the front of the lorry and hammered on the dividing wall with the cab. The engine changed pitch, the gearbox whined and the Horch came to a trembling halt. Watson could see the twin regiments of snow-covered pine trees that lined either side of the road. It looked like the spot where Sayer was killed. But then, so did every kilometre of that particular stretch of road.

'Be quick,' said the old man.

Watson followed the younger guard down onto the icy road surface and, leaning on his cane, headed off for the trees.

'Here!' the guard said. Watson glared at him and carried on to the treeline. 'Halt.'

Watson did another mime, this time pointing to his backside and squatting. The younger man laughed. Watson carried on trudging into the privacy of the woods, with the German bringing up the rear.

'Now!' Fingerless shouted, when the white silence had enveloped them. Watson pointed to a thick trunk with his stick and indicated he would go around the other side. The German nodded.

Once there he undid two things, his trousers, and the ferrule from the walking stick. Then he waited, watching his breath smoke in the still air.

'Finish?' the guard asked.

Watson gave a grunt.

'Finish. Now.'

Watson half-emerged, one hand on the trunk of the pine, breathing hard. He groaned and held his stomach. He shook his head to show he couldn't move.

'No. Come.' Fingerless sounded panicked.

The guard stepped in close. That was when Watson used the carefully sharpened end of his walking stick – a point, created by the Dräger scalpel, carefully hidden under the brass ferrule – to drive the pointed wood into flesh and bone.

Snow had begun to swirl from the black sky once more and Gunther was taking shelter, contemplating his pipe when he saw Watson's face appear at the rear of the truck. He held out a hand to pull him up. Watson responded with a Mauser rifle aimed at the man's chest and a finger pressed briefly to his lips.

The guard's eyes darted to the trees, hoping that his young companion would be on hand to club Watson to the ground. Then he appreciated where the rifle must have come from.

'*Tot?*' he asked.

Was the lad dead? Watson dodged the question.

'I'm not going to kill you,' he said in a low voice, even though he was certain the driver couldn't hear him over the thud and rattle of the idling engine.

'No?'

'No. Just do as I say.' Watson, resting the weighty Mauser on the floor of the lorry, but keeping his finger on the trigger, made a series of signs. The guard nodded. He handed over his rifle and the Luger pistol he had in a holster at his belt. Then Watson snapped his fingers and mimed turning a key. The guard understood. He handed over a bunch and, without further instruction, snapped his right hand into one of the dangling shackles.

Watson placed the two rifles on the ground and examined the Luger. There was a small lever with the word *gesichert* next to it. *Sicher* meant safe, so he assumed this indicated 'safety on' or something similar. He moved the lever and a red dot appeared.

That was when he heard the sound of the approaching vehicle, coming down the road behind them.

He pointed the barrel of the Luger at the guard and put a finger to his lips. Gunther nodded again at the implicit threat. Then, holding his loose trousers up with his left hand Watson skirted around the truck so he was on the tree side of the vehicle.

There was a door mirror there, but it was cracked and covered in a light dusting of snow. The chances of being spotted by the driver were slim.

The newcomer was a car, not a lorry full of troops, of that he was sure, for it had a lively engine with a pleasingly high note compared to the old thumper in the truck. The driver could reach a decent speed on the ice and Watson surmised he would be in no mood to stop.

Sure enough, the whining increased in volume until the vehicle was level and then thrummed by. Watson had let out a breath of relief when he heard the brakes engage and the shush of tyres slithering on snow. The saloon had stopped. The gears crunched into reverse and the wheels spun for a second before finding grip.

Watson ducked under the truck. Crouching down, he could see the wheels and the panting exhaust. '*Etwas falsch?*' shouted the car's driver.

There came the squeak of the lorry's window being pulled down. '*Bitte?*'

'*Was falsch ist?*' the other repeated. '*Sie Hilfe benötigen?*'

'*Nein. Toilettenpause,*' the driver said. Toilet break. '*Danke.*'

'*Vorsichtig sein, von dem Hügel in Thürgin. Es wird sehr eisig.*'

'*Ich werde. Danke.*'

Something about an icy hill ahead, Watson half-translated. Just a concerned fellow traveller. Sure enough, the car moved off, slowly at first and, once the tyres had bite, speeded up, the engine note climbing and descending with each gear change.

Watson opened the passenger door and, as sprightly as he could manage, climbed in next to the driver, gun held steady.

The driver's eyes widened and his hands went up. He was not the walnut-faced man who had brought him to Harzgrund. This was another, barely into his twenties.

Watson reached over and took the cigarette that was stuck to his lower lip.

'*Tun Sie was ich sage, und du wirst leben. Verstehen Sie?*' he said. Do what I say, and you will live.

The lad had turned quite pale at the threat and he nodded more vigorously than was necessary. His nerves were audible when he spoke. '*Was soll ich tun möchte?*'

'What I want you to do is turn the lorry around.'

'Huh?'

Watson raised the gun to eye level so the driver was staring down the barrel. '*Wenden Sie das Fahrzeug.*'

'OK. OK. *Sie sind der Chef. Aber warum?*'

'*Wir gehen zurück zum Lager.*'

We're going back to the camp.

FORTY-SEVEN

'We have nothing to offer now,' said Mrs Gregson, staring at the two bodies in the bedroom. Buller was sprawled on the bed, his throat cut, having leaked so much blood it was difficult for her to ascertain whether her theory about the methods Miss Pillbody had used to lure him in close were correct. No matter. She had managed to get Buller in within striking range, near enough to grab him and slice through skin, cartilage and blood vessels. The cut-down shotgun he favoured lay next to him.

Victor Farleigh was lying outstretched by the door. He had been killed with a piece of cutlery. Exactly what it was – spoon, fork or knife – wasn't clear because only the handle was protruding from the eye socket. But it had been driven in with considerable force.

'He's been shot as well,' said Nathan, pointing to a burned patch on his jacket. He flipped the coat open to reveal a leather harness that would have held a pistol. 'So now she has a gun.'

'How did she manage it? I was so careful. We were so careful.'

He shrugged. 'Does it matter now? You are right, we have nothing to offer.'

'What do we do?'

Nathan stood and straightened his clothes. 'I telegram Mycroft. He can get someone to clean up this mess—'

'No, Nathan. What do we do about the exchange?'

Mrs Gregson felt her eyes sting with tears of frustration. To come this far, to spring a monster from prison, drag her over the North Sea, only to have her . . . win! That was what was so galling. Somewhere along the way she had outwitted them, secreting tableware about her person. Perhaps she hadn't used keys to undo her chains – it was possible she had managed to filch something to pick the lock. The pins and grips perhaps, when Mrs Gregson had done the prisoner's hair back at the safe house. Had she counted them as she should have? No. Of course, a Sie Wölfe would be trained in such things as secreting pins about her person and picking locks.

'Damn it!' she shouted out loud. Now her witless scheme had cost the lives of three people.

'We have a choice,' said Nathan. 'We can go home. Or we can go to the bridge as mere spectators.'

Something fizzed in Mrs Gregson's brain, sparking like electricity. She fought off a feeling of light-headedness. She wasn't going to be overwhelmed by this. She quickly crossed to the bed and scooped up Buller's shotgun.

'It's no good looking for her,' said Nathan. 'The border is a matter of miles away. Miss Pillbody will be in Germany in no time.'

'I'm not going to look for her.'

'Then what?'

'We do have something to exchange for Watson, you know.'

'What?' asked Nathan.

Mrs Gregson levelled the shotgun at his stomach. 'You.'

'You are certain nothing has come through for me?' Von Bork asked.

'Nothing, sir,' said the communications clerk.

'Nothing from Kassel?'

'No.'

It was at Kassel that Watson was to be transferred to a faster, more comfortable vehicle and driven to the crossing point, a drive of about five hours by Adler. He was expecting a telegram to confirm that the change had been made.

'Let me know the moment anything does arrive.'

'Yes, sir.'

Von Bork stepped outside and lit a cigarette, looking at the scruffy collection of former farm buildings around him and the newer concrete structure that dominated them all. He was at the barracks of the border guards, the *Grenzschutzkompanie*, which consisted mostly of grizzled veterans, with a few battle-damaged front-liners moved to softer duty. There were some young men, whose parents or benefactors had greased the appropriate palms to keep them away from the trenches or, like the communications clerk, had skills that could not be found among older heads.

'Von Bork, there you are.'

He turned to see Admiral Hersch, well wrapped against the cold in a new leather coat, striding across to him. 'Sir. I didn't expect to see you.'

'Ach, I thought I'd best come along, keep an eye on the film people. Make sure they don't get in your way.'

'Of course,' said Von Bork, realizing that the admiral wanted to make sure that credit for any propaganda coup would go where he reckoned it was due. To him. Hence the new coat – he intended to be on camera, recorded at the scene for posterity. Von Bork made a mental note to wear his smartest uniform and his own best topcoat.

'Your man Watson is here?'

'He is on his way.' He knew that much. Kügel had at last telegrammed to confirm the doctor's departure. But that was some time ago and the message that he had reached the changeover rendezvous was worryingly late. Perhaps they had broken down? Perhaps he should have insisted on a train to bring him. Or an aeroplane. Ah well, it was too late now.

Hersch checked his watch. 'So we have, how long? Seventeen hours?'

'About that.'

'I have inspected the kitchens and the cellars here. Quite inadequate. I suggest we go into Geldern for a decent dinner. Or we could cross the border into Venlo.'

'I'd rather stay this side tonight, Admiral.'

'Of course. Well, we'll crack open a bottle of Sekt, too, for a little celebration.'

Von Bork knew Holmes wasn't in the bag yet. With Watson lost on the road somewhere, there was still plenty of opportunity for things to go awry. Surely Hersch was aware of that too? 'I would rather celebrate after the event, sir.'

The admiral slapped him on the back, the hide of his leather coat creaking as he did so. 'Forgive me. I'm not prematurely celebrating our bagging of the Great Detective. I have just heard that one of my Sie Wölfe escaped from Holloway prison. Ilse Brandt. One of the very best. By which I mean, in peacetime even we would probably lock her up and throw away the key. Quite, quite ruthless. And a damn fine fuck, to boot. The newspaper reports say she is dead, but I'll take that with a pinch of salt until I have confirmation. If she is at large in England, then they had best watch out.' He chortled at the thought. 'She will cut a swathe through them like a reaping machine.'

'Won't she try and make it home?' asked Von Bork, dropping his cigarette on the floor and grinding his heel on it.

'To Germany? Almost certainly.'

'Then that will be the time to break out the Sekt, surely.'

Hersch jutted out his lower lip as if contemplating this. 'The woman has spent many months in British captivity. There is no knowing what they have done to her.'

'Meaning?'

'If she does make it home, it might be safer to treat her as a hostile. Like a potentially rabid dog.'

'Quarantine her?'

'That,' said Hersch, gently but firmly moving Von Bork towards his car. His streak of sentimentality meant that it pained him to utter the next option. But he knew his affection for Ilse was a weakness he could ill afford. 'Or put her down and have done with it.'

'My name is Isle Brandt but it is so long since I used it I almost think of myself as Miss Pillbody now,' she said to the young Dutchman. 'The lonely, sweet, naïve Miss Pillbody. But it is time to put her away. Ilse, you see, had a husband who was killed by the British. A Zeppelin man. So proud of that machine, he was. The new frontier, the way to the future. But it didn't turn out that way, did it? Giant bags of gas that can immolate men in a second. It doesn't bear thinking about how they died. How they still die. Watching the envelope split asunder and faced with the choice – let the fire consume you or jump to your death. But there you are. He died, and I decided to offer my services to the Kaiser, to the Imperial She Wolves. Hersch might be a callous bastard but he knows how to train a unit of women. Fifty of us began. Thirty-two survived. That's really what we are trained for. To survive. And survive I will. By whatever means necessary. You seem like a nice young man. I am so glad you helped me. Money, very generous. Some schnapps, most welcome. And a hiking map from the local Wanderclub, which has helped no end, and a compass. I'm not stupid, though. I can't just stroll up to the border and announce my return, like a prodigal daughter. How suspicious would that be? Hersch would suspect I had made a deal with the British. Hersch taught us to suspect everyone. I don't even trust myself now. So, I have to prove myself, I suppose. Give them proof of my credentials, that I am still loyal. But that's not your concern. Not any longer.'

She took another gulp of the schnapps. The handsome young man opposite hadn't said anything. He couldn't. Not since she had walked up behind him, put a cushion over the top of his head and fired two shots into the fabric, the muzzle of the pistol pushed firmly into the stuffing. It hadn't been a clean kill, he had thrashed about, although she was certain that was just a flurry of spinal reflexes. She had been able to place a third round into his heart to put a stop to that. There had been some noise from the discharges, despite the muffling, but nobody had come banging on the door of the house where he had invited her to take coffee while she decided how best to find her lost companions. Poor Stijn. Where would she be without such kind men to help her on her way?

After she had drained the schnapps, Ilse performed a fast but thorough search of the upstairs. She found an airing cupboard with clean sheets and towels she would use to stanch her little feminine problem, the one that had horrified Buller so much when she had smeared her face with it, feigning a bloody coughing fit. In a locked cupboard, easily forced, she found a vintage Beaumont-Vitali hunting rifle. It was a Dutch design, but with an Italian magazine system. Handsome, well-balanced, but with only open sights. She rummaged deeper in the cupboard and, among the waders and oilskins, found a pair of binoculars, which she slung around her neck. It was a few more moments before she discovered a box of the rifle's obsolete cartridges – the 11.35 x 52R – without which the gun was simply a rather elegant club.

She took the booty back down to the kitchen, laid it on the table and rummaged in the larder. The excitement of her escape had left her feeling peckish. She selected a carton of eggs. She set about boiling three of them on the range, while singing a song she had heard at a prison concert: "'When I think about my dugout, Where I dare not stick my mug out, I'm glad I've got a bit of a Blighty one!'"

She liked the jaunty tune but not the sentiment. It was about a soldier glad he was wounded badly enough to be shipped home. What sort of message was that for the troops? Not one a singer could peddle in Germany, that was for certain. They would find themselves hanging like ripe fruit from a lamppost.

While the eggs boiled she checked Stijn's other provisions in the larder. Fresh-ish bread, milk, cheese, bacon. More schnapps, a flagon of wine and a crate of beer.

Yes, she had all the supplies she needed while she decided her next move, certain that, one way or another, things had come full circle. Ilse – Miss Pillbody – had begun this part of her life's journey out on the mudflats of Essex, and made an uncharacteristic mistake in not executing Holmes and Watson, trusting instead for nature to take its course and drown them in the incoming tide. But the pair had cheated death and had punished her for her slackness.

She removed the eggs from the water and placed them in the pretty china eggcups she had seen on the dresser. As she cracked the tops of the shells, she vowed to herself she wasn't going to make the same mistake twice. This time bullets, not the waves, would do the job.

FORTY-EIGHT

Darkness had descended prematurely by the time the camp came into sight and snow was falling with increased vigour, the flakes the size of sovereigns. Thanks to the wet and streaked windshield, the *Lager* fence lights were blurred starbursts ahead, guiding them in, but Watson tugged at the driver's sleeve.

'Don't turn. Not here, carry on,' he instructed, the gun indicating the direction. '*Nicht hier. Auf der Straße.*'

The driver looked at him, his expression apprehensive. '*Um dem russischen Lager?*'

'*Nein.*' They weren't going to the Russian camp. In fact, Watson wasn't sure where they were going. He would know it when he saw it.

Watson peered into the screen. The headlamps, such as they were, were mainly picking out the dancing walls of snow. 'Keep to the right. *Halten Sie sich reichs.*' It was difficult to see where the road began and ended. He navigated them by the diffuse string of camp lights to his left until they were suddenly gone and said, 'Left wherever you can. *Links!*'

'*Es gibt keine Straße.*'

'Not a road. A track. *Eine Fährte. Hier.*'

In truth it was more guesswork than anything else – he wished he had paid more attention to the local geography when Kügel had taken him out in the Argus – but two striped poles splayed at drunken angles suggested the entrance to something and the truck swerved off the road, slowing as it hit deeper snow. Ahead, another two marker poles suggested the way. '*Ja, ja,*' Watson urged.

The lorry bounced and bucked its way forward, wheels, axles and engine all protesting as it was forced to head-butt its way through the drifts. The driver was a blur of activity, at one point reminding Watson of a man playing a theatre organ as much as steering a truck. The road, if that was what it was, was leading them down a gentle slope behind the camp, which was soon looming above them on its plateau.

Watson was just feeling pleased with himself when the lorry lurched and crashed to a standstill, sending him arcing forward and cracking his head on the windshield. The engine gave a huge shudder and stalled. They had hit something buried under the snowfall.

Watson leaned back, groggy from the blow, and he felt hands on him, clawing for the gun. He managed to pull the pistol away, raise it and bring it down as hard as he could. It made contact and the driver yelped in pain like a cowed dog. Watson pushed him away.

He waited until his vision stopped pulsing into darkness and back before he took stock. With his free hand he stroked his forehead. No blood. The driver, though, had broken skin above one eye, which was leaking two thin rivulets onto his brow.

'Do that again and I will kill you. *Töten Sie.* Understand me? *Verstehen?*'

'*Ja,*' he replied, his fingers probing his wound above.

'You have a flashlight? *Sie haben eine . . .*' he groped for the word, '*Taschenlampe?*'

The driver nodded and indicated a metal box attached to the dashboard in front of Watson. He opened it to find a squat torch, the sort that clipped onto bicycles. It would have to do.

Watson climbed out of the cab and, keeping the gun levelled at the driver as he walked around the front, opened the second door and ushered him out. They stumbled through the snow to the rear, where Gunther was still bound with the prisoner transport shackles.

'Where are we?' the old man asked.

'The camp. Or at least at the back end of it. You, up. Up. *Schnell.*'

The driver climbed into the rear. Watson indicated that the guard should manacle him too. He did so.

'Both hands for him. *Zwei.*'

He did as he was told. 'Now the feet.'

'Where is the young one?' the guard asked as he snapped the cuffs on.

Watson took a moment to appreciate he meant the other guard, Fingerless.

'The one who killed my friend Sayer?'

Gunther's features sagged, like melting wax. 'Orders.'

Watson nodded. He supposed it was. 'I could gag both of you now. But I doubt anyone will hear you shouting through this snow. If I hear you, however, I'll come back and shoot you both. No matter who is doing the shouting. Stay quiet, stay calm, you'll see tomorrow. Is that understood?' His head was swimming as he spoke. Making the threats and keeping his face looking as if he meant them was an exhausting business.

'*Ja*,' said Gunther.

'Tell him.'

There was a burst of rapid German and the driver, apparently still dazed from being coshed with the handle of the Luger, nodded woozily.

Watson turned to face the night, and flakes that had grown to almost saucer-size, and set off into the darkness, the yellow, pencil beam of light guiding him towards the escarpment at the rear of the camp. He examined the surface of the fallen snow as he went, but it was smooth and untrammelled. Nobody had walked this way recently. This was all a huge gamble. But he couldn't leave the camp without knowing the truth. Steigler had taunted him that he knew nothing. But he knew this – there was some way into the tunnels that linked the rec room with the isolation hut. Peacock had told him that. He had said he had seen freedom, smelled it. You didn't get the scent of liberty behind wire or underground. So there had to be some way out of the camp. And the most likely way was through some old gold workings.

Gold was the answer, his inner voice had told him. But he had assumed that meant it was about the precious metal – the very embodiment of human greed. But somewhere deep in his unconscious he had known that there were other elements to the extraction of gold. Cyanide, for one. An easy way to kill three men when you knew they drank the camp liquor in a ritual toast. Steigler had given him the jar of alcohol to test, but he only had the doctor's word for it being the self-same liquid the men had drunk. He was beginning to think the doctor's word was worse than worthless.

And the second was—

A firework went off in his cranium and his heart thumped in his chest in excitement at what was before him. The beam was shining not on rock, but on wood, albeit wood painted to look like rock at a casual glance. This was it; this was the entrance to the tunnels. He looked back over his shoulder towards the lorry, but it was lost in the backdrop to the white speckled world that had enveloped him.

Watson put the torch down on the snow and used chilled fingers to explore the wooden panel before him. It was not a door. There was no sign of hinges. It appeared to be simply placed against the smooth face of rock. Yet no amount of pulling would shift it one way or another. The ends of his fingers, already raw from the skin loss, began to bleed after a few minutes of exploring every crack and crevice around the periphery of the barrier. Despite the cold he was sweating and breathing was painful, the air sharp in his lungs and his bad knee ached – he had left his walking staff pinned through the young German guard.

Energy drained from him like water from a punctured canister, pooling at his feet, so that he felt like an empty vessel. Which he was, an old hollow man, jousting at windmills, without even a Sancho Panza for support.

You have me, Watson.

No, I don't Holmes, you're not you. You are a mere vocal simulacrum of you. I thank you for being there. You have helped keep me sane. Even offered decent advice. But you aren't flesh and blood. You aren't real.

He turned, put his back to the wooden façade and allowed himself to slide down, so his buttocks were in the snow, his knees to his chest. He wasn't strong enough to break down the panel. Perhaps if he could get the lorry closer, he could pull the door off with ropes. But how could he manage that? It had thumped into a rock or a fallen log under the snow. It was stuck and probably damaged.

Alarmingly, he knew now in his heart that the game was up. He was quite done in. It was remarkable he had kept going this long. He wanted to keel over and lie down, feel the crisp snow against his cheek, let it wick the warmth out of him, surrender to the—

Shush!

—surrender to the embrace of cold earth and endless oblivion.

Will you be quiet! Listen.

Watson did, but all he could hear was the moan of a sly wind. There was nothing out there.

Watson, sometimes, you really do test my patience. Not out there. Behind you.

Watson turned his head, so that one red and raw ear pressed against the painted planks. Sure enough he could hear something – a man coughing and spluttering. Hawking in the throat. And then, footsteps. Followed by a snatch of conversation, low enough to make the words a mere rumble, but human voices all the same. There was only one conclusion to draw.

Someone was coming up the tunnel to the outside world. And the moment they opened the hatch, they would see from the churned snow that he had been there.

FORTY-NINE

From his table in the front corner of the working men's café, Sherlock Holmes had a perfect view of the Knok bridge that spanned the Meuse. All he had to do was casually wipe away the steam on the windowpane with his sleeve and there it was. The crossing was an ugly beast, he thought, practical but unlovely, with irregular and unharmonious metalwork, hinged in the middle, supported by a four-square, plain slab of concrete that rose from mid-stream. Nobody had put any care or affection into it; he doubted those who had constructed it were particularly proud of their handiwork or gave it a second thought.

During his coffee-fuelled shift in the café, Holmes had seen bankside activity on both sides of the span. A film crew checking angles and the light on the German side. Mrs Gregson striding about, trying to look nonchalant and disinterested, yet clearly taking the measure of the location. With her a man he couldn't place, but when he got out of the car to open the door, he got a good look at him. Military, colonial, but not in uniform. One of Kell's? What was that about? Mrs Gregson's loyalties and affections were clear. But the man? A lover? No, they were not familiar enough with each other. A suitor? Ah, now possibly. Was Mrs Gregson using her feminine charms on him? Shame on her! He laughed to himself, imagining her bluster when he accused her of undermining her suffragette principles.

And what was he to make of the others who drove by three times in an hour in a Ford? Three men, one slouched in the rear as if trying to hide. Not Dutch, judging by the clothes. English, or at least British. Civilians, but he could tell the pair in the front were servicemen in mufti, one a senior officer to the other, judging by the interactions he had witnessed.

And then there was the little tug that scooted up and down the German side of the river, back and forth, back and forth, never with a load in tow. What to make of its mindless wanderings? Or was conjecture on that a step too far? Perhaps it had simply been a tug.

Where was Mycroft in all that activity? He was sure he would be in there somewhere. Because he would have found out that his brother had been less than forthright with him. And when he discovered what he was planning, surely Mycroft would try to stop him sacrificing himself for his friend.

Is that what he was doing? After a fashion, he supposed. Von Bork and others would try to break him, that much was certain. But he doubted it would be purely physical coercion. That would be counterproductive. Parading a broken, abused Holmes before the world, slack-jawed and dead-eyed, would have no currency whatsoever. They had to be cleverer than that. Which meant they had to be cleverer than *he*.

Was this hubris? There was a time when he would have wagered his intellect against any man, saving perhaps Mycroft in his pomp. But he was well aware that his faculties had faded, although they were sharper than they had been in those months of despair before Watson had diagnosed that there was a physical cause to his decline.

No, he was confident, but not over-confident, that he could if not best the Germans, then thwart them. And if not? He was prepared for that. Secreted about his body, in a manner that would fool even the most fastidious of searchers, was the poison. To the casual observer it looked as if the toenails on his feet had coarsened, thickened, ridged and yellowed with age. But the nails of both big toes were false, the cement holding them on impregnated with the poison itself. It would be like licking a stamp, albeit a rather unsavoury one, perhaps, but it would be quick and Hua, the Chinese doctor and herbalist in Limehouse he met around the time of the 'Twisted Lip' adventure, had assured him it would be relatively painless. Although, as Hua admitted, he could hardly guarantee that, and Holmes would be in no position to ask for a refund. He rather liked Hua's sense of humour.

So, all was set. He had even clapped eyes on Von Bork, although as he had intended, the German had not recognized him. The man had filled out from the well-toned sportsman Holmes had known. But his eyes were bright, alert and hungry. Hungry, Holmes appreciated, for revenge.

There was just one thing in this complex intermeshing of scenarios that puzzled him. One piece missing that was skewing the balance, the one that was at the very heart of all this activity. Where on earth was Watson?

FIFTY

Watson scurried away from the panel as the voices approached it. He retreated seven or eight paces then flattened himself against the surface of the genuine rock face. The snowfall was thick enough that he would be hard to spot, but the traces of his movement on the ground were unmistakable. He double-checked that the safety catch of the Luger was off.

There came the squeak of wood moving over wood. The rotating pegs that held the panel – or some such device – were being turned. The top moved outwards, while the bottom stayed in place. A thin light spilled out from the sides of the opening and he felt horribly exposed, but he couldn't move now.

There came the sound of heavy, forced breathing and coughing.

'Jesus Christ, I got a faceful of that.' Another huge intake of breath. 'I think I've burned my lungs.'

'Go outside.'

'Are you kidding? Have you seen it out there? Bloody snowing like Christmas. We need gas masks.'

'Ach, no we don't, we won't be doing this much longer. As Link said, time to shut it down. Mustn't get too greedy.'

A bitter laugh.

'What?'

'I didn't think Link knew there was such a thing as too greedy.' Another wheeze. 'OK, let's get this over with.'

The panel moved again, a few inches back towards closing. 'Give me a hand here.'

'No, leave it. Get some fresh air in the tunnels m'be. Ma eyes are stingin' too. We'll close it afterwards.'

Footsteps echoed off rock walls as the pair retreated. Watson couldn't quite believe his ears. Boxhall, the man who made the coffins and had damaged his lungs, yes. But the other? The accent was unmistakable. Hardie, the Scottish priest, had been in on it too.

Watson spent what seemed like a long time pondering his options, but in truth there was only one. With the Luger tucked in the top of his trousers – safety back on – he approached the wooden entrance cover and levered it open, inch by careful inch, wincing at every squeak and groan it made. Eventually he had created enough of a gap for him to step through into the dank chill of the old mine. He pulled the panel back up to roughly where it had been, the weight of snow at the base helping keep it in position.

He looked up the tunnel. This section was lit by a string of small electric bulbs, which gave a feeble illumination. He risked switching on his torch for a few seconds and was gratified to see a curve to the walls, which meant he was probably invisible to

Boxhall and Hardie for the moment, who were up around the bend. The floor was dusty but flat and quite even. The pattern of holes and markings suggested there had once been a narrow-gauge railway running into the hillside, but that had probably been torn up for scrap or possibly reuse in a working seam.

He turned off the torch and pocketed it, then reactivated the Luger with a flick of his thumb. Quite what he intended to do he wasn't sure but he was aware of one thing – the death they had in store for Cocky, if he still lived, was hideous in the extreme. He couldn't not act with the burden of that knowledge.

You are a good man, Watson.

Or a bloody fool.

The floor rose gently as he walked and he, too, felt something attack his eyes and sinuses. His tongue tasted metal in the air and prickled when he swallowed. Watson rummaged in his pockets and found a handkerchief, which he tied around his face, like a highwayman of old. It wasn't much, but it helped a little.

Oh, how he wished Holmes was with him. He would not only know what was ahead but would have worked out a strategy. Watson had no plan. He would have to decide moment by moment. But how many people were up ahead in the gloom? How many would one old man with a pistol and a limp have to face down? He paused and the chill of the mine settled around him like a damp blanket. That was when he noticed that he was shivering. And it wasn't entirely due to the cold.

A cough and a few words spliced from a conversation rolled slowly down the mine workings towards him, growing fuzzy and incoherent as they came. How far around that bend? Ten yards? A hundred? Perhaps more. He had no way of judging.

Watson waited until the worst of the shivers had subsided. If this was to be his end, then it would be death in a noble cause. Not a blaze of glory, perhaps, but a blaze of gunfire.

He took a deep breath and, crouched just below the string of lights, he started forward at a determined pace. The ground rose again, taking him closer to the surface but within a hundred yards the slope had all but disappeared. He was moving over even ground as quietly as he could manage, but, careful of his knee, he was favouring one leg slightly and dragging the other. To his ears the rhythm of his footfall sounded like the boom of a bass drum followed by the slide of cymbals. He only hoped the men ahead were too busy to notice they had a marching band coming their way.

On his right there was a series of side-tunnels, all dark, the blackness swirling within. He wondered where they led. Deeper into the earth, no doubt, as the miners struggled to extract more and more gold as the gilded seams near the surface petered out.

As he rounded a sharp bend the fumes became stronger and he had to press the handkerchief to his mouth, although it could do little to help with the moisture streaming from his eyes. He fought the urge to cough and splutter. Thanks to the occasional oil lamp the light was stronger here, and ahead, their outlines blurred by his tears, he could see Boxhall and Hardie, standing at the top of another small rise, busy admiring their handiwork. They were alone. In the wall next to him he could see the metal rungs that led up to the isolation hut, but the hatch up there was closed. If his calculations were correct, the two men were actually standing right under the graveyard.

Watson stood fully upright, pulled down the kerchief, puffed out his chest and hailed them with a confidence he did not feel.

'Stay where you are and put your hands up.'

The two men turned and looked at him. Neither showed any inclination to raise his arms in the air.

'Major Watson,' said the priest with a little laugh. 'Now, I didn't expect—'

'Move that trough. Now!'

'Which is it to be? Not move and put up our hands or move that trough?' asked Boxhall.

The trough in question was a large porcelain vessel, around twice the size and depth of a bathtub, and fitted with wheels. Twists of vapour were rising from it, the source of the burning fumes. It was full of sulphuric acid, a chemical used in the processing of gold. Here, though, it was positioned under one of the false graves. It was intended that Captain Peacock would come down, straight into a solution that would do its damnedest to dissolve any evidence of him.

'Look, Major,' began Boxhall, 'it's not at all what you think—'

The gunshot sounded like a thunderclap and for a moment Watson thought he had missed. Then a large patch of the porcelain, near the base, fell away, and the acid began to gush out.

'Jesus Christ!' shouted Boxhall, hopping on alternate legs as the fluid flowed towards him.

Father Hardie slipped behind the trough and pushed it, propelling it down the slope towards Watson. The metal wheels rumbled as it came at him, spewing its corrosive cargo. He sidestepped it, but his face was enveloped in the fumes from the agitated liquid and he spun into the opposite wall, blinded, as the vat crashed to a standstill, its contents still gurgling and hissing out onto the floor of the workings.

Watson wiped his eyes with the back of his sleeve and blinked. 'Hold it!'

Hardie had picked up a length of wood and had taken several steps towards him.

'Drop that.' A wave of the Luger. 'Now.'

Hardie looked down at it and opened his fingers. The timber clattered onto the floor. He took a step back away from it. The standoff resumed, Watson holding the gun, the two men, weaponless, almost daring him to fire at them. Acid hissed around Watson's feet. He was glad, once more, of his Trenchmasters.

'What now?' asked Boxhall. 'We can't stay here all night.'

Watson didn't answer. He didn't have one. The fumes from the spill were even stronger now and he felt his airways burning with them. They had to move soon.

Watson did not recognize the next sound to come down the tunnel but when Lincoln-Chance strode into view from behind Hardie and Boxhall he realized the man was clapping.

'The great Dr Watson! Come to prevent more deaths. How? By shooting everyone?'

'You'll hang for this,' said Watson.

'Possibly,' said Link, stopping the ironic applause. 'But just as likely we'll all disappear with a great deal of money to our name.'

'Hardie, you are a man of God. How can you justify this? It's barbaric.'

Hardie's eyes flicked to the floor. 'I was a man of God. I want no part of a deity that could create this war.'

'I wouldn't worry,' sneered Watson. 'I doubt He wants any part of you.'

'So,' asked Link, 'what do you propose? I really don't believe you are going to shoot all of us? I don't believe killing is in your character, Major.'

'Oh, I've done my share.'

'On a battlefield, perhaps. But in cold blood?' He took a pace forward.

'Stay where you are,' Watson warned, extending his gun arm further.

'Or else?' Lincoln-Chance was level with the other two now. He brushed his fringe back into place, ever conscious of his looks. 'And how do you propose to get the three of us back above ground without one of us taking that weapon from you?'

'I'll do my best. You aren't armed.'

'No, but I am,' said the voice from behind.

Watson didn't turn. 'Steigler?'

'Indeed, Major. How fortunate that I was in the bone room, making a bit of space for Peacock. The acid doesn't dissolve them completely, you know. But it makes them more . . . manageable. But now, what a pretty pickle you have got yourself into. All you had to do was go to the border and you'd be free of all this. But no . . .'

'I think the gallows will find space for you, too, Steigler.'

'I think not. I think Henry here and I will be heading for Switzerland sometime soon. The first genuinely successful escape from Harzgrund. And a blot on Kügel's record. How sad.'

'Hold on,' said Hardie. 'What about us?'

'Your share will be waiting for you back at home,' said Lincoln-Chance. 'I'll get all the legal gubbins out of the way.'

'Isn't it strange how lies ring like a cracked bell?' said Watson.

'These men trust me,' Lincoln-Chance insisted.

'We could all go,' said Boxhall. 'A mass break-out.'

'Impossible,' said Lincoln-Chance. 'We'd never all make it to the border.'

'Whereas Lincoln-Chance will have his old bobsleighing friend with him to guide him through,' said Watson softly. 'If that's all he was. Just a friend.'

'Don't be ridiculous,' snapped Lincoln-Chance. 'What are you suggesting?'

Watson gave an inward smile. He had riled him. And an angry man was sometimes a careless one. 'Harry Kemp intimated to me that there was sex of some description in this camp. So it could be you are setting yourselves up for life as a happy couple at the expense of everyone here.'

'You are disgusting.' Lincoln-Chance took a step forward, his fists clenched.

'Henry!' snapped Steigler from over Watson's shoulder. 'He is just trying to provoke you. I am afraid, Watson, you are barking up the wrong tree. Now will you please put that gun down.'

Watson flicked on the safety and let it fall. The clang took seconds to die away. 'Still, if I were Hardie, Boxhall and the others, I'd be wondering about what you were up to while they languish here. Is there really honour among thieves? Among men who will do such terrible things to their countrymen?'

'Aye, he has a point,' said the priest.

'There is only one point here,' said Steigler, 'and that is we have to make sure Major Watson disappears for ever, without trace. Is there another acid bath?'

'Yes, one more,' said Boxhall. 'In the stores tunnel.'

'Fetch it. We'll make sure the disappearance of Watson is a mystery that even Sherlock Holmes couldn't solve.'

Boxhall turned to leave and two things happened simultaneously. First there was a groaning from the roof of the tunnel and, in a shower of dust, Captain Peacock came hurtling through the trapdoor, and at the same time Watson was enveloped by the boom of a pistol's discharge and felt the punch of the round as it struck between his shoulder blades, sending him senseless towards the cold and acid-streaked floor.

FIFTY-ONE

Ernst Bloch had considered writing a farewell letter to Hilde, but in the end thought better of it. The tone, he knew, would be pessimistic, sorrowful, and he didn't want his final missive to convey any form of sadness. He wanted to tell her how much she had meant to him and how he still cherished the thought of that one night in Brussels. He had fought day after day to keep the details of those hours fresh in his mind, but in vain. The memory of her scent had faded and he viewed the room as though through gauze. But her face, her smile, the shine in her eyes, they were still pin sharp.

Now he enjoyed one last cigarette in the twilight, crouched in a corner of the graveyard, his hand cupped over the end to hide the glow. Hide it from whom, he wasn't sure. Carlisle and Balsom were a few metres away, talking in low voices. They had his haversack, the rifle and the ammunition, which would be handed over to him at the last possible moment. They still didn't trust him. As if he had any alternative apart from going along with their scheme. Apart from when he had a full set of papers. Then he might just . . .

'I can smell that cigarette from Eindhoven. Put it out.'

It was Jasper, the smuggler, with two other men. All three were dressed head to toe in black.

'We aren't over there yet.'

'No, but there are KMar border patrols on this side,' replied Jasper. 'Not many, but you don't want to be answering their questions about what you are doing in a graveyard after dark.'

Bloch dropped the cigarette and stood on it. Jasper turned his attention to Carlisle and Balsom. 'You have the money?'

Carlisle tossed over an envelope and Jasper caught it and shoved it in his jacket without counting the contents.

'It's all there,' said Carlisle.

'It better be.' From another pocket Jasper took out a folded set of papers. 'Here you are. Proof of entry.'

'Thank you,' said Bloch.

'Your luggage?'

'They have it.'

Carlisle held up the haversack. 'We hand it over at the border.'

'You are not coming to the border,' said Jasper firmly. 'We take it from here.'

'What sort of fool do you take me for?' hissed Carlisle. An owl seemed to answer the question with a hint of derision in its hooting.

'No kind of fool,' said Jasper. 'Simply that this isn't your country or your river. Bastian and Karel here, they know the way down to the water, how to get across, where to land the boat, the path to take, how the wire fence swings open. Everything. What would you be? Ballast?'

Carlisle made to speak, but Jasper held up a hand. 'Look, we have entered into a contract. We are to deliver your friend over there. Why, we don't know and don't care. You have paid a fair price, we will deliver a fair service. Now, it might be that your German friend here decides he doesn't want to go across after all. It does happen. People change their mind, get an attack of nerves . . .'

The Dutchman's eyes seemed to bore into Bloch.

'But you have paid us. Therefore we will get him into Germany even if we have to cosh, gag and bind him. Understand?'

'But we have to take your word for that,' said Sergeant Balsom.

'Yes, you have to take my word for that. The word of a . . .' he spat a few shreds of tobacco from his tongue, '. . . Dutchman. You might think it doesn't have as much currency as an Englishman's, but I have only survived doing this because I am as good as my word. Now, you can wait here if you like. We won't cross until it's fully dark in about . . .' he looked at the sky, which still had a faint glow in the west, '. . . about one hour, maybe a little more. We'll be gone for another three hours doing our other business. So if you don't mind being cold, you are welcome to stand around. Or there is a little tavern three hundred metres to the left of the church. Nothing fancy, but you can stay warm and have a drink while you wait.'

'We'll be here,' said Carlisle, to the obvious disappointment of Balsom, who was already imagining the glow of the tavern's fire and the taste of its beer.

'Hand over the luggage, then.'

Jasper took the rifle and pack and gave one to each of his men. 'Best be going. I'll see you back here. You,' he pointed at Bloch, 'stick close to Karel, the one with your rifle.'

Bloch wasn't sure why, but he shook hands with Carlisle and Balsom as if this were a parting of old friends, rather than gaolers and prisoner, and set off after Karel. Jasper was behind him. As they emerged from the graveyard onto a cinder track that led towards the river, he felt the Dutchman's hand on his shoulder. 'Just so we're clear, German, what I said back there was mostly true.' A blade glinted with starlight in the corner of Bloch's eye and he stiffened. 'Relax, I'm just showing it to you. And just making the point.'

'What point?' Bloch asked as they slipped into the darkness between two tall, gabled houses.

'That if you do anything stupid, anything that might betray us to your fellow Germans, you'll be dead before you hit the ground.'

FIFTY-TWO

Watson was drowning, water cascading over his face, streaming up his nose and down his throat. He spluttered and coughed and ejected a stream of it into the air. He rolled to one side and dry retched.

'There you are, Dr Watson.'

It was Harry, cradling him in his arms. He tried to struggle upright but the servant held him tight.

'Careful, sir, you've had a bit of a shock. I was just washing the acid off your face.'

'Hell, we've all had a bit of a shock.'

Watson blinked and tried to focus on the figure looming above him in the dim light, the man who had just spoken. It was Kügel.

'What happened?' Watson asked. 'How is Peacock?'

'Dead,' said Harry. 'Whatever they gave him to mimic death didn't mimic at all, it was the real King's Shilling. He landed on Captain Boxhall. Broke Boxhall's arm.'

'Good.' Watson managed to sit up and look around. The tunnel was empty except for the two other men, a pair of

German guards and a body lying face down in a pool of liquid, the acid softly sizzling as it digested the flesh. 'Who is that?'

'Steigler,' said Kügel.

Watson felt a stab of pain in his back. 'He shot me?'

'No, I shot you,' said Kügel.

'I don't understand.'

'One of your two prisoners escaped from the truck: the driver, I believe. He came around to the camp gate and raised the alarm. I couldn't understand what the hell you were doing back here so I followed the man around to the truck, with some of my guards. I saw the entrance, and then I heard that fool Steigler talking and had some idea that he'd been fleecing me—'

Watson had to laugh at that. 'It was a damn sight more than fleecing. It was murder.'

'That, too,' said Kügel. 'So I shot him. And I am afraid the bullet went through him and hit you. Hard, but not hard enough to penetrate.'

'Badly bruised, probably,' said Harry.

He'd happily take another bruise, Watson thought, rather than a bullet in the spine.

'Lincoln-Chance and the others? Hardie? Boxhall? What will you do with them?'

'I've put them to work, for the moment. But I'll keep them in solitary until I can break them. I need to know how many prisoners knew what they were up to.'

Watson had considered this. 'I am not sure Critchley did. He might be Senior Officer but he never struck me as particularly incisive. And he was in awe of Lincoln-Chance. Harry, did you?'

'No, sir, on my life. Blimey, I knew they was gettin' people out but . . . no. Not this. Not murder.'

Watson hoped that was true. 'How did you get down here, Harry?'

'I was in the rec room when I heard the shots. From under the floor. I knew something had gone wrong but I honestly thought the guards must have discovered the escape route. I thought about making myself scarce, but I also thought there might be wounded. So I crept down here just in time to see Cocky fall through and the commandant shoot you.'

'You're a good lad.' He turned his face to Kügel. 'There is someone else you need to speak to. Brünning.'

'Feldwebel Brünning?' Kügel asked in some astonishment.

'Yes. There had to be a German dimension for this to work, more than just Steigler, someone who could make sure the tunnels weren't discovered. But whether Brünning knew the true extent of the enterprise and its ultimate aim, I can't be certain.'

'Either way, he is a traitor.'

'I suppose he is. You'll need me as a witness?' Watson asked. 'I think I can piece it all together.'

'I will need a written statement, that is all. You won't be here, Watson, to act as a witness.'

'I'm not sure Dr Watson should be moved,' said Harry. 'He's not a well man.'

'He'll have to be. Von Bork has been on the telephone and burning up the telegraph wires and the damned radio waves about your disappearance. You'll have to be driven all night, but he is insisting you are in Venlo by dawn.'

Watson groaned. The thought of hours in that truck was

depressing. Then he remembered. 'I think it might be damaged. The Horch. We crashed it into a snow bank.'

'You can take my car, then. The Argus. It might be more comfortable, after all.'

There was no 'might' about it. 'Thank you.'

'No, thank you. I knew you would get to the bottom of this and unmask Steigler.'

'What? You suspected Steigler all along?'

'Of course. What kind of idiot do you take me for?' Kügel gave a cruel smile and Watson knew he was busy rewriting his own version of the whole story. Another reason he was happy to lend Watson the car, to ship him away as quickly as possible. With Steigler dead, every misdemeanour in the camp, from profiteering to pitiful rations, would be laid at the doctor's door when the Red Cross and the new commandant arrived. Mad Bill would be the hero. Only the British would dare contradict his new version. And who would believe them after how they treated their own men?

'If Lincoln-Chance or the others should be shot while escaping,' warned Watson, 'I would take a very dim view of it.'

'You'd be sorry? After what they did?'

'Justice has to be done, Kügel. Real justice. Not the summary kind. They murdered fellow countrymen. A British court should decide their fate.'

'Wait until the end of the war, you mean?'

'If need be,' replied Watson.

'You are assuming you know the outcome of this war. That Great Britain will win. It might be that all courts are German courts. Help the Major up, boy.'

He put his arm around Harry's neck, struggled to his feet and they began a slow progress down the tunnel back towards the rec room. Above them he could hear rhythmic thumps into the earth, sending down little fountains of soil. 'What are you doing up there?' Watson asked.

'Excavating the graves.'

'In this weather? It'll take hours to make a dent in that ground. And it's freezing. Your men won't like it.'

'My men? Oh, no, Hardie, Lincoln-Chance and the others have plenty of time. They'll keep going until someone tells me the truth.'

'There's a good chance you're going to work them to death.'

'I doubt it. If one of them isn't talking by tomorrow morning I'd be very surprised. A hot drink and a chance to save their own neck does wonders after a night of digging up coffins.'

'You'd know all about that. Saving your own neck, I mean,' Watson said sourly.

Kügel threw back his head and laughed. 'Not so Mad Bill now, eh?'

As they approached the ladder that would take them up to the recreation room, Watson stopped, as if catching his breath.

'Just a few more yards,' said Harry.

'You know, you are wrong about me not knowing the outcome of this war.'

'How's that?'

'As we said, the Americans are coming, Commandant. Not tomorrow or next week, but sooner or later they'll be over here on European soil.'

'You could be right. But then again, it might be the making of me. As we also said, I speak their language, after all. Yes, sirree, I truly do.' He stood aside and presented the ladder, like an usher showing a patron his seat. The smile faded and the joviality vanished from his voice. 'Now, Major Watson, perhaps you could get out of all our hair and get to the Dutch border. I do believe you have an appointment there.'

Watson was surprised, to say the least, when Kügel decided to join him on the cross-country trip to the exchange point. The snow was easing, Kügel had left the capable Hauptmann Musser in charge and Watson sensed that the commandant wanted to hand him over personally to Von Bork. After all, he was going to need allies when the full story of his camp emerged.

Watson was provided with a blanket, a flask of schnapps, a hot-water cylinder and some bread and sausage for the journey. Once again the driver was Emil, the scarred *Feldwebel* with the eye patch, and Watson hoped that one eye could judge distance well enough to manage in the prevailing conditions. It was difficult enough with two.

'There is one other thing,' said Watson as Kügel made to get in the car. 'You will need the help of the guard or the truck driver to locate the exact spot, but there is a young lad in the forest. The other guard. The one I got the better of.' Damn, an old man's pride was leaking into his voice. A stab between his shoulder blades reminded him he had hardly come through this unscathed. 'He's wounded and will be quite chilled by now.'

'Not dead?'

'Not when I left him. He had a skewer driven through his

foot. He is gagged and tied up with both my belt and his own. You should send someone to pick him up.'

Kügel went off to make the arrangements. There was a chance the boy had succumbed to hypothermia but Watson was oddly indifferent to that. He had considered running the boy through with the sharpened walking stick, but something had stayed his hand. Yet part of him felt he would have been justi-fied, given that the lad had shot Sayer in cold blood. He wasn't sure, however. His moral compass was spinning wildly, as if he had ventured too close to the magnetic pole.

The car bounced on its springs as Kügel climbed in. 'I know you want to sleep but first I need you to fill me in on events.'

Watson opened his weary, stinging eyes. The German was right. He needed to sleep. 'Events?'

'When did you suspect they were murdering their own people?'

Watson shuffled more upright in the seat as the Argus moved off and took a hit of schnapps from the flask. 'First of all, I hope you will take some responsibility for this.'

'Me?' Mad Bill's eyes widened, as if in shock. 'What have I got to do with this? I didn't dream up this cockamamie scheme. I haven't, despite what you think of me, murdered anyone.'

Watson felt he could speak freely, given that Kügel clearly wanted to play him as a card to Von Bork and his superiors. 'Not directly, perhaps. But you created the atmosphere in the camp, the one of naked greed. If you had money, or access to it, you thrived. If not, you starved. It was like a perversion of the American way that you admire so much. Survival of the fittest, the thriving of the most rapacious.'

'There was an element of that, perhaps,' admitted the commandant.

'No perhaps about it. Into this environment come men who discover there is a way out of the camp. Through the old gold workings. But it's useless. Escaping the camp is just the first step, the easy one. Getting across Germany and over a border? Almost impossible. So the tunnels are useless . . . unless they could use them to convince others that they work.'

'And you suspect who of initiating this?'

'Lincoln-Chance.'

'And your suspicions were aroused?'

'They put me in one of the coffins. To show the mechanism. I honestly think they meant to kill me but then began to worry that I would be missed too much, thanks to Von Bork. He has, in a way, saved my life.'

'Go on.'

'When I inspected the underside of the coffin, I burned my fingers.' He held up his hand. 'Look. No skin on the tips. Acid. Why acid? Because of the acid extraction method for refining the gold. And what else is used in the process?'

'I don't know.'

'A powerful poison. Toxic enough to pollute the waterways. You said so yourself, gold ravages the land, poisons the water.'

'Ah, cyanide,' said Kügel.

'Precisely. I believe the three men at the séance were poisoned with cyanide. It was why they had to be buried so quickly – the symptoms post-mortem are easy to spot.'

'They were killed simultaneously?' Kügel asked. 'All three?'

'The Greek tradition of summoning the dead is, apparently,

to cut the wrists and then make a ritual toast to the spirits they are about to contact. So all three would drink, and die, at the same moment.'

'And they were killed because . . . ?'

'Because they were about to tell all and sundry that Brevette was not at home having tea in London, but had perished. Which he had. I suspected that because the postcard from the Coburg was a forgery. It has recently changed its name, but nobody in the camp knew that.'

'Except you.'

Watson nodded. 'By a stroke of luck, a casual mention in a letter.'

They were on the long straight road past the pines now, plunging downhill into the snow-flecked night. The one-eyed driver was travelling faster than Watson himself would have risked, but he was exuding an air of absolute confidence in himself and the big roadster. After a few moments of silence Kügel spoke, his words tentative. 'But if the séance had contacted Brevette, and he was dead, surely that means . . .'

'It suggests the séance was genuine,' said Watson. 'As has been pointed out to me before. It means that they really did get in touch with the dead.'

'Which we both know can't be true.'

'No,' said Watson. 'I must agree with you.'

'Do I detect some doubt, Major Watson?'

'No.'

How often have I said to you that when you have eliminated the impossible, whatever remains, however improbable, must be the truth?

Too often, Watson thought, far too often.

'So it was all about the money? They simply pocketed what-ever they charged for this fictitious escape?'

'Not quite. There was more at stake. The men were persuaded to make a new will and give power of attorney or probate to one of the escape committee. I suspect by the time peace came and the men returned to England, those wills would have been altered to make new beneficiaries. The signature would be genuine, after all. Although I equally suspect Steigler and Lincoln-Chance would have found a way to cheat their fellow conspirators. The survival of the cruellest, you see.'

'Devilish.'

'Indeed. Now, if you'll excuse me I need to get some sleep if I am to participate in whatever scheme Von Bork has for me.'

'I think that is straightforward. I am not privy to the fine details. But in the time-honoured fashion, you are to be exchanged for someone more valuable than yourself.'

Watson slumped down in the seat. It would probably be some German general he had never heard of. Unless . . .

But no. He didn't want to think beyond 'unless'.

FIFTY-THREE

Snow was not a sniper's friend. And it was starting to fall thick and fast as Bloch climbed the last few steel rungs that led to the upper tier of the observation tower. He glanced up at the sky. There had been evidence of stars up until two hours before, right up to when they had entered the small boat for the almost silent paddle across the river. He had watched Jasper's men deploy their oars, but he still had no idea how they made the blades slice through the water and rotate them for the next stroke with hardly a ripple or a plop. Practice, he supposed. He was in the hands of experts, which was some comfort.

The snow was blowing in from the east, so Jasper had said, and might grow into a full storm. In which case . . .

The Dutchman hadn't finished the sentence. Jasper was no fool. A lone man, with a rifle, wanting access to the highest point around. Clearly, Bloch hadn't crossed the Meuse with the intention of sightseeing. There was precious little of value to see in this pancake-flat stretch of the country. In which case, Jasper was suggesting, should the storm materialize, he might find his mission aborted due to impaired visibility.

Once he was up on the ledge, Bloch hesitated. It was three metres wide, made of steel plate and ran around the entire circumference of the top of the structure. So, in fact, he was standing on the edge of a steel doughnut. If he stepped off the edge it was an eighteen-metre drop to the floor below, that one made of concrete. He had to keep his wits, and his balance, about him.

His eyes had had plenty of time to adjust to the gloom. Jasper had used his flashlight sparingly and its lens was masked with layers of muslin, so it gave a glow equivalent to a candle. Just enough for him to show Bloch the tower entrance and illuminate the sequence of steps, stairs and ladders that would take him to the top, and to warn him about the hibernating bats that clustered together two floors below, away from the worst of the weather. He wished he could be so lucky, for the snow was spotting his face now. It would do the same for the scope. And judging distances through a snow flurry, with its shifting, ethereal light, especially at dawn, was tricky at best.

What was to stop him just packing up and going now? Going back down, finding a German border guard and giving himself up? Nothing. Nothing at all. Except . . .

Carlisle would have thought of that. Or if not Carlisle, then one of his superiors. Who knew if there wasn't an agent of England lurking downstairs who, having made his own way over the border, was ready to put a bullet through his head if he emerged before daylight? At one point Jasper had been convinced they were being followed, and had sent Karel back to investigate, but he had reported that they were alone on the eastern bank, that nobody had crossed after them.

Then perhaps the British already had a man in place. And, of course, it was possible that agent, if he existed, had orders to kill him once he had done his work.

Almost anything was on the cards – there were simply too many variables. Which meant, in the end, Bloch had to take the simplest course of action. He had to shoot the Englishman and leave, and if someone was going to try to stop him . . . well, good luck to the man who came between him and Hilde.

A dog yapped on the Dutch side of the river, the sound carried across the water and the refrain was picked up in Germany. A sharp exchange of barks was followed by silence as streamers of snow fell around him. He pulled his collar up and sat, back to the wall, while he took the rifle from its protective case. He had often practised stripping down his weapons blind-folded and this was easier than that – a silvery shine from the clouds seem to bounce off the snow, which meant he could see the gun well enough. He ejected the single round and rolled it in the palm of his hand. One shot, one chance, one kill for Hilde. Make it count, he thought.

Bloch reloaded the bullet, slid the gun back into the case. He would check it over again at first light, which was a good few hours away. He didn't feel like doing it, but the sensible option would be to climb back down, find a dry spot and grab some sleep. But even as he thought of it his head lolled and he drifted off so quickly, he failed to hear the soft tread of feet on the iron rungs below.

'Wake up!'

His eyes cranked open, gummy and sore.

'We're here.'

Watson tried to move but a spasm in his neck caused tracks of pain to shoot up the side of his head and across his shoulders.

'We're here,' Kügel repeated in a softer voice.

Watson grimaced in response. He had slept in an awkward position and his joints had set rock hard within his body. He felt like he had an exoskeleton as he unfurled his arms and straightened his legs, as if his skin might snap and crackle, like a stamped-on cockroach's. 'Give me a minute. What time is it?'

'Almost eight.'

Watson levered himself up in the seat so he could look out of the window. There was a shimmering light in the east, and a glow from the snow-covered ground. About an inch had fallen but it had stopped now. They were parked near a river with, ahead of them, beyond a border fence, a broke-back bridge. Around them were a number of vehicles, lorries, military staff cars and civilian transport. It looked as if the circus was coming to town.

'Is all this for me?'

'I expect so,' said Kügel. 'I think you are the biggest event this part of the world has seen in some time.'

'That's difficult to credit.' Watson wiped his eyes and tried to focus on the steel span over the Meuse. 'That bridge is open, isn't it?'

'For the moment. Come on, stretch your legs, Watson. You want to walk, not hobble to freedom.'

Emil, the one-eyed driver, was yanking open the door as the German said this and a blast of cold air whipped over Watson's face. It felt momentarily invigorating after the stuffiness of the roadster, like a roll in the snow after a sauna, something he had experienced in Sweden all those years ago when Holmes was on the trail of Ricoletti and his abominable snow-woman of a wife.

Watson threw off the blanket and swung his legs out. The driver helped him unfold from the car and Watson placed a hand on top of the door for support. He wondered about the pulsing in his back, until he remembered the bullet that had passed through Steigler but, thankfully, not him.

While he stood, stooped and stiff, two men had approached and begun setting up a hand-cranked camera. They intended to record his humiliation. 'Will you tell them to stop?' he asked Kügel.

'This is not my show any longer.' He pointed into the strengthening light, where a sleek black limousine was approaching from the direction of a barracks. 'It is Von Bork and Admiral Hersch's.'

'I can make it worth your while.'

'How?'

'I can tell you who is behind the whole enterprise at the camp.'

'You've told me. Lincoln-Chance.'

'No. I haven't.'

Kügel stamped his boot into the snow. 'Why not?'

'Because I have only just come to what I feel is the correct conclusion. It was someone invisible.'

'You are talking rot, my friend. First the dead come calling, then an invisible man.'

'Get them out of here and I'll tell you.'

'Hey,' said Kügel, waving his arms, as he approached the film men. '*Haben Sie etwas Respekt. Geben Sie dem Mann etwas Privatsphäre. Er braucht Zeit, sich zu rasieren, und auf einigen frische Kleidung.*'

Watson hoped he was right. A shave and a change of clothes would be most welcome. He stroked the stubble on his chin. And a trim of his moustache. And a cup of tea.

The limousine had pulled to a halt and a familiar figure with an unfamiliar grin was getting out. Von Bork.

'So,' asked Kügel impatiently, aware that he was about to lose his prisoner, 'what do you have for me?'

'I kept wondering who poisoned the three at the séance. Who spiked the drink with cyanide? Who better than the man who looked after the rec room? The man who could get the hooch? The man who suddenly appeared in the tunnels to help nurse me. Harry Kemp.'

'Who?'

'The lad who was cradling me after you shot me.'

'Him? An orderly?'

'Precisely. A servant. Invisible.'

Kügel looked doubtful, as if he couldn't quite believe that a non-officer could operate such a Machiavellian scheme. 'He is just a common soldier. A private.'

'Is he? Could a common private have recovered my boots from Lincoln-Chance? And he recognized Latin, I am sure, when it was spoken as I was leaving the camp. He said his Latin wasn't so good. Not that he didn't know any. How many Boots or grooms have even a smattering of the classics? And he told me he didn't speak German, yet he understood well enough when Steigler told him, in that language, that a certain inscription might be appropriate. And Steigler called him Harry – yet how would a man like Steigler know a servant's Christian name? No, the lad was no servant.'

'An imposter? An officer all along?'

Watson nodded. 'In a strange way, the orderlies have more freedom than the officers. They come and go as they please around the camp. And think on this. The orderlies and the officers have separate *Appells*. A man, an officer could actually appear at both, and wouldn't be missed.'

'I'll be damned.'

'Let's hope so.'

Before Kügel could reply, Watson heard his name being called with something approaching delight. 'Major Watson! At last! I was beginning to give up hope. I am sure you would like to freshen up before our little event gets under way.'

Von Bork's gratified smile was so wide, so full of victory, that it left Watson in no doubt the identity of the man he expected to get in return for him. Von Bork was about to net Sherlock Holmes.

'Why are we here?' Nathan asked.

Mrs Gregson gave a petulant shrug and looked out of the car window, over towards the bridge. She knew that she had been behaving badly since Miss Pillbody's escape, that she was mourning the loss of her prisoner more than she was the two murdered men, but she couldn't help it. All that planning and effort . . .

'I'm sorry,' said Nathan. 'But you know what I said was true. They wouldn't exchange me for Watson. What do I know that would be of value? And it would be treason to hand over a serving intelligence officer.'

'I know, I know, don't snap your braces, Robert. It was just a moment of madness, pointing the shotgun at you like that. It is I who should apologize. Besides, you are probably right – you don't know much that they don't know already.'

'I'm beginning to think you really must have feelings for Major Watson. Feelings you could never have for me. I'm curious to meet the man who can melt your cold heart.'

'Don't get your hopes up. It isn't about his appearance, Robert.' And, she added to herself, there was no telling what the months of imprisonment had done to him physically.

She watched a figure approaching the bridge, swinging a bunch of keys and levers on a chain. She couldn't hear, but he looked to be whistling. 'What's the time?'

'Eight thirty,' said Nathan after consulting his pocket watch. 'I don't think it's going to get much lighter.' He peered at the sky, as dull as oxidized zinc plate.

'No, probably not. And I think that man there, in the blue, I think he is the bridge operator. It's the man who shouted at me to get off it.'

Sure enough the man stopped to one side of the crossing and used a key to open the metal control box.

'Come on,' Mrs Gregson said, opening the door of the car.

'Where are we going?'

'To the bridge.'

'Why?' sighed Nathan. 'What's the point?'

'To be there when Sherlock makes his move.'

'And?'

'We improvise.'

*   *   *

A sniper is like a god. Sitting on high, deciding the fate of the humans who move across the earth, oblivious to how easy it would be to snuff out their lives. Like the workman scuttling over the snow to his buttons and switches at the bridge, unaware of the crosshairs coming to rest on his body, then moving up to the head, then back again. Or the cameramen gathering on the other side, somewhat closer to the shooter than the workman, more vulnerable as they fussed over their wooden boxes and portable lighting rigs. Or the officers clustered around the limousine, the pair in leather coats laughing and stomping their feet, the third glum and withdrawn.

But none of those was the target. This god had only one in mind, to be plucked out of this life and propelled into whatever the next held.

There was a movement, caught from the corner of an eye, from the Dutch side. The visual field of the telescopic sight swung across the bridge and river, the image on the lens blurring as it did so, before coming to rest and back into focus. A touch on the ring to sharpen it a little. Ha. The show was beginning.

The noise from the bridge carried to the tower. The low squeal of moving parts being spurred into reluctant motion. The hiss of a piston. The span looked to judder along its length as the folded section began to move as cables tensioned, hydraulics pumped and pulleys spun. The pivoting section was moving out over the water, ready to reconnect Holland and Germany.

Now the crosshairs moved onto the land, pausing on each person in turn: the participants in this drama and the spectators who had wandered over from the café. Each one a hair-trigger pull away from sudden death.

Just one shot in this rifle. What a pity.

The sniper moved the graticule once more. Ah, yes. There. That one. Then, the sniper's mantra, spoken softly on the slowly exhaled breath: *Target acquired.*

FIFTY-FOUR

By the time Watson returned from the barracks the snow had stopped, the clouds had thinned and a low sun, its glow muted by a haze, had appeared. Watson was out of the car, flanked by Hersch and Von Bork. He had shaved, bathed and been given a change of clothes, but it all felt very superficial. He required a far deeper cleansing after what he had witnessed at the camp. The activities of Lincoln-Chance, Father Hardie, Feldwebel Brünning and young Harry Kemp had mined the depths of depravity. He was certain he was right about the boy. He had deduced the lad was a spy, sent to keep an eye on him, but not that he was most likely a ringleader. That had come to him only when he had been half delirious with exhaustion in the car.

'Shall we?' asked Von Bork.

Watson surveyed the scene before him. Beyond the wire border fence, the bridge was slowly cranking into its closed configuration. The cameramen had taken up position near to where the moving span would eventually touch the German bank. The cameras – two of them – were pointing in his direction, their operators' hands on the handles, ready to start cranking when he began the long slow walk towards his freedom. Other film men were clustered around them, one with a megaphone, others holding stalks with lights on them, although he suspected the newly arrived sun made them unnecessary.

Von Bork consulted his watch and then peered across the river, apparently unhappy with what he could see.

'I do hope this isn't a waste of time,' said Hersch.

'He'll be here,' said Von Bork with as much confidence as he could muster. 'Let's go to greet the bridge when it completes its journey.'

He placed a hand in Watson's back and the three of them moved forward, followed a few yards behind by four border guards, each with a Mauser rifle at the ready. A larger contingent of troops was deployed around the striped pole that marked the border, some four hundred yards from the riverbank. On either side of the pole and its hut the frontier fence began, stretching off over what had once been Dutch soil. The two Germans and their escort walked through the gap in the fence where the pole lay in its cradle, and carried on down the gently sloping no man's land to the bridge and the cameramen, who had now begun to turn their handles with an even, steady motion.

Watson, too, now scoured the crossing at the Dutch side of the river. But he could see no sign of his old friend. There was a car drawn up and, emerging from it, a man and . . . a woman.

The moment of identification caused him to stop in his tracks and both Hersch and Von Bork had taken a few strides before they noticed that they had outpaced their 'parcel'. 'What is it?' asked Von Bork. 'Watson?'

He could see that flame-coloured hair flying like a red flag as she reached up and removed her headdress. The sight of her caused palpitations in his chest, generating a touch of vertigo as his heart faltered.

Watson quickly decided it was best not to give anything away to the Germans, to show no potential weakness. 'I simply . . . can't quite believe I am so close to going home.'

'Well, you are,' said Von Bork. 'Although from what I heard from Kügel, it was a close-run thing.'

Watson nodded. 'My own people nearly got me.'

'How ironic would that have been?' asked Hersch.

'Yes. I'm wondering how I'm keeping my sides from splitting.'

'Come along,' said Von Bork. 'We have a rendezvous.'

Watson walked slowly to catch them up. 'He won't come, you know.'

'Who?' Hersch asked.

'The man you hope to swap me for.'

'Ah. You have managed to work it out, have you? I think you underestimate his affection for you, Dr Watson,' said Von Bork. The 'doctor' was stressed, to remind him of days before the war, of the bond Watson and Holmes had once shared. As if he needed any help with that. It was burned into his very being. Even when they were apart, Holmes was an integral part of his thought processes. That, he now fully appreciated, was what the voice in his head was. The little part of him that would always be Holmes, that would always try to think like Holmes. So not, in one sense, an imposter at all, just a gift from a friend.

It was Hersch's turn to put a hand on his back to propel him forward. 'We'll soon see, won't we?'

'He won't come,' repeated Watson.

At least, not in any way you'll be expecting.

Moments earlier, Mrs Gregson had opened the door of the car, stepped out into the sunshine that was busy melting the snow. Now Nathan had emerged and was moving around the bonnet towards her. 'You have your pistol to hand, Robert?' she asked him.

He tapped the pocket of his coat, feeling the weight of the Webley as it shifted. 'Of course.'

'And you know what to do if need be?'

'I do. Just a flesh wound.'

'Just a flesh wound,' she repeated, although she was well aware that a bullet in any part of the body had serious consequences. Especially for an older man like Sherlock Holmes.

She exited and stood for a moment, looking at the bridge and its operator as moving metalwork swung the last few yards to its resting place.

Across the bank on German soil she could see dozens of people, both civilians and soldiers, but there was only her and Nathan to represent the Allies, and the bridge operator for the Dutch, along with a few of his fellow countrymen some way down the bank who had come out from the café to watch the proceedings. So little happened hereabouts she would imagine that the swing bridge closing was a big event.

She moved across the snow-speckled ground, scanning up and down the river in case she had missed something, but this was a peculiarly featureless stretch of countryside, the only building of note a black tower some distance to her right, and that appeared to be situated on the German side of the water.

As she reached the threshold of the bridge, where the heavy wooden planks began, she pulled off her headdress and shook her hair free. The red cascade of loose curls was her signature, the one thing she could be sure Watson would recognize from across the span of the crossing.

Was that him? There was a man over there, flanked by two Germans in shiny leather greatcoats and senior officers' caps. Behind them, a quartet of riflemen. That must be Watson, although he seemed diminished, but then he would be, after his ordeal. Tentatively, she raised a hand, hoping for a signal of recognition back. The man's arms remained at his side.

'Wait here. I have to secure the bolts.'

It was the bridge controller who had spoken, coming past her at a walk that was almost a run. As he went the strides seemed to lengthen with the urgency of his task, and the man who had seemed hunched into his working man's jacket appeared to add an inch or two to his height. And he had spoken in English.

No, it couldn't be.

'Holmes!' she hissed. 'Holmes, wait.'

The man looked over his shoulder, just a glance, but those piercing grey eyes told her she was right. He broke into a faster pace but she was after him.

Target moving.

She could sense the consternation at the other end of the crossing. One of the German officers had taken a step onto the as-yet-unsecured bridge, which oscillated under his weight. He, too, had perhaps appreciated that Holmes had been in plain sight this whole time.

'Sherlock, wait, please,' she pleaded.

'Stay out of this, Mrs Gregson,' he growled. 'I know what I am doing.'

'I am glad one of us does. Wait, damn you!'

Target in crosshairs. Trigger tensioned. Wind zero.

Younger and fitter than Holmes, and driven by a deep desperation, she reached him before he was halfway across.

'Mr Holmes—'

He pushed her away and she turned back to Nathan. 'Robert. What are you doing? Shoot him! Shoot his legs!'

But Nathan stood rooted to the spot next to the car, his pistol still in his pocket, as if frozen into inaction.

Take the shot.

The crack of a high-powered rifle echoed over the flat landscape, the sound reaching those around the bridge some moments after its bullet penetrated the flesh of the upper arm, found the collar bone and was deflected downwards, severing the pulmonary artery as it went, ploughing through soft lung tissue until it nicked the aorta, causing the chest cavity to fill with blood, before it punched its way out between the ribs, leaving its victim to crumple down onto the wooden surface of the bridge.

A volley of shots followed from several directions, the bridge's metalwork sparking and flashing with the ricochets. Most of the onlookers, feeling the air about them snap and crackle, flung themselves down to the ground but two witnesses to the assassination, one from either end of the bridge, broke into a sprint.

In that moment, few noticed that the waters of the Meuse next to the German bank had started to bubble and boil as a glistening black shape emerged from its muddy resting place.

The two figures collided close to the centre. There was a brief tussle and the pair of them pitched sideways. Their balance gone, Holmes and Watson fell through a gap in the iron latticework of the bridge and, still intertwined in a desperate embrace, plunged into the icy waters of the river below.

FIFTY-FIVE: EPILOGUE

The convalescent home had a decent view over the wintry South Downs from its veranda, where the patients spent much of the day. Watson wondered if this particular establishment had been deliberately chosen to torment him, to remind him of where his former friend had once cultivated his bees and his honey. Most of the other occupants of the converted mansion were wounded soldiers, for the most part missing limbs or gas-blinded. Watson felt something of a fraud. All he had lost, he thought, sitting in his bath chair, blanket over his thighs, was his will to live. That and about three stones in weight.

He was scanning the advertisements in the *Argos* when the matron announced he had a visitor.

'Who is it?'

'A Mr Holmes.'

'Mycroft Holmes?'

'I believe it is.'

He carefully folded the paper and laid it on the table next to him. 'Very well. Show him in, please.'

Mycroft stepped from the shadows of the day room and onto

the glassed-in veranda and pulled up a chair, taking his time in sitting, showing the care of a man cautious with his ageing joints.

'Watson,' he said once he had settled.

'Mycroft.'

'How are you?'

'Getting stronger, despite myself.'

'That water was very cold. The shock to a body of our vintage . . . it takes time to heal.'

Watson didn't answer.

'You might like to know that a Red Cross investigation team, operating under the Geneva Convention, is at Harzgrund. The Germans have agreed to co-operate fully, to hand over any evidence of wrongdoing on the part of prisoners and to deliver the perpetrators to British military authority. Men will be hanged for what they did in that camp, Watson.'

'The thought gives me little pleasure.' In truth, there was little in life that gave him much pleasure these days.

'I have something for you.' Mycroft handed over a parcel.

'What's this?'

'Notebooks. Pencils. You have a story to write.'

Watson threw the package on top of the newspaper. 'I don't want to write any of this. Not Harzgrund. Not that bloody bridge.'

Mycroft was not surprised by the mix of venom and despair in Watson's words. The mental scars of that day would clearly take even longer than his body to heal. 'No, not that. The Harwich Von Bork affair. It turns out that Mrs Gregson sold that story, and the promise of several others, to Greenhough Smith to finance her little escapade. He wants to call it "His Last Bow".'

Watson nodded his approval. The Von Bork affair would prob-
ably be Holmes's last official appearance, at least chronologically.
There were still earlier adventures to relate, he supposed, 'The
Girl and the Gold Watches', for one, but the tale of that night in
August 1914, when he bested Von Bork, would be a fitting place to
end his tenure in the public eye. 'How much did she get?'

'Two hundred pounds, so he says.'

'Well done her.' Watson looked the older man in the eye. 'It
was more than an escapade, you know. Wrong-headed, perhaps,
but at least she tried.'

'And so did we.'

'By positioning a sniper to kill Sherlock?'

It was Mycroft's turn to be silent.

'And a very poor sniper at that. Missed his bloody target
completely.'

Watson could sense that something was troubling Mycroft,
something he didn't quite know how to express.

'Didn't he?'

'That's not entirely true. At least, we don't believe it is.'

'Tell me,' demanded Watson.

'Perhaps when you are a little better.'

Watson gripped Mycroft's arm. 'Tell me.'

'The sniper – our sniper, that is – was under orders to shoot
only if Sherlock was in German hands. We had a plan in place to
make sure that didn't happen.'

'The Holland.'

'It was Churchill's idea.'

'Churchill is full of . . . ideas,' said Watson slowly. 'Not all of
them good.'

Watson had discovered once he and Holmes had been
dragged onboard that the Holland was an experimental class
of submarine, most of which had been lost or scrapped.
Holland 6, though, a minelayer designed for penetration of
estuaries and rivers, was still extant. Churchill had persuaded
Jackie Fisher of the Board of Invention and Research to release
it for a special mission, which involved travelling through
neutral waters, to emerge on the German side of the Meuse at
the appropriate time.

'It worked,' said Mycroft. 'The marines did a good job of
pinning down the enemy while you were fished out of the
river. It is a shame we were late – a small tug that had been
depth-sounding for us missed a mud bank. We were grounded
for a few minutes.'

A few very precious minutes, thought Watson. 'You were
saying about the sniper.'

'Churchill had a man named Bloch released. German sniper.
He was promised freedom no matter what happened, but if Von
Bork had my brother in custody, he was to shoot Sherlock. At
least, that's what Churchill told me.'

'And you believe him?'

Mycroft hesitated. 'It's possible he told him to shoot Sherlock
the moment he crossed over to the German side.'

'That sounds more like Churchill.'

'But without Winston we wouldn't have had the Holland. I
wouldn't have been on board to help save you. It was a belt-and
braces approach. Give him credit for that.'

'The sniper?' prompted Watson. 'What happened to him?'

'Dead.'

'How?'

'Throat cut.'

'By whom?'

'The one who took his place on the tower. As far as we can ascertain, that is.'

Watson leaned forward. 'You are talking in riddles.'

'Miss Pillbody was on the tower. It was she who pulled the trigger.'

Watson reacted as if he had been given electro-therapy at full voltage; his body arching into spasm.

Mycroft reached over and poured him a glass of water. 'Nurse!'

'No, no . . . I'm all right.' He took the water and gulped, spilling some down his front. 'Miss Pillbody? That damned woman again. How?'

Mycroft explained about the escape from Holloway and the subsequent murder of two men in Venlo, including his own agent. 'She killed a local man and took his hunting rifle. We think she was looking for a suitable spot to shoot at the bridge when she saw the tower and instinctively knew that it was the location we would choose to try and silence Sherlock. Her training would tell her that.'

'So Mrs Gregson's death wasn't an accident? Miss Pillbody meant to kill her.'

'Possibly.'

Watson remembered the moments after the bullet struck, how he had turned round and punched Von Bork so hard his nose had split, and then tossed him into Hersch. His run over the bridge towards the body and his confusion when a Dutch worker had come straight at him. The shock of recognition when he was confronted with Holmes. The anger when Sherlock wouldn't let Watson go to the crumpled, lonely figure of the woman he . . . the woman who, by filling his imagination and dreams, had kept him alive through his incarceration.

The tussle that took them over the bridge to the waters where Holland 6 had already broken the surface and was disgorging a line of Royal Marines, marksmen every one. The volleys that kept the Germans' heads down while they were extracted from the water. The delirium, the total physical collapse that followed. Yes, he could recall every hideous moment.

Mycroft passed him a handkerchief, ostensibly to mop up the spilled drink from his waistcoat, but also to dab away the tears on his cheeks.

'The other shots, after the one that . . . after the first one?'

'Again, mostly Miss Pillbody with the hunting rifle. Less than accurate. We had no idea who or what she was aiming at till now. I'm afraid she got clean away, though. She could be back in Berlin, for all we know. But rest assured, when this war is over we will run her to ground. You might be pleased to hear that Von Bork is to face a military trial for overstepping his authority. That's the story they are giving the Red Cross, anyway. The plan to ensnare Sherlock was all the work of a rogue officer, pursuing a personal vendetta.'

Watson was only half listening. 'I never got to say goodbye to Georgina. Not properly. He denied me that, your brother.'

'When this is over we'll bring her body back for a proper burial and service. But the Dutch were furious about their neutrality being compromised. Although the Holland 6 was in

German waters, technically at least, when it picked you up, it had to pass through Dutch sections of the river to get away.'

'I don't give a fig for Dutch neutrality.'

'I realize that. My brother did it for the best, you know.'

'I didn't even get to see her face!' Watson snapped. 'Just for a second would have been enough.'

Mycroft sighed. 'I appreciate that you must miss her. Even I understand that.' Mycroft indicated the newspaper. 'That's not the way forward, though.'

'What isn't?' Watson asked suspiciously.

'A séance. Or any other bogus way to contact the dead. Wherever they are, the dead are always beyond us.'

Watson looked puzzled. 'How did you . . . ?'

'When I asked Matron how you were doing, she said you were strong enough to consider a trip to Brighton this Saturday. I see from the newspaper there that there is a public meeting of the British Society for Psychical Research, with a famous author or two speaking on the matter of life after death, on that very day. It will be very busy. You aren't alone in hoping this life isn't the end. Not by a long chalk.'

'I don't believe. And yet, there was one case in the camps that I keep wondering about.' Watson outlined the details of Brevette and the séance where he apparently told Hulpett that the captain had not made it home. Hulpett, apparently, was not one of those who knew the truth about the fate of the men who entered the trick coffins. He was onboard solely for his experience as a solicitor. And so he had told Lincoln-Chance about his qualms, sealing Archer's fate and, for good measure, the medium's fellow voyagers to the afterlife.

'It could be a coincidence,' offered Mycroft when Watson had finished.

'Do you believe in coincidence?'

'On the 30th of June 1916, *The Times* crossword had clues that gave the answers "Somme", "offensive" and "Albert". And the next day the Battle of Albert began, the first part of the Somme Offensive. The poor man who set the clues was hauled off and virtually hung by his ankles. Turned out to be a complete coincidence. So, yes, sometimes the stars do align and coincidences do occur. Look, you know that Harry Houdini has spent much of the last few years debunking mediums and the like. Sherlock has done his fair share of explaining supernatural phenomena. Good Lord, man, you were there for most of them.'

Watson's chin dropped onto his chest. 'I know. I am a foolish old man.'

'And, as I said, you miss her.' There was a touch of impatience in the voice. 'It might have been for the best, you know, that you didn't see her on the bridge. She was already dead,' said Mycroft, putting a hand on Watson's knee. 'Sherlock knew that. He wanted to save the living . . . there was no time for mourning.'

Watson did not answer.

'If you insist on exploring the possibility of the continuation of sentience, there was always one case that baffled Houdini and every other investigator, including Madame Curie.'

Watson turned and looked at Mycroft. 'Don't mock me.'

'It's true. A woman in Paris, Eva Carrière, has received some acclaim, although I also hear she is something of a sexual exhibitionist. Personally, I am not convinced, but I think it might be more interesting than the hysteria that will ensue in Brighton. People *want* to believe so badly, you see. It doesn't make the dead come calling.'

'Well, thank you all the same. I shall do some research on this Carrière woman. But perhaps you are right. It is just so hard to accept that I will never see her again.'

'That is the worst part.'

Watson's head flicked up. 'Until now?'

'What?'

'You said, about the shots on the bridge, the wild firing. You said you had no idea what she was firing at "until now".'

'No.' Mycroft chewed his lip. 'This is . . . difficult.'

The matron appeared with some tea and biscuits, interrupting them. When she had left, Watson asked: 'How is it difficult exactly?'

'To reopen old wounds.'

'The old wounds are not yet healed, Mycroft, they will reopen easily enough. What do you have?'

Mycroft reached into his jacket pocket and extracted a piece of paper. 'Three days ago the body of one of Kell's men was discovered in his London chambers. He had hanged himself. Robert Nathan. You know him?'

Watson indicated he didn't.

'I met him briefly. Competent enough fellow, although rather in thrall to—' Mycroft pulled himself up short and cleared his throat. 'He was assisting Mrs Gregson. He left a note. Much of it is rambling – he had drunk a fair quantity of alcohol before he did the deed. But this is the relevant page.'

Watson took it and, with a shaking hand, read the scrawl,

which was blobbed with water stains. Tears, he guessed, dropping as the man wrote.

> Some say evil is a contagion. That it can infect others, like influenza or typhoid. I believe that now. I believe the woman Pillbody to be a creature of pure evil, capable of corrupting all who come into contact with her. Why else would I have conceived of such a wicked plan? Wicked and foolish. It was I who arranged her escape in Holland. I who gave her the means of picking the locks to the manacles that bound her. I did not know she was going to kill Farleigh and Buller. That was not my intention. Before I released her, I gave her a price, which she agreed to. Kill Dr Watson on the bridge. Oh, how depraved it seems now. But at the time it seemed the perfect solution. If Watson were dead then there would be no exchange – Sherlock Holmes would not fall into German hands. And Mrs Gregson would be free of her infatuation for the man. And I would be free to pursue her without

Watson refolded the paper and handed it back, struck numb by the words. 'I wish Pillbody had killed me, not Mrs Gregson,' he said. 'The man was right. It would have solved the dilemma at a stroke.'

'He is also right about Miss Pillbody being evil,' said Mycroft. 'Cruelty is her currency. She had one accurate shot. By killing Georgina, she struck at both you and at Nathan.'

'It was stupid of him. You might as well try and control a hungry tiger as Miss Pillbody.'

'Those shots on the bridge, from the hunting rifle, I suspect they were meant for you. Mrs Pillbody probably thought she might as well kill you as agreed. So Sherlock saved your life by pulling you into the water before she got her range.'

Mycroft concentrated on drinking his tea, biding his time until Watson had composed himself and dried his tears once more.

'How is he?' Watson asked at last. 'Sherlock?'

'Back in London for the time being. He, too, suffered from his submersion. And from the events on the bridge.'

'He knows about this Nathan and what he did?'

'I told him this morning.'

Watson remembered his tea and took a sip. It was almost cold.

'He's outside,' said Mycroft softly.

'Who is?'

'Sherlock.'

A shake of the head. 'I don't want to see him.'

'He said you wouldn't.'

'It's all too painful.'

'He said that too.'

'Then why did he come?' asked Watson tetchily.

Mycroft frowned. 'He said the most extraordinary thing to me when I pointed that out.'

'Which was?'

'I quote: "I am not always right, you know, Mycroft. And on this occasion, I would very much like to be in the wrong." Imagine that. Admitting to me that he was fallible.'

'Imagine,' Watson repeated sourly.

'There is something else you should know,' said Mycroft

cautiously, as if tiptoeing through a minefield. 'There is a case he needs help with.'

'A case? Isn't he past taking cases?'

'An old adversary has apparently reappeared,' he replied solemnly.

'Really?' Watson tried to feign disinterest, but he knew Mycroft would have picked up on the signs of his curiosity being pricked. Some time passed before he could wait no longer. 'Which one?'

'He didn't say. I am merely his brother, not his . . .' Mycroft let Watson's exact status hang in the ether.

Watson drank the rest of his tea in silence. Eventually, he put down the cup and saucer and picked up a biscuit. He felt a strange mixture of emotions. The weight of years and shared experiences, a near-lifetime with Holmes, pressed down on him physically like a great weight, but somewhere deep inside he could feel something – his soul? His spirit? – floating with a lightness he had not known for many weeks now.

'All right, Mycroft. It would give me considerable pleasure to prove the Great Detective wrong.' He took a bite of the ginger nut to mask his smile. 'Send him in, will you?'

APPENDIX

The Girl and the Gold Watches
by John H. Watson

It was April 1890 (and not 1892 as some accounts would have it), as the debilitating bone-chill of a lengthy winter had finally begun to relax its grip on the metropolis, when my friend Sherlock Holmes turned his attention to what the daily press were calling The Rugby Mystery and some others The Girl and the Gold Watches. Holmes had recently completed his investigation into a most gruesome business, involving jealousy and murder. The solution to the case had put him in a rather sombre mood. 'What is the meaning of it, Watson?' he had exclaimed, not for the first time. Peering into the darkest corners of the human soul often caused him to recoil in revulsion at the depravity of his fellow man. 'What object is served by this circle of misery and violence and fear? It must tend to some end, or else our universe is ruled by chance, which is unthinkable. But what end? There is the great standing perennial problem to which human reason is as far from an answer as ever!'

That resultant brown study, a cloud of melancholia that wrapped itself around him like a winter fog, persisted for some weeks, to the point where I feared he might reach for solace once more in the seven per cent solution. I sought permission – freely granted – from my wife to move back to our old rooms in Baker Street that I might keep an eye on him until the black dog was driven away. And sure enough, as the thermometer rose on a certain bright Monday morning, Holmes stirred himself from his regular position, curled on the sofa with a newspaper, and began to pace the floor of our Baker Street lodgings, a practice I knew sometimes drove Mrs Hudson on the floor below us to distraction, for it could last many hours.

I lowered my own newspaper – I was studying an article about the recent rash of card-sharping incidents across the city and the methods the fraudsters preferred – and peered at him. He looked like a freshly coiled spring and something burned in his eyes. I knew that look of old and it warmed my heart. 'Yes, Watson, you are thinking that my hibernation is at an end.'

I felt a surge of relief course through me. 'You don't have to be the world's only Consulting Detective to deduce that, Holmes.'

'Quite so. But, as your faculties are in such good order, you'll be well aware that we are about to have a visitor.'

I listened for a footfall on the stairs, but could hear nothing. And as he had not been near the bow window that overlooked Baker Street and often provided him with an early indication of our visitors – not to mention their profession, history, dietary preferences, whether or not they owned a dog and were married or no – I was perplexed as to how he could be so certain our morning reading would be interrupted. Holmes frowned, as if his timing was a little off, and then smiled when there was a ring at the bell.

'Well, Holmes,' I said, with, I admit, a little sarcasm in my voice, 'are you going to tell me anything about our visitor, even before he enters the room?'

'Well, he came to London by train, arriving at Euston, of that much I am certain. He will be smartly, but quite cheaply attired. Prominent whiskers, probably in his thirties, I would surmise, and a little portly for his age—'

'Holmes,' I said. 'Really. It's too much.'

'You know of The Girl and the Gold Watches Mystery?'

'Of course,' I said. The singular events on the Manchester-bound express train had been the subject of much speculation in the press for weeks. 'The Rugby Mystery. In fact, I do believe I first brought it to your attention.'

'In the hope of arousing my curiosity.'

'Indeed,' I confessed.

He snatched up the folded newspaper from the couch and waved it at me, as if trying to shake the newsprint loose. 'But I knew that, should no solution present itself, the case would eventually find itself at the door of this very building. And so it has proved, if somewhat tardily. It says in here that the railway authorities and the police are seeking outside help this very week.'

'And you have assumed this outside help is you?'

Holmes rose to his full height and peered down that thin, hawk-like nose of his. 'My dear Watson, who else is there to turn to?' The slightest of twinkles in his eye served to undercut the arrogance of his remark. But not the truth of it.

Mrs Hudson showed our visitor into the sitting room. He was indeed in his thirties, ruddy faced and stout, with mutton-chop whiskers and wearing a suit that, although clean and pressed, was not of the best quality. He already had his bowler in his hands. 'Gentlemen,' he said, looking from one to the other of us. 'Excuse my calling without an appointment.'

'Nonsense,' said Holmes, beckoning him to a chair. 'You gave more than adequate notice of your arrival, Mr Henderson.' He gave the newspaper a tap and tossed it aside.

'I assume I am addressing Mr Sherlock Holmes?' the man said, unperturbed that Holmes already knew his name. Perhaps, in no small part to my writings, the public had come to expect him to be something of a mind-reader. If so, it was his own fault. For my part, I could only assume that Henderson was mentioned in the newspaper account, that Holmes had deduced that a railway police inspector – for that was what I assumed he was – from Rugby would not be a young man nor, being a policeman and a provincial, particularly smartly dressed. (The whiskers comment baffled me, although I wouldn't admit it; it was only much later that I discovered the newspaper in question had published one of the new experimental half-tone photographs of Henderson, which I thought was a shabby trick on Holmes's part.)

'You are correct. And this is my friend and companion, Dr Watson. Now, what can we do for the railways?'

'I am employed by several railway companies in the role of detective. I do have police training, you understand, but I am engaged in a private capacity as an investigator.'

So not a police inspector. 'And for your discretion, I would imagine.'

Henderson sat down. 'It is true that many cases are resolved without recourse to the civilian police. But not the matter I have come to consult you about. I am sure you are familiar with the facts regarding The Rugby Mystery.'

Holmes now folded his frame down onto the sofa, one arm running along the back. 'I know of the case, but the facts . . . no. I know only what I read in the daily press, which, as you appreciate more than most, Inspector, hardly amounts to the same thing. Facts are often smothered by speculation and innuendo, not to mention mischief and prejudice.'

Henderson smiled knowingly, showing yellowed teeth. 'Quite so, Mr Holmes.'

'As Watson will no doubt point out, I have said on previous occasions that it is a capital mistake to theorize before one has data. Insensibly, one begins to twist facts to suit theories, instead of theories to suit facts. It bears repeating, Watson.' The detective twirled a hand in my direction. 'Now, Mr Henderson, I have but the vaguest grasp of the details, so assume we know nothing. Lay out the relevant facts as if to a jury. I will only interrupt to clarify a point. Should I ask Mrs Hudson to fetch you some tea before you begin?'

'No, thank you, Mr Holmes.' He cleared his throat. 'The known facts of the case begin on the 18th of March. That is, almost a month ago.'

Holmes made a slight sucking sound, which I assumed was displeasure at the length of time it had taken to consult him. The crime scene would be very, very cold ground at this remove.

'There is a five o'clock train to Manchester every weekday evening from Euston Station.'

'I know it from Bradshaw's,' said Holmes. 'Just three stop-pages and an approximate travelling time of four hours and twenty minutes. Very popular with businessmen from the North who wish to save the expense of a hotel in London. The weather?'

'Inclement. Squally, I would say.'

'Yes,' I began, 'wasn't the 18th the day we spent the night watching for—'

Holmes shot me a glance that pierced me like a jezail bullet. At first I thought he was annoyed at the interruption (even though he had hardly stayed true to his statement of not inter-jecting unless to clarify a point). Then I realized he did not want me to mention the persons at the heart of the case to which I referred. It was still to reach the divorce courts. 'We were soaked through,' I finished feebly.

'Despite the poor conditions, the train was fairly well filled,' continued Henderson. 'The guard on the train was a tried-and-trusted servant of the company. His name was John Palmer and he had worked for the railway for twenty-two years, without a blemish or a complaint. The station clock was upon the stroke of five and Palmer was about to give the customary signal to his driver, when he noticed two belated passengers. A man and a woman.'

'The guard furnished a description, I believe.'

'Indeed he did. The man was exceptionally tall, dressed in a long black overcoat with astrakhan collar and cuffs. As I have already said, the evening was an inclement one, and the tall traveller had the high, warm collar turned up to protect his throat against the bitter March wind. He appeared, as far as the guard could judge, to be between fifty and sixty years of age. But vigorous with it. In one hand he carried a brown leather Gladstone bag.'

'But no other distinguishing features?' asked Holmes. I must admit I was watching my friend as much as the policeman. It warmed my heart to see him so engaged.

The railway detective shook his head. 'No. Palmer said, had he known what was about to happen, he would have studied every aspect of the man. But as it was, he simply thought him one more passenger among the hundred or more he would see that evening.'

'Quite so. And the lady?'

'No fuller a picture, I fear. Tall and erect, walking with a vigorous step, which outpaced the gentleman beside her. She wore a long, fawn-coloured dust-cloak, a black, close-fitting toque, and a dark veil which concealed the greater part of her face. The two might very well have passed as father and daughter. They walked swiftly down the line of carriages, glancing in at the windows, until Palmer overtook them.' At this point the policeman fetched a notebook from his pocket and flicked the pages until he found the desired passage. '"Now then, sir, look sharp, the train is going," he said to them. "We'll have First Class," the man answered.'

Now Holmes's fingers were pressed together, forming a pyramid, and his lips were pursed. I could almost hear the great brain humming like a dynamo as he conjured the scene of steam and haste. 'Proceed.'

Henderson looked down at the notes once more. 'The nearest carriage, which Palmer opened, was occupied by a small man with a cigar in his mouth. Now this man's appearance seems to have impressed itself upon the guard's memory, for he was prepared, afterwards, to describe or to identify him. He was a man of thirty-four or thirty-five years of age, dressed in some grey material, sharp-nosed, alert, with a ruddy, weather-beaten face, and a small, closely cropped, black beard.'

'That is a very precise description for such a fleeting contact,' I said, gratified when Holmes nodded that the same thought had occurred to him, 'especially when he was so vague on the other players.'

'But he swears those are the facts.'

'Then we should give him the benefit of the doubt,' said Holmes.

'The gentleman with the astrakhan coat was not happy. "This is a smoking compartment. The lady dislikes smoke," he said. Now Palmer, being a good servant of the railway, thought the express might be late. So he slammed the door of the smoking carriage, opened that of the next one, which was empty, and thrust the two travellers in. He says he fears he might have been brusque, which pained him, but he is a punctilious man and it was now one minute after five. So he sounded his whistle and the wheels of the train began to move. The man with the cigar was at the window of his carriage, and said something to the guard as he rolled past him, but the words were lost in the bustle of the departure. Palmer stepped into the guard's van, as it came up to him, and thought no more of the incident.'

'Why should he?' I asked. 'Nothing untoward has happened so far.'

'Patience, Watson,' said Holmes with a slight smile on his lips. 'Mr Henderson, I feel we are about to reach the crux of this matter.'

'Indeed we are. Some twelve minutes after its departure the train reached Willesden Junction, where it stopped for a very short interval. Now, before you ask, Mr Holmes, an examination of the tickets has ascertained beyond doubt that no one either joined or left it at this time, and no passenger was seen to alight upon the platform. At five fourteen the journey to Manchester was resumed, and Rugby was reached at six fifty, the express being five minutes late. At Rugby the attention of the station officials was drawn to the fact that the door of one of the First Class carriages was unlatched. An examination of that compartment, and of its neighbour, disclosed a remarkable state of affairs, Mr Holmes.'

Holmes leaned forward now, fingers still pyramided together and his eyes blazing. 'Pray, proceed, Mr Henderson.'

'The smoking carriage in which the short, red-faced man with the black beard had been seen was now empty. Save for a half-smoked cigar, there was no trace whatever of the recent occupant. The door of this carriage was fastened. In the next compartment, to which attention had been originally drawn, there was no sign either of the gentleman with the astrakhan collar or of the young lady who accompanied him. All three passengers had disappeared. On the other hand, there was found upon the floor of this carriage – the one in which the tall travel-ler and the lady had been – a young man fashionably dressed and of elegant appearance. He lay with his knees drawn up, and his head resting against the further door, an elbow upon either seat. A bullet had penetrated his heart and his death must have been instantaneous. No one had seen such a man enter the train, and no railway ticket was found in his pocket, neither were there any markings upon his linen, nor papers nor personal property that might help to identify him. Who he was, whence he had come, and how he had met his end were each as great a mystery as what had occurred to the three people who had started an hour and a half before from Euston and then Willesden in those two compartments.'

'But there was one other peculiarity,' prompted Holmes, 'about this young man. Much commented upon at the time.'

'Yes. In his pockets were found no fewer than six valuable gold watches, three in the various pockets of his waistcoat, one in his ticket-pocket, one in his breast-pocket, and one small one set in a leather strap and fastened round his left wrist.'

'The obvious explanation,' I offered, knowing I would be knocked down, but enjoying the show all the same, 'was that the man was a pickpocket, and that this was his plunder.'

Holmes turned his gaze to me. 'Yes, my dear Watson, but note that all six were of American make and of a type that is rare in England. Three of them bore the mark of the Rochester Watchmaking Company; one was by Mason of Elmira; one was unmarked; and the small one, which was highly jewelled and ornamented, was from Tiffany of New York. The other contents of his pockets consisted of an ivory knife with a corkscrew by Rodgers of Sheffield; a small, circular mirror, one inch in diameter; a readmission slip to the Lyceum Theatre; a silver box full of Vesta matches, and a brown leather cigar case containing two cheroots – also two pounds and fourteen shillings in money. It was clear, then, that whatever motives may have led to his death, robbery was not among them.'

'I thought you knew only the vaguest details,' offered Henderson, unable to hide his amazement.

To Holmes that list amounted to the vaguest details, but I said nothing.

'As already mentioned, there were no markings upon the man's linen, which appeared to be new, and no tailor's name upon his coat. He was young, short, smooth-cheeked, and delicately featured. One of his front teeth was conspicuously stopped with gold.'

'And what action was taken upon the discovery of the body?' asked Holmes.

'An examination was instantly made of the tickets of all passengers, and the number of the passengers themselves was counted. It was found that only three tickets were unaccounted for, corresponding to the three travellers who were missing. The express was then allowed to proceed, but a new guard was sent with it, and John Palmer was detained as a witness at Rugby. The carriage that included the two compartments in question was uncoupled and sidetracked. Then, on the arrival of Inspector Vane, of Scotland Yard—'

'Vane?'

'You know him, Mr Holmes?'

'Only by reputation,' he replied, with a thin smile that gave little away.

'And of myself as company detective, an exhaustive enquiry was made into all the circumstances. That a crime had been committed was certain. The bullet, which appeared to have come from a small pistol or revolver, had been fired from some little distance, as there was no scorching of the clothes.'

'The clothes have been retained?' Holmes asked.

'Yes. You are welcome to examine them, Mr Holmes.'

Holmes nodded his appreciation. 'But I assume no weapon was found?'

'None.'

'Which, along with the lack of scorch marks, suggests this was not a suicide.'

'My conclusion exactly, Mr Holmes. Nor was there any sign of the brown leather bag that the guard had seen in the hand of the tall gentleman. A lady's parasol was found upon the rack, but no other trace was to be seen of the travellers in either of the sections. Apart from the crime, the question of how or why three passengers, one of them a lady, could get out of the train, and one other get in during the unbroken run between Willesden and Rugby has been exercising us.'

'Could the guard throw any light on this?'

'John Palmer said that there was a spot between Tring and Cheddington, where, on account of some repairs to the line, the train had for a few minutes slowed down to a pace not exceeding eight or ten miles an hour. At that place it might be possible for a man, or even for an exceptionally active woman, to have left the train without serious injury. It was true that a gang of platelayers was there, and that they had seen nothing, but it was their custom to stand in the middle between the metals, and the open carriage door was upon the far side, so that it was conceivable that someone might have alighted unseen, as the darkness would by that time be drawing in. A steep embankment would instantly screen anyone who sprang out from the observation of the navvies. The guard also noted that there was a good deal of movement upon the platform at Willesden Junction, and that though it was certain that no one had either joined or left the train there, it was still quite possible that some of the passengers might have changed unseen from one compartment to another.'

I ventured a theory. 'A gentleman might finish his cigar in a smoking carriage and then change to a clearer atmosphere. Supposing that the man with the black beard had done so at Willesden – and the half-smoked cigar upon the floor seemed to favour the supposition – he would naturally go into the nearest section, which would bring him into the company of the two other actors in this drama.'

'Bravo, Watson,' Holmes said softly and sincerely. 'But what happened next? The line has been examined, Mr Henderson, with thoroughness, I presume?'

'Yes. And near Tring, at the very place where the train slowed down, there was found at the bottom of the embankment a small pocket Testament, very shabby and worn.'

'Obviously well loved. Which suggests there might be an inscription?'

'It was printed by the Bible Society of London, and bore an inscription: "From John to Alice. 13 Jan 1856," upon the fly-leaf. Underneath was written: "James. 4 July 1859" and beneath that again: "Edward. 1 Nov 1869," all the entries being in the same handwriting.'

'It does not sound as if the owner would part with this willingly. Which suggests foul play indeed.'

'Hence the coroner's verdict of "Murder by a person or persons unknown", Mr Holmes.'

'There were rewards offered for information, I believe,' I interjected.

'The usual time-wasters, I am afraid, Dr Watson. It was the unsatisfactory ending to a singular case. Unless, of course, you can help, Mr Holmes.'

Holmes took a breath so deep it threatened to deplete the air in the room. 'I cannot promise, Mr Henderson. It is, as you say, a most singular case and I would change nothing about your investigation.'

Henderson reddened with pleasure.

'But I need some time. Having furnished me with the facts in such a concise way, you may consider your duty done. You left your card with Mrs Hudson? Good. I hope to be in touch shortly.'

When Henderson had left I let Holmes ruminate for ten minutes, eyes half-hooded, and returned to my newspaper. When the lids lifted I asked: 'Well, Holmes?'

'Well, my dear friend. Do you have any appointments this evening?'

'None, Holmes.'

'Good. Then perhaps you would do me the kindness of accompanying me on a journey.'

'Where to, Holmes?'

'Rugby, of course. Pass the Bradshaw's, will you?'

The Manchester Express left that Monday evening at two minutes past five, with the usual cacophony of steam, whistles and slamming carriage doors. Holmes and I had a carriage to ourselves, a smoker in the same portion of the train as the one that the gentleman with the cigar would have occupied.

We both used the opportunity to light a cigarette and, replete after a late lunch in Simpson's, I felt like snoozing. Holmes was having none of it. He was on his feet as soon as the train left the station, examining the doors and latches and, at one point, throwing himself on the floor and rolling under the seat.

'Can you see me, Watson?'

'Of course I can. And it is filthy down there.'

He emerged covered in fluff and cigar stubs, and brushed himself down. 'There was a remarkable theory put forward. The fact that the young man's watches were of American make, and some peculiarities in connection with the gold stopping of his front tooth, appeared to indicate that the deceased was a citizen of the United States. His linen, clothes and boots were undoubtedly of British manufacture. So, it has been surmised, he was a spy on the trail of some secret society, recently arrived in this country from America. He was concealed under the seat, and that, on being discovered, he was for some reason, possibly because he had overheard their guilty secrets, put to death by his fellow passengers.'

'Including a woman?'

'Are not women conspicuous in the nihilistic and anarchist movement?'

'But why would he have so many watches about his person? And you can't conceal yourself under a seat. And what role does the smoker play in that theory?'

'Good points. But remember, Watson. When——'

'——when you have eliminated the impossible, whatever remains, however improbable, must be the truth,' I completed.

'Admirable, Watson. I see some of my methods are finally taking root. Now, we will be at Willesden soon. I suggest when the train stops we move one carriage forward, to that non-smoker where the young man met his death.'

We were not alone in the second carriage. There was a young lady and her father, who had been down from Lancashire on business and wanted to show his daughter the metropolis. Neither seemed to recognize that a Great Detective was among them and, after some polite words while the lamps were being lit, he went back to his book and she embroidering an antimacassar. Holmes sat on the inner side of the carriage and glanced frequently at his pocket watch, as if impatient for something to happen.

'Tring,' he said absent-mindedly, as the train slowed. 'The works must still be in place.'

'Watson,' he said eventually, 'I took the liberty of bringing a flask. Perhaps you would like a sip for fortification?'

I thought it rather improper to drink in front of the young woman and turned to look at our fellow passengers. At that moment I heard the slamming of the door and looked around to see that Sherlock Holmes had left the carriage.

All three of us watched in incredulity as a local train rattled our windows as it passed, leaving a trail of grit-laden steam in its wake.

'What's going on?' demanded the businessman. 'Where's your friend?'

'Please stay calm,' I said. 'This is entirely normal behaviour for Mr Sherlock Holmes.'

'Sherlock Holmes!' exclaimed the man. 'I thought he looked

familiar.' He tapped his daughter on the knee. 'And you were complaining we hadn't seen anyone famous.'

Her expression suggested that she had hoped for someone more celebrated than a well-known detective. I, meanwhile, dropped to my knees and examined beneath the seats but, as I expected, I found only discarded rail tickets and dirt.

Then, in the space he had recently vacated, I saw the flask he had mentioned and, pinned beneath it, a small note.

> Apologies for the parlour trick, Watson. Either it worked, and I am now on my way south once more, somewhat circuitously, to Baker Street, or I lie mangled and lifeless on the track. If the former, I shall see you there as soon as possible. If the latter, it has been a pleasure and privilege to have known you. You really are a fixed point in a changing world.

I sprang to the window and lowered it, thrusting my head out without concern for any approaching train on the downline. The light was already fading but, through the dispersing trail of smoke left by the local, I could just make out that there appeared to be no hideously crushed detective lying on the track.

It was late in the evening when I finally made it back to Baker Street. Holmes was still up, smoking a pipe, a fire blazed in the grate, as the nights were still chill. There was a plate of cold meats set out by Mrs Hudson at Holmes's request and I set about it with some relish.

'Apologies again, Watson,' said Holmes.

'Leaping between moving trains, Holmes? It was a foolhardy thing to do—'

'Which is exactly what I expected you to say if I had revealed my plans beforehand. Bradshaw's told me there is a local train running through Harrow and King's Langley, which is timed in such a way that the express must have overtaken it at or about the period when it eased down its speed to eight miles an hour on account of the repairs of the line. The two trains would at that time be travelling in the same direction at a similar rate of speed and upon parallel lines. As I have just demonstrated, it is entirely feasible to cross from one to the other.'

I finished off the last of the food. 'That tells us how one might disappear from a train. But not why. Nor why murder was perpetrated.'

'Whatever may be the truth,' said Holmes, 'it must depend upon some bizarre and rare combination of events, so we need have no hesitation in postulating such events in our explanation. In the absence of data we must abandon the analytic or scientific method of investigation, and must approach it in the synthetic fashion. In a word, instead of taking known events and deducing from them what has occurred, we must build up a fanciful explanation if it will only be consistent with known events.'

'Really, Holmes? That goes against your usual methods.'

'It sometimes does one good to ring the changes. We have nothing to lose here. There is no urgency, apart from to track down the killer, whom I suspect is already long out of Scotland Yard's reach. But having come up with our theory, we can then test this explanation by any fresh facts that may arise. If they all fit into their places, the probability is that we are upon the right track, and with each fresh fact this probability increases in a geometrical progression until the evidence becomes final and convincing.

'You recall that the lamps of the express had been lit at Willesden, so that each compartment was brightly illuminated, and most visible to an observer from outside. It is within everyone's experience how, under such circumstances, the occupant of each carriage can see very plainly the passengers in the other carriages opposite to him.

'Now, the sequence of events as I reconstruct them would be after this fashion. This young man with the abnormal number of watches was alone in the carriage of the slow train. His ticket, with his papers and gloves and other things, were, we will suppose, on the seat beside him. He was probably an American, and also probably a man of weak intellect. The excessive wearing of jewellery is an early symptom in some forms of mania.

'As he sat watching the carriages of the express which were – on account of the state of the line – going at the same pace as himself, he suddenly saw some people in it whom he knew. We will suppose for the sake of our theory that these people were a woman whom he loved and a man whom he hated, and who in return hated him. The young man was excitable and impulsive. He opened the door of his carriage, stepped from the footboard of the local train to the footboard of the express, opened the other door, and made his way into the presence of these two people. The feat, on trains going at the same pace, is by no means so perilous as it might appear.'

I lit a cigarette. 'I'm not sure I'd like to test that theory again. Now you have got our young man, without his ticket, into the carriage in which the elder man and the young woman are travelling.'

'Yes, Watson, and it is not difficult to imagine that a violent scene ensued. It is possible that the pair were also Americans, which is the more probable as the man carried a weapon – an unusual thing in England. If our supposition of incipient mania is correct, the young man is likely to have assaulted the other. As the upshot of the quarrel the elder man shot the intruder, and then made his escape from the carriage, taking the young lady with him. We will suppose that all this happened very rapidly, and that the train was still going at so slow a pace that it was not difficult for them to leave it. A woman might leave a train going at eight miles an hour. As a matter of fact, we know that this woman *did* do so.

'And now we have to fit in the man in the smoking carriage. Presuming that we have, up to this point, reconstructed the tragedy correctly, we shall find nothing in this other man to cause us to reconsider our conclusions. According to my theory, this man saw the young fellow cross from one train to the other, saw him open the door, heard the pistol-shot, saw the two fugitives spring out onto the line, realized that murder had been done, and sprang out himself in pursuit. Why he has never been heard of since – whether he met his own death in the pursuit, or whether, as is more likely, he was made to realize that it was not a case for his interference – is a detail that we have at present no means of explaining. I acknowledge that there are some difficulties in the way. At first sight, it might seem improbable that at such a moment a murderer would burden himself in his flight with a brown leather bag. My answer is that he was well aware that if the bag were found his identity would be established. It was absolutely necessary for him to take it with him. My theory stands or falls upon one point, and tomorrow I will call upon Mr Henderson and the railway company to make strict enquiry as to whether a ticket was found unclaimed in the local train through Harrow and King's Langley upon the 18th of March. If such a ticket were found my case is proved. If not, my theory may still be the correct one, for it is conceivable either that he travelled without a ticket or that his ticket was lost.'

'Remarkable, Holmes.'

'You don't sound convinced, Watson.'

'And neither,' I ventured, 'do you, Holmes.'

To which he gave a peal of laughter. 'Perhaps not, but we shall see what tomorrow brings.'

It was actually two days before the glum tidings arrived. No such ticket as hypothesized by Holmes was found; secondly, that on the night of the murder, thanks to a boiler problem, the local train had been stationary in King's Langley Station when the express, going at fifty miles an hour, had flashed past it.

Holmes took this news remarkably well, perhaps because an intriguing note had arrived from Montague Place from a governess with a singular problem. 'I am sure that the solution to this puzzle will present itself eventually,' he said. Neither of us realized then that it would take five long years for The Rugby Mystery to be solved and, in the interim, my great friend would appear to be lost to the world for ever.

I recall it recorded in my notebook that it was a bleak and windy day towards the end of March 1895 that Holmes received a telegram over breakfast. He scribbled a reply and said nothing more of it. A few hours later there was a measured step on the stairs and a moment later a stout, tall and grey-whiskered gentleman entered the room.

'Mr Peredue. Come, please be seated. This is my friend and companion Dr John Watson.'

'I have read and greatly enjoyed your works, sir. Most engaging.'

'Aren't they?' said Holmes. 'Although Watson does have a rather romantic streak when it comes to reporting our cases. And a tendency to tell stories backwards. How was the crossing?'

'Crossing?'

'From the United States.'

Peredue frowned at this. 'Rough, since you ask. It took me a day or so to recover. How did you . . . ? My accent?'

'Sir, I would have placed you as from New York or its environs before you uttered a single word. The cut of the jacket, the cuffs on the trousers, the pearlized buttons on your waistcoat . . . or should I say vest?'

'Waistcoat will do. I haven't gone entirely native.'

'When did you leave Buckinghamshire?' Holmes made an aside to me, in case I wasn't keeping up. 'Peredue is an old Bucks surname.'

'It is. My people emigrated to the States from there in the early fifties.'

Holmes took his customary place on the sofa. 'Come, arrange your thoughts, Mr Peredue, and lay them out in due sequence. Watson, make yourself comfortable, because you are about to hear the solution to The Rugby Mystery.'

I needed no more encouragement to give Mr Peredue my undivided attention. At last! Five full years since Holmes hopped between those trains.

'My family settled in Rochester, in the State of New York, where my father ran a large dry goods store. There were only two sons: myself, James Peredue, and my brother, Edward Peredue. I was ten years older than my brother, and after my father died I sort of took the place of a father to him, as an elder brother would. He was a bright, spirited boy. But there was always a soft spot in him, and it was like mould in cheese, for it spread and spread, and nothing that you could do would stop it. Mother saw it just as clearly as I did, but she went on spoiling him all the same, for he had such a way with him that you could refuse him nothing. I did all I could to hold him in, and he hated me for my pains.

'At last he fairly got his head, and nothing that we could do would stop him. He got off into New York, and went rapidly from bad to worse. At first he was only fast, and then he was criminal; and then, at the end of a year or two, he was one of the most notorious young crooks in the city. He had formed a friendship with Sparrow MacCoy, who was at the head of his profession as a bunco steerer, green goodsman and general rascal.'

'We have heard that name before, have we not, Watson? But not for some time.'

'They took to card-sharping, and frequented some of the best hotels in New York. My brother was an excellent actor. In fact, he might have made an honest name for himself if he had chosen. He would take the parts of a young Englishman of title, of a simple lad from the West, or of a college undergraduate, whichever suited Sparrow MacCoy's purpose. And then one day he dressed himself as a girl, and he carried it off so well, and made himself such a valuable decoy, that it was their favourite game afterwards.'

'Ah,' said Holmes, then put a finger to his lips, as if to remind himself not to interrupt.

'They had made it right with corrupt politicians of Tammany Hall and with the police, and nothing would have stopped them if they had only stuck to cards and New York, but they must needs come up Rochester way, and forge a name upon a cheque. It was my brother who did it, though everyone knew that it was under the influence of Sparrow MacCoy. I bought up that cheque, and a pretty sum it cost me. Then I went to my brother, laid it before him on the table, and swore to him that I would prosecute if he did not clear out of the country. At first he simply laughed. I could not prosecute, he said, without breaking our mother's heart, and he knew that I would not do that. I made him understand, however, that our mother's heart was being broken in any case, and that I had set firm on the point that I would rather see him in Rochester gaol than in a New York hotel. So at last he gave in, and he made me a solemn promise that he would see Sparrow MacCoy no more, that he would go to Europe, and that he would turn his hand to any honest trade that I helped him to get. I took him down right away to an old family friend, Joe Wilson, who is an exporter of American watches and clocks, and I got him to give Edward an agency in London, with a small salary and a fifteen per cent commission on all business. His manner and appearance were so good that he won the old man over at once, and within a week he was sent off to London with a case full of samples.'

That explained the watches on the young man who, clearly, was this gentleman's brother.

'It seemed to me that this business of the cheque had really given my brother a fright, and that there was some chance of his settling down into an honest line of life. My mother had spoken with him, and what she said had touched him, for she had always been the best of mothers to him and he had been the great sorrow of her life. But I knew that this man Sparrow MacCoy had a great influence over Edward and my chance of keeping the lad straight lay in breaking the connection between them. I had a friend in the New York detective force, and through him I kept a watch upon MacCoy. When, within a fortnight of my brother's sailing, I heard that MacCoy had taken a berth in the *Etruria*, I was as certain as if he had told me that he was going over to England for the purpose of coaxing Edward back again into the ways that he had left. In an instant I had resolved to go also, and to pit my influence against MacCoy's. I knew it was a losing fight, but I thought, and my mother thought, that it was my duty. We passed the last night together in prayer for my success, and she gave me her own Testament that my father had given her on the day of their marriage in the Old Country, so that I might always wear it next to my heart.

'I was a fellow traveller, on the steamship, with Sparrow MacCoy, and at least I had the satisfaction of spoiling his little game for the voyage. The very first night I went into the smoking-room, and found him at the head of a card-table, with a half a dozen young fellows who were carrying their full purses and their empty skulls over to Europe. He was settling down for his harvest, and a rich one it would have been. But I soon changed all that.

'"Gentlemen," said I, "are you aware whom you are playing with?"

'"What's that to you? You mind your own business!" said Sparrow, with an oath.

'"Who is it, anyway?" asked one of the dudes.

'"He's Sparrow MacCoy, the most notorious card-sharper in the States."

'Up MacCoy jumped with a bottle in his hand, but he remembered that he was under the flag of the Old Country, where law and order run, and gaol and the gallows wait for violence and murder, and there's no slipping out by the back door on board an ocean liner.

'"Prove your words, you . . . !" said he.

'"I will!" said I. "If you will turn up your right shirt-sleeve to the shoulder, I will either prove my words or I will eat them."

'He turned white and said not a word.'

I recalled that newspaper article I had been reading the very day when Henderson had called. 'He would have revealed that he had an elastic band down the arm with a clip just above the wrist,' I said.

'Yes. It is by means of this clip that they withdraw from their hands the cards that they do not want, while they substitute other cards from another hiding place. I reckoned on it being there, and it was. He cursed me, slunk out of the saloon, and was hardly seen again during the voyage. For once, at any rate, I got level with Sparrow MacCoy.

'But he soon had his revenge upon me, for when it came to influencing my brother he outweighed me every time. Edward had kept himself straight in London for the first few weeks, and had done some business with his American watches, until this villain came across his path once more. I did my best, but the best was little enough. The next thing I heard there had been a scandal at one of the Northumberland Avenue hotels: a travel-ler had been fleeced of a large sum by two confederate card-sharpers, and the matter was in the hands of Scotland Yard. The first I learned of it was in the evening paper, and I was at once certain that my brother and MacCoy were back at their old games. I hurried at once to Edward's lodgings. They told me that he and a tall gentleman (whom I recognized as MacCoy) had gone off together, and that he had left the lodgings and taken his things with him. The landlady had heard them give several directions to the cabman, ending with Euston Station, and she had accidentally overheard the tall gentleman saying something about Manchester. She believed that that was their destination.

'A glance at the timetable showed me that the most likely train was at five, though there was another at 4.35, which they might have caught. I had time to get only the later one, but found no sign of them either at the depot or in the train. They must have gone on by the earlier one, so I determined to follow them to Manchester and search for them in the hotels there. One last appeal to my brother by all that he owed to my mother might even now be the salvation of him. My nerves were over-strung, and I lit a cigar to steady them. At that moment, just as the train was moving off, the door of my compartment was flung open, and there were MacCoy and my brother on the platform.'

'In disguise,' said Holmes. 'Because Scotland Yard was after them? Yet you recognized them?'

'I did. MacCoy had a great astrakhan collar drawn up, so that only his eyes and nose were showing. But that nose, that great red beak, I'd know it anywhere. My brother was dressed like a woman, with a black veil half down his face, but of course it did not deceive me for an instant, nor would it have done so even if I had not known that he had often used such a dress before. I started up, and as I did so MacCoy recognized me. He said something, the conductor slammed the door, and they were shown into the next compartment. I tried to stop the train so as to follow them, but the wheels were already moving, and it was too late.

'When we stopped at Willesden, I instantly changed my carriage. It appears that I was not seen to do so, which is not surprising, as the station was crowded with people. MacCoy, of course, was expecting me, and he had spent the time between Euston and Willesden in saying all he could to harden my brother's heart and set him against me. That is what I fancy, for I had never found him so impossible to soften or to move. I tried this way and I tried that. I pictured his future in an English gaol; I described the sorrow of his mother when I came back with the news. I said everything to touch his heart, but all to no purpose. He sat there with a fixed sneer upon his handsome face, while every now and then Sparrow MacCoy would throw in a taunt at me, or some word of encouragement to hold my brother to his resolutions.

'"Why don't you run a Sunday school?" he would say to me, and then, in the same breath: "He's only just finding out that you are a man as well as he."

'"A man!" said I. "Well, I'm glad to have your friend's assurance of it, for no one would suspect it to see you like a boarding-school missy. I don't suppose in all this country there is a more contemptible-looking creature than you are as you sit there with that Dolly pinafore upon you." My brother coloured up at that, for he was a vain man, and he winced from ridicule.

'"It's only a dust-cloak," said he, and he slipped it off. "One has to throw the coppers off one's scent, and I had no other way to do it." He took his toque off with the veil attached, and he put both it and the cloak into his brown bag. "Anyway, I don't need to wear it until the conductor comes round," said he.

'"Nor then, either," said I, and taking the bag I slung it with all my force out of the window. "Now," said I, "if nothing but that disguise stands between you and a gaol, then to gaol you shall go."

'"Oh, you would squeal, would you?" MacCoy cried, and in an instant he whipped out his revolver. I sprang for his hand, but saw that I was too late, and jumped aside. At the same instant he fired, and the bullet which would have struck me passed through the heart of my unfortunate brother.

'He dropped without a groan upon the floor of the compartment, and MacCoy and I, equally horrified, knelt at each side of him, trying to bring back some signs of life. MacCoy still held the loaded revolver in his hand, but his anger against me and my resentment towards him had both for the moment been swallowed up in this sudden tragedy. It was he who first realized the situation. The train was for some reason going very slowly at the moment, and he saw his opportunity for escape. In an instant he had the door open, but I was as quick as he, and jumping upon him the two of us fell off the footboard and rolled in each other's arms down a steep embankment. At the bottom I struck my head against a stone, and I remembered nothing more. When I came to myself I was lying among some low bushes, not far from the railroad track, and somebody was bathing my head with a wet handkerchief. It was Sparrow MacCoy.

'"I guess I couldn't leave you," said he. "I didn't want to have the blood of two of you on my hands in one day. You loved your brother, I've no doubt; but you didn't love him a cent more than I loved him, though you'll say that I took a queer way to show it. Anyhow, it seems a mighty empty world now that he is gone, and I don't care a continental whether you give me over to the hangman or not."

'He had turned his ankle in the fall, and there we sat, he with his useless foot, and I with my throbbing head, and we talked and talked until gradually my bitterness began to soften and to turn into something like sympathy. What was the use of revenging his death upon a man who was as much stricken by that death as I was? And then, as my wits gradually returned, I began to realize also that I could do nothing against MacCoy that would not recoil upon my mother and myself. How could we convict him without a full account of my brother's career being made public — the very thing that of all others we wished to avoid? It was really as much in our interest as his to cover the matter up, and from being an avenger of crime I found myself changed to a conspirator against Justice. The place in which we found ourselves was one of those pheasant preserves that are so common in the Old Country, and as we groped our way through it I found myself consulting the slayer of my brother as to how far it would be possible to hush it up.

'I soon realized from what he said that unless there were some papers of which we knew nothing in my brother's pockets, there was really no possible means by which the police could identify him or learn how he had got there. His ticket was in MacCoy's pocket, and so was the ticket for some baggage that they had left at the depot. Like most Americans, he had found it cheaper and easier to buy an outfit in London than to bring one from New York, so that all his linen and clothes were new and unmarked. The bag, containing the dust-cloak, which I had thrown out of the window, may have fallen among some bramble patch where it is still concealed, or may have been carried off by some tramp, or may have come into the possession of the police, who kept the incident to themselves. Anyhow, I have seen nothing about it in the London papers. As to the watches, they were a selection from those that had been entrusted to him for business purposes. It may have been for the same business purposes that he was taking them to Manchester, but – well, it's too late to enter into that.

'I don't blame the police for being at fault. I don't see how it could have been otherwise. There was just one little clue that they might have followed up, but it was a small one. I mean that small, circular mirror that was found in my brother's pocket. It isn't a very common thing for a young man to carry about with him, is it? But a gambler might have told you what such a mirror may mean to a card-sharper. If you sit back a little from the table, and lay the mirror, face upwards, upon your lap, you can see, as you deal, every card that you give to your adversary. It is not hard to say whether you see a man or raise him when you know his cards as well as your own. It was as much a part of a sharper's outfit as the elastic clip upon Sparrow MacCoy's arm. Taking that, in connection with the recent frauds at the hotels, the police might have got hold of one end of the string.'

'The mirror,' said Holmes. 'I should have known.'

I kept quiet. I had been reading that article about card-sharpers and it had mentioned the very same device and technique. Yet my mind had not made the connection. That, of course, is the difference between Holmes and the rest of us – his brain would have seen the link at once.

'I don't think there is much more for me to explain,' Peredue continued. 'We got to a village called Amersham that night in the character of two gentlemen upon a walking tour, and afterwards we made our way quietly to London, whence MacCoy went on to Cairo and I returned to New York. My mother died six months afterwards, and I am glad to say that to the day of her death she never knew what happened. She was always under the delusion that Edward was earning an honest living in London, and I never had the heart to tell her the truth. He never wrote; but then, he never did write at any time, so that made no difference. His name was the last upon her lips. Once she was gone, I felt I owed it to the authorities to travel here and put the record straight and take my punishment. But before going to Scotland Yard, I thought I would offer the explanation to you, as

I followed the news carefully, and knew you had been consulted.
It must be very vexing to a man of your unblemished record—'

I suppressed a smile, knowing that there was a clutch of cases
that represented a blemish. Norbury, for example.

'Oh, I would not bother with Scotland Yard, Mr Peredue,'
said Holmes.

'No?'

'No.'

'I will convey the basic facts to Chief Inspector Vane. I am sure
he will decide that unless you can produce Sparrow MacCoy,
there is little point in reopening the case.'

'But I—'

'Lost a well-loved brother. None could have done more to try
and save his soul. I am grateful you have drawn a line under The
Rugby Mystery.'

'Very well, Mr Holmes. There's just one other thing that I
have to ask you, sir, and I should take it as a kind return for all
this explanation if you could do it for me. You remember the
Testament that was picked up. I always carried it in my inside
pocket, and it must have come out in my fall. I value it very
highly, for it was the family book with my birth and my brother's marked by my father in the beginning of it. I wish you would
apply at the proper place and have it sent to me. It can be of no
possible value to anyone else. If you address it to me at Bassano's
Library, Broadway, New York, it is sure to come to hand.'

'I am sure we can locate it and have it returned.'

When Peredue had taken his leave, to visit the grave of his
brother and arrange, anonymously, for a headstone to be
erected bearing his name, Holmes turned to me. 'Watson, no

doubt one day you will wish to write of these events, of the time when Sherlock Holmes developed a theory so preposterous, it was only trumped by the truth. But have a care. Peredue did aid the escape of a murderer, albeit an accidental one, and leave the law, and a certain Consulting Detective, scratching their heads. Strictly speaking, he should face the courts. Perhaps you should allow some time to pass before putting pen to paper.'

Time has indeed passed and two of the principals are no longer with us. James Peredue perished in 1907 when the *Larchmont*, a paddle steamer, sank after a collision off the coast of Rhode Island, en route from Providence (where Peredue owned a fine home) to New York. Sparrow MacCoy sharped one too many cards and was shot dead in a gunfight in San Francisco in 1906, just days before the earthquake. Mr Sherlock Holmes is retired, tending his bees, his reputation secure and robust enough to survive a tale in which he played the part of the mistaken detective.

AUTHOR'S NOTE

Although *A Study in Murder* is fiction, the details of the POW camps in Germany (including the sanctioned strolls in the countryside, providing a form was completed giving the officer's word they would return), the prisoner aid services in the UK and the exchanges for POWs to live on licence in Holland and Switzerland are all based on fact. Harzgrund is inspired by the rather grim Holzminden, where the commandant really did run the camp for profit. No prisoners were dissolved in acid, although there was a largely successful mass escape through tunnels in July 1918. See Jacqueline Cook's *The Real Great Escape* and Neil Hanson's *Escape from Germany*. There really were work camps in Germany like the one described for the Russians, which presaged the conditions and brutality found in Nazi concentration camps twenty-five years later. *The War Behind the Wire* by John Lewis-Sempel is a sobering and thoughtful overview of the life of POWs of all ranks and the harsh regimes they often endured.

Watson's story about Sparrow MacCoy & Co. is based on Arthur Conan Doyle's 'The Man With the Watches'. Like 'The

Lost Special' this is one of his tales that, while not part of the Sherlock Holmes canon, has the feel of a Holmes tale (in fact an unnamed 'amateur detective' and an 'amateur reasoner' pops up in both). I have reworked it to put Sherlock at the centre of the puzzle, even if, as in *A Study in Scarlet*, the answer to the crime ultimately lies off-stage from Baker Street.

The Connaught in Mayfair was once called the Coburg and changed its name in 1917 (although a little later than here).

The Holland class of experimental submarines did exist, but Holland 6 never got off the drawing board, except within these pages. And if you happen to be in Venlo, don't go looking for the bridge at Knok. There isn't one there. We novelists have to be allowed to make some things up.

As always, I would like to thank Clare Hey, Sue Stephens, James Horobin, Jamie Groves, Carla Josephson and all at Simon & Schuster, as well as Susan d'Arcy, David Miller, Christine Walker and Deborah Ryan for their enthusiasm, help and support with this series.